metatron's daughters

book two: the lost race trilogy

DEBORAH RILEY-MAGNUS

Metatron's Daughters
Book Two: The Lost Race Trilogy

Published in the United States of America by Little Pen Press

Paperback ISBN: 978-0-980273-4-0
EBook ISBN: 978-0-9980273-5-7

Book and Cover Design by Natalie Preston

YESTERDAY

As I pushed my reluctant self through what felt like a wall of warm water and took my first step into the unknown, all I could do was take a moment to explore what I knew to be real and true. A week ago, I was just a girl getting her freedom from an orphanage. I'm no Little Orphan Annie and there's no Daddy Warbucks on my horizon. It turns out I'm Nephilim, Pure Nephilim, in fact. That means I have six ridiculous, massive wings that tend to sprout when I get ticked off or really scared, and a war I never knew about just around the corner. Turning eighteen was way more complicated than I imagined but, hey, those rainbows looked so cool.

Raising my eyes, I gasped in the thick, fragrant air of the strange plane Cole, Cia, and I had entered through the portal in a dying peach grove. We were not on Ocracoke Island anymore, that was certain. The colorful ribbons of light twisted and interlocked, crisscrossed the sky from every angle, and created a glow so odd and brilliant I had to squint.

"Gracie!"

I turned to Cole's voice. Such a good, strong voice. My ears told me he was right beside me but I could see he was easily twenty feet away. Then the voice turned garbled, bubbled, and came as an irritated shout.

"Gracie! Damn it! Stay close!"

I thought I was staying close. The rainbows weren't the only distraction. A vibration buzzed at the tip of my head like a constant whispered warning. I swear I saw angels, just like the ones carved and painted all over Ariel's Gate Orphanage, floating above me and pointing in a hundred different directions. Then I blinked and *poof* they disappeared. What was real and what wasn't? What would, and easily could, vanish in the blink of an eye? Everything that ached in my heart, every loss, every death, every painful discovery over the past few weeks expanded and pressed against the walls of my chest.

"Gracie! Don't stray!"

Okay, Cole couldn't be yelling at me like that. We're not a couple, or whatever we almost became, anymore. I snorted and took another glance at the sky. Tiny lightning bolts crackled from the arcs of each rainbow. A million streaks of light flashed and shot up from all the other colorful sparks surrounding me, closing in on me, prickling and poking at me. Something was not right about that place.

A boney hand gripped mine. I focused on it, the cool touch, the tight clasp. It had to be Cia but she was nowhere in sight. The woman was so ancient and so comforting, the best memory I had. She brought us into this place to find… something. What were we looking for? I forgot. I swung around and that hand held me tight, pulling, pulling, pulling, until my face slammed into her chest. Arms squeezed around me then a set of wings wrapped us both. Cole protected, Cia's breath was heavy and anxious, and me? I just let the panic run its course, shiver through my body then still. I swear I could hear the surf, but all around me was nothingness. How would we ever find our way back?

"Listen to me!" Cia shouted into my ear, making me wince. "This place is designed to confuse and deceive. Stay close!"

"I'm trying."

"I got her," Cole bellowed and his voice caused ripples in the thick air.

"No, you don't!" I broke free of his grip, focusing as hard as I could on his and Cia's strangely distorted faces, then pointed ahead. "Lead the way."

"We can't lose you, baby. I can't lose you." Cole whispered but it was so loud Neptune, deep under water on another planet, could have heard him.

"No one's going to get lost. Cia, take us to the treasure." Yep, that's right, we were seeking buried treasure. I remembered. Heart pounding, I stomped ahead, Cia at my right and Cole at my left. The ground felt wonky, like it wasn't quite solid and I found myself walking with my knees loose and bent for balance. I wanted to look to Cole for comfort, but I was still mad at him. It had been made clear that he and I were to stand together for the challenges ahead, but I wanted more. At least once I wanted more. Now, gasping in the heavy atmosphere of a dangerous and confusing alternate plane, I knew I'd have whatever fate saw fit to give me.

"Why is it so hard to breathe?" I choked and gasped again.

Cia's hand tightened on mine. "We're traveling under a protective veil. It's temporary, and if we don't move quickly, it will dissolve before we can get what we came for."

I nodded then suddenly, as though I'd awakened from a dream, everything stilled. The sky was normal, the ground under my feet was firm, and Cole was sweating bullets digging and digging in the sandy dirt. Had time slipped ahead? Were we still inside the portal? I held tight to Cia's fingers and glanced around. Empty. Open. A desert of nothingness. The Sahara? Mars? "Where are we?"

"This is the safe place where I protected Esther. Close your eyes, Gracie, just for a second then open them again. The illusion will clear and you'll see."

Okay, that was better, but really, was it? If this was a safe place in the middle of all that crazy, how could my twin sister have ever grown up normal? I was raised in an orphanage thinking I was all alone in the world. So, Esther had her challenges, too. I'd need to explore that concept further, but after seeing her naked with Cole, I had no interest in that now. Maybe later. Much later, in fact.

My head swiveled slowly, wanting to take in everything around me. If this wasn't the illusion, what was it? The alternate plane might be a hundred planes at the same time, or it could be only one diabolical plane floating and twisting over and through itself inside the real world. Who made it? God or the devil? The answer to that would give me something to grasp onto, and a better idea of how to trust such a place. The surroundings were so like where I grew up, I could hardly believe it. The gardens flourished, the air was sweet, the little houses were neat and well taken care of. The only real differences were that the old weeping willow tree was nowhere in sight, and neither were people—Nephilim, demon, or otherwise. For all its familiar beauty, it was desolate.

Cole grunted and stepped on the shovel, driving it deeper for another load. He ran an arm across his brow and continued. Poor guy looked like he had some experience at digging up buried treasure.

"We're nowhere near Ocracoke," Cia explained. "This is the portal near Nassau."

I handed Cole my bandana to wipe away his sweat. Commandeering it without even a nod of thanks, he tied it over his soaked hair and kept burrowing.

"So, these portals are how your pirate seemed to appear out of no-where, not a ship in sight. Tricky guy." I marveled. I have to admit, it was still a stretch to believe that Edward Teach—the famous pirate known as Blackbeard—was Nephilim, once Cia's lover, and astute enough to create a treasure that could help us through the coming war.

"He was one of a kind. On this plane, there are about three thousand portals." Cia knelt and looked into the hole. Cole was waist deep. She shook her head and reached for the other shovel. "Not even halfway, we need to reach it faster." But before she could slide into the hole that had started to look like a grave, I snatched the shovel from her hands.

Sitting on the edge I gripped Cole's shoulder and slid in. I might have a messed-up foot but I'm not helpless. With a grin, he moved to one side while I began working on the other.

Cia, down on her knees, talked in a hush. "Every portal on the planet leads here. This is the place of the Counting."

"What's the Counting?"

We looked up at her and she blinked then nodded. "I see. You don't know. This isn't the first time the Nephilim have dropped the ball, children. It is the fifth. No living Nephilim was alive the last time, and there are no records of the Countings." She gave a shrug. "The Tribunal is big on bonfires. But we ancients know. Many of us have seen, even assisted with, the Countings of the past. When the balance is off, all Nephilim are commanded to this place to be counted and face judgment if necessary."

I looked to Cole. "So," he said. "No battle? No war?"

"That depends on the Counting," she stated. "It depends on how much each side wants balance, or imbalance. It depends on a lot of things. I will tell you this much." Her wrinkled face puckered as though she might cry. "In all my knowledge, all that's been passed down to me from other ancients, and all that I know from the 1802 Counting, it has never been this perilous, this dangerous… this far from the center. And Lucifer has created his race of battle heat demons to push the imbalance even further."

"There weren't battle heat demons before?" I had to know.

"Later. We'll get all that information later. For now, dig."

Cole pushed his shovel and so did I, again and again until we heard a thump. It sounded exactly like it did in the old black and white pirate movies, too. We dropped to our knees and pushed the last of the sandy dirt aside. A flurry of activity followed, scrambling out of the whole, slipping ropes under the trunk, then raising the thing to the surface with grunts, groans, and a few well-chosen obscenities. It was heavy enough to be loaded with gold doubloons and pieces of eight, but I knew it wasn't.

With a turn of a key that had hung around Cia's neck for as long as I'd known her, the lid was lifted. Scrolls and heavy books were set inside in neat piles. We gathered them and followed her through the rainbowed world. Her protective covering dissolved, making it easier to breathe on our escape, but as we walked, the plane became heavily speckled with black battle heat demons heading one way or another, paying no attention to us at all.

"So very odd," Cia whispered as we stepped near the portal to our world.

Passing through I heard a grunt, a small gasp, then the usual sounds of the island. Bees droned, birds chirped, a distant sea gull called, normal. The grass felt soft and comforting as I dropped onto it, enjoying the sensation of gravity as it's meant to be.

I shook my head, thrilled to have survived the expedition and pleased to be back in a world that made sense. Well, sort of. A battle heat demon rushed past me, into the peach grove then disappeared. One set of eyes actually looked into mine as the air sizzled with its passage. "Wow."

"Maybe they're too focused on their assignments to give a damn about us." Cole grunted under the weight of his heavy booty. He reached down to help me to my feet. I turned and tripped over the big book Cia had carried. It was safe on our side of the portal, but where was she?

"Cia!" I yelled as loud as I could, aiming my voice into the invisible portal. Cole dropped everything and stomped toward it. "No! Stop!" He turned, his eyes ablaze with concern and determination.

"Gracie, they have her!"

"We don't know how to find her," I stated, so cool and in control, except for the tears soaking my face. "We can't get her until we understand all this. Otherwise, they'll have us, too."

We stood, staring at each other while despicable, slimy demons walked right past us and into the portal. "We need to get her, but we need to know how first." I sniffled and fought the need to fall against his chest and sob. How could we have lost Cia? She was our ace in the hole, the only person with the answers to all my questions.

Cole added the book to his load and led the way, his shoulders and ethereal wings drooping in despair. Looking back, I half expected to see Lucifer himself laughing at me.

PART ONE

"The grim fact is that we prepare for war like precocious giants …"
~ Lester Pearson 1897–1972

1

ickness twisted Cole's gut. He'd received his second quickening just days earlier, an awakening of yet another inexplicable and terrifying power, and still he couldn't see how to fix this. Why on earth should there be an entire race of part-human part-angels if they couldn't fix this shit?

Cia was gone and with every passing moment he knew the chances of getting her back were dissolving like salt in water. The old house creaked against a raging storm. Outside the window, the occasional slither of demons whipped past, heading toward the peach grove. To the place of the Counting. The place he couldn't figure out if his life depended on it.

Thunder rattled the door then a gust of wet blasted into the room. He turned to see Gracie standing there, dripping rain in the dim light, watching, waiting for him to do something. Already he was failing her.

"I have an idea." She didn't lash out or show her disappointment. Gracie stepped forward, like she was afraid but brave as ever. "I'm pretty sure we can do this together," she whispered and held out her hand. "We can."

For eighteen hours straight he'd been agonizing, sweating, and crying over the maps and books, unable to comprehend anything at all. Time was running out. They could try to rescue Cia, or they could try to rescue their entire race. How the hell was he going to explain it to Gracie?

"Where've you been?" He grabbed a ratty blanket from the sofa and wrapped it around her.

"I went to the tree… tried to talk with my father. He was a no-show. Maybe the great Metatron doesn't like thunderstorms." She shrugged and sat, looking over the maps, scrolls, and opened books spread haphazardly on the floor, a few still fluttering from the wind's fury seeping under the door.

"It could be worse than that. Maybe it's too late to get any help from him. From any of them. Raphael said we're going to be on our own when this all comes down. It was our race that made the promise to protect the balance, not the archangels."

She tossed up her hands, spraying rainwater across the room. "Right, they didn't make any promise, they just made babies. Us. Damn, damn, damn."

They sat in silence for several moments, listening to the squall roll away as the dawn whispered in. Somewhere a boat horn called. The day would go on like any other on Ocracoke. When the storm passed, ferries would race across the water, coffee shops and businesses would open, humans would go about their lives oblivious to the fact that Nephilim exist and have forgotten to keep a vow. That the earth was struggling under the horrific weight of it all. That they, too, would suffer for a failure that could, and should, have been corrected.

For the second time since Cia's disappearance, Cole lost his temper, but this time it was bigger, more powerful, more dangerous. It would destroy far more than the tea kettle he'd tossed against a wall. Desperate to save the house, he charged outside and blew the gasket he couldn't hold back any longer. "Stay back, Gracie!" he shouted. She shrieked and turned her back, huddled for safety and protection just as flames blasted from his eyes and mouth, from his fingertips, from his feet, from his very heart. For the first time since Afghanistan, he felt the full weight of his specific responsibility. He had to do what was needed. He could not fail.

Cole struggled to let off steam in a safe direction. They needed Cia's house. It was the only one standing on the three acres of Gracie's property. It was sturdy enough and kept the rain out. But just outside the front door, the rickety fence was ashes and the overgrown garden, burned to the drenched ground. Nothing sparked or flamed, it simply fizzled out into the sodden dirt. If he had to do it, at least he felt he'd controlled it. Angel Fire, he called it. The first of his two awakened powers. Angel Fire had only come to him twice, both times in desperation. His second power was always present and ached in his eyes and his chest. It also brightened his mind.

"Holy shit!" He charged back inside and knelt at the maps, pushing books and scrolls aside, focusing as hard as he could. "Good God, Gracie, I wish I had your memory."

"Why?" It was a small, shaky voice but she was there, right at his side.

"Remember how I recognized the portal at the peach grove?"

She nodded.

"I saw lights like that inside, too. Across all that space, I saw portals all over the place. The problem is …" He shuffled maps and turned them, held them up to the light then smiled and drew in a deep breath. "Holy shit! That damn pirate is a Godsend!"

She drew closer, looking at the same parchment. "Um, what are you talking about?"

Laughter bubbled, freshening and cooling the heat in his throat. "Our portal is blue, like a dark, rich, royal blue."

"Uh-huh, and?"

"The portal near Nassau was green. Hot, lime green."

"Okay."

He gripped her shoulders, grinned, and planted a kiss on her lips. His heart fluttered and his body reacted but he had to keep everything in perspective. He leaned in for another brief kiss but before she could protest or remind him that he was still in the doghouse, he pointed to the map. "Look, look real closely. Gracie, they're all marked, by color and location. Numbered and noted. Blackbeard had the same awakening power I have. Or at least something like it. He saw the same colors, was able to identify the portals, then he mapped them out for us. Do you know what this means?"

"I have no clue. Cole, you're so tired. Maybe you need some sleep? Maybe some water? Your voice is raw and—"

"I need you to listen to me and trust me, baby. I can navigate the portals. I can travel like Teach did, go anywhere, recruit like crazy. I know how to find the Free-Winged. I can gain their trust, their vow, bring them here."

"What about their soul swords? They'll need their weapons if we have to fight."

"I'll deal with that when I have to. Maybe I can regenerate them. Who knows?"

Her brow was curled but her breath came fast and hard.

"Think about this. Those portals can bring Nephilim from all over the planet to the Counting place, Gracie! They just need to know how to get in. I can do that. I can recruit all over the world and I can guide our army through as many portals as we need." He stood and paced a wild circle around the maps. "Tobias needs to know about this. Someone needs to get out to the other segments of our race and tell them. We can do this, I—"

"And what about Cia?" Her eyes glistened with sadness and he wanted to hold her close. That wouldn't make a leader of her. That would only make her more dependent, or more rebellious. Neither was the best version of Gracie Caine.

"If we take the time to search for Cia… baby… we all die, the human race suffers, and eventually the planet implodes. You know I'm right."

She said nothing, just watched his face, her eyes locked on his.

"You know I'm right. And you know Cia would agree. I'm sorry, Gracie, I wish—"

"No. No more." She gasped back a sob then pulled the largest map up to the kitchen table. "How long will it take you to figure out a plan? Where will you start?"

~*~

"We had a deal!" Esther slammed into the house, crashing the door into a table holding a crystal vase that shattered across the painted tile floor. Lucifer—her lover, her master, and the precariously-perched future ruler of the earth—stood and made a *tisk-tisk* sound.

"We made many deals, my little love. Which one are you ranting about today?"

Heart racing, she checked her attitude. One doesn't shout at the devil without consequences. "Why is Cia here?"

"Cia? The ancient? What a pleasure. She's never visited us before." His brilliant blue eyes glittered with mirth. "Bring her in."

"I can't. Luc, she's burned! One of the demons hurt her and she's…"

He raced past. Outside the sky was clear and bright, the sun speckled over the infinity pool as a slight breeze rippled the perfectly chlorinated water. The patio overlooked beautiful Santorini. It appeared Lucifer was in the mood for spanakopita. Yesterday Esther and the devil lived in the French Alps. The day before, South Africa. The man was never satisfied or content. Things always changed. Everything but Esther.

On the cool slate walkway lay the trembling ancient. Lucifer squatted close, careful not to touch her with the toe of his sandal. A hand waved across her face and her eyes opened. "Are you all right, my old friend?"

The woman was severely burned. Flesh on her arms and face bubbled and crisped, turned bloody then black as night. She gave a well-practiced scowl. "We are not friends." It appeared all she could manage.

"Luc, you promised!" Esther fought tears, but mostly the desire to swing her biker boot into his balls.

He lifted Cia into his arms with surprising tenderness and was gone, off into the bowels of the house. Now she was really in trouble. Esther debated, should she pace and wait, or follow? She followed.

The quaint stone and plaster had dissolved and shifted into sterile hospital hallways, but before she could locate Cia, Lucifer stepped in front of her, a wall of big, tall, dark, and too handsome to be real. Esther looked up, worked her expression and gave a sigh. "Is she better?"

"You know better than that. They are battle heat burns."

"So," Esther shrugged and pushed back her black and fuchsia hair. "Fix her. I know you can heal her. All angels can heal people. Just fix her!"

His hand gripped Esther's arm tight, drawing a squeal. "I hope that's a sound of delight." He pulled her to a room, pushed aside the privacy drape and with no effort at all, tossed her onto the bed. They were naked without removing a stitch, a trick Lucifer especially liked. He mounted and penetrated then looked down into her eyes.

Esther kept her expression cool. It was a well-practiced continence. He was angry and it was all her fault. There was always a little hurt, a little blood, a little humiliation. It was how he liked it. Until Cia arrived damaged by the demons' touch, Esther had always felt that sex with the devil, even when he was this annoyed, was worth the life she received in return. The hurt was bigger this time, and there would be more blood than normal but she could take it.

"So, will you fix her now?" she said, ignoring the ache in her belly after he grunted his searing fruition.

"You haven't told me your plan yet."

"What plan?" Esther shifted on the narrow mattress and lay her head on his chest.

"You know what I'm asking."

His voice had gone gravelly and she had to fess up. She might look like a tough gal, but when push came to shove, she always knew her rightful place. "I told you. He doesn't want me. You saw it. He literally threw me off of him!"

"Don't be so damn dramatic. He gave you a bit of a heave. Cole Masters is playing hard to get. I know this Norema well. He may be Makha'el's grandson, but he has enough human blood to hear my commands. He can be had, I know it. I've led him to the dark a thousand times."

"And has he once given you a vow?" Esther's heart nearly burst. What the hell was she thinking, talking to him like that? Lucifer was silent, he stood from the bed and clothing formed over his flesh, this time New York chic down to his Italian leather shoes. He straightened his tie. "No," she chose to continue. "He hasn't given you a vow but I have. Luc, doesn't that count for something? Anything?"

"You have a duty to keep trying. You are perfect, my little love. Not like your gimp of a sister. He will choose you. You just need to keep trying. After all," and his eye twinkled in an ominous way, "you got me to choose you, right?"

She followed him down the hall, naked as a jay bird. "Clothes, please!" Poof, a pink seersucker linen shirtwaist dress from the 1950s, and pinching high heels. Ugh.

The Devil turned on a toe, looked her up and down, nodded with a grin then put his hands on his hips. "You're no angel, Pure Nephilim or not. In my name and for my cause you have seduced many, all as good or better than Cole Masters. Many of those men and women have become my own race, my own army! Turn on the charm. One ejaculation inside your belly and he's mine. Esther." He gasped and raised his hands to the sky. "Can you imagine the dark warrior Makha'el's grandson could become?

"But… know this. I hear from a few of my brothers that as long as Cole and Gracie are together, they can't be taken. Split them apart. Get them to look away from each other. Work your magic. Or perhaps…" He made an abrupt about face and headed back the way they came.

"What?" she followed him into hospital hallways.

"Perhaps the demon who brought Cia to you has solved that problem for us. Perhaps you need only watch the portals and wait for Masters to play the hero. After we have him, Gracie will follow to save her love." His laughter rattled the walls.

"No one but Cia and I understand the portals. He'll be lost before he even gets near us."

"So, plant your pretty ass in the peach grove and wait for him."

Esther blinked, sickness building inside her.

"Now!"

~*~

Too late. I couldn't talk him out of going alone so Cole was gone. Off to recruit the Free-Winged of our race, all those poor lost souls who got their wings without having the slightest clue what they are. I was concerned about him, I was angry, and I was definitely jealous. How could he leave me stuck all alone at Cia's house, waiting like a forlorn housewife for him to come home from work? What if the demons attacked? Well, I knew the answer. Six wings and a powerful soul sword would take good care of that. I just wish I had the heart of a warrior to go with all the power.

At least Cole had gone into town and activated my cell phone before he left. I stared at it, willing it to ring, but nothing. Where was he? Did he survive stepping through the portal he chose? What was he doing? "ARRRGGGH!" This much frustration could kill a person.

I huffed, grabbed my dad's book, and sat under the big weeping willow tree. Dad's book was something magical. My dad is Metatron, God's scribe. He's the bookkeeper, the writer of stories, and the keeper of records. When Dad writes stuff, it shows up in that peculiar book. The coolest part is that I'm the only one who can read the symbols. Only a few days ago I sat under that tree and he talked to me. I heard his voice inside my head and he filled my brain with knowledge. Too bad he isn't well versed on broken hearts and love matches, but the fact of the matter is that we're at war. There's no time for such foolishness anyway. I sighed. Loud. With gusto. The breeze pushed the hanging boughs around and there he was. Metatron. Holy crap!

"Daddy!" Like the child I once was, I leapt into his open arms and held on for dear life.

"So much joy in the feel of you, my dear Gracie," he whispered then set me on my feet. "There's little time. Watch the book, I'll send information as I receive it. You have new arrivals on the way. You must be strong, my daughter."

I nodded and stood. Man, he was a tall guy. Looking up I tried to smile. Guess it didn't happen.

"He will do well, Gracie. Cole has a mission. Let him gain warriors for you. Watch for word from Michael Allerton. Keep your—"

"Allerton? Isn't he still with Tobias?"

"No. He has been given a mission as well. Much is brewing all around and all will report to you, my daughter. All will look to you for guidance. Keep your strength. Fight your fears. Stand with those worthy of you… but watch out for those who are not."

With that, he dissolved into thin air. For a moment I wasn't even sure if it really happened. I reviewed all his words. It sure sounded like an important communication and it was real, so real I smelled the scent of him, the scent I recalled from babyhood. He was there, and he was gone. If Cole was right, one day soon my dad would be gone completely. All the archangels will go silent. It's not their war, it's ours. Soon we'll be on our own.

I stepped out from under the tree, jittery and worried, ready to jump out of my skin, then I looked around me. The land was big and open, surrounded by trees but cluttered with fallen branches, the remains of downed shacks and houses. If people were coming, I had to get it cleaned up. A laugh escaped my throat. I, a club-footed gimp, was going to clear acres of crap? Now how the hell was I going to do that? Esther's jeep was parked behind Cia's house. Her keys were on the kitchen table where she left them the day after her sexual attack on Cole. The attack I'm still punishing him for. Maybe it's time to let that one go?

All I knew about driving came from Cole during our silent escape from the Emmaus Magic Show. I could steer. I could press on the brake. The other pedal must be the gas, but what was that third pedal, anyway? Whatever. I shrugged and turned the key.

The vehicle was off like a bolt of lightning. I stopped, gasped for air, then did the right thing. I shuffled through the glove compartment and found the owner's manual. It took hours for me to figure it all out. Clutch. Brake. Clutch. Gas. Clutch. Accelerate. Clutch. Brake. Slow down. Stop. Four boxes of garbage bags and a million scratches and bruises later, it was far from done but the place was as good as it was going to get for now. Every chance I got, I gawked at my phone. Nada. Well, I sure wouldn't be sitting around pining for Cole. I had a mess of work to do. At least I could sort of envision a camp for preparing warriors. The sun kissed the horizon and I headed to the house in search of a hot shower and some food.

Wrapped in a towel and staring into the steamy mirror, terror shook me. For the first time in my entire life, I was alone. Totally alone. I had always been surround by other students, House Mother, teachers. Even when I used to hide in Makha'el Lecture Hall, I wasn't alone. I knew everyone was just down the hall, in classrooms or the gym. At that moment, I had no idea where my friends, or Cole, or Allerton, or even the Emmaus Magic Show was. I shook it off.

"Just a new dynamic," I said to the me in the mirror. "Another part of life Ariel's Gate never prepared us for. Normal people are alone a lot. This… is normal." I shook it off but still listened for strange noises as I left to dress. A demon could climb into an open window, or push through the door. A stranger could try to break in. Then I took a deep breath. "Or," I said, bold as can be, "nothing at all might happen." Normal people didn't panic just because they were alone.

My duffle was full of smelly, filthy clothes. None of that would do, especially if Dad was right and I'd be receiving guests. Cia had a washing machine, but that wasn't happening, not tonight. Walking into Esther's bedroom the air felt heavy, like a threat to my very existence. No matter. This Pure Nephilim was on a mission. I needed clean underwear. I found a pair and ran out, slipping on water drops I'd left on the wooden floor.

Did I want to wear those panties? Hell no! With drama worthy of my beautiful, nutty, late friend Jenny Perkins, I wadded the flimsy fabric and threw it back into the opened door. Maybe Cia had some underwear.

I gentled my way into the ancient's bedroom. A sensation of love and compassion, wisdom and loss wafted like the scent of roses. The weight of her possible death nearly crushed me, but I held strong. "This is how leaders handle adversity," I said softly, but a tear rolled down my cheek. Just one. It was all I could spare. I found undies, a pretty tie-dyed skirt, and a white jersey. Looking around I knew that for as long as I was alone, I'd rest and dream in the distinct protection of Cia's room.

My feet moved slowly, partly from exhaustion, but mostly because I felt respect and reverence in that house. There were photos everywhere. Women's faces came to life as I looked into the dusty frames. Women I remembered, women I loved. There were children everywhere, playing in the gardens, climbing trees, crowded on Cia's tiny porch, laughing around a Christmas tree. I was only five when I was taken from this beautiful place, but I recalled every moment of my time here, and now I even remembered playing with my twin sister—all those beautiful twin memories Esther had removed from me with her own Nephilim power to stop my sadness over leaving. I wondered, were we really that close? That devoted to each other? Was that the last pure and good thing she did before pledging to the dark? Was it pure? Was it good? Or was it manipulative? I so wanted to believe we treasured our sisterhood.

Every photo was filled to the brim with happiness and bliss. It was shocking to realize that they all were dead. All but me and Esther… and hopefully Cia. What kind of a disease could take them all like that? A devil disease for sure. So many little Nephilim, innocent, lovely. So many women, all lovers to archangels like my dad. All gone. Leaving me to… do what? Be the leader? Wage a war? My stomach turned as I set a frame back on the mantle. Me. Because I'm the only Pure Nephilim left on the good guys' side. At that moment I hated Esther more than ever.

I pulled my phone from a pocket hidden in the peach and blue swirls of my skirt. "Where are you?" I whimpered, then shouted. "Where are you, Cole!" Like that was going to work. I tried not to imagine him in so much trouble he couldn't dial a phone. I hoped he was safe and just busy doing what he left to do, but, hey… what about me? I missed him so bad my chest ached. We'd been together every single day since leaving the Gate. Did this mean I loved him? Of course, I loved him. I loved Ben and Ryan, and poor dead Wally and Jenny. But was I in love with Cole? I missed his touch, his soft lips, his voice. Oh hell, maybe in love, maybe not. Maybe that was too complicated a topic for tired and hungry.

I shuffled to the kitchen and checked the refrigerator. Cold air drifted to me and I wondered, who paid the bills? The electricity, water, gas for the stove? Food? Esther was gone now, and wouldn't likely be sending cash to cover expenses. Maybe I could take her job at the *Hell to Pay Pub*? I could dye my hair like hers. They'd never know, right? Except for the fact that I have a messed-up foot, refuse to wear her awful clothes, or be a bartender. What's in a pina colada anyway? I could learn. No Wi-Fi at the cottage, but I could go to a coffee shop in town and get online with my laptop. Never thought I'd be a skanky bartender but at least it would take care of the utilities. Then I worried, what if someone recognized the jeep and wanted to know where Esther was? Crap, crap, crap.

I ate leftover soup, worried about the expenses, prayed for Cia, thought about Cole, and, oh yeah, wondered about who would be coming to join me. If the great Metatron was correct, I was meant to lead all of us to victory. The jelly-kneed gal. Me.

Weakness overcame every muscle and my body dribbled like melting ice to the floor. The vibrant colors of Cia's skirt billowed and wrapped around me like a hug. Could I do this? What was fear, anyway? Something I couldn't exactly define. What did I fear? Well, failure. Dying. Being inadequate was up there, too. But none of that was exactly it. I had nothing to be afraid of until I could clearly identify what lie ahead. This was just fear of the unknown, and that could be easily remedied. Knowledge always trumped fear. Leading people into battle was an abstract, an idea, a conundrum. I remembered everything I'd ever read or studied about war and battle strategy. Napoleon. Hannibal. George Washington. General Eisenhower. Captain James T. Kirk. David and Goliath. Joan of Arc… gulp. That was me. Crap.

My eyes drifted closed, my brain deciding that clearly, I was in no state to explore further. I slept until the sun glittered through the kitchen window and footfalls sounded on the porch.

2

He had done his best, and done it the only way he knew how. Michael Allerton was raised in the safety of the Nephilim orphanage system, thinking he was a foundling like most of the children there, wondering, hurting, constantly curious whether his parents were dead or just didn't want him. It was painful. It was life changing. It was important. He grew up in Ariel's Gate and worked hard to fulfill his dreams of someday running the place, making it as nurturing as possible so that the children would never experience the agony he had.

It was a no-brainer for him to take his own son, the love child of a strange relationship mixed with passion and the need to feel like someone's important someone. Maybe the affair was foolish, maybe it was necessary, but after the infant arrived, Michael had no other choice. Rachel was not the motherly type by her own proclamation, so he took the child, named him Ben Wheeler, and watched him grow into a strong, beautiful young man under his careful eye and distant but heartfelt care as headmaster of Ariel's Gate.

Ben was never supposed to know. He was to be spared that discomfort. So, when he confronted Michael on the flight from Charlotte to Los Angeles, at first it seemed the earth would stop spinning. Ben knew because of his quickening received soon after Acclimation, a power of perception. The discussion was hard, but the solution was achieved. Ben would tolerate and assist Michael on his all-important mission to gain warriors for the cause, and the dad would forever forgo any right to offer fatherly advice. At least until Ben found a way to forgive him. Seemed fair enough.

None of it mattered in the light of their urgent responsibilities. It was showtime and Michael stood in the wings beside his son. The stage was austere, just a podium, a microphone, and a few chairs. He peeked around the edge. Holy shit, this was going down whether he was ready or not.

The venue director, a proud Norema, had informed them that there were over ten thousand people in the auditorium. Standing room only. Gregory Parkland, Grand Regent of the Americas and head of the Nephilim Worldwide Intelligence Bureau sure knew how to make things happen. Now it was Michael's job to take it home.

Ben's hands visibly shook as he leaned to see the audience. "How the hell can you do this? Just stand in front of all those people and talk? I think I'm going to puke."

"You'll be fine. I'm not afraid of talking, I'm afraid of not getting through to them. Here we go."

They stepped onstage surrounded by loud applause. As they walked together toward the podium, the director whispered that he was looking forward to hearing the speech. So was Michael. He had no clue what he was going to say. He'd been like that his whole life. Whether in front of the Tribunal, leading conferences, or serving as keynote speaker at Nephilim conventions, he never planned a speech. He read the audience and leapt into the void. Maybe this time he should have brought a parachute. At least a first-aid kit.

He gulped and awaited the introduction. Ben and the director took seats behind him, his son shooting a nervous thumbs up. Michael drew in a deep breath then stood at the podium and opened his arms. His massive dark wings spread wide with the action, tugging at his back in a way that intensified his responsibilities to God, man, and his race. His mind reached out. He stood silent until the applause quieted. His previously empty mind thrummed and clicked, pieces fell into place and he knew exactly the right words. This would not be as gentle as he'd hoped. Scanning the massive gathering, stuffed wall to wall and wing to wing before him, he opened with a prayer.

"Brothers, sisters, may our glorious Father be with us as we explore our uncertain future together on this fateful day. May He wash us clean with purity and honesty, courage and strength, vision and hope. May He bless us with grace and tolerance, open our minds, and help us see the truth."

"Amen."

The crowd spoke in unison and Michael wondered how they knew his prayer was finished. How they sensed his rhythm. All eyes were bright, intense, surprisingly ready. But were they?

"I have no gentle preamble for this. We are ending." He stood, silent and waited. Many faces tightened, some dropped in sadness, others looked prepared to challenge, and still others remained blank, disbelieving. "Look around. There is no doubt the balance is off… completely, and devastatingly off. Can any one of you deny this?"

"Humans are at fault far more than we are!" The shout rose from the audience and Michael shook his head sadly.

"No, my brother. We have failed. Otherwise it would have never, *ever* gotten this bad. It's time to face facts. It's time to realize that our time is almost up."

No one even whispered, no one shuffled a foot, or rolled their eyes. Facts were facts and these facts were all too obvious.

"So, what are we to do?" Michael stepped off the stage and walked among the attendees. "You have a few choices. You can ignore the call. You can pretend that your primary responsibilities are to yourselves and your families. You can pray and hope for balance to magically return. If you're considering any of those options, you need to seriously review your Acclimation lessons. I hope you took notes, because there are a few very important points to remember."

He walked deeper into the room, looking into terrified eyes, wishing he didn't have to do this. Wishing the world was different, better, balanced. Ben was right. Why should they join the fight? Tough love was the only way to get through to Nephilim living cushy, comfortable lives. This was going to be a hard sell. He sighed then gave a glare, meaning to get his point across without delay or confusion. He wanted to shout but instead spoke softly, pulling all their attention to him.

"See, we will all die if the balance is not regained. Let me repeat that for you. We… will… all… die. Not eventually, mind you. The moment it's clear that balance will never be regained, that's it. Over. Done. That's fact. How will you take care of your families then? Especially those of you with human children? Human extended families you love and care about? You'll be leaving them all behind to deal with a damaged and ravaged world we were supposed to protect… and you will have done nothing to stop it." Michael shook his head and pushed a hand through his hair. "Are you ready to face the purge? Face our Father, knowing you did little to honor our promise to Him? That we just sat aside and watched an evil imbalance overcome the human race and the planet?

"I know, I know. You all took a pure vow to serve our Father within the human race and you've faithfully done that. Many of you truly believe you're not to blame for this mess but you are Nephilim. I am Nephilim. We all dropped the ball. It is our failure… as much as the failure of those who took no vow, or those who took a warrior's vow of service with a soul sword in hand. It started many years ago with a mysterious disease that killed hundreds of our breeding females and far, far too many of our young. We were all aware. We took no action. We imagined it couldn't affect the balance enough for serious concern. Just an unfortunate deadly flu. Nothing major. But this imbalance grows every single day, every single moment. Look around. When was the last time you saw so many battle heat demons? Right in the middle of everything? Everywhere?"

Mumbles rose and rippled through the crowd, heads turning back and forth like swirling wind blowing a field of wheat.

He turned and walked back toward the stage, all heads following his trek, many faces fearful, but many becoming more and more angry. Too late to change his approach now. Michael pointed to a woman sitting in the end seat. "Can't you see the devastation caused by allowing such imbalance?" She nodded and bit her lip. He moved on, focusing on a well-dressed man. "By standing aside and watching?" The man pushed back in his seat. Michael turned toward the back of the room. "Seriously? Blaming the human race? It has always been *our* responsibility to protect the human race and their planet. We are the interlopers, the intruders. We are the race God did not intend. The race that convinced Him we could maintain the precarious balance between good and evil on earth to earn our worthiness. Seemed simple enough, huh?

"So now it's a mess and we face a purge. That's a lot to take in, my brothers and sisters." Michael drew a long breath and released it. "A hell of a lot to take in. What a freaking dilemma. What a damn mess. That I must come to you now and beg for your help. Beg you to come and do what our fathers', fathers', fathers vowed we would do since the beginning of human life on this planet."

He returned to the podium, and moving in a business-like manner, flipped through a folder he brought along. "Let's see… there are nearly ten thousand orphanage system awakened Nephilim in this room. Every one of you chose to serve our Father among the human race but we're facing the end unless something changes. Unless we reestablish balance. What went through your head at the point of making your Acclimation vow? What did you think? How many times have those thoughts raced through your heart since that day? Every time you hear a news report about terrorism, earthquakes, devastating floods and tsunamis? Every time madness overtakes human behavior? What do you *really* think?" He watched the squirming crowd. "Do you think, 'hey, not my problem, not my fault.' Or do you think, 'wow, something's really off kilter here.' Do you feel it in your bones, your muscles, your heart, aching through your wings? Something is really, seriously, *dangerously* off kilter." He paused a moment, watching the terrified faces in the audience.

"Once, long ago and at the tender age of eighteen, you sat before a guide. You listened and learned about your race, your future, your role to play. And, you were given a choice. I've guided hundreds of acclimates, I've witnessed hundreds of awakenings and many, many quickenings. I strongly believe in giving an acclimate the choice for how they will serve God. At eighteen, all of you chose to believe that God is here for you and at that time, it was a good and right choice."

Another moment of silence, a moment of respect for their choice, a moment for them to reflect on the horrific situation. "Well," he finally said. "Things have changed. I am here to ask you that question again. To ask you to help save our race, to step out of your comfort zone, to take up your regenerated soul sword and bring about balance or die trying, because face it… we will be purged from existence if we fail. We have one last chance to redeem ourselves. One last chance to stand together and prove our commitment to the promise made to our Father. And so, I ask each and every one of you…" He closed his eyes and gathered his strength. "Are you here for God, or is God here for you? Will you take up your sword, or live quietly and hope… *hope*… that we get through this terrible time without your help?"

His mind rang loud in prayer and fear and he felt his son's hand settle on his shoulder.

"Wow, maybe a little too rough, Dad," Ben whispered.

"Maybe. Maybe not. Either we get lynched, or we start regenerating soul swords." And Michael waited.

~*~

Tobias grinned like a lunatic. He loved the carnie life, the packing and moving, the shows, the battles, the performer warriors and most especially, the magic alive within his control. His energy expanded with each recruiting effort and regenerated soul sword. As another Counting war loomed, he felt joyful, ready to dance a jig. For a man so many thousands of years old, he sensed his own rejuvenation with the prospect of the coming clash. Tobias loved battle more than anything.

His life left little room for sentimentality. Without the overwhelming passion for Dawn, his stunning, young, red-headed Nephilim lover, he knew he'd be void of all emotion. It was the cost of being an ancient. Not that anyone would rationally request such a long life. After a century or two, it all starts to become unbearable. Watching the human race repeat horrifying mistakes ad nauseam has caused many an ancient to put a rope around his neck. He was a lucky one. He'd discovered his value early on. Connecting with the Nephilim and their cause made everything not only bearable, but exciting and challenging. In all his memories, nothing like the Counting to come had ever presented itself before. This one was big. The biggest, if he had anything to do with it, and Tobias certainly planned to have a lot to do with the coming Counting.

In the beginning, the world was so young and he traveled with Raphael. At first, he didn't realize what Raphael was, or even what he himself was. The realization of being an ancient is so very subtle, so diabolical, so hidden in the psyche of the recipient, that it takes decades to discover. The dubious gift of eternal life is bestowed by something ugly and manipulative. A connection never sought and seldom recalled. Raphael knew what was happening and cared for Tobias until the time came to give him the truth—and all his options. Tobias chose to work with the Nephilim race, feeling it was truly his calling and the best way to spend eternity. It didn't take long to realize that Nephilim were half human, and made all the stupid human mistakes. Between battles he would bide his time for the real fun—the repeated Countings that would shift reality until the world fell back into place.

No human or Nephilim alive had been around during the last Counting. Only the ancients and the archangels—who always took a powder when the real test presented—knew what was about to happen. But this time circumstances held greater difficulty. Lucifer had perfected his race of battle heat demons, and for some unfathomable reason, a young girl was supposed to lead the Nephilim race to victory against such creatures. Preposterous.

Tobias blinked and sniffed, closed his eyes in delight. Cookie had again outdone himself for breakfast. Last show, maybe ever, and the food would be extraordinary! Cookie had set out a buffet elegant enough for a five-star Manhattan hotel dining room. Fresh fruit, eggs prepared multiple ways, quiches, potatoes, fried chicken, baked fish, fresh vegetables tossed in herb scented olive oils. It was a feast for heroes, and every one of his troupe would be such. Bravery and courage, commitment and stamina, the true qualities of Nephilim warriors.

Even enjoying the spread, bitter sadness seeped into Tobias's coffee. It was all in the hands of the Nephilim big boys now—the Michael Allertons, and Cole Masters, and Gregory Parklands of the world. They'd set the tone, meet the warrior quotas, then all were to follow a little girl. Insanity.

Tobias itched under his skin, irritated to have been left out of that assignment but a much bigger one lay ahead. Gracious Caine, so young and inexperienced, needed Tobias and he would be there every step of the way. Teach her. Guide her. She was a kid. She'd listen. He grinned again. Who else could manage things while she batted her pretty eyes and wondered about the world she'd possibly never understand? Tobias hated the Orphanage System for just that reason. How could they turn out battle-hardened warriors if they were pampered and elegantly educated?

Deep inside his soul he already knew what to do. He would push his own ideas for true solutions to the repeated mistakes Nephilim make. Ah, but he wasn't Nephilim. He was a mere ancient, hanging around, Counting after Counting, just to assist the half-angel-half-humans toward survival. It was a seriously difficult life, pulling with desperation to make them see the real light, the one that identified eternal success. Humans don't get it, archangels don't get it, or at least his many, many centuries of knowing Raphael gave no indication that the superior celestial beings understood. Only one did, and that one repeatedly threatened everything. One. Lucifer. The answer. And only Tobias could see it. He knew a way to help the Nephilim race more than survive, he knew how to make them thrive.

As an ancient, his was a thankless job but it had its rewards. The tart apple pie attested to the positive perks of living thousands of years. There was always something more enthralling, more enticing, more delicious, and more dangerous around every corner. He was ready to face the most dangerous of all.

After brunch and conversation, his camp was enthusiastic for what lie ahead. They were toughened, confident, and well trained. Tear down, pack it all up, and head for the ferry. Already Tobias had sent forth his own magic to assure his show would occupy the last four ferries sailing to Ocracoke. He would immediately choose a prime space on the Caine girl's property and set up camp.

Arriving first gave him time to establish superiority over the coming rogue warrior troupes, and the girl. What he wanted was to make sure this would be the last Counting the Nephilim would ever face. He was playing God, he knew, but Tobias was also damn good at it. His warriors would follow his lead, even if they were unsure of his motive. His goals and intentions would drastically shift his reality. Tobias would no longer be listening to his advisors, his lover, or his even fellow-ancient, Garta. He had a plan, and the plan gripped and ground every muscle and cell of his mind and body, honing him for the win. The leadership he deserved, and the hopes he had always desired for himself among his Nephilim friends.

Garta caught his eyes and he heard her thoughts. *Oh Tobias, what are you up to now?* He smiled and wiggled his fingers playfully at her, then he had his beautiful lover take a piece of pie to the old healer. Watching Dawn's lovely hips sway, he sighed. He would love her before they left, but not again until after the Counting. Such delights were too distracting. He knew this all too well. Tobias was first and foremost a leader and a soldier. Soft things were for times of peace. It too would be folded up and packed away with the colorful strips of fabric that made his big top, and the pretty twinkle light that lined the walkways through his elusive carnie.

And Tobias wondered, as he did before every Counting—would he see any of it again? Or would he finally be able to triumph over all evil?

3

The pirate's maps and books were amazing, creating a convoluted network of portals identified by color and description. However, those descriptions left a lot to be desired. Edward Teach lived in the late 1600s and died in the early 1700s. Most of the locations he mapped had no name, others weren't even populated at the time, although several warned of vicious natives. He described the climate and general topography, and he understood that the future would present differently. A mountain was a mountain and apparently Blackbeard had little concern that it would move or crumble to the ground.

The inland locations were noted for the color and the letter L, whereas the east coast and west coast of America—where a pirate could more comfortably explore—were marked with a star. At the time there wasn't much to plunder along the American west coast, especially north. The rugged and desolate coastline troubled pirates, leaving little hiding coves or cover. The southern west coast was another story altogether back then, offering a pirate most of what he wanted. Teach listed names like Monterey, many miles north and many miles south of contemporary Monterey.

All of the notations along the shorelines of America and now Canada and Mexico received a grave notice of danger. Piracy was not real popular among the governing class in the seventeenth and eighteenth centuries. Everything Cole studied had to be taken with a grain of salt and a lot of imagination. How far north of Monterey was Los Angeles? San Francisco? These were two primary target cities for his search. Where the homeless live, and where the terrified, confused, and struggling Free-Winged of his race hid.

So many colors, so many locations, so much unclear. He had no actual plan when he kissed Gracie and prepared to leave. He knew which lighted portals were closest and figured it might be smartest to move fast, take each portal one at a time, then make his own notes, plow ahead to locate his needed warriors, then move on to the next. Cole ignored the nagging fact that it could take years. He'd do his best. At least it wasn't 1798 and thankfully, he wasn't a pirate.

There would be other challenges to deal with.

Cole stool still as death just inside the portal, praying that none of the many rushing demons would touch or notice him. His eyes darted left and right, gauging the landscape of that odd place, comparing it to the abbreviated map he'd made, folded tightly and tucked inside his back pocket. Good God, losing that map would mean losing everything. At least Gracie was keeping Blackbeard's treasure safe in the house. He could always go back and re-draw his tiny cheat sheet if something bad happened. But nothing bad was going to happen.

He was standing in the most dangerous part of his journey, close to the battle heat demons and the devil himself. All Cole had to do was get from there to his chosen portal, the bright yellow portal that should be closest to him. Easy-peesey, but not so much. Logical dimension was a relative term inside the eerie Alternate Plain, and he needed to adjust his thinking. A great place to start would be to put his concerns for Gracie, all alone at the house in Ocracoke, aside. Like that could be even remotely possible. So, Cole decided to let his concern for her charge him ahead. The sooner he finished his assignment, the sooner he'd get home and help her save the world. He grinned. Right.

Most of his adult life he'd slithered into and out of illegalities and dangerous situations. Would it be prudent to do what he was best at, or should he try something different? Maybe run as fast as possible to the yellow portal? Maybe slink around, low and quiet, careful not to catch any demon's attention? What would Blackbeard do?

He chuckled then proceeded toward the chosen portal without hesitation or hurry, strolling along as though he belonged there. At the moment before he leaned into the brilliant yellow entry, he jumped back and almost screamed like a girl. The biggest, most complicated battle heat demon Cole had ever seen stepped out at him. It was massive, six heads, so many arms and legs he couldn't count in his panic. At its back stood the shattered stumps where wings once existed. Nothing seemed alive on that creature. Its stench was nauseating, the reek of burned flesh and sulfur. Ugly, glowing eyes seemed to examine him from head to toe. One set blue, another brown, still another, black as coal. He held his breath as it slithered closer, blackness dripping like thick molasses from every point of the creature—nipples, elbows, chins, knees. It leaned within an inch of his face and Cole closed his eyes, awaiting the pain ahead. Its heat radiated, making Cole feel the tightness of a Badlands sunburn across his nose and cheeks. Then suddenly, the air around him cooled.

It was gone. He blinked, breathed deeply then tightened his fists to stop his hands from trembling. Nobody said this would be easy. Easy was no longer in his lexicon. Easy was dangerous and kept a soldier from watching diligently for the real and sudden danger all around. Still breathing hard, he stepped through the bright yellow portal.

Blackbeard described the portal location as a safe, hidden forest surrounding the small town of New York, but it was no longer safe, hidden, or a forest. It was on the curb, less than a foot from the street. Before Cole could adjust his eyes, all hell broke loose.

Swoosh! Whomp! The sound of shattering glass and crushing metal greeted him. That, and bitter cold air. Autumn in the Big Apple felt a whole hell of a lot like winter. Or, did perhaps the portals play with time as well as location? That would be really, really bad. He wrapped his arms around himself and hunkered against the wind. A few yards away was the source of the noise, a taxi wrapped around a telephone pole. The driver seemed fine, dialing his cell phone and cursing the pole rather than the weather. Cole cursed too. He hadn't thought to pack for this kind climate. Stupid. Nothing but clean tee shirts and socks. He had cash and could get himself a warmer coat, but maybe that wasn't the best idea. If he wanted to connect with the homeless Free-Winged, he had to look like one.

The sky spit icy rain and he stepped carefully. Nothing about the light confirmed it was the same morning he left Ocracoke. Grey and wet, it could be evening or midday. At least the street sign was clear. He'd stepped through the portal right at the East 106 Street Central Park entrance. Now he'd know where to go to get back home. He drew a sigh of relief.

Not surprisingly, there were almost no people on the street. It was a Sunday morning and ugly as hell, not the kind of day for a pleasant stroll in the park. Around the corner, greeting him like a kind hostess, stood a newspaper box. He squinted into the dirty, ice-speckled glass. The date was correct, thank goodness. The last thing he needed were time-travel-voo-doo-science-fiction complications.

"Hey!" came a grunt from behind and Cole turned.

"You Grissom? Joe Grissom?"

But before Cole could answer and maybe ask a few questions of his own, a fist smacked hard at the back of his head and he felt himself being quickly dragged by his backpack. Half-conscious and reminiscent of his drinking days, Cole went into self-preservation mode. Loose and dangling like a dead man, he permitted the assailants to pull him along the slippery pavement. His outlaw lifestyle raced toward him like a speeding train. Would these guys beat him? Kill him? Steal his backpack, his phone, money, and worst of all, the map in his pocket? *Shit, shit, shit!* As they dragged him around a bend and into an alley, he noticed a sign in a bus stop booth. In what was turning out to be a challenging day, was what he saw possible?

There was a large, professionally taken photo of Michael Allerton, all suited and head masterly. The headline was simple, cryptic, and sure to be effective.

EDUCATED TO FLY? TIME TO TAKE UP YOUR WINGS AND FLY AGAIN

Professor Michael Allerton at Pier 94

Three dates only. November 5, November 6, and November 7

For reservations call 1-800-777-6407

Either the world had shifted or crap was happening Cole wasn't aware of. Last he knew, Allerton was taking orders from Tobias. Seemed there was someone above Tobias after all. That made Cole feel a little better, until he was tumbled down a flight of metal stairs.

"Hey! Damnit!" he shouted and leapt to his feet, fists ready and a bloody nose dripping down his chin.

"Oh, uh, so are you Grissom?"

"If I was, is this how you'd treat him?" Cole ran the sleeve of his soaked jacket under his nose.

The one asking the questions seemed normal, just dirty, homeless and a little concerned. The other one, round, in his early twenties and definitely confused, danced from foot to foot like he had to take a piss. Wringing his hands, he asked again. "You Grissom?"

"You gonna hit me again?"

"No, sir."

That's when he finally noticed the light at their chests and the ethereal wings hanging lank and embarrassed at their backs. He'd found the Free-Winged, or, more accurately, they'd found him. Now what? Desperately seeking a clue, he focused on the light at their chests. Both were a dull blue. They were following orders, but were they good orders, or was Cole's lights about to go out? Should he play Grissom, or find another route around getting bashed in the head again? Both options looked ugly to him.

"Who's Grissom?" Cole asked like he had the right to be asking questions.

Just as the normal one made to charge, the odd one reached out and stopped him. "He's like us," grunted the fat dude.

"He ain't Grissom."

"We're gonna get our asses in a shitload of trouble if we don't get Grissom. Leave him alone, Haling. We gotta follow orders."

"Orders from who?" Cole demanded and both men stepped back. He focused on the fat kid. "What's your name?"

"Ice. Spelled big I, big C, and little E."

What the hell did it matter how it was spelled? Cole shook his head to clear it. Looking closer, he could see that ICe was more than just an over-weight homeless Free-Winged. He was a little slow. Maybe a bit autistic. His odd movements looked familiar. There were a few such students at Ariel's Gate. They were loyal, strong, but often confused kids desperate to please everyone. "Okay, ICe, who's giving you orders?"

And damned if Haling didn't get him again. All Cole could hope for was limited brain damage. The man packed one hell of a punch. He didn't wake until much later, tied up and bloodied, sitting in a makeshift cell somewhere deep under the city. Cold, hungry, and pissed off. Outside the cell made from pieces of discarded metal dog crates, sat a man. Bald. Norema. And the longest eyebrow hair Cole had ever seen.

"Joe Grissom, I presume?"

The man just gave a grin.

~*~

Michael stood, fully suited, his tie loosened, cuffs of his trousers rolled up, and his bare feet sinking into the cool California sand. A warm breeze defied late October as he knew it, and the restless ocean tickled at his ankles. Malibu. Unreal. Unaware. Unthinking. He was still reeling from the success of his first speaking engagement. More than eight-thousand regenerated soul swords. Eight-thousand additional warriors for their side. Not bad, but all around him, as he stood with his son watching a painful, beautiful sunset, slithered hundreds of slimy battle heat demons. Was Lucifer producing followers faster than they could?

"Are we gonna be able to do this?" Ben asked with a sad sigh, reflecting Michael's thoughts.

"Relax, buddy. Enjoy the beach. Just two more days here, two more shows. We head for San Francisco on Thursday. Too cold for sun worshiping there. Then New York. I hear it snowed in Manhattan last night."

Ben shuffled his feet, splashing water. "Is Gracie okay?"

"She is. Raphael is with her."

"And where the hell is Cole? What a good for nothing piece of shit! He was supposed to take care of her."

Michael's heart thumped. He'd watched the close friendship develop between Gracie and his son over the years—as their headmaster. Not as Ben's father. If he could have been Ben's father, he could have, well, done a lot of things differently. Maybe helped his son to see things with a less selfish point of view.

"Cole's recruiting, too."

"No. How? Bad idea. He's really kinda useless. What's he got that—"

Michael swung around with a quickness he didn't intend. Ben jumped back, wide eyed and nervous. "What?"

"You don't understand yet," Michael said with a growl, his fist tight at Ben's collar. "You need to start understanding. There's too much to do to make this easier for you."

"Okay, okay." Ben carefully peeled his father's fingers from his tee shirt. "So, hit me with it. Tell me everything."

"Inside." Michael turned and headed to the hotel, hoping Ben was right behind. He was.

"Why are there so many of them?" the kid whispered, eyes following several demons who casually sauntered around the beautiful lobby.

"Methinks sunny California might be good recruiting ground for the bad guys, too."

In the room with a spectacular view of the demon-infested beach, Michael ordered room service then slid out of his jacket and carefully lay it over the chair. These were the times he wished he smoked. He sat on the edge of one bed, pushed back his hair and pulled in a deep breath.

Ben reached for the television remote, then slowly put it down. "This is some bad shit, isn't it?"

Michael nodded and actually sniffled back a tear. "Yes."

"Hey, man. You did good! Who knew you could be so convincing?"

Michael gave a tilted glare.

"Yeah, well, you did go all headmaster on them a few times, but mostly you were really… well… convincing."

Michael sat hunched and exhausted, looking down at the locked fingers between his knees.

"Dad… please tell me everything."

His heart skipped a beat, then skipped another before Michael actually grinned. He looked into Ben's innocent face and sighed. "I don't know if you can deal with all this, but you have no choice. Do you realize that you, Gracie, and Ryan are the only three Nephilim of your entire generation to survive?"

"No, you sent them all away and they're just not eighteen yet, that's all. They're fine, they're just—"

"All dead." Michael watched his son struggle with such a reality. He explained his desperate attempts to save the Nephilim youth of Ariel's Gate, but he, along with every other headmaster around the planet, had failed. As soon as the children left their orphanage, they were killed one way or another. "I don't know how to explain it, but Cole Masters has done the impossible. He brought four of you safely through Acclimation."

"So, who killed poor Jenny?"

Visions of the too-pretty Jenny Perkins slipped across Michael's memory. How many times had he reprimanded her for turning her drab school uniform into a showpiece fit for a New York fashion runway?

She reminded him of Dawn St. Mary. Charming, kind, determined. Poor Jenny was gone, but Dawn had landed beautifully on the arm of the loyal and powerful ancient, Tobias. Michael liked Jenny's spark, her growing resolute nature, even the relationship she had with Ryan Sutcliff —although it was far more promiscuous than acceptable. Jenny was a symbol of the future, the kind of Nephilim to support either side of the spectrum, as a fighter and a supporter. Such a terrible loss. Michael cleared his throat. "I'm told it was an accident. That no one could have stopped it. She wanted to perform on that damn trapeze and the cables weren't set or calibrated for the weight yet."

"Maybe a demon screwed with the cables?"

Michael just shrugged. "No matter, she's gone. We're left with three of your generation, one a remarkable Pure Nephilim poised to lead us all to victory."

"She can do it, you know. She's so smart and strong. Gracie can do whatever you need from her."

"It's what we *all* need from her… our race, the human race, and the planet. That's a lot of weight to put on one young woman's shoulders." Michael rummaged through the courtesy bar, opened a small bottle of vodka, gulped it down and considered another. Not yet. Not now. Maybe never again. Such false comfort could only derail his efforts. "You miss her, don't you?"

"Gracie?" Ben dropped back onto the mattress with a bounce. "Yeah, but we're not, you know, involved or anything."

"I know," Michael said softly and watched Ben squirm a little, stare up at the ceiling and tighten his lips. "But we need to talk about Cole."

"What about him?"

"Cole Masters is the direct grandson of the archangel Makha'el, our Father's chief warrior. Cole is powerful, Ben. He's been quickened several times since his Acclimation. You need to give that man some respect."

"Why, because he can swing a sword better than me? I can learn, ya know."

"Ben, are you jealous of Gracie and Cole's relationship?"

"What relationship? I know that girl. She doesn't open her legs for just anyone!"

"Are you that protective of her? Or are you that blind to the powerful dynamic Cole and Gracie bring to our efforts?" He sat next to his son.

The kid was quiet for a long time. Michael did what he couldn't stop doing since Ben learned the truth. He looked at his son's good face, strong heart, and considered the powerful quickening that made the boy acutely aware. So why all the questioning? Was he looking for confirmation? Did Ben need to hear it from his father? Or was he looking to punish Michael? What was causing such a deep disconnect in an awakened Nephilim with the power of perception? Could it be…?

"Ben, is there something you need to talk about?"

"Nope. When's dinner coming?"

"Ben. Think. Use that brilliant brain of yours. That powerful perception you've been given. Tell the truth. Did I say anything here that you didn't already know?"

Silence.

"Did you—"

"No. I knew everything you told me. I know exactly how Jenny died. It feels like I was actually there and saw it!" Tears welled in the boy's eyes and he gritted his teeth, tightened his fists. "I knew they were all dead. I knew. I knew. Dad… I don't want to know this shit! It's too hard."

His instinct was to embrace his son and comfort him, but something in Ben's energy warned him off. "How can I help you?"

"Leave me alone."

Michael gulped and prepared to take another walk on the beach, give Ben the time he needed.

"No, don't leave me alone. Make it stop."

"I can't. It's your gift."

"How the hell is this a gift? Already I'm so fucking different from everyone else I know. I can't have this, too. This hurts too much." His eyes blinked and he focused on Michael who sat steel still. "I feel," he whispered and Michael leaned closer. "I feel like I'm split into thirty pieces… and every single piece is alive somewhere else. Where am I, Dad? Where am *I*?"

Michael swallowed hard, starving for another hit of vodka. "Ben, you're right here, in Los Angeles, with me. We're doing our part."

"Cole's in trouble in New York. He already knows we're going to be there. One of Parkland's advertisements or something. I'm not sure he'll catch up with us. I'm not sure he'll survive."

"It's not your job to worry about this stuff, buddy. It's just your job to know, have the perception, and let it work with all the other energies toward fruition."

"What fruition? He gets himself dead?" Tears slipped down Ben's face and he ignored them. "I can't know all this. Did you know that Tobias thinks he's going to run the show in Ocracoke? That Raphael loves chili dogs? Did you know that Gracie cries for all of us when she's alone? That her father is Metatron?"

Michael's jaw dropped. This was astounding. "Ah, of course. That makes sense. There are legends that Metatron is the author of that book."

"Did you know Gracie has a twin sister? Another of our generation… still alive?"

Michael gasped and shook his head.

"Dad, her fucking name is Esther and she's blood bound to Lucifer!"

When did Michael stand? How could he possibly control his sudden urge to run and hide? "Fuck," he whispered, pressing a hand to his aching chest. "Oh, holy hell."

Ben was gripping his hand tight, probably sensing his flight inclination. "Holy hell for sure. But Dad, there's more."

How could there possibly be more? Michael nodded, waited for the next bomb to drop.

"Dad," Ben spoke in a whisper.

Michael sat, once more looking into his son's eyes, prepared for any-thing. His hand tightened on Ben's arm and he nodded encouragement.

"Dad, I think… no. I'm… not sure I can deal with all this? You thought I was being thick, not understanding, but I do. Too much. There are a hundred worlds shouting at me at the same time, letting me in on way too many secrets. I know my mother's name is Rachel and she didn't want me. I know you always wished Cole was your son so you could guide him. I know so much and it hurts. Dad, I'm not normal. I mean, I'm not a guy like other guys. I'm… I like men. And *that*… alone is way too much for me!"

The boy fell silent and Michael ran a hand over the top of Ben's head, pushing hair from his eyes to see them better. "And?"

"Something's wrong with me."

"No."

"I can't deal with this coming out of the closet thing and the crazy ass power of perception!"

"And?" Michael's heart pounded in his throat.

"I'm not strong enough."

"That's what you think? Is that why you've been a royal pain in everyone's ass since Acclimation?"

"No, it happened later. My… quickening. Just before we met with the Emmaus Magic Show people."

"And you're pissed about all this… why?"

Ben dropped back onto the mattress. "Don't you get it. It's too much?"

"No, son. It's never too much. I'll help you through all these transitions, but you have got to be honest with me."

"Sorry I didn't tell you about… you know."

"That you're gay? No big deal."

"You're not disappointed, or pissed off or anything?"

"I am what I've always been, ridiculously proud of my son."

A knock at the door signaled dinner, but they didn't speak another word until long after dark, laying in their beds, far too charged up to sleep. Emotions raced through Michael. Would Ben do something stupid? Was he considering suicide? Did he really think he was cursed and not gifted with the power of perception? Worse yet, how could Michael explain it all and comfort his son at such a terrible time of personal confusion and fear?

He gazed across the room through the darkness, praying for strength. He couldn't lose the son he loved so much. Not Ben. Not because he was too busy, or stupid, or incapable of guiding him through the rough roads ahead.

"It's okay, Dad." Ben's voice floated over the sound of the surf drifting through their opened window. "I'm so not brave enough to off myself. Cole told me once that it's really hard to kill oneself. I know he's right. All I think about is the people I'd hurt."

"Me, Gracie, God." Michael blinked tears, wetness sliding down into his ears.

"Can you teach me how to control this power thing?"

"I can try."

"And the other thing? I feel better, knowing you're not going to hate me, ya know."

"Go to sleep. We have a busy day tomorrow."

Sickness wafted all around Michael's dreams. Like Ben, he felt pulled in a hundred directions. His eyes fluttered open to a brightening morning. The quiet dawn spoke to him and he nodded. He'd do everything he could to help Ben. He'd show his son how any Nephilim controlled power. One step, one choice, one commitment at a time.

But the nagging fear remained. Was Ben ready for it? Could he handle it?

4

Knock, knock.

I rubbed sleep from my eyes, fluffed my hair and Cia's colorful skirt, and walked across the kitchen. Unsure if I'd see an entire army or a lost demon, I took a deep breath and opened the door. Ryan Sutcliff stepped in and wrapped his arms around me. He didn't say a word. He just held tight and trembled, and I knew he was crying for Jenny—love of his life and my roommate for years at the orphanage—now dead and gone. My heart broke for him and all I wanted to do was sit him down and learn how it happened. Jenny was such a strong, capable Nephilim warrior. How was it possible for her to just cease to be?

My questions would have to wait. Behind Ryan, still tearful but shaking himself into the football quarterback hero he once was, stood the beautiful Raphael, glowing with inner light but wearing a serious expression, tattered jeans, and a black Iron Butterfly tee shirt.

"Gracie." The archangel's voice was like silk and really good chocolate. "There's a lot to teach you, little general."

I blinked and sighed. "There's so much to do around here. The land needs to be cleared for the camps. Someone has to make sure there's enough firewood and water. I need to get a job and pay the utility bills, and somewhere in there, I really need to learn how to cook. There's nothing left but soup." I blinked and rubbed my eyes again. Was I still sleeping? Why was I talking like a crazy person? Or maybe I just didn't want to hear what Raphael was about to tell me. "Uh… maybe we can get stuff done today and talk tomorrow?"

"Tomorrow is too late to begin." Picking the keys off the hook near the door—like he already knew they'd be there—the archangel tossed them to Ryan. "Buddy, can you work on clearing the land?"

Ryan brightened and looked like a kid with a new toy.

"Hey, read the manual!" I called out as he left the house. I'd hate to lose the clutch and have to figure out how to pay for a replacement. Looking into Raphael's beautiful eyes, I knew the least of my concerns was a clutch.

He sat at the table. I made a pot of coffee then settled in with a sad sigh.

"It's not so bad, Gracie. You father tells me you love to learn. This is your history. The story of the Nephilim race."

Maybe archangels didn't care about the tiny details. Maybe Raphael knew something I didn't know about how the water bill would get paid. Maybe, I thought, looking into his powerful eyes, it didn't matter. I love to learn. Dad was right. Already my heart pounded in my ears. Sipping hot, black coffee, I tried to smile then nodded, ready to learn everything I could.

"There have been several Nephilim wars and Countings since the beginning of man, but I will tell you of only the four most important. Starting with the War of the Lilies.

"From the very beginning, there was trouble. My beautiful brother Lucifer had his issues with Father's plan, with the dimensions, the magic. Perhaps with everything, and he made no bones about it. Father was tolerant, even jovial in the beginning, allowing his children, us, the archangels and angels, to tuffle and nip like puppies to find our place in it all.

"In those times, the world was so very different. A playground for us all to explore and appreciate. A spectacular piece of artwork in light and color, heat and ice, solid ground and flight. It took our Father far longer than seven days to create the heavens and the earth. It took millennia, and the process was slow and curious, laden with discovery and reinvention, shifting and solidifying, soft and hard. We, His original children, were a part of all this and in Lucifer's eyes, we were and would always be His favorite creations. The Morning Star was spectacular, and he still is. His heart was bigger than any of our hearts. He loved our Father with unconditional fervor and trusted that all would continue with celestial beings holding His complete favor.

"Then things became very complicated. The dawn of man, and the ever-controversial gift of free will bestowed upon the human race.

"Wait," I interrupted. "I don't understand."

Raphael tilted his head, then blinked, so I asked my questions.

"What's with this whole Lucifer is a good guy stuff? He's the bad guy. God doesn't love Lucifer. He can't."

"He does, Gracie. Our Father loves everything he made. Including Lucifer."

"No, no. He can't!" I stood and tried to pace, then gave up the awkward hobble for a glare down at him. "He's the devil. He's evil. Look what he did! He created those demons, look how he pulled poor Wally Dean to him. There was nothing really bad about Wally, he was just scared and… confused. That's being manipulative and only the bad guys—"

"Gracie, listen to the immaturity in your words. You are full Pure Nephilim. You must grow up and you must do it quickly if you're to lead your race to victory."

My heart skipped one beat. Another. I gulped, and shouted, sure it was the only way I'd get the words out of my mouth. "What if I don't want this? Any of it? I'm no leader. I'm just like Wally, terrified and weak."

"Weak?" It was the archangel's turn to shout and it rattled the windows.

I sat back in my chair and tried not to look into his eyes. Man, I was in trouble.

"How can you call Wally weak? He was the first, the only battle heat demon who has ever torn himself free of Lucifer's hold! It cost his life, Gracie. That's not weakness, that's the kind of courage you all need. That's the resilience you have. The power. The possibilities are endless if Wally, just a scared, confused kid, could accomplish such a feat."

I sighed and finally raised my eyes to meet his. "I'm scared. I don't think I want to do this. I'm not a leader."

He smiled. "Ah, but you are. I've been watching you from my bulldog point of view all your life. You, my dear, are a born leader. I'm charged with arming you, giving you the knowledge to make you stronger and stronger. Will you hear this history willingly, Gracie? I can put you into a dream state, so it may be easier to receive it all."

"No." I didn't want that. I wanted to be aware of everything he said, even if I didn't agree with it. I didn't want to fail, either. If Raphael thought I could do this, if Allerton and Cole thought I was capable… maybe I am. "No. Tell me. I'll try not to interrupt."

"That would be appreciated," the archangel said, then slumped down in the chair, sipped coffee and closed his eyes to continue.

I closed my eyes, too, wanting to hear his words and allow the visual of all he said to move in the darkness, like a movie or play, a magical, real, honest story.

"Where was I?" he began and I felt myself settle into what was to come.

Ah yes, the dawn of man and the gift of free will bestowed upon humankind. Until the moment the first man and woman opened their eyes to the garden provided for them, we—the angels and archangels—were the Father's only children. Yes, there were animals and creatures of the seas, creepy crawly things and tiny furry beasties. They were fine and fun to play with, but then came man… and free will was given to him.

Many who like reading the Bible prefer to believe the fiction that

Lucifer tempted Eve with the forbidden fruit and caused all the trouble that got so many of his brothers tossed from the heavens. There was no forbidden fruit. There were no rules in the garden. Only life and love and comfort and joy. No one was punished and forced from the garden. The earth, as it was wont to often do back then, simply changed and shifted. It was still being molded and formed. The world was unstable, dangerous. Not as constant as it seems today. This planet is continually changing.

At first, the first man and woman were wonderful companions. They were fruitful and created many children. Human women were glorious, so beautiful it was often hard to take our eyes from them. They triggered deep love and admiration from us, often more love than from the men of their own race. When the upheavals began, we ran in to help. There were earthquakes and exploding volcanos, terrible storms of flaming rocks and falling stars, causing cataclysmic disturbances all around the garden that is this planet. We were able to guide many to safe places, take care of the wounds, console the bereaved, and bury the dead.

It was during this time of fear and destruction that the gift of free will reared its head and caused the rift never to be repaired. Once we felt the humans were safe, we settled among them. For a millennium we inbred with the beautiful human women, as we have no women of our own race. Our children ware magnificent, special, powerful… especially after receiving their wings. But as life became more and more difficult on the planet, the human men became confrontational and territorial, and many women refused to continue to lay with us. This was acceptable, and no woman was ever forced. Many hearts were broken and emotions ran high.

But worse than all that was when the humans began to refuse our assistance for protection. It was their free will that gave them that power, and they were endowed with abilities even we could not claim. They lived short lives and chose to live them the way they wanted. Vast, tight communities became discontented with their brothers. Clans split off, battles for food and survival became common. Man killed man and we could no nothing but watch.

When the Father set the first rule, that man should love his neighbor and love God as they love themselves, few took heed. This is when things got very ugly. Lucifer, the Father's biggest advocate and second only to Makha'el in command of His armies, petitioned Father. He begged, he pleaded, he cried to the Father to remove free will from the human race. Lucifer was sure that such a gift could only hurt our Father again and again, for eternity. He paced before Him and stated his case—the weakness of the human race, the stupidity, the uncompassionate nature, and clear tendencies toward evil. When Father refused, Lucifer went a little nuts.

He campaigned among us and drew many to his side, then attempted once more to present his case to God. The Father shook his head sadly. "My dear Morning Star, can you tell me what makes you any different from the human race?"

"I have no free will, Father. I must obey you. They only obey when they wish to. We are far more loyal, far more powerful, completely committed to You."

"Are you, Lucifer?"

"I can prove man is worthless, Father! Just allow me to show you."

At that moment thunder split the skies and heaven and earth were one. All stood before Him—man and angel, Nephilim and Lucifer's followers. The proclamation was sure to begin the war, and Father knew it. I knew it. We all knew it. It was called The War of the Lilies, because it was the test of free will.

God said to Lucifer, "Do as you must." But before my brother could respond, he and all his followers were cast into a below place, far from Father's grace.

Lucifer and his minions lost their ability to heal, among many other unique powers. They could create illusion and shift the visual world around them, but not their own reality. They could whisper in a human's ear, but never force that human's hand. Lucifer took it as a challenge to prove his point. To this day the devil continues to tempt in hopes of convincing our Father to remove free will from the human race. This would accomplish two objectives in Lucifer's eyes. First, it would protect our Father's heart from the pain of being disobeyed. And second, it would reinstate the archangels and angels as God's most beloved race.

The War of the Lilies began with a strange disease that killed most of the Nephilim born of love between a human woman and angel. Those that survived were counted and found inadequate. Some of these Nephilim were my own children, grandchildren, and great-grandchildren. Some were my brothers who were still loyal to God. Like Lucifer, we petitioned our Father for mercy. The War of The Lilies was the beginning of a pact between God and the Nephilim race. A vow that continues to be broken, leading to wars and Countings ever since.

Often, I hear talk of the story of Noah and the agreement between God and man. That story is a version of the War of the Lilies, Gracie.

"What was the pact? What did Nephilim agree to do in exchange for survival in this world?" I asked through a tight throat. Raphael had surely put me into a dream state. How else could I have grasped such a story? I wanted to cry, to shout, to jump around and scream about it all. Did Lucifer really do this to protect God? Was that possible? All those bible stories that entertained us as children were just a tiny bit of the truth. Ah, well. It wouldn't be the first time humans told a story to their advantage.

Raphael stood with a grunt and stretched his arms high. "The Nephilim vowed to protect the human race and the planet. To maintain balance on earth." He looked down at me. "Not to rule the world, or be more powerful than humans… just to protect and keep balance."

"So, how the hell can we do such a thing with Lucifer out there doing his thing? Making demons and not fighting fair. It seems like he has all the advantage."

"First of all, Gracie, you've been here a mere eighteen years. Lucifer and the rest of us have been here since the beginning. There's a lot you can't possibly comprehend yet, but you will."

I glared and he grinned.

"And second, what is balance, little one? How can you gain balance if there aren't two sides? See?"

I blinked. "Huh?" But bile crawled up my throat and the facts suddenly smacked me in the gut. "Balance. It takes…"

"Dark and light. Hard and soft. Sweet and bitter."

"Good… and… evil?"

"Exactly."

"So, the need for balance is because of the devil?"

"Not exactly. It's because of everything. And the Father knew this. At times He has positioned someone at a precipice, poised to take on the dark role, just to create true balance."

My belly rolled. "Lucifer fell into that role," I whispered.

"As did a few others throughout time and history including Judas Iscariot, and many, many more. Gracie, balance can only be maintained if it's threatened, and someone must stand firm on both sides of the scale. There can be no life without both good *and* evil."

I had no words. Of course. It made perfect sense. I rubbed the back of my neck and wanted to start praying, that old fashioned begging kind of prayer we all do when we're scared to death. Nothing Raphael said felt very encouraging, because that all-important balance was tipping the devil's way and I was supposed to somehow win the battle.

"Over generations," the archangel continued, and I listened through the imagined screams, terror, and bellows of war, "balance becomes impossible and another war or Counting is required to remind the Nephilim of their promise." He walked to the refrigerator, opened it and stuck his head inside. "Is there anything to eat? I'm hungry."

My mind spun with images of Lucifer and heaven and the place below God's good grace. How could I think about food? I had a billion questions. What about Esther? She was sitting at the devil's side. Were she and I part of that good and evil balance? No. I refused to believe it. Esther was a victim. Not the devil's minion.

"This soup any good?"

I blinked. Raphael, like any goofy guy, rummaged through the refrigerator, opened the Tupperware lid and sniffed.

I rolled my eyes, took the container from him then tossed it into the sink. "I told you. We need to shop for groceries and I guess I have to learn how to cook."

"Nah, I saw a lot of restaurants on the way here. Let's track down Ryan and get some lunch."

This archangel was a conundrum. He was nothing like my father. Metatron was succinct and straightforward. He found humans a curiosity, but Raphael seemed to find us fun to be around. Perhaps he'd lived among us for so long, he knew how we function. His stomach was more human than Dad's, that's for sure. A war was coming with an impossible Counting we were sure to lose, and all Raphael could think about was food. Before we even climbed into the jeep, he announced his preferences with a big, contagious smile. A chili dog, nachos, and a beer. So not angelic, if you ask me. But then again, this particular archangel was once a dog that drank from the toilet.

5

The day started so well. Esther woke beside her lover, dressed, and left to please him with new recruits. But before she could even leave for the earth, Cia was dropped at her feet, burned and nearly dead. Then, the argument. She knew better but couldn't help herself. Sometimes even the prodigious Lucifer was wrong.

It should have been a great day. Esther held a pleasure and joy deep in her heart. She'd known for weeks now but said nothing to Luc. Maybe this one she'd hold. This one she'd love. Maybe it would stick around long enough to be born.

But something just wasn't right. Esther knew it, she just couldn't accept. Lucifer was her touchstone, her heart, her all. As a child he'd spend blissful hours playing with her in the fake compound on the other side of the portal. She never wanted for anything. They explored fantasy worlds and played with dragons. They laughed at strange mixed-up animals and she often slept in his arms. He was the consummate babysitter, nanny, teacher, friend, and confidant, and as she grew and turned fourteen, she already understood that she clearly belonged to him. Her blood vow was taken in the act of lovemaking. He was gentle and kind, compassionate and patient. He was her hero. The best person she knew anywhere.

Lucifer was often frustrated and angry, but Esther understood. He had a magnificent plan that had to succeed. He'd been working at it for so long… since, well, the beginning of time, if he was telling her the truth. His plan would change everything and make it better for everyone. Unfortunately, it would kill a lot of people, Nephilim, and even parts of the beautiful planet earth along the away. "But, my little love," he'd often whisper, warm in bed, cuddling her close as he told and retold his vision of the new world to come. "It's all for the best, you see. All for the best." And she believed it, until Gracie showed up. He had told her that her beloved twin was long dead. Obviously not. He didn't even seem to care that he'd been caught in a blatant lie. Something about this twist made Esther feel shaky, unsure, even a bit more thoughtful about trusting him so much.

Gracie was exactly like Esther, Pure Nephilim, unique in the world today. But deep in her gut Esther felt profoundly inferior to her twin. She had never felt that way before and she couldn't stop wondering why. Had Luc been honest with her about other things? Or maybe he really didn't know her sister was still alive? He'd promised her a huge portion of the world to come, but Gracie seemed far more poised and capable to handle that new world.

Covertly peeking around trees and shrubs, she'd watched her sister learn how to drive the jeep and work so hard to clear the property. Luc said many were coming to fight at Gracie's side, but how many could she possibly get? Lucifer had millions and was creating more demons every day. Was it just sibling rivalry, or did Esther sense something real and solid in her twin that was lacking in herself? To Esther, Gracie was a dynamo ready to make a big impact on the devil. Should she warn Luc? Or would that just bring about another temper tantrum that could hurt the baby?

With that thought, discomfort bit and burned in her womb. Pressing a hand against her belly, she glanced toward the Ocracoke portal. Did she really want to sit there and wait for Cole? Grab him, struggle with him, try to seduce him? Feeling as bad as she did? Her hand cradled the ache below her belt. Was it worth it? But could she deny the devil? She loved Luc, but, for the first time ever, she wondered, did he love her? He was generally good to her, but did he love her? The pain intensified and she almost cried out.

Luc told her that he could heal anything that bothered her. He never did, explaining that her pain, be it a skinned knee or broken arm, made her stronger for the time her strength would be needed. The growing ache tormented her, but she'd not speak of it to him. He wouldn't help her anyway. Tears dripped from her eyes, pulling black mascara down like drawn lines. She was losing it. Again. It had happened a few times before, but stupidly, she thought it would never happen again after her awakening. Either she'd never again conceive, or she'd never again miscarry. Why did she imagine such a thing? Pure Nephilim was not archangel status. Pure Nephilim had powers, but not really great powers. He'd repeatedly told her so. She'd never be as powerful as Lucifer. But shouldn't she feel something? Some surge of energy? Some… power? All she felt was, human.

Esther took a deep breath and stepped ahead. With a wave of waffling energy, she slipped onto the earth realm. "Oh!" Sudden agony made her double over. She didn't want to lose this one. She felt like she needed this baby. It would be her only hold on Luc. With the war so close, he might easily toss her aside for Gracie, just like Cole did. No, Cole didn't toss her aside for Gracie, he loved Gracie. Could she count on the same from Luc?

The misery ebbed and flowed with her thoughts, one moment bearable, the next, excruciating. Sweat gathered on her brow and she found it hard to breathe. Esther had to think of something else. Something good. Blinking, she tried to remember how beautiful the peach grove once was, how fragrant, how comforting. Like the giant weeping willow, both the grove and the magic tree had gone silent and dead. So much lost.

Dizziness gripped her. She gasped and blew it out slowly. The baby was fighting to stay with her, she just knew it. A grim chuckle drifted from her lips and she leaned back against a dead peach tree. Rosemary's baby. Facts were facts. She could conceive, she was fertile and taken to Luc's bed often enough. The problem was that it never held. Wouldn't it be nice to keep one? How would her life change?

A dark, ominous shiver slid like a snake up her spine. That was senseless, dangerous thinking. The last thing Luc wanted was a domestic life. He would rule everything soon. Kids were not in that plan. Neither was the weakness of pregnancy or motherhood. He wouldn't want that at his side.

She tried to stand but instead sat still as death in the trees and watched Gracie, dressed in Cia's favorite skirt, leave the house in the jeep with two handsome men. Esther knew that Morning Star, most beautiful of all celestial beings, desired her day and night, but what the hell was it about her plain, crippled sister that attracted so many pretty guys?

And, she wondered again, where were her own Pure Nephilim powers? When would she receive her first quickening? Could those powers save the baby? Was something wrong with her Pure Nephilim celestial part? Luc told her everything, told her how most Nephilim are terrified to get their wings, horrified of their awakening, and all because no one thought to let them just sleep through the traumatic transformation. It was the gift he gave to her, blessed slumber without terror or fear. When she woke, there was no pain from torn flesh as wings emerged, no sudden awareness of new powers, no soul sword. Luc had taken care of it all. It was the first and only time he ever healed her. He boasted of her massive wings, so beautiful and strong, how much her damaged back bled, how he stopped the flow and erased any sign of the wounded flesh. Luc explained the need to hide her soul sword to protect it for the battle to come. It was the kindest thing he'd ever done for her.

But looking at Gracie, she saw clearly that her sister was different. She glowed. She was brave and strong in ways Esther never was. Part of her hated her twin, but the biggest part of her loved the girl. Her sister completed her. That's what twins did. It's why Luc wanted Gracie, too, to have all the power on his side, to make them both stronger, but Gracie looked perfectly sufficient without Esther.

With a sudden shift, pain soared through her body from head to toe. Something was seriously wrong. Esther turned, vomit spraying from her mouth. Three battle heat demons stood to watch and she waved them off. The idiots were likely to carry her through the portal and burn the hell out of her, like they did to poor Cia. One lowered a face close, while a second head, attached at its back, peeked over with a strange, lop-sided expression of curiosity. "I'm fine," she grunted. "Don't you have something to do?"

They always did that, watched over her, or just plain watched her. The idea suddenly occurred to her—did they hate her or care about her?

Oh dear. She'd never thought that way before. Before. Before her awakening. When this stuff happened, she knew she was protected and nothing bad was coming. The pain intensified and she actually felt something slide free from her body. Tears of agony and sadness ran down her face but Esther Caine, the devil's woman, didn't cry over crap like this. She was never like this before. Never so human. So weak. What a mess.

She carefully stood and went to the empty house. It smelled of Gracie, and cookies, and loss. Esther showered and tried to think of more important things. She had a quota. If chasing after Cole wasn't in the cards, she'd need to at least return to Luc with no less than twenty recruits. That felt impossible. She dried, dressed, and looked around. The shabby old house was her home, as much as life with Lucifer was her home. All she wanted was to slide into her own bed and rest, but there was no telling when Gracie and her handsome entourage would return.

She was still dealing with heavy bleeding. Esther couldn't stay there, but she also couldn't just go on like nothing had happened. She couldn't tell Luc. He'd be pissed she hadn't confessed the pregnancy earlier. It was time to think of herself. To make her own decision. She needed to rest and recuperate. She'd deal later with building the perfect lie, for now it was a matter of survival and she knew Luc wouldn't heal her. He would punish her. What if he refused to heal Cia as part of that punishment? More tears fell, big and persistent, as she gingerly walked toward the peach grove.

No recruiting would happen that day. Determined not to die, she chose to do something else. She chose to hide, and there was only one place safe enough for her on earth. Weak and growing weaker by the moment, she stepped through the portal and to her favorite place. Whatever happened, she'd be taken care of there.

~*~

It was so strange, watching Raphael work his magic over everyone. The diner was quiet, high season now past and the weather teasing at a chill. The cook had no chili, but whipped up a batch just for the archangel's hot dog. Ryan, restless as usual, started drumming his hands on the table, eyes closed, hearing music in his head and ignoring my frustrated expression. Boys will be boys, I guess, but I didn't need Ryan to be a boy. I needed him to be a man. Didn't he realize there was a war coming?

My mind spun with everything Raphael told me. Half of me knew it had to be true, the other half battled to protect my stupid sense of fairness. If Esther could side with the devil, she shouldn't get God's love. But two statements kept repeating inside my head. *God loves all his creation.* And, *you can't have good without evil. That's what balance is all about.* Don't you just hate when archangels make sense?

Burger and fries for me. Grilled cheese for Ryan, and Raphael's chili dog had finally arrived. I think he was drooling. Looking at my lunch mates I couldn't help but recognize how remarkable my simple life had become. Honestly, even with all the conflicting concepts in Raphael's lesson, I couldn't wait for the next. I'd gone from a bookworm who only believed what was printed on the page, to a warrior, relying on the storytelling power of an archangel. I had to admit that I was excited. This life, as frightening and dangerous as it is, as terrifying as the battle ahead could be, is far more interesting than the normal life I thought I wanted. I just had to keep some of my practical nature intact as things progressed. Metatron had told me to be strong against those who could be against me. I think I can do that. It felt good to set that scared little girl aside and feel like a woman of substance for a change. Well, at least I was trying.

I sighed and dug my phone out, gave it a glare then dropped it back into my pocket. Deep in that pocket, Cia had left a few personal things—a tube of Chapstick, a fingernail clipper, a few quarters. Every time my fingers grazed the items, I fought fears that I might never see the beautiful ancient again.

"Where's Cia?" Raphael asked, orange grease dripping to his chin.

His question startled me. "Are you psychic?" I had been able to block Tobias's mind-reading powers. Was I going to have to deal with Raphael's?

He shook his head and pulled a thin paper napkin from the dispenser to mop up the mess. "No. Every time I've ever been to Ocracoke, she's been here."

"I think she's dead." Tears fell and Ryan squeezed my hand.

The archangel nodded sadly. "Gracie, if that's true, remember. Cia lived a very long and productive life."

"So what? Does she have to die? I mean, what's the point of being an ancient if you can't keep on living?"

"Hell," Ryan grunted between stealing my French fries. "Can you imagine how boring that could get? Living forever?" He shook his head then sighed, despair dimming the blue of his eyes and he melted into a softer version of himself. "Sorry. I'd give anything for just one more minute with Jenny."

"Death is part of life, even for the ancients." Raphael waved for another chili dog.

I pushed my plate away and checked my phone again. Thirty-six hours and no news. Was Cole hurt? Did he forget all about me? Was he that insensitive? I just needed to hear his voice. My soul hurt, every muscle strained, even my heart seemed to beat slower when he wasn't with me. For the first time I realized, it wasn't that I, the fairer sex, needed a man around. It wasn't that I loved him so much I couldn't live without him. It wasn't even that I was still mad at him and wanted to shout into his ear about it. It was that I *had* to be with him, and even if he had to be far away from me, I had to know that his heart was with me. It's our connection. The power that bound us together, for each other and for the cause. I couldn't help but chuckle at that thought, feeling a little like a starving Russian peasant rebelling against czarist rule. I wanted all my comrades at my side. We had the devil to fight.

Still, why hadn't he called? Was he really in trouble? I fingered the phone and sighed.

"Hey, you got your phone activated? Cool." Ryan grabbed the device and started playing with it.

"Hey, wait, I need that. I'm waiting for a call!" I struggled to get it from him and he held it away, grinning like a lunatic.

Raphael leaned back, his arms spread wide like wings across the back of the booth and smiled his angelic smile. No help was coming from that front so I kicked Ryan under the table. Hard. He jerked and shouted, then his iced tea tipped, pouring across the wooden surface and right into Raphael's lap. The archangel wasn't smiling anymore. Four women, a waitress, two customers, and, I swear, a lady walking past the restaurant on the street, ran to help clean up the spill—and gaze into the beautiful face of Raphael. He looked pleased with himself.

"You know what," I hissed when they left, still reaching for my phone, well out of grasp because of Ryan's ape-long arms. "Raphael, you *are* a dog," I hissed, anger oozing from my words.

Oops.

Silence.

We all stilled. I blinked. Then Raphael gave a loud guffaw that led us into peels of laughter. I giggled so hard my belly hurt, and Ryan snorted over and over again. He had the weirdest laugh in all of Ariel's Gate. I sometimes wondered if that was why he laughed so seldom. To avoid embarrassment. But we weren't embarrassed, we were rolling in joyous revelry. Good God it felt good to laugh, to be young, light, full of life, unburdened by what lay ahead. Even for just one moment.

"So, who's supposed to call?" Ryan stood, now his gorilla-long legs were in play. I gave up trying. "Ben?" he asked. I glared. "Allerton?" A bigger glare. "Cole?" He winked and I nodded sadly.

The happy mood was gone. "Oh." Ryan shrugged and ran his fingers over my phone. "When was he supposed to call?"

"The minute he reached his destination safely. I'm… I think… I'm afraid he might be, you know…"

Ryan looked to Raphael who gave an approving nod. "So." His fingers moved swiftly. "You call him."

He handed me the phone and I could hear it ring. Holding my breath, all I could do was pray that Cole would answer.

6

ole squirmed under the stranger's glare. He glanced around. It was dank and damp, cold and smelled something awful. But he had a bigger concern. Recalling that Allerton suffered a loss of power when held captive deep under the Tribunal's courthouse, concern flared. He was definitely underground, but had no clue how deep. "So," he said, trying to sound cool and nonchalant. "I suppose you're not Joe Grissom. Who are you?"

The man's clothes were shiny from years of dirt and grime, but his face was clean and freshly shaven. His hair was smoothed back and hung down below his shoulders, yellow as the sunshine. That face was strong and chiseled, and his shoulders and chest muscles were, too. If he wasn't a destitute Free-Winged, Cole would have suspected the man was a romance novel cover model.

"All that matters… is I know who you are. Cole Masters."

Cole almost panicked then gave in to his fearful curiosity. He'd been unconscious for a while. He dragged his backpack close and dug through. His wallet, ID, cash, notes, clothes, even his cell phone, were all there.

He looked up.

"Hey buddy. We're homeless, not thieves. Everyone here's struggling. We manage. No need to fucking steal, even from strangers who have no damn good reason to be here."

"Where's here?" Cole worked to steady his heart. The guy said they didn't steal, but he didn't say anything about murder. Visions of Gracie floated in his mind. His original thought was to bring her with him, but thank God he hadn't. She'd be right there at his side, caged like an animal, cold, hungry, terrified. "Answer me!" he finally shouted.

"I don't gotta say nothing 'til we know everything we need to know about you. Could take a while."

"I'm hungry," Cole said with a frustrated huff. How long was *a while*?

"Don't worry, we'll feed you." Cole's brow knotted and the man grunted a laugh. "We don't eat outta no garbage cans, mister. Some of us work and we all share the cash. Eat pretty good, too. Food's on its way."

Cole shuffled his butt for more comfort on the cement floor. Light drifted in from behind and to the right, it seemed like natural light. If so, he'd keep his powers, but no matter. So far there appeared no good reason to shoot flames at the guy. All Cole wanted was to help, and in turn, get them to join the cause. Maybe this guy was too far down the food chain to make any conversational headway with, but he might be able to learn the lay of the land from the nameless one.

"So, tell me how that works? Making a paycheck is a big deal, it can get someone out of places like this and to a better place."

The man growled like an animal. "Then who's gonna take care of all the rest of the gargoyles? The ones that can't work, can't see, can't hear, got missing limbs, or missing brain cells?"

The man's eyes glowed and Cole feared he was about to witness a quickening power he might not survive. "Calm down. I just asked. So, you take care of each other. You know, I'm a... gargoyle, too."

"Yeah, but we don't know you, so your ass stays here until we figure you out."

"You could just ask me, you know."

"Not my job. *Ahhh…* here comes dinner!" He stood and almost jumped at ICe as the big kid entered, McDonald's bags in hand."

"Hey ICe," Cole said casually, like it was normal to sit in a cage. "What ya got there, buddy?"

"Um, burgers, cheeseburgers, fries, and fries." He turned to the jailor. "Pollo said he gets this food, and I'm supposed to watch him for a while. You can leave."

"Good. Did you eat, buddy?"

ICe nodded and sat. "Old Mamma's waiting. I left bags for you with her."

Cole ate like it might be his last supper, closely watching ICe play with a string between his fingers, knotting it into a long, crocheted chain that wrapped repeatedly around his wrist. "Hey ICe, thanks for the burgers."

ICe shrugged, focused on his chain.

Cole licked ketchup from a cheeseburger wrapper, wondering when he'd last ate. Breakfast with Gracie. How long ago was that? A day? Two? "Hey, ICe, how far underground are we?"

"Not far. Too far down and it starts to hurt. McGuire found this place. Calls it a sub-basement. Up there is an abandoned building." His finger pointed up then returned to knotting, knotting, knotting.

"You nervous?"

"Uh-huh."

"Why?" Cole grinned when the man looked into his eyes. "Everything's fine."

"It ain't," ICe whispered. "Those black things are everywhere. Jeff's missing, Callie got sick when she touched one. Now she's dead." His broad butt scooted closer. "I'm scared."

Cole sighed. "I know. But if you can get me out, I'm sure I can help you all."

"Can't."

Bing Bong Bing Bong

And ICe suddenly leapt to his feet. "Ahhh!"

Cole's phone, loud and reverberating against the cement walls had scared the crap out of the poor guy. "Hey, hey it's cool. Just my phone. See, it's nothing. It can't hurt you."

ICe pressed his hands to his ears and squeezed his eyes tight.

Cole answered the phone, sufficiently quieting it and the trembling big man. "Hello."

"Where the hell are you?"

Gracie! It was Gracie, and even with that terrified, angry sting in her voice, it was the most beautiful thing he'd heard in a while. "Hi, uh, I'm here. I got through. New York."

"And?"

"Sweetheart, I… um… I can't talk right now. I'm okay at the moment. But I need to get back to what I was doing."

Silence.

"I love you, Gracie."

More silence.

"I'm sorry, baby. This isn't a good time." Four burly men were stomping their way to the basement and dismantling the cage. Cole stood and backed away from the men. The racket was ridiculous and ICe had run for quieter places. "Honey, I gotta go."

"I love you, too."

Thank goodness she'd said it. Those men weren't going to patiently wait one more minute. He dropped his phone into his backpack, shrugged it over a shoulder, and waved a hand. "Lead the way."

~*~

Cia woke with a start, pain searing through every inch of her body as a crackling screech vibrated all around her. It couldn't be her own scream. Her throat was crisp with demon burns. Confusion made her fingertips tremble and with great effort, she forced her eyes to open.

"Ahh, my dear Selancia," Lucifer said softly as he turned from his work across the room. Behind him panted a demon, or perhaps it wasn't quite yet a demon. There were too many legs, arms, and heads, but the creature's flesh was just bruised, not yet black as dripping tar. On the floor lay two sets of bleeding wings. The tips of one still fluttered like a fish desperate for water.

Lucifer removed bloodied gloves and tenderly ran a finger across her brow. She grimaced at his touch and gave an animal-like growl.

"I can't help you, Cia. I want to, but you know…" He shrugged, his face sad but unbearably handsome.

"It's your weakness." Cia forced a painful grin.

The devil's expression subtly shifted from compassion to annoyance, a sure sign that Cia should stop, but she didn't. She couldn't. This was her first and only chance to really speak her mind. To hurt him.

"You," she said with a grunt, attempting to sit up. "You are the weakest of all His angels. You can't heal… you have no foresight… you have no—"

"Enough!" It was an outraged shout, and yet his hands gently assisted her, piling pillows at her back and adjusting her sheets. "You ancients are so damn arrogant. Like you know something we don't."

"We do. I know you are weak, and I know I will die here in… in… what is this place?"

He smiled and his face was radiant. Hands out, he spun like a proud child. "This is my laboratory, Cia. Can you imagine the things I've accomplished here?"

The victim across the room whimpered.

"I have created an entire race all my own! A loyal race who comes willing to my side and gives of themselves. A race of warriors that the

Nephilim can't conquer, and the humans will fall to and worship." He rolled a stool close and sat near her face. "I have done what no other has even imagined! Some of my celestial brothers are waffling, Cia. They seriously consider joining me. I don't actually need them. Millions are already mine, and more are running from fear and confusion right into my loving arms."

"Loving?" Her voice was a miserable squawk.

"Yes, my dear. They know I love them. I've given them everything they need! Power, leadership, guidance, guaranteed success. In a single generation I will have changed the world. I've been cultivating my warriors since the day they were born. Leaning close and whispering. Promising. Showering them with rewards. They are mine."

Cia glared. "Is that what you did to Esther?"

"Esther? Oh my, no. Can you imagine tearing away the wings of a pure Nephilim? Those wings have far too much power to destroy. It never mattered with my little Esther, there was no need. She joyfully lay with me and we are one. She does my bidding, and doing so as an intact pure Nephilim gives me all that power you think I don't have."

"Heal me."

"I can't, Cia."

"Then take me to Gabriel."

"No. I have far too much to do here to waste time with that old, self-righteous curmudgeon."

He held a water glass to her lips and she sipped but never moved her eyes from his. An intense glare, as though she really did have power over him—a kind of tightened fist around his throat. Few played chicken with Lucifer, but they'd been long at this game. They'd made a deal and he broke it. Of course he did, but how else could she have kept Esther safe in such a place for so long? He promised not to harm the child. In his eyes, fourteen was far past childhood and Esther was free for his taking. The blood vow was simple. The rest, knowing Esther's extreme independent nature, surely complicated things for the devil. That was

Cia's greatest hope.

"Don't die, old woman. Esther will never forgive me."

"You break promises all the time. Why would she be surprised?" Oh, how she wanted it to sound like a threat, one he should fear, but her ancient body was decaying from the inside out, the blackened burns seeping deeper and deeper. She could hardly bear the pain.

The creature across the room screamed and her vision shifted to its blackening body. As she was dying, it was coming into its power. "What have you done?" she gasped.

"My job, Cia. Maybe you should rest, my dear."

"I will never do as you say, Morning Star. Never." And with those words, she closed her eyes. Her life had been too long, too hard, too full, and she was far too tired to fight any longer. With very little effort, Selancia left the life she'd been bound to for hundreds of years. Her soul slipped and swayed and went to a quiet place to recover. All her cares and worries for the planet, Metatron's beautiful twin daughters, and the Nephilim race melted into oblivion. But she wasn't far enough to escape the sound of Lucifer's bellow. It sounded like a cry of agony. Selancia had finally had the last word.

Standing over the dead ancient, reverence and sadness overwhelmed the devil. Tears burned his face raw and his heart ached. "Goodbye, my old friend." He whispered the ancient words and with the wave of his hand, Cia's destroyed body dissolved into the air, gentle sparks lifted and lost their light. The sound of sobbing caught his attention and Lucifer sighed. This, he would have to deal with.

In the far corner stood an eight-foot-high bell jar. It glowed like an opal, wavering with color and light. A subtle heat and vibration emanated from it, and the distinctive scent of ripe roses wafted through the air as he neared. Step by step, Lucifer wanted to pause and admire, hold his breath, tremble with fear. Inside that glorious jar sat his pride and joy, the most powerful of all his experiments. It was the element sure to turn the tide and win him the earth forever. Tender hands covered the sobbing face, but he knew that face well. Massive six wings drooped and lay, dripping down her back and into a puddle at her knees.

Lucifer let his heart lighten with pride and he walked around the bell jar. She was magnificent, and the most difficult part of getting her was awaiting Esther's awakening. He was ready for that critical moment, and as the human half of Esther slept a deep mystical slumber, the winged Pure Nephilim arrived and was trapped, stolen from her other self. She was his slave until he would reunite them again, only moments before the coming battle. By that time, even Esther's defiant free will would always bend to his every whim. Esther's heart required the painful scar of Cia's loss, as well as the loss of many others along this journey to toughen and harden her. He would break her spirit, just as he'd stolen her Nephilim half.

She must suffer, as she was suffering that moment, alone and afraid, bleeding and imagining she was hiding something from him. Of course, he'd known of her condition. It was nothing he ever wanted, and the devil made sure to poison the seedling of life early. Every time. Unlike his brothers, he held no love for human or Nephilim women, no interest in fathering Nephilim children, only irritation at their free will. They were humans with wings, nothing more. Ahh, except for the specimen in the bell jar.

Difficult times lie ahead and his plan was meticulous. Esther the human and Esther the Pure Nephilim were an integral part of his success strategy. For now, he was happy just to know his secret. Esther had no clue that she'd lost her celestial self. He'd augmented her senses with his own influence, energies he wanted her to be used to and comfortable with. After his triumph she would sit at his side, be his queen, and help him rule over everything for a brief while. He will have proven forever that his Father was wrong—that giving the human race free will was bound to hurt Him. The Father would reward him for proving such a flaw and bring him home, even permit him to rule over the earth, a planet filled with beings that would no longer have free will. Lucifer would once again bask in the glory of God forever. Esther might not make it to that level in heaven. She'd have quite a few sins to pay for, thanks to his own manipulation, but they were her choices. All her own sins, selected with her free will.

Lucifer smiled and returned his full attention to the demon's transformation.

The irony of Cia's comments made him chuckle. Weak? He was far from weak. He could not only take multiple mundane Nephilim and turn them into singular, powerful, killing machines, he could also split the human from the Pure Nephilim. He turned and winked at the sobbing, translucent creature in the bell jar. "How's that for powerful!" he said.

7

Wow, it was all happening so fast. We got back from lunch and Tobias was there, standing, hands on hips with a grin as wide as can be. That man was pretty pleased with himself. He pointed here and there while various trucks and campers slowly shifted until they formed the exact, perfectly compact camp he wanted. He turned and opened his arms wide. "My dear Gracie!" he bellowed, like I wasn't mere feet from him.

That was so not the reception I expected, seeing as how Cole and I slipped out of his camp a week ago without so much as a good-bye. I noticed that the largest of his vehicles, all those eighteen-wheelers, were nowhere in sight. Thank goodness, there'd never be room for them all, especially after the remaining forty-some eastern rogue warrior camps arrived. I couldn't help but wonder where the camps not heading to Ocracoke would gather. Did they know about the portals already? Were they mustering near one of those magical doorways someplace else in America? Or maybe they were just awaiting instructions from higher up.

I stepped closer to Tobias and he embraced me like a bear.

"This is good land, little one."

"I know," I grumbled into his substantial chest.

Finally released, he held me at arm's length and looked me up and down. Satisfied, he waved an arm. "Go on, everyone's waiting to say hi."

No longer interested in me, he turned to Raphael and I had a strange feeling Tobias was about to share secrets maybe I should know about, too.

"Go on." He gave me a gentle shove and I stepped away. Ryan shrugged and walked with me.

The camp was a pared-down version of the usual carnie camp. No Ferris wheel, no food trucks. The communal tent was there. Small sleeping tents and campers lined up neatly, like little suburban streets. Someone actually put up a street sign with two arrows—one direction said *Battle Ground Road*, and the other said *Salvation Avenue.* Good to see that someone had a sense of humor about this mess. Without all the show elements to deal with, the neat little camp came together quickly.

Beauty Low, the prettiest bearded ringmaster I've ever seen, was sitting comfortably under her camper awning, watching the goings on. She smiled and we joined her, I on her blue striped lawn chair, and Ryan, sitting cross-legged on the ground, his eyes observing everything. Was that his quickening gift? Being able to see and evaluate stuff faster than any normal man? Crap, I hoped so, because I couldn't make heads or tails of what was happening around me. I thought this was going to be a gathering of warriors waiting to fight. It didn't look or feel anything like that.

"It's so good to see you, Gracie." The light at Beauty's chest glowed a brilliant gold. She was magical, according to Cole. She held things together, like the performances and the maintenance of protective veils. "This is going to be so exciting, children."

"What? War?" Ryan shook his head. "Where's the training tent?"

"Training's over, young master. Real preparation for war requires expanding our quickening powers… so…"

She winked and I shrugged. "What?"

"Performances, Gracie! There will be many, many performances by all troupes before the Counting. Forty-one powerful rogue warrior troupes all in one place. As I understand, it hasn't been done since the last Counting. This should be spectacular." She sipped lemonade from a tall glass then signaled for us to go on into her camper and get some if we liked. I didn't. Naturally, Ryan did. He came out with a box of cookies, too. Beauty's eyes twinkled. "Bought those just for you kids," said the health-conscious ringmaster.

Watching her, recalling Tobias's greeting, and observing the kind waves and smiles from passing showmen and women, I couldn't help but feel strange. A little patronized.

We walked all the way around the camp, chatted with Billio, the snake man, Ballister Green who invited Ryan to stay in camp with them, and even Benny Beans, the dwarf clown, still, as always, in full face paint. Ryan seemed to be enjoying the reunion, but I sensed a gritty discomfort. As we passed Cookie, sweating over a really big, really hot grill, he scratched his chin and tossed a sweaty arm over Ryan's shoulder. "Ya know," the camp chef said, "God loves barbecue."

Ryan laughed, but I felt my brows knot.

"It's true, Gracie. It's in Leviticus. Look it up."

Heading toward the house, I couldn't help but look back a few times. Tobias had arrived first and chosen the most strategic area in the open field—a slightly raised area where he could see everything from the front of the camp, to the distant tree line in the back, and even past the house. He didn't take up too much space, and last I saw, he'd already mapped out a place for each coming show. I never got the impression that Tobias was the head honcho, chief leader of all rogue warrior groups, but it looked like he thought so. Was I going to have bickering and alpha male crap to deal with? "Don't you think something's fishy about all this?"

The sun was setting and Ryan, being chivalrous and all, was walking me home. He stopped, thought a minute, then shook his head. "Nah, those people were always friendly."

This felt a little too friendly. Like they were hiding something from me. So much for my presumption about Ryan's super power. Whatever quickening he'd had, if he even had one, wasn't going to help me figure out what was really going on.

Darkness fell and I stuck to the house, Blackbeard's maps, Dad's silent book, and my own thoughts. I gulped back concerns for Cole. He was definitely in some trouble. I could hear it in his voice when we talked. The idea shook me to the bone. What would I do if something happened to Cole? I couldn't think about that, I had to think about things I could actually do something about. One of the clowns brought me a platter of barbecue and I swear, God would've loved it. Cookie was the best part of the Emmaus Magic Show if you ask me. Proof that straight forward, honest food really runs an army, not political machinations.

For hours I sat on the porch, listening to the distant sound of people and realizing just how alone I was. I sat until the night chill became too much. Inside and wrapped in a blanket, I watched camp through an opened window and munched candies. Across the way, firelight and camp lamps flickered. Latrines had been dug in the woods and the swivel of flashlight beams came from, and went into, the trees. Laughter and music rose and fell, soft and poignant. Powerful. Compelling. They were preparing for battle, but it felt more like a bunch of campers just having a good time.

It was so hard to know where I fit in. No one was telling me anything. Cole was trapped somewhere in the Big Apple, Tobias had commandeered Raphael, and Ryan was deep in the fun trenches with his carnie friends, most likely trying to forget his own loss. I blinked and my breath caught. Heart pounding, I watched as a black figure blocked out the twinkling camp in the distance. It moved past, then returned. Frozen in place I focused as hard as I could.

Long, boney, shiny black fingers settled on the windowsill. Would it come inside and kill me? What was it waiting for? I was prime for the taking, too terrified to even make a squawk. Then, slowly, a head came into view. Its eyes were pale blue and one winked at me. Then, with calculated slowness, the demon's fingers reached for, then dragged a piece of dropped candy from the windowsill and slid it into its mouth. A mouth that smiled. Then it turned and sauntered away toward the peach grove.

Well, I knew something no one else in the world knew. Battle heat demons liked M&Ms.

The front door opened and I jumped out of my skin, letting loose with the screech I'd been holding for what seemed like forever.

"Just me, Gracie." Raphael plopped onto Cia's ragged sofa and dug into a slice of lemon meringue pie.

"Did… did… did you see…"

He licked his plastic fork and leaned back. "What's on your mind, Gracie?"

What's on my mind? What's on my mind? "Everything!"

"Breathe. Everything is moving as it should."

I lowered to my seat and pointed out the window. "Tobias?"

"He's just being Tobias. The time to rein him in will come but for now, he's handling a lot of the logistics you don't have time for."

"All I have is time." I really had to stop glaring at the archangel. He was there to help me, which was more than my own father seemed to be doing. Three days, and not one update in that crazy book. No new advice, no guidance. Zippo. "What am I supposed to do? Worry about Cole, eat biblical barbeque, and watch magic shows?"

"And learn. It's time for your next lesson."

Tears gathered and dripped down my face. "No, I'm too tired for a lesson today."

"Come," he said with a voice that sounded like a wind chime. "Sit next to me here on the sofa. This is a long, difficult lesson and you'll receive it far better as you sleep."

"What if more demons come?" Melting into the sofa cushions, I leaned my head on his shoulder.

"The camp will take care of them. Just close your eyes. This is the story of The Battle of the Corroded."

My eyes drifted closed and his voice dissolved into the bubbling of water running in a stream. Images and sound, sensations and wonder filled my head and it felt like a memory, but a memory of things I'd never experienced before.

The ground shuddered and quaked and I was down on my hands and knees. Under my fingers, the dirt was gritty, black, like volcanic sand, still steaming. Above, the sky was a vivid green, unnatural and blazing with white lightning strikes. Each crash thundered and vibrated under me, each flash was blinding and hot.

It was so loud, shouts and screams everywhere. Looking over, I saw Raphael standing beside me, but he was not the Raphael I knew. This was a tested warrior, his sparkling armor splattered with blood, his expression one of determination and rage, his powerful arm raised, a sword glistening in the eerie light and ready to strike.

I tried to call out but no words came from my mouth. All around the world trembled. I struggled to stand, reaching out to hold on to Raphael but he'd taken flight. High above was a raging battle that rained blood down on me. On the ground stood strange beings, darkness in their eyes, their black hair wild and tangled in their even blacker wings, and their flesh, white as snow. Many lifted to fight in the sky. On the ravaged earth others stood. Their words were their weapons and as they spoke, the dead climbed to their feet, sought a weapon, and returned to clash against God's angels.

A massive strike of lightning blasted many of the creatures again to death, only to be regenerated again, and again. Fighting terror, I ran as hard and fast as I could, but the wind blew me back, twisted me around until I sat on the ground, legs out like a child in front of a television, bound and absorbed by the scene before me.

That's when I recognized it. Craning my neck and focusing high above, I saw blessed Makha'el, his glorious golden armor aglow, his voice a bellow, his powerful weapon pointing south as his army did as they were bid. Somewhere in that battle was my father, or maybe his job was to sit along the sidelines and record the combat for posterity. Perhaps for the ceiling of Makha'el's beautiful hall at Ariel's gate. The white winged angels were the archangels, fighting for God. The black winged angels were the ugly black-haired creatures. Were they Nephilim? Nephilim gone bad? I knew it to be true, even as my heart begged for proof otherwise.

Bodies of the black-haired creatures dropped and died all around me, blood gushing, bone and muscle wrenched in unnatural positions. Shouting came from another one and poof, *up the dead arose. A word came to me like a whisper, like a terrible dream or amazing paranormal experience. It was soft yet hideous. Dangerous yet extraordinary. Vague and terrifying. Necromancer. Necromancer. And I knew. The Battle of the Corroded was the first time my own race had gone afoul. Necromancers brought the dead back to life and as this conflict continued, booming and crashing all around me, tears fell from my eyes. Why are we all so corrupt? What did those immoral Nephilim want? To live forever? To be more than the archangels that spawned them? To be in control? Wasn't that always the case? Sobs continued as angels battered and splintered almost every single necromancer in the air and on the ground. They were fighting for the earth. For the human race. Fighting for the things the Nephilim race was supposed to protect.*

And suddenly, darkness swallowed everything. A single beam of light drifted from the heavens onto the single, remaining Necromancer still alive. He fell to his knees, begging mercy, but a command dropped from heaven, booming, pulsating.

"You alone shall survive," the voice said. "You are now human, but you may only die when you have passed on the curse of eternal life to another human. Heed my warning! Only if you are worthy, will you truly die. Only if I'm ready to call you home to me. You are the Corroded. You will create the race of ancients who will eternally pay for the sin you have committed."

I woke with a start, shouting in the ancient language I learned from Metatron. "Bac a ghoi pha! Annre faanea!" *There is no honor! Have mercy!*

My trembling shoulders were tight in Raphael's arms. "Hush, Gracie. Hush, now."

"Oh, good God! What did I see?" I jumped from the sofa, spun around and tried hard to catch my breath. "What was that?"

"I think you already know."

Slowly returning to the sofa, I decided that either Cookie's barbecue was bad, or I'd just witnessed the Battle of the Corroded. "What did they want? The… the… necromancers." I whispered that last word.

"Dominance over God, over the earth, over man. They were Nephilim who chose never to follow the vow, never to maintain balance. Never to be faithful."

"And…" I swallowed hard.

"The last standing necromancer was cursed to live forever."

"He became an ancient?"

"Yes. And they could only die after serving God, and man, and the Nephilim race fully and for as long as the Father sees worthy. They would create another ancient then wait, hoping for death and redemption. Some ancients have made several ancients, yet still await blessed death."

"How do they do it? Make other ancients?"

Raphael shrugged then sighed. "It's more of an intention than an action, as I see it. I was assigned to walk with Tobias many, many thousands of years ago. I was his companion and his guide, but still, he created more and more ancients. A woman he found interesting, a man he hated, a child he felt had little to lose by living forever. He was selfish, and still is in many ways. Can you imagine such a curse, Gracie?"

I nodded, unable to breathe through the stench of death and blood inside my nose.

"I hope I helped him all those years ago. I know that what I learned by walking at his side taught me much about ancients. First of all, they are human, because the last necromancer on that battleground was stripped of his celestial elements. An ancient has no real power over a Nephilim. Ancients do develop some powers after being unexpectedly turned, but worst of all, they have no idea they'll be living a very long time. They only discover the curse after they watch everyone around them age and die. After they watch the world slowly change and evolve. After they realize they can't do anything for anyone except those unique beings called Nephilim. It's a trying life."

"Am I supposed to feel bad for Tobias?"

"Yes. He didn't ask for this. And he has served the Nephilim race very well for a very long time. This will be his third Counting battle. It's possible he's earned his way home. But…"

"Yeah. That's a big *but*. Is he really more knowledgeable than any other ancient about the Counting?"

"Not at all. At least one ancient on the way here to Ocracoke is far older that Tobias. She is the oldest ancient alive today. Her name is Rashee, and she has never once made another ancient, but even she is not more knowledgeable. She's just more experienced."

All I could say was, "Wow."

"You'll meet her tomorrow. For now, get some sleep." He stood and playfully pulled at my feet until I was flat on the sofa, then he dropped a blanket over me.

"Oh, Raphael." I yawned wide, already under whatever sleeping spell he'd hit me with.

"Yes?"

"M&Ms."

"What about them?"

I had already drifted to a pleasant place where no war or battle frightened me or made my heart pound. Somewhere in the distance I heard him say, "Sweet dreams, Gracie."

8

sther struggled, even walking was difficult. She'd lost so much blood, her head was light and her fingers, freezing cold. She'd almost toppled down the steps, but her salvation was right there to catch her.

ICe was running up the steps, the glint of terror in his eyes and she reached out before he slammed right into her. "Hey, buddy, it's me."

He blinked, looked up, then behind, then into her eyes. "Esther! It's you."

"Yes," she said, fighting a gasp of pain as chilling air raced over her fevered body. "ICe, I need some help. Will you help me?"

She dropped into his arms and he held her tight, as though he needed comfort more than she. "What's wrong?" she mumbled into his meaty arms.

"I dunno… I dunno… noise. Lotsa noise." His body trembled against hers and she hugged his neck tight.

"Remember what we talked about, ICe? Noise is not going to hurt you. Noise is just noise."

"Loud, so loud!" And he sobbed then looked down at her weakened frame. "What happened to you?" He wiped snot from his nose and cuddled her more gently. "Someone hurt you?"

"No, no. I need to rest, that's all."

Cradling her like a baby, he rushed her through dark walkways and doors all the way to his own private, and very quiet, cubby. He settled her onto his wooden cot and covered her with a sleeping bag. Hands hovering, his eyes scanned every inch of her. "Something's missing. Someone took something from you, Esther. Did it hurt when they took it?"

"No, no, nothing's missing, ICe. I lost something, that's all. Everything else is fine." She rolled to her side, sighed and drew in a deep breath.

ICe danced from foot to foot. "It's gone. Your light's gone. Who hurt you?"

Esther sat up and reached for the big man. "Hey! Nothing's missing. Come now, be calm. We don't want noisy people coming to see what's going on in here, do we?"

"No… no… no."

"Help me, ICe. I know you can. Just like last time, remember?"

He shook his head, stepped back until he stood at the far wall, then rocked back and forth. "What happened to you? Someone hurt you. Are they gonna hurt me, too?"

"I am hurt, ICe, but nobody hurt me. I lost a baby. A tiny baby that was growing inside me and it died. It left me. Remember, it happened before. This time it feels a little worse, that's what you see. I'll be fine. Only your sweet kindness can help me. Please, come sit with me." She gasped but tried to hide it with a smile. "You don't have to do anything, just hold my hand." Whatever had scared the man was likely to cause bigger repercussions if she couldn't calm him down. She could bleed to death. Half of her was still human and that human part was susceptible to getting dead. Death was not in the plan. "You know I need you, ICe."

"I couldn't help that guy."

"What guy?" Her hand reached out and he took a step closer.

"The guy with the noise, then they took him away, took apart the cage and the noise, the noise, the noise!"

"Hush," she whispered. "It's fine. That guy didn't need your help. I do. Come, hold my hand."

Another step closer.

"I brought some snickerdoodles," Esther said with a big grin, pleased that she'd remembered to steal them from Cia's cookie jar. "Just for you."

Another step closer. ICe sniffed and inched a bit closer.

Blood gushed from Esther and she feared this was it, the end. "Please, ICe. Hold my hand."

Another inch closer. He snapped the bag from her fingers and dove in, crunching away. Finally, he sat on the cot and reached for her fingers. "You're cold… and you're hot," he said, spitting crumbs.

Esther closed her eyes, sensing his power begin to slide, like warm water, over her. As it seeped deeper and targeted her pain, the bleeding slowed and she sighed. "You're the best, ICe," she whispered then slipped into a place of comfort and well-being. Her mind drifted to the day she'd first met Isaak Cambridge Effingham, III.

She was sixteen and exploring the portals. Her natural curiosity drew her to the distant portals, not the ones closest to Cia and the real Ocracoke. On a specific afternoon, after promising Luc she'd find new recruits for his army, she slipped through a closer, unfamiliar portal and right into bustling summertime New York City. Amazed at what she'd been missing, she spun on her toes and took in the splendor of the big, dirty, crazy city. Strolling casually, wearing short shorts and a yellow tank top, boasting her newest shoulder tattoos, and loving her currently pink hair, she watched carefully for people who seemed a little different. She didn't know how they looked or felt different to her, but they always turned out to be exactly what Luc was looking for.

She followed one down into a subway, then into a tunnel. A little afraid, she considered turning back, but as more and more odd people gathered and followed the first, her curiosity got the better of her. She was sucked right into the group. No one questioned her or demanded an explanation for why she was there. They gave her some food, offered her a place to sleep, then talked among themselves.

Esther thought, this could be the easiest place on the planet to recruit. They were trusting, they were gullible and easy-going, and strong. They called themselves gargoyles. Of course, they would, with the wings and all, but was it like a club? Didn't they know they were really Nephilim?

It would be two years before Esther would receive her own wings, but she had a good, strong sense of what the Nephilim world was all about. Cia had been telling her about it since she could understand. Stories of the archangels and Nephilim were told right along with Grimm's fairy tales and Harry Potter.

She knew all about the Nephilim, but it seemed the gargoyles didn't. What a treasure trove she'd discovered. She could exploit them easily enough, until every last one of them was part of Lucifer's army.

Then something happened, and a big, slightly slow gargoyle took her under his wing. She'd accidentally tripped in the darkness and broken her ankle. Now she was in serious trouble. What would Luc do to her? He'd make her hobble like a cripple as punishment for being so clumsy. The ankle would never heal correctly, then she'd be exactly like her twin.

Tears dripped down her cheeks. How could she have been so stupid? Was she stuck with the gargoyles? Should she even dare to go back to Luc? Cia would be far more compassionate, but Luc preferred that she spent her days and nights with him. She reached down and touched the swelling ankle, inhaled and let out a dramatic sigh. "I am so screwed."

"No, no, no." The big man grunted his substantial butt down onto the cement floor and leaned over her foot. He touched her ankle gently, closed his eyes, and Esther could actually feel her bone knit back together. A raggedy old woman brought her a blanket, and another woman with two toddlers hanging onto her pant leg, brought a bottle of aspirin.

Even with her injury, she'd not become the sole focus of gargoyle attention. No one worried what she wanted or how she came to be there.

They just seemed to worry that she was taken care of. Over the next few days, she kept her leg up and watched the goings on around her. They all took care of each other, and when any one of them was sick, or hurt, they came to Isaac and he touched them. They were better in moments.

Esther had never experienced such kindness in her life, except from Cia. Like a flash of lightning, her resolve and blood vow to Lucifer became slightly fractured. She knew, without a doubt, that the gargoyles would forever be her secret. That none of them would ever join Luc's armies. As she prepared to leave to locate a different place to recruit in the big city of New York, she sat with the healer and offered him some cash.

He shrugged and focused on his fingers.

"You're a strong healer, Isaac."

"I hate my name. You have to say it all, every time, Isaac Cambridge Effingham, III. I hate it."

"I just call you Isaac."

"No… no… Old Mamma said. You have to say Isaac Cambridge Effingham, III. Every time. Otherwise it's not me. It can be any Isaac. But I'm the only me."

Esther thought a moment. "Would you like another name?"

"What name?"

"Something that only you have. Something super easy to say."

He blinked his curious brown eyes.

"Your initials are I, C, and E, so how about Ice for a name?"

His brow curled, then his teeth bit on his lower lip and his eyes closed in deep thought. "Only if it's spelled with a big I, a big C, and a little e."

"Sure, why not. But… why the little e?"

"Because my daddy wasn't a good man." His face turned red and his breath caught, then he rocked on his feet and looked up at the ceiling.

"I understand." Esther reached out and touched his massive arm. "So, from now on I will call you ICe."

"Big I, big, C, and little e," he boasted with pride. Then he frowned. "Will you come back?"

"Yes. I promise." And she did. Once every month Esther gathered canned goods from the *Hell to Pay Pub* where she worked and took them through the portal to the gargoyles. She'd gather all her tips and leave them in ICe's cubby. But most importantly, she'd do everything she could to redirect Luc's other recruiters away from the area, stating that the Nephilim who called themselves gargoyles were inferior and far too weak for the devil's army. Lucifer would not be pleased. That was enough to deter any recruiter. They all knew that if they didn't please Lucifer, they could find themselves next in line for the devil's factory, and life as a battle heat demon warrior.

Over the years Esther had located many, many of the lost Nephilim, all over the big cities, all homeless, but none like the gargoyles. Most were bitter, dangerous, uncontrollable. Many she'd taken to Luc were rejected and destroyed. That bothered her. Didn't they have the right to die on their own terms? She never permitted herself to think the same way of the recruits who would, and had already, died in small scrimmages for Lucifer. They willingly gave their blood vow, just as she had. It was their choice. Only recently, while eavesdropping on Gracie, had she heard the words "Free-Winged." It made sense. They knew nothing of what they were before it happened, so they did the only thing they could. They hid. They followed no leader, they'd make terrible battle heat demons for the devil, but would they do any good for the other side? Was she leaving a big, ripe, recruiting territory open for the opposition? Should she reconsider trying to recruit more of them? The next crack in her vow to Luc came as a shock to Esther, but it was already indelibly written on her heart. Why not just leave the Free-Winged out of the equation? Whatever they did, they did.

The bleeding had completely stopped and ICe had once again saved her life. She owed him and the gargoyles so much. But she couldn't help but be curious. "ICe, what happened to the man in the cage?"

His head shook and his eyes glazed over, so obviously it wasn't good. Either that, or ICe had let his imagination run away with him again.

"You stay another day. You're still weak."

She grunted to her feet, and tried to smile. "It's okay. I'll rest when I get home. Thank you so much for helping me, my friend."

"Always, anytime, anyplace, forever, Esther."

She left, slipped through the portal, stepped into Luc's world and slid directly into bed. When he discovered her return, he'd ask questions and she'd tell him she caught a bug. He'd reprimand her for being so foolish, and she'd bicker that he sent her out into the world to collect recruits for him, and that's where the germs and sickness lived. He'd shout that it wouldn't make her exempt from his carnal interest. She'd escalate the argument and threaten to leave. Then he'd soften and let her rest. It didn't promise he wouldn't nudge her late at night, but at least she could sleep for a few hours.

~*~

The next rogue warrior traveling show to arrive blew my mind. No kidding, *pow*! They rolled in at dawn, all fitting on one single ferry. They were elegant and perfectly matched, the sides of every camper painted red with gold elaborate curlicues around the show name. *Rashee Mystics*. The campers followed Tobias's instructions and flowed into the area he'd chosen for them. At least he'd honored the oldest ancient on the planet with a space right next to his.

In comparison, even from a distance, Rashee had won the coolest show on the property award—three rows of perfectly parked identical red and gold campers. They made the Emmaus Magic Show look like a rag tag gang of gypsies. The Rashee warriors even dressed to match. Brilliant white turbans above rusty faces, loose gold silky pants, deep red romantic shirts, and a black sash tied around every waist. Beautiful men and women, all looking like they were already performing.

The back of each camper was a painting with the likeness of the Hindu god, Ganesh. If I remembered my studies correctly, Ganesh was the god of beginnings, worshiped before any major enterprise. How appropriate was that? Already I liked these Rashee Mystics.

I walked a little closer to the camps, staying far enough away to respect Tobias's perceived superiority. The day was cloudy and rain threatened. I still hadn't heard a word from Cole, and my stomach was tense with concern. Was he dead? No, I'd know. Did he really screw up? Or was he working hard to recruit for our side?

A demon stopped next to me and just stood there, watching the Rashee Mystics get settled in. When I worked up the nerve to look at it, my skin crawled, but all three faces gave a casual glance before it left—no doubt to report what it had seen. I couldn't help but wonder. Were those demons as bad as all that? Or were they maybe just not afraid of me?

Tobias bellowed a welcome to the new arrivals, but a tall, stunning woman dressed in a traditional sari, elegant and form fitting, walked right past him toward me. I looked behind, fully expecting Raphael, but I was all alone. Uh-oh.

"You are Gracious Caine?" Her voice was as smooth as the silk of her sari.

"Uh-huh. Um… yes."

"I am honored to meet you, Pure Nephilim Gracie. We are privileged to fight at your side."

She touched my arm and led me back toward the house. I gawked at her. I had never seen a woman so beautiful. All I could do was listen and nod like an idiot.

"We have gathered four-thousand-twenty-three recruits. They await our call in Philadelphia. We have received word from the archangel Metatron that you have uncovered ways to bring all recruits into the Counting plane. Is this so?"

Another dumb nod.

"Is there a portal in Philadelphia?"

I led her into the house and spread Blackbeard's maps across the kitchen table. Her elegant long finger trailed the parchment and she smiled.

"We are good. And how about Vermont, New Hampshire, and Maine? A branch of my recruiting staff has been very busy there as well."

And it went on and on. Rashee's people were recruiting in fifteen cities, most with a recorded portal. All we needed now was for Cole to come back and show her guys exactly where the entries were.

"Did Metatron really talk to you?" I asked while nervously pouring a cup of tea for the youngest-looking oldest women alive.

She smiled and nodded, sniffed the tea then carefully sipped. "Yes. He is most proud of you, Gracie." We sat in silence for a long while, but it didn't feel uncomfortable. I realized that as more warriors gathered on the land, and everywhere else, things were moving in the right direction. Maybe we'd get through this after all. When the great and powerful Rashee left, she left behind a sensation of warmth and calm inside every room in Cia's house. It was just the opposite of how Tobias made me feel.

While I rinsed out the tea cups, I thought about her words. Hopefully she meant that Dad was proud of me *and* Cole. He was taking the risks, facing the danger. Cole. Where the hell was Cole?

Rain fell and I sat at the table, munching cookies and exploring the maps. Why did Metatron tell Rashee about the portals, but not Tobias? Or did he tell Tobias, and was he thinking he knew some big secret I didn't? I wasn't sure why I was so suspicious of the man. He didn't do anything to deserve it. I just plain wasn't sure I trusted him and that had to change. He might be a big, boisterous, pompous, very old dude, but that didn't make him my enemy, did it? The enemy was the demons, and they hadn't tried to hurt me once since the battle at the Emmaus Magic show. One casually hung out with me while Rashee's band was setting up camp, another ate my M&Ms. Often I noticed demons walking around the house or sitting near the magic tree. Something was very odd. There's trouble in Oz when you can't recognize the good guys from the bad.

But some things were moving ahead perfectly. The maps were amazing, showing hundreds of portals all over the American, South American, and Canadian territories. If Raphael was right, Allerton and Ben had already recruited and regenerated soul swords in Los Angeles and were doing it again in San Francisco. From there, ten more major cities including New York, Phoenix, Las Vegas, Salt Lake City, Dallas, St. Louis, Miami and some I couldn't remember.

Hopefully Cole was convincing the Free-Winged in New York to fight at our side, then he could move on to other cities where they hid. There was a lot of recruiting needed if we were going to survive the Counting, and should the balance be severely off, the battle that might follow.

All I could do was wait, and I'd become so not good at waiting. I looked at the phone. Right there in my hand it vibrated and gave a goofy bonk. Afraid it was about to explode, I dropped it onto the table. Then the screen popped up and I tapped the white field.

I'm good, but it was touch and go for a while. Will let you know more as soon as I can. Don't call, just wait for my next text. I'll try to get back there to see you in a few days. Love you.

Okay, so that was a text. Cool, and hopefully it was from Cole, because I couldn't imagine anyone else saying "love you" to me. Even though it looked like good news, I was not comforted. I wanted to just call him, but he asked me not to.

Noon of the longest day of my life. I found an umbrella and walked around the open areas, wondering how all the camps would fit, curious if Tobias had selfishly taken the biggest area for himself. I thought about everything I knew from Dad's book, Blackbeard's maps, and what Rashee had told me. There were forty-one rogue warrior groups in our division, and there were another two-hundred-ninety groups around America. Also gearing up for the Counting on our side of the planet were 300 coalition warrior groups in Canada, South America, and Australia.

Dad was clear in the book that the European, Asian, Russian, and African coalitions were working together to make their way to the Counting as well. That seemed like a lot, but the Free-Winged were the unexpected factor, the turning point that could change everything. How was it that only one guy, my guy, was responsible for all of them? I needed answers.

As rain dripped from the metal spokes of my umbrella and I kicked sandy mud with my twisted foot, the strangest thing happened. A stretch limo pulled up at the house and the chauffer—a *real chauffer* with a hat and everything—holding a big black umbrella, escorted a dapper-looking man onto my porch.

Company. Time to go home, and with a little luck I'd get to there before Tobias, who was running on the slippery grass, awkward as a goose on land. I was much closer but slowed down, just to see what was about to happen. Tobias beat me to the porch, out of breath and smiling like a lunatic. A real dignitary had arrived. This time I'd make the good tea Rashee had gifted to me. It smelled like flowers and sunshine. It looked like we were going to need that.

9

n the midst of all the confusion, he'd shot a quick text to Gracie, hoping she'd be cheered that he could connect at all. Standing in front of twenty-some burley Free-Winged, all looking like they were out for blood, Cole realized he might never see her again. He had to make sure that didn't happen. His mind stuttered, tried to grasp the goal of his mission, but analyzing the expressions in the men's eyes, the strain, the fear, the body language, he settled on asking one question first.

"What's happened?"

Three giants looked at each other. One was a man, black as night with a massive puff of hair hallowing his head. Cole decided he'd call that guy The Electrician. Even his expression appeared shocked.

"Are you Joe Grissom?" the man asked.

"You know I'm not. My name is Cole Masters. Who the hell is Grissom?"

The crowd shifted on its feet, looked to each other, whispered and grunted. Finally, The Electrician spoke. "Where's McGuire?"

"How the hell would I know?"

More shuffling, and now shouting. Cole listened carefully and caught slips of information, bouncing around like balls in the dark space. He raised his hand and bellowed. "Hey! Listen up!" In that miraculous moment, he became the marine he once was. That would hopefully serve him and keep him alive one more day.

They all turned and glared, but had at least silenced.

"Am I to understand that McGuire is missing? Kidnapped?"

Eyes dropped and feet shuffled. The Electrician nodded.

"When?"

"A week ago. Without McGuire, nothing works."

So, McGuire ran this show. A group like that had to have strong guidance of some sort. "Yeah, I understand that, but what I need to know is who kidnapped your leader?"

More nervous movement.

"You," Cole pointed to the yellow-haired romance novel model. The guy straightened and looked like a deer in a headlight. "Yeah, you. Tell me everything you know."

The information poured like honey. Apparently, McGuire was accosted on rounds to other gargoyle locations.

"Whoa," Cole interrupted. "Other locations? How many locations?"

The Electrician jumped in, his voice low and rumbling. "We got eighty-four locations."

"Just in New York?"

Heads nodded.

"How many… gargoyles. All together?"

Shrugs and head scratches then finally a smaller man pushed ahead from the back of the pack. "Gargoyle population in New York City vacillates between eight and nine-thousand, depending on the time of year. Higher in the summer because of the mild weather. There are gargoyle groups all over the country, too, and McGuire takes care of all of us. I once estimated around sixteen million gargoyles nationwide, but without real records, I could be a little off."

Cole lowered to sit on the ground and they all joined him. He wondered. Was the guy talking about gargoyles, or the Free-Winged in general? Too complicated to ask that, so he cleared his throat. "How? How does this McGuire take care of so many?"

The small guy sighed and smiled. "Good things. Good thoughts. Good works. A code of ethics. Like that."

"Uh-huh. I see. What's your name?" Cole asked.

"Custer. That's Greg Grease," he pointed to The Electrician, "and he's Pollo."

Cole lowered his face to hide a grin. Pollo. Well, at least now he had a name for Mr. Pretty. "So, if everyone's taken care of, who would kidnap McGuire?"

"Mister," Custer said with a grunt. "There are way more winged things hiding in New York City that aren't gargoyles. They're dangerous. Criminals. Murderers. Folks McGuire could never bring in and manage."

Cole's head was spinning. "And you think one of those took McGuire?"

"We know." Custer looked to Grease. The black man pulled a crumpled piece of paper from his grimy pocket and handed it over.

We got McGuire. Get $10,000 together then maybe you can get your leader back. You got six days. Look for Joe Grissom.

Cole read it over again and again, hoping to find a clue that could help. In the back of his mind, he couldn't help but think about the numbers. If he could get McGuire back for the gargoyles, he might be able to bring in between eight-thousand and sixteen-fucking-million warriors. If not, who knew what was going to happen next? He flipped the paper over. Nothing more. "When did you get this?"

"Right after McGuire disappeared. We're all looking for this Joe Grissom. We were sure it was you."

Cole shook his head and leaned back against a wall. "And the ten-thousand bucks?"

"There's no way we can get that." Poor Custer groaned.

The gargoyles looked to each other then at Cole. Funny, with their leadership lost, he'd become their answer to everything. So, he'd lead.

"Okay, here's what we're going to do. We're going to pretend we have the cash."

Eyes blinked, a few whispered and nodded agreement.

"Get a sack," he told Pollo. "Custer, how much cash do you think you can pull together?"

Custer's mouth twisted and his eyes closed while the calculations raced. "About two hundred. Nowhere near enough. I'm afraid they're going to kill McGuire, then we're really in trouble."

Cole couldn't have agreed more, but for different reasons. "No. No," he reached into his backpack. "Let's see. I can drop another two hundred on top of that. We'll cut up a bunch of newspaper the same size as cash and stuff it all in the sack with the cash on top."

"Wait." Grease stood his entire height and looked down a broad nose at Cole. "You'd put your own money in?"

"Why not? You need McGuire back, right?"

"But," Custer chimed in, hands wringing and sweat gathering at his temples. "They'll never go for it. It won't work."

"Trust me. Those guys will be just as thrilled with four hundred as they would be with ten grand." Cole watched their concerned faces. "We're going to get McGuire back. Now, exactly where did you find this ransom note?"

"Stuck to the door at street level." Rollo handed Cole a dirty straw purse, but it would work fine for the ruse.

"So, can someone make a really big sign and stick it in the same place?"

"Sure," Custer was already on his feet. "What should the sign say?"

Cole grinned. "Joe Grissom, we're ready."

It had been a while since Cole planned a heist, but this operation felt just as exciting. If he won, he'd get the unique opportunity to recruit massive numbers. The plan had to be perfect, and already he knew who he wanted on his team. ICe, for distraction. Custer as spokesperson. Grease as the muscle. And finally, Pollo as the traitor. If they pulled this off, he'd be surprised, but also thrilled to know how valuable they could be in real battle.

~*~

Ben was suffering. He missed Gracie more than he imagined possible. They'd been best friends since she arrived at the Gate, but now he felt willing to share his deepest secrets and pain. Gracie would understand. She'd be able to help him. Soothe him. The quickening power of perception was destroying him, feeling more like a terminal illness than a gift, and no matter what he tried, it constantly plagued and terrified him. From the moment dawn brought his mind to awareness, it started. Pounding. Pummeling. Thrashing. Worry alone caused him to toss his cookies at least once a day.

Michael told him it was only his job to know what he knew, not to do anything about it, but that seemed wrong. He knew Cole was walking into real danger. He knew Gracie was about to be stretched beyond her limits. She was followed by demons all day and all night long, several sleeping outside her bedroom window. Tobias was heading for big trouble with even bigger consequences. And Esther, Gracie's twin, had just suffered a dangerous miscarriage. Even healed, Ben knew, absolutely and without a doubt, that the girl's womb was damaged beyond repair. Now why on earth did he have to know something like that?

Then there was Michael. Ben wanted nothing more than to accept the man as his father, but the closeness he needed was just out of reach. Michael was trying so hard to help him. Was it too little, too late? Or was it because of the desperate situation his race was facing? He did as he was told, ate when Michael asked him to eat, slept when he was expected to sleep, and almost every day he sat at the back of a stage and watched his father perform the miracle of bringing Nephilim back into the fold and regenerating their soul swords.

The routine wasn't working. He was still tormented, sensing awareness of many, many experiences, none of which were his own. And he wondered—exactly what was his quickening power of perception good for? What was the point? Every single moment was a fight to pay attention to what was happening to him, and push aside what he knew was happening to someone else. There was one problem. A lot of what was happening was happening to people he cared about. How was he going to explain that? All Michael did was repeat that he only needed to know, he wasn't responsible to do anything about what he knew. It made no sense. It was stupid, and probably impossible, too.

Finally, immediately after another successful speaking engagement in San Francisco, Ben erupted. "So, what the fuck is this damn power for?"

Michael rubbed his brow and sighed. He paced the empty stage, then suddenly brightened. "I'll show you!"

The coordinators for San Francisco were two professional Nephilim. Chester Finniss, a powerful Norema in his sixties, grey haired and knowledgeable. Chester's mannerisms reminded Ben of Gandalf from *Lord of the Rings*. Chester listened well, and considered everything he saw and heard. Ben wondered, what was the old man's special power? His assistant was a younger man, only a year older than Ben. His name was Kevin Hatch. Kevin was Calanine, extremely handsome and extremely self-focused. Kevin made Ben a little nervous. He couldn't figure out if he liked the guy, or hated his guts.

The last of the stage crew was wrapping up electrical cords. Michael had done two speaking engagements in San Francisco, and at the last minute was booked for two more tomorrow—the first starting at one, and the next at seven in the evening. The news was getting out, and more and more Nephilim were interested in hearing the message. It was going to be a hectic, busy day.

"Chester," Michael called out. "I wonder if I can use the stage here tonight, and after both engagements tomorrow?"

The old man shrugged. "Sure. Why?"

Michael looked suddenly energized. "Sword practice!" He left for the dressing room and returned with both his and Ben's soul swords.

"Uh… Dad, it's kinda late? Like already two in the morning." All Ben wanted was some blessed, silent sleep.

"This is more important, Ben. I'm going to show you what your power of perception is for and… how it works for you." Michael pulled off his suit jacket and rolled up his sleeves. He kicked off polished black leather shoes and stood in the center of the stage in stocking feet, grinning like a lunatic.

Ben grunted up from his folding chair and shook his head. "If this doesn't work, I'm liable to slice off your head. I'm just that tired, and that pissed off."

"Good. It'll keep you focused."

Chester called for Kevin who quickly dragged the heavy podium into the right wing then stood and waited. The old man shouted, "Now!"

"Wait! Wait!" Ben shuffled out of his leather jacket and kicked off one shoe before Michael stepped forward and swung.

Kevin laughed and Chester shouted. "Watch his blade, Ben. Anticipate its angle, its speed, its target!"

Jumping away from the next swing, Ben yelped. "How the hell am I supposed to do that?"

"Use the force," bellowed Michael. "You can do this more than anyone on the planet. It's your power. Use the for… *ack*!"

This time it was Michael who escaped a lunge. He spun and lowered, then leapt when Ben's sword leveled at his knees. "Good!"

Ben stepped back, kicked off his other shoe, focused on his father and thought hard. Then another idea came, this time from someplace deeper inside his soul. *Don't think. Know.* And with that, Ben just knew.

The swordplay went on for an hour amidst shouts and cheers from their two-man audience in the wings. Michael lunged, thrust, twisted, and swung, and Ben escaped every single approach, again and again.

"Kevin!" Michael called, running an arm across his sweating brow. "Get your sword."

"Hey!" Ben shifted and escaped yet another dangerous sweep of Michael's blade. "No fair!"

Kevin, stocking feet and down to his tee shirt and jeans, inched his way into the circle. He stepped slowly, sliding his feet sideways, his grey eyes intense. All Ben could think about was how many muscles the dude had, how they were bulging inside the white tee shirt, and that those biceps alone made it an unfair fight.

Michael lunged and Ben almost lost an arm. "Use that power, Ben. Use it!"

Again, he emptied his mind and let only what he needed to know float in. Two swords sliced the air around him, spun and clanged, once Michael even lost his sword and dove to retrieve it. Then he stepped back, breathless and drenched in perspiration, leaving Ben and Kevin to continue the match.

There was no match. Ben slipped and slid like a dancer in water, escaping everything that came his way. The sound of metal on metal clanged, reverberating through the empty theater. Then Ben decided it was done. He twirled the sword in his right hand, recaptured it with both hands and snapped up, causing Kevin to lose control of his blade—soaring high, end over end, then dropping, its grip safely in Ben's hand. Now with two weapons, he quickly stepped in and slammed both blades into the floor at Kevin's sides.

Kevin huffed to catch his breath. Their noses were almost touching, they were so close. Ben could smell the man's sweat, and see the texture of the sunburnt flesh on his nose. His dark hair lay plastered to his wet brow, and he smiled a smile that could make Ben melt.

"You are spectacular," whispered the loser. "But such a whiny crybaby." Kevin took his sword from Ben's fingers and walked away.

That's when he heard the applause from Chester and Michael. He shrugged, trying not to watch Kevin leave. Swallowing his mixed feeling of rejection and reward, he turned to his father and bowed like a champion. "I get it. I get it now. It's all about focus, right?"

Chester followed Kevin, stage left, and Michael wrapped his arms around Ben, squeezing him like a bear. "Exactly."

"But…" Ben lowered to the floor and desperate for air, lay flat on his back, arms wide. Michael sat cross-legged beside him.

"But, what?"

"How do I know which things to focus on, and which things to ignore?"

"Ignore nothing, buddy. Everything is important in some way, just not as vital as some of your insights. Controlling your power of perception is going to take a lot of practice, but you have to trust yourself. You will know which things are bigger. I bet you already know. Tell me some of the perceptions you're having right this moment."

"Okay," he rolled to his side and supported his head in hand. "Um… The black tribunal judge is heading to Ocracoke."

"Ah… that one's easy. That judge, Terry Fennimore, is Jenny's real father."

"Oh." Ben sat up. "So that's important."

"Is it? Considering our goals?"

Ben closed his eyes and considered. "Maybe not so much."

"Tell me another insight."

"Cole's getting his ass kicked."

Michael shrugged. "Is that more important than the first insight?"

"Kinda. I like Cole." Ben sniffed and pushed his hair back. "But… honestly, it can't be the first time he got the shit kicked out of him."

"Do you sense he'll survive?"

"Yeah. I do."

"Something else."

Ben drew in a deep breath and let it out slowly. He thought hard. "Honestly, I'm not sure anything is really that important. Except maybe… but maybe not."

"Tell me," Michael looked with intensity into Ben's face.

"It's Tobias… I'm just not sure yet what he's brewing or how it'll effect things, just that it's not good."

Michael rose with a grunt. "Anything Tobias does is important. Keep an eye on that one."

"That, and all those demons following Gracie around." Ben retrieved his soul sword and stood with a stretch.

Michael turned on a dime and grasped Ben's shoulders in both hands. "Tell me more about that. That could be a big, big deal."

"They're not touching her, or attacking her, or anyone gathering in the camp either. They're acting, well… sort of passive, but I bet they're spying, you know."

"Yes, that's possible, but I once witnessed something like that, when demons, hundreds and hundreds of them, didn't attack, they just stood still as stone… docile."

"When was that?"

"Right after Gracie's Acclimation."

Ben was speechless.

10

Stepping up onto the porch, I turned to close my umbrella, but listened to Tobias talk, and talk, and talk to my guest. Then, before I could even face them, I heard something that made me want to laugh out loud.

"Tobias, man, don't take this the wrong way, but… shut the fuck up. Is this Gracious Caine?"

Tobias, wide eyed, nodded to the affirmative. A well-manicured hand shot out to me and I shook it. That was probably the first time in my life I ever did that, but it seemed appropriate.

"Gracie, my name's Gregory Parkland. I'm the Regent of the Americas, and head of the Nephilim Worldwide Intelligence Bureau—the Nephilim secret service."

"Oh, wow."

"Gracie, sweetie, go put on a pot of coffee, Greg and I have important things to discuss." Tobias was relentless, I'll say that for him.

"Actually," Parkland grinned. "Tobias, I need you to go back to camp and bring Ballister Green and Pete Koeffer."

"Why?" Tobias looked like he'd missed a memo and was way out of the loop.

"Because I need to speak with them." Parkland settled his hand on my back and waved toward the door. "Oh," he looked back and Tobias looked hopeful. "And have Cookie send food and coffee."

"Um, what can I do for you?" I asked once we were comfortably settled in Cia's living room.

The man crossed his legs and smiled, looking at me, gauging me, measuring me. I squirmed.

"You are as spectacular as expected, my dear. But I wonder… do you have any idea what's expected of you?"

Tears gathered in my eyes and all I could do was shake my head. He didn't reach across the sofa to comfort me. He didn't sigh or tilt his head compassionately. He simply drew in a breath and spoke words I really needed to hear. "I'm gong to try my best to explain it all to you. It'll take a little while, as will my business with Tobias and his motley crew. Tell me, is there a guest room in this cozy little house?"

"Yes, but wouldn't you be more comfortable at a hotel in town? There are several, some really nice, and—"

His head shook. "I'll be here several days and Tobias plans to initiate the protective shield tomorrow night at the latest. I need to be close to things right now, just for a few days." He glanced toward the door where Tobias was already rushing inside, dripping rain all over the floor.

"Green and Koeffer are on their way. Cookie's got a spread ready and boxing it up as we speak. Now, what's up? And…" he nudged his head toward me, "does the young lady need to be here? Why burden the child with matters of state?"

"You still don't get it," Parkland said quietly. "This child is the *state*. She's our ace in the hole, our secret weapon, our power. She's our direct line to Metatron."

"Yes, yes, of course, but she's just a—"

"I'm not a little girl," I spat.

"Just trying to protect you, Gracie," Tobias glared, but made his voice sound kind.

"Ah, but she's here to protect us, Tobias. There will be no more of this. It's time to get our ducks in line."

My stomach turned. Me? Protect them? Holy crap. Where the hell was Cole? I wanted Cole.

"Forgive me," the ancient actually bowed to Parkland. "I'm old. I think *old* sometimes. How can I help Gracie carry her responsibilities?"

Parkland let out a frustrated sigh. "I'm here to give her some guidance, as for carrying her responsibilities, her Pure Nephilim power is already prepared for that."

"Yes, yes okay. On… ah… on another subject. I can report that Cole Masters is not in camp, he's off somewhere trying to—"

"Do you seriously imagine I need a report from you about things outside this camp?"

Tobias blinked and I was starting to feel bad for him. I wanted him to stop talking so he could stop embarrassing himself.

"Certainly. Yes. I understand, but there's something else. Mr. Parkland, I have a plan, something never tried before, and I'd love to discuss it with you. At your convenience, of course."

"We'll see if I have any time after we get through the fiasco at hand. Ah, refreshments and Mr. Green. Please have a seat. Where's Koeffer?"

Green and Tobias glanced at each other. "Pete Koeffer is tied up, sir," Green offered. "Fifteen camps are arriving today, and another seven before midnight. He's clearing land and—"

"Get him. Now."

It wasn't a shout but it felt like one. Tobias nervously jumped to his feet, and Ballister Green left without a word. Parkland reached to the coffee table, covered with sandwiches, cups of potato salad, a tureen of hot soup, bowls and spoons. If I wasn't so freaked out, I'd have dug in too.

"What happened?" I whispered to Parkland and he sighed.

"It's about your friend, Jenny Perkins."

Now I knew I wouldn't be eating a thing.

It took mere moments for Koeffer to show his face, standing inside the doorway like a lost giant. His bulging arms and chest made the room seem too small for air. He was the strong man in the ring, and a strong man for just about everything Tobias needed. I once saw him lift a vehicle out of the way so Tobias could rearrange the camp. I wondered then, as I did every time I saw him—was that extraordinary strength his quickening power?

Green squeezed in around the big man and sat on a chair, pushing his long, wet hair back from his narrow face.

"Koeffer. Sit," Parkland said through a full mouth. "Eat."

The man shook his head slowly, looking down at his feet. Everyone looked at Koeffer's feet until Parkland brushed crumbs from his hands and leaned back on the sofa.

"Okay," he began. "A lot is happening in the world, children, and a lot will shift in ways that can, and will, affect our efforts if we don't nip this shit in the bud. First and foremost, and," his eyes trailed to each of us, "this doesn't leave this room…" He waited for nods all around and that's when I realized I really had made it to the adult's table. "The International Tribunal system has fallen," he stated. "Many are insisting that it's just a reorganization, but it's nearly dissolved already. Thanks to Michael Allerton's efforts, knowledge of the current desperate situation has gotten out to the unaware Nephilim population, leaving the Tribunal system at a loss for explanations. Being left out of such a dangerous loop has made Nephilim the world over pretty angry. I've ordered all prisoners released, which they still haven't done. One thing I didn't have to order, was an end to Tribunal litigation. No one's dealing with them. The general opinion is one of complete distrust, and a judicial system without respect is useless.

"That brings me to the primary reason I'm here. Tribunal judges are basically out of work with nothing to do… and one is on his way here."

"Why?" Green said with a distasteful expression. "They can't fight, they don't even believe there's a fight ahead!"

"Well, that's a little complicated. For centuries, high power and affluent Nephilim sent their newborns to the Orphanage system to protect them. Most of those children were given new names."

I raised my hand. What a stupid geek I am. Parkland nodded. At least he didn't laugh. "I guess I understand, now that I'm out of Ariel's Gate, why people sent us to the orphanages, but… why change some of the names?"

"For additional protection. In the case of a Tribunal judge, it assured that someone with a grudge against a verdict wouldn't take it out on the child. You need to understand, Gracie. Every single one of you are, and always have been, precious and vital. There's always a Counting coming, at some point, at some century. Every Nephilim is important."

"So, why are the Free-Winged allowed to happen?" I piped. Why were Nephilim permitted to just toss their kids out before they turned eighteen without the slightest clue of what they were?

"That practice has been illegal for a millennium. It's just not a law we can enforce. Our race is secret. We're to be seen as mere humans by the human race. Enforcing such a law would cross a few lines we just can't cross and still remain clandestine. And… broad-based laws established by the Tribunal never received a lot of respect outside the upper-class Nephilim race."

Green gave another snort. "The asshole judicial system was flawed, and continually grew more flawed and corrupt." He glared at Parkland who just shrugged.

"Trust me, power plays are overwhelming among our race. Look at Teddy Roosevelt… Mussolini… do you think anyone could have stopped them? They played for power. So did the Tribunal system, and they didn't care how they got it. You won't believe who's been sitting in their cells for years and years."

"Will the released prisoners fight with us?" I know, I should have kept my mouth shut but this stuff was fascinating.

"If they can, they will. If they've been held in the underground cells for too long, they may never regain their strength, but they can help in other ways. It's one of the reasons I'm here."

"So, can we cut to the chase?" The irritation in Tobias's voice was evident, just like the irritation in his expression.

"The chase?" Parkland glared. "Okay, big boy. How's this for getting to the point? Terry Fennimore, High Black Tribunal Judge of the Eastern United States Tribunal is on his way here."

"What the hell for?" Tobias said, but looked directly at his two men, both now focused on Parkland.

"His daughter was Jennifer Perkins. Ring a bell?"

My heart thumped. The room went dead silent, then, without warning, Tobias boomed. "An accident! This is about a stupid accident?"

"Or murder," Parkland said quietly.

Again, silence. I fingered the fringe on a pillow at my side. Murder? Could someone have murdered Jenny? Someone in the Emmaus camp? I could hardly breathe.

Parkland leaned back on the sofa. "Green, tell me exactly what happened."

All set, and Cole's blood was racing. "Let's go over this again, people."

Custer started. "We go wherever the kidnappers tell us to go. Then I make the negotiation."

"And what is that negotiation?" Cole quizzed.

"Oh, uh… we offer the cash, plus we trade you, a big dignitary, for McGuire."

Pollo piped in, "Wait. He doesn't look like a dignitary."

Frustration frayed Cole's every nerve, but Pretty Boy had a point. Not the right clothes. Not the right face.

"You could be some kind of techie business entrepreneur," Custer suggested.

"Nah, he don't look that smart. How about… movie star?"

Cole shot a glare Grease's way. "Do I look like a damn movie star?"

"More than you look like a dignitary."

"It could work," ICe offered. "None of us ever get to see any movies, so…"

"Good point, but we do see those billboards all over town."

Even Cole had to agree with that.

"Oh! Oh! I know!" Buster actually jumped up and down. "How about a Broadway star? He could be the lead in that play, what's it called? Blackwood. Yeah, Blackwood! You know, the one where the main actor wears a mask through the whole thing? We never see his face, even on billboards."

Excited discussion followed and Cole shouted, "Hey! Come on. Let's focus, guys. It's almost midnight and news from the kidnappers should arrive any minute."

"Well," Buster was still grinning like a lunatic. "That could really work."

"None of us go see plays, either," ICe said, shaking his head like this was the most difficult conundrum in the world.

"It's fine, that'll work. So, after the negotiations?" He turned to Custer.

"If they go for it, we make the trade. In which case, you will somehow, like magic, free yourself. How're you going to do that, anyway?"

"Not your problem. And if they don't go for the bait?"

Pollo rubbed his hands together. "I tell them you're all lying, and that this guy isn't a… what is he again?"

"Broadway star," several voices chimed.

"Then I tell them I think they should keep McGuire. We'll keep our money." He held up the bulging straw purse.

Cole nodded. "That should rile them up. They're homeless, desperate, and they want the money more than they want your leader. What happens next?"

Custer patted ICe on the arm. "Then we make lots of noise and ICe reacts. Greg starts punching people."

"Remember, I need real distractions going on because I'm going to run and try to locate McGuire. Any ideas what kind of place they'll take us to?"

Heads shook.

"No problem, we'll figure things out as we need to. Now, tie my hands at my back. Grease, you're in charge of the prisoner. Um… that's me."

The big black man shook his head solemnly as he tightened the ropes. "You really do think we're all idiots, don't you?"

"No, no. I just want it to go well. I don't want anyone to get hurt, don't want you guys to lose your money. I just—"

A crashing boom, then shouts and bellows came down the hallway. ICe covered his ears and Grease started shouting. Custer stepped forward, standing his entire five-foot-nothing, trying to appear in charge.

Cole wondered what the hell he was thinking, trying such a thing. Already it had gone bad. He expected the kidnappers to lead them to their digs, not to come roaring into the gargoyles' place. On the bright side, maybe they brought McGuire. He could only hope.

Brave little Custer tried to negotiate, the goons just laughed, then demanded that Cole recite something from the play. He said the only thing he could think of. He saw the movie *Rocky* once and the line really stuck. It was etched in his brain. He drew in a deep breath and tried to project his voice the way a stage performer might.

"Nobody's gonna hit as hard as life, but it ain't as hard as you can hit. So, how hard can you hit, and keep moving forward? It's how much you can take and keep moving forward. That's how winning is done."

Cole was proud of that delivery. It was honest, powerful, even poignant, given the situation. He almost smiled and took a bow.

"So," a monster with tattoos everywhere spat, "hit him."

And they did, and all hell broke loose. Even ICe was slapping his hands at the men.

"Wait! Wait, the deal!" Poor Custer was still playing his role, and Grease just slammed his substantial fists into any part of a body that presented. They were outnumbered and Cole's team was beginning to back away. At one point, all the attention was on making poor ICe bleed.

Cole had enough. "Get back!" he yelled, struggling to his feet. "Behind me! Now!"

Heat built to a staggering pressure inside his body and it happened, not quite as controlled as the day on Gracie's porch, but just as effective. When Cole roared for his men to take cover, so did the bad guys. Almost all of them found safety behind a wall. Two were burned, one badly, but Cole was on a roll. Angel fire singed and broke the ropes at his hands. Brilliant flames flashed and bounced off the cement walls as he focused his energy at the kidnappers.

"Custer! Negotiate! Now!"

The little guy bravely stood at Cole's side. "You want to live… you give us McGuire! Right! This! Minute!"

Another blast shot from Cole, now with his hands free, he raised his flaming palms toward the enemy.

Two kidnappers raced outside, returning only moments later with a small man, his head under a burlap bag, his hands tied. Immediately, the bad guys ran. There was no chase from the gargoyles.

Grease looked into Cole's bloodshot eyes. "How'd you do that, man? Teach me how to do that shit. I wanna do that shit."

Cole knelt beside one of the wounded. "Pollo, can you get these two up to the street? Flag someone down and get them some help. Just don't give any clue how they got burned. Say you found them that way. Say they ran out of a building across the street, or were tossed from a passing car. Do not let anyone get suspicious and start looking down here." They quickly dragged the wounded up and outside.

Cole looked around, fire had singed everything and there were a few flames still alive. He stomped one out and pointed. "Grease, Custer, put out these fires, clean this up." They quickly worked to make the place safe again, although it was still filled with smoke. Cole wished he had some kind of power to make it dissipate, just to make sure no one came to investigate.

"We may need to get the hell out of here, fast." He coughed and walked to the prisoner in two long strides. He untied swollen hands and dragged the sack from McGuire's head, then stepped back. His heart thumped.

McGuire was not only a woman, but a woman Cole had met once before. The gargoyles' McGuire was really Carla Shreveport. Cole had met her in a Wichita pub. He was on his way to bigger things, and she was on her way to the loony bin. Carla Shreveport was the only reason Cole even knew about the Free-Winged.

"Well, well," she said, rubbing her wrists. "Strange… the people you run into in strange places."

"Damn!" He grinned for the first time since stepping through the portal at East 196th Street. "We have a lot to talk about."

She seemed wobbly but stronger than expected. "Yeah. First things first. Everyone, to the south exit. We'll disperse, then meet up at Hallingport. Grease, gather the sick and, ICe, can you help him? Help him get Old Mamma out safely?"

"Yes!" ICe wrapped his arms around her and ran off.

Cole just scratched his head and followed, grateful to get away from the smoke.

11

Ballister Green looked shaken. I'd never once seen him anything but in control and confident about himself. When he started giving his testimony, I thought I'd start crying for Jenny all over again. My hands in fists, I listened and kept my mouth shut, wondering exactly who I could and couldn't trust.

"The girl was fascinated with high wire performing. I started her training on a balance beam, then on a low wire, three feet off the ground. Jenny was a natural… and an exceptional warrior." He rubbed his eyes. "I told her we'd take her up to the high wire at 4:30 the next day. While I was off doing other things. Koeffer here was setting the correct tension on the cables, adjusting the pressure and checking all the ties. He was also going to stretch the safety net."

"Did he do those things?" Parkland asked, his eyes hard on Green.

My heart pounded a mile a minute.

Green nodded. "He was in the process of doing it all. Pete?" He handed the baton over to the big guy and all our focus shifted.

"Yes, I was doing it. At around three, I needed a tool, so I headed off for it. Without that wrench, I couldn't attach the net right or finalize the tension."

Silence.

"And?" Parkland obviously wanted answers, but he wasn't playing bad cop. It looked like he just wanted to know what happened.

"And, when I got back, she was already on the ground."

My eyes watered.

"It wasn't even four," Green jumped in. "I clearly told her four-thirty. I timed it so that Pete could get his work done and we could practice first with the net, showing her how to fall… then the trapeze. She just didn't wait, Parkland."

"Anyone else know she was supposed to wait? Any witnesses?"

Koeffer nodded. "That boyfriend of hers. He was there at the dinner table when Ballister told her the time. He was with her when I got back… she was already dead."

"Ryan saw it happen?" I said with a gasp.

"Ryan Sutcliff?" Parkland asked and all heads nodded. "Get him in here, now!" And this time, he did shout.

Green left in a rush, but Tobias just shook his head. "It was a damn accident. This shit happens. What's the big deal?"

I gasped. All eyes glared at him and he cleared his throat.

"Okay, okay, that was insensitive. I've lived a long time, little girl. Sometimes sentimentality is overrated. In this case, it's a lot of hoo-ha over a simple accident."

"Sit down and shut up, Tobias." Parkland was starting to look a lot less like a dignitary and more like a pissed off headmaster.

"But it was just an accident," Tobias said softly as he resettled on the overstuffed chair.

"It would be," Parkland said with a sigh as he reached for his cold coffee, "if Koeffer here had never been accused and found guilty of a crime by none other than—"

"High Black Tribunal Judge of the Eastern United States Tribunal, his honor, Terry Fennimore," I said, my voice cracking.

All eyes turned to the weightlifter I wondered if he'd run. If he'd kill us all and escape. If he'd go after Parkland. He blinked and cleared his throat. "I was exonerated. I never committed any crime."

"How long did you spend in the deep prison?" Parkland poured the giant a cup of coffee and handed it over.

"Three years."

"And there's no bitterness? I read the trial transcripts… it was Fennimore who fought to make sure you did prison time."

"So what?" The big guy finally sat down. "Mr. Parkland, I've been out for fifteen years. I have no reason to hold a grudge. I live the life I want. I get to fight and perform for my race. I did not try to kill that girl. If she waited until the work was—"

The door opened just as a crash of thunder roared, shaking the whole house. Green and Ryan were drenched. "This is him, Ryan Sutcliff," Green announced.

Ryan shook his hair, spraying water like a dog. Then he looked around. "What's up?"

"My name is Gregory Parkland and I'm asking a few questions about Jennifer Perkin's death."

"Are you with the Nephilim police?"

"No." Parkland grinned and Ryan relaxed. "Can you please just tell me what happened, what you saw when Jenny died?"

Ryan's eyes found mine and I tried to look encouraging. "Well," he began, cleared his throat, and started again. "All she wanted to do was get up on that damn trapeze. I was there when Green offered to teach her. He said four-thirty. We actually had an argument about it. She wanted to start earlier. I wanted to… you know… mess around. Jenny was so headstrong. I never won those fights and she was halfway up the ladder before I started yelling. Bennie Beans, the clown, and a few others came running. We all shouted for her to come down. No go. She looked beautiful up there, so bold and brave. So damn sure of herself, and if she'd have waited, I bet she could have actually performed up there. But…"

"Go on, Mr. Sutcliff."

Ryan looked at Parkland, huffed and blinked back his tears. "Nothing was ready. We were early, and she should have known it was important to wait. Her hands gripped the trapeze and she looked down with a wink. With a jump, she was swinging. It's like it happened in slow motion. I saw wires and cables fray and twist, wild in the air, then she fell. When she hit the ground, it was right at my feet. Everyone else ran for help, I just yelled and yelled at her, figuring she'd open her eyes and fight back, but she was twisted and broken… blood poured from places where her ribs… her arm… one of her legs… split open, white bone poking through her beautiful skin. And her head. So much blood. Her ears, mouth, nose. I knew Jenny was dead before anyone got back to help her."

"I'm so sorry, son. Sorry you had to see that, but please understand… we're going to need you to tell that again in the near future."

Ryan's head shook, his eyes bloodshot and shiny.

"It's important for the truth to be told."

"Fine." And Ryan left the house, leaving the door wide open.

It had stopped raining.

Esther was dreaming. She was an infant, laying back to back against her other half, her beloved twin, Gracie. When they woke, they'd stay as still as possible until Gracie would giggle, jiggling Esther and she'd giggle, too. It was bliss, beautiful. Happy. She rolled to her back and sighed, eyes closed, savoring the dissolving dream memory then a broad hand tenderly lay on her still aching belly.

"No." She pushed it away.

"No?" Lucifer's voice was soft and she opened her eyes.

"No, not now. Not today." And she braced herself.

His palm was warm and light over her loss and she tried to push him away again, but his lips met hers in a tender kiss and he whispered, "My love, I am so sorry that you've lost another one."

Esther pushed herself up and sat back against the head rest. "Another one?" She blinked sleep out of her eyes, determined to see his expression clearly.

"Yes, my dear. I understand, it's hard for you."

He had her off guard. Since they became lovers, he had always taken the upper hand, total control, never apologetic, always clear about what he wanted and how he wanted it. How could she have liked that? Why did she let it happen? She swallowed hard then carefully controlled her voice. "So, you knew… about the other miscarriages?"

He nodded sadly, then sat at her side and pulled her head to rest on his shoulder. "I am so sorry. I fear my seed is too strong for your womb, but I can correct the problem, my dear. I can assure that you'll never conceive again."

Pulling away she slowly stood and turned to face the devil. "No, thanks."

"No?" This time his voice and expression were not so kind.

"No. I want a baby."

"I… I know, but the pain, the bleeding. My sweet Esther, I fear I'll lose you." His hand reached for hers and she stepped back out of reach. "Come, now. No need to be like this. You know I love you more than life."

Esther snorted a quick laugh. "Are you watching soap operas again? You never say things like that."

He too was on his feet, and faster than her vision could follow, he stood and glowered down at her with menacing eyes. "Isn't that kind of talk what you want?"

"I want the truth."

"Do you, now?"

"Always!"

He gripped her wrists and tossed her onto the bed, then stilled and drew in several calming breaths. "You're overwrought. Still in pain. Don't argue with me, Esther."

"Don't touch me," she said with a hiss.

"Let me love you. It will heal you."

"You never heal me!"

Lucifer looked like he'd explode but she stared up at him, her wrists still tight in his grip. "I'm teaching you lessons, you ungrateful—"

"How many times have you lied to me?"

Innocence spread across his face like peanut butter on bread and Esther knew she was on to something. "Lie to you? Why would I lie to you? You are my lover, my sweet Esther, everything I need to meet all my goals. Why would I—"

"Where's Cia?"

"Why, she left. She was cured and she walked out, right through the damn peach grove. I escorted her there myself."

"You cured her?"

"Of course, I did."

"In your laboratory?"

He freed her wrists and leaned back. "That's enough. No more of this shit, woman."

"No more lying, Luc. Or I swear, I swear—"

"You swear what? That you'll leave? So, leave? I've got the best of you already. I don't need this." He stomped out of the room and Esther followed close behind.

"What else do you do in your laboratory?"

He swung a turn and leaned down, nose to nose and shouted, "Keep this up and you'll find out!"

Still, she stood strong, even though every nerve in her body trembled with terror. "And you would hurt me?"

Lucifer, the devil, future ruler of the whole world, blinked. "No," his voice was a soft rasp. "I would never hurt you. That's why I want to make sure you never conceive again, so that you can't be hurt again because of a random mistake of nature."

"Random? You fuck me every single night."

"Let me sterilize you, it will be so much safer." He looked like he was begging. Obviously, abstinence wasn't an option for the devil.

"No, Luc," she said, allowing tears to fall. Those tears had nothing to do with what he said. She already feared she might never conceive again. Her tears were over his many deceptions, all the times she never should have trusted him. Believed in him. Lucifer was a trickster and she had been tricked far too often. He was also the only person she'd permitted herself to love. Like a chilling ocean wave, she was drenched with everything she'd lost, everything she might never have. "Tell me the truth. Cia's dead, isn't she?"

He turned and walked away. Question answered. Esther returned to her bed. She needed sleep, space to mourn, time to decide what to do next, and to determine if she was capable of doing anything at all to change her life.

~*~

In the time it took for Koeffer to be proven innocent, at least until the judge showed up, twenty-eight camps had arrived and were shuffling into place exactly as Tobias had mapped out. It was going to be magnificent. All paths led to the large center area. Bits and pieces of fabric and various show tents were being sewn together to create the big top. Cooperation among all the camps so far was stellar, and it just might turn out exactly the way Tobias imagined. This would be a big top to outdo any performance venue in history, and Tobias was pleased.

With the camp.

But not with anything else.

Something vital had altered. A crack in the underpinning had shifted and for the first time in Tobias's very long, very illustrious life, he felt discounted, set aside, ignored. Naturally, his own camp was still faithful and loyal, but not as much as he expected. Koeffer and Green never told him the whole story of that stupid girl's death. Granted, he had shrugged it off as simple misfortune, but it was inexcusable that they never explained Jenny's part in the outcome. They'd let him down, but what could he do about it?

Ballister Green was his recruiter, and even though there were no more recruits to gather and the rogue warrior societies had come to the final stages of preparation, the man held the distinguishing powerful ability to regenerate soul swords. That meant he had a hidden power too valuable to reveal itself until the moment it was needed. He couldn't, in good faith, even reprimand Green.

Koeffer, however, could be, and had already been, assigned punishment. Cookie finally had the help he'd always requested. The strong man could peel potatoes until the end of the world for all Tobias cared.

"Tobias?"

His eyes squeezed tight. "No, Dawn."

"But—"

"Whatever you want… the answer's no!" And he stomped off into the darkening woods, thinking, thinking, thinking. His head throbbed and his chest ached. Could no one see what was happening? That it would all end this time? That it was hopeless?

Parkland's arrival had fully eliminated any control Tobias had over Gracie. As an ancient, one of the oldest still alive, he'd seen three Countings and even more wars. Tobias knew, without a doubt, that there was no way that girl could do a damn thing to help them. It was folly to think so. When he again requested time to discuss his plan, Parkland brushed him off saying, "Later, if I have a minute." The man treated him like a bothersome child. Didn't Parkland know what was coming? How bad this was all going to be? Did he care?

Raphael, his friend since the beginning of his ancient life, had forsaken him. The frivolous archangel preferred the company of the Pure Nephilim, a very pretty girl, over a real leader. But naturally, it didn't matter to Raphael or any of the celestials. They'd all be hiding when the real shit hit the fan. They'd be safe until it was all over, leaving their Nephilim children, grandchildren, and great-grandchildren to face the consequences of their failure. One might think that with this crap happening again, and again, and again, the archangels would learn a lesson, take control, teach their children better, instead of just sitting by and letting them repeatedly *free will* the whole planet into near extinction.

The smell of wet sandy dirt and the distant sound of ferry horns pierced his thoughts. Tobias sat on a felled log, covered his eyes, and for the first time in his life, he cried. He'd seen too many wars and Countings, and he knew how to stop it all. He knew. No one else could do this, so—he sniffed and grumbled, pulled a sleeve across his eyes and gave a sad sigh. Why do what had always been done before? Yes, the fighting was satisfying, but to what end? Even if they survived this one, it would be just another run at another Counting, another war, another battle. It was time to do what he intended to do. It was for their good; they'd know that when it was over. There was no need to seek approval or support. He didn't need anyone to help him stop this madness.

He'd told no one about his plan. Other ancients were oblivious on how to deal with things like this. Most, even Garta, old as she was, were still coping with the curse of being an ancient. He'd gone numb to that concept. There was one action only he could take. He had the age, the stamina, the power, and the commitment. The only ancient older than him anywhere was Rashee, and her ridiculous penchant for peaceful resolution had always fallen on deaf ears. When push came to shove, she swung a sword beside her Nephilim warriors just like everyone else.

It was time. He stood. He sat back down. He let his mind go over the strategy, roll across centuries and centuries of death, battle, and

Countings. It was definitely time. He just wasn't sure how to start. So, he decided to pray.

"Uh, it's me, Tobias. I never prayed to the Morning Star before. Never talked to Lucifer. Never imagined I'd do this, but here I am. Where are you?" He stood and stepped to the right, scanned the trees as darkness dropped from the sky. Tobias headed toward the dead peach grove where he'd seen several demons come and go.

"Lucifer. It's Tobias. I'm praying to you. I need to talk to you. I have a proposal you will want to hear." A demon raced past and disappeared into nothingness, leaving behind the scent of burned flesh. His breath caught and he panted. "Where are you?"

Looking back, he noticed the camp lighting up, campfires, flashlights, and glittering lanterns transformed it into a fairy city and he couldn't help but smile. What a life he'd lived. He would be saving so much, protecting so much. He would assure that there'd never again be a Counting. He'd be remembered for longer than he'd lived. A laugh hissed from deep in his chest. Maybe the devil was busy. He'd try again tomorrow night, and the next, and the next until he could put his plan into action. Walking back, he heard a dark chuckle that made the hair on the back of his neck stand at attention. "Nope," he said casually. "Tomorrow." And he walked, a little faster than normal, back to camp.

12

arkland motioned for me to sit at the kitchen table. He set a plate of food in front of me and when my brows rose, he licked his fingers and shrugged. "Yeah, I can cook. Eat."

Dinner was a chicken casserole filled with creamy sauce and vegetables. Surprisingly delicious.

"My wife," he said between bites, "hates everything domestic. We have cooks and housekeepers, but sometimes it's nice to just get my hands dirty and make a meal. It's a good place to put my energy."

Okay, I understood. He wanted me to think he was just a normal guy. Poor Mr. Parkland had no idea that I knew nothing about normal. I smiled. "It's really good."

"Good. You can wash the dishes."

I groaned.

"But not just yet. Let's talk for a while. Let's talk about your responsibilities."

"Okay," I replied, hoping it didn't sound as frustrated as I felt.

"First, tell me. What do you think those responsibilities are?"

What? How could he ask me that? As much as I wanted to ace this test and give the right answers, I also wanted to make a few points. "Honestly? I have no clue. No clue why I'm the one responsible for anything. No idea where I'm supposed to get the knowledge or strength to lead people anywhere. Look at me. I'm a gimp, a girl, barely a woman, and actually, damn scared. Who would listen to me? Who would follow me?"

He'd listened well, now he was about to talk and I was terrified at what he was about to say, sure that a reprimand was coming. I braced myself.

"Let's start at the top. Why are you responsible? That one's easy. Genetics. Because you are Metatron's daughter. A Pure Nephilim. The knowledge will come from your father, Raphael, me, Cole Masters, Allerton, and other sources."

"Tobias?"

"No. Not Tobias. Celestial beings and Nephilim are the only beings who can see the things you don't see about yourself. We can see your… for lack of a better word… magic."

"Yeah, right. Does magic lead warriors and win wars? I am a weakling!" I waved a hand toward my twisted foot.

"Gracie, that's only your human form. Koeffer's strong form covers his true quickening power. Transformational compassion."

Mind blown. "Really?"

"Yes, really. When you are the being you were born to be, you are spectacular. We can see that about you all the time, though you only know it when your battle blood is up. That's because you have little experience with your celestial existence."

"And how do we fix that? Trust me, when I have my wings, I can hardly fit inside this room."

He laughed. "Gracie, you have your wings all the time, and you fit just fine. It's time to understand all this. You know, I have a few special powers of my own. One of my quickening powers was received about twelve years ago. It's taken a long time to figure out how to use it best."

"Does it help you with your job?"

"Not that power. I also have the power of perception that informs me of everything I need to know."

"So, you don't have a big office building full of spies and technology?" I pushed my empty plate aside.

"Like James Bond?" he said with a grin. "That would be cool, but no. I have a small building with a few very reliable, very loyal Nephilim operatives. It's my little secret. If you tell anyone, I'll lose all my funding."

I liked Gregory Parkland. He didn't focus solely on the horribleness of everything happening. He liked to lighten things up a bit. It felt positive, not as terrifying. "My lips are sealed."

His eyes darkened a bit and I figured he wanted to get down to business. "To use this power, I will be talking to you, but while I explain things, you'll be in like… an… alternate reality."

"Like a dream?"

His head shook. "More like a fantasy, I'm told. This process is how I train my operatives so that they clearly understand their duties and responsibilities. It helps you to not only hear and digest my words, but visualize them in form and color, whatever way your particular Nephilim mind understands best."

I leaned back in my chair. "Why do you need to do that? Why can't you just tell me?"

"Do you trust me, Gracie?"

I was terribly close to falling back into that *yes sir*, *no sir*, student I once was. It was a comfortable place, but I'd been sitting in that cushioned pocket for way too long. Raphael was correct, Tobias was handling the small details for me, but I should be on top of things. Now I had to decide if I wanted this head of the Nephilim Secret Service to do some mind control on me? Did I trust him? "Honestly, I'm not sure who I trust and who I don't trust anymore. Allerton let us all think we were orphans, that we were heading for a great life with tons of promise."

"He was protecting you, and if things were different, you would be starting a great new life. It's—"

"And what's up with that whole Tribunal thing? They hid a coming war from all of us? How was that right?"

"It wasn't, and the Tribunal is paying for it."

"Why did this happen?" I stood, pushing my chair back so hard it fell to the floor. "Why me? Why now?"

Parkland leaned back and his eyes became soft, understanding. "The battle heat demons had just begun their reign of terror right after my Acclimation some twenty odd years ago. Trust me, Gracie, I asked the same questions then. The reason I rose to my position was because the Tribunal hired me to shut down all rumors of demons, and destroy every single rogue warrior band on the planet."

"And you took the job?" I retrieved my chair and sat. This might get interesting.

"I did, but with one and only one intention. To protect those who protect us. The orphanage system. The rogue warrior bands. The coming Counting required a double agent to gather the intelligence and powers we were going to need to survive."

"So, you appointed yourself as savior?" That was mean, but I felt mean. I felt empowered to ask, no, demand answers for why my world was in such a mess. The problem was, this wasn't the guy to be yelling at. This guy was trying to fix it.

He cleared his throat then picked up the dishes and set them in the sink. "Again, I'm asking. Do you trust me?"

"You're telling me you know stuff going on all over the place, right?"

"Yes."

"Then I want to know some things first. No nebulous answers, Parkland. I want real, solid answers."

Returning to the table he locked his hands together and waited. "Shoot."

"Is Cole alright?"

Parkland was silent for a moment, that dark, floating light crossing his eyes again. "Cole is fine. He's bruised, a little battered. He's just connected with a very valuable Free-Wing coalition asset."

"And?"

He smiled. "He'll contact you when he can. He's very busy, just like you are."

"But…" okay, I was just going to say it. "Cole and I are supposed to work together."

"You are. There's another, too, who will complete the power, but that's later."

"Is Ben okay?"

"Ben? Oh, Ben Wheeler. His real name is Ben Allerton."

I gasped and his hand patted mine across the table.

"Ben's good. He's with Michael, recruiting across the United States. Someone else is covering Canada, another recruiter is in Mexico. Yet another is doing the same job in South America. Others are doing it in Europe, and—"

"Yes, I understand all about the coalitions in different parts of the world. What I want to know is… do you really think we can pull this off?"

"Let's hope so."

I was quiet, letting it all filter through my brain, my bigger, more sensitive brain thanks to time with my father. Metatron filled it with important data and the ancient Celestial language. Was I supposed to open that brain up to Parkland and his superpower?

"Do you trust me?" he said softly.

Drawing in a deep breath I screwed up my mouth and looked at the ceiling. "I don't want to, but I think I should. Again, why do you have to tell me things this way?"

"It gets more information across, faster."

"Is it like when Raphael puts me to sleep? Will it feel like a memory?"

"No," he laughed. "Nothing about me is as powerful as Raphael. It's just my power. I like to perfect it when I can. I can just tell you, but I think… no… I know you'll get more from my words this way."

Still thinking, weighing, considering. I lowered my eyes to the table. What if I did this and he messed me up? But he hadn't messed anything up. He was taking care of everything. Letting the Tribunal collapse, possibly even the architect of that collapse. Building massive recruiting efforts all over the world. None of us knew when this would all come down. We had to just trust that our efforts would be enough, and in time.

"Do you trust me?" he asked again.

I had to answer, "Yes." Gregory Parkland had proven himself.

~*~

Cole was ready to beg, but knew it would be useless. "You have to see the reason, the plain logic of it all," he said, his voice raw from talking, talking, talking.

McGuire had led every last one of the gargoyles from the fire site to safety in a deserted Harlem parking garage. All of them huddling on one floor made it a tighter fit, but they were thrilled to have her back, safe and sound. Once they'd all settled for the night, he began his speech. The one he'd been mentally rehearsing since stepping through the New York portal. The only problem was, she wasn't buying it.

"No," she said, sipping cold coffee from a McDonald's cup and pushing a hand through her dirty hair.

"No? Don't you understand? We're all going to die if we don't do this. Every single one of us. Gargoyles, Nephilim, humans, animals… the earth will die. Nephilim need to show up for the Counting. Carla, this is fact."

The night was chilly, but warmer than the day he'd arrived. She tightened a raggedy blanket at her neck. "I will not put my people in danger, mister. It's taken me years to grasp the fact that I'm Nephilim. These people never have, they can't. Not emotionally, not mentally, not at all. No how. I struggle to take care of them… to teach them how to take care of each other. Why the hell would I put them in danger for crap we didn't do? Crap we didn't even know to do? It's plain stupid. No."

"Carla, please. Be reasonable."

She waved a hand and turned her back to him.

He scooted his butt around the dirty floor to face her.

"I said no."

"Damn it, Carla… I put myself in danger to save you."

She blinked. "Yeah. Why did you do that? You didn't even know who McGuire was. Not that I imagine you'd have done it for me if you did, after all—"

"Especially if I knew it was you. It's that important. Every single one of us is important."

She shook her head. "*Every* one?"

"Every single one."

"Even Nunzio, who raped me and tried to kill my gargoyles? Tried to kill you?"

Carla was still a beautiful woman, now a little rough around the edges and tarnished from living so long on the streets. His memory of meeting her never faded. She was drinking gin and tonic, he was on his fourth beer. They'd talked a bit, but mostly touched each other in the dark corner of that bar. She wanted sex in the men's room and he obliged. It was raw, hard, fast. Then, as she sipped her final drink, and just before the cops came in to raid the place, she told him she would be committing herself to a mental hospital in the morning. When he asked why, her only response was a shrug and to whisper the word, "Wings." Cole had just received his dishonorable discharge from the U.S. Marine Corps, so he figured he'd head west, learn a few things about living hard and ignoring his own wings. It felt better than committing himself like Carla. If he only knew then what he knew now, he could have changed both of their lives.

Cole took a deep breath, watching Carla examine her hands, ignoring him. What if she never changed her mind? He needed as many Free-Winged as he could get. He had to shoot for the stars. He even had to reach for the bad Nephilim like Nunzio. Was he getting greedy? Should he be happy with Carla's sixteen million gargoyles? No. All of the Free-Winged were needed. Every single one.

Then he realized, getting them all, bringing the bad guys into the fold, just might be the incentive Carla needed to change her mind.

"Even Nunzio. Every single one," he stated.

"But if we're all going to die anyway, why bother?" She leaned back against the grimy wall. "What's the point?"

"Carla, I remember you. In that bar. How you fought off all those cops, all those men, even that crazy dog."

"The dog just got in the way," she said with a grunt, obviously enjoying the compliment.

"You love a fight. This is the fight of a lifetime. You love our race. Why else would you work this hard to take care of the Free-Winged? You've taught them so much, made them survivors. You should have seen how they fought for you."

Her head shook slowly.

"You're a fighter. A warrior. We need you… we need your people. Most of all I need you to help me convince Nunzio's coalition to join us."

She gave a loud snort. "Like that could ever happen. You make it sound like we'll all be buddies, off for a night on the town."

"Carla, think of poor ICe. He, of all of us, doesn't deserve to die without understanding what he is, or how he can help save the world. The whole world."

"I need time."

"We don't have a lot of time." He stood and brushed off his jeans. "Not a lot of time at all. Tell me where I can find Nunzio." Cole lifted his backpack and pulled out some cash. Dropping it into her lap he shrugged. "To help with what your people lost when we all ran."

She rolled up the cash and rubbed her eyes.

"Nunzio? Where is he?"

"He'll kill you."

Cole grinned. "Don't bet on it. While you're thinking, I'm going to work on him."

"You're fucking crazy."

"I'm doing it. I have to. I have no choice."

She rolled her eyes and slipped the cash into her bra. "It's your ass. He's usually at a pub called East Gags. He won't be alone."

"Fine. I need an answer by tomorrow." And he left into the New York night.

Metatron's Daughters, Book 2: The Lost Race Trilogy

13

eautiful San Francisco. It was a super successful engagement. The last session, standing room only, and not one Nephilim left without a soul sword, instructions to be prepared, and to watch for information on where and when to muster. Ben was beginning to think this just might work. He was never so impressed with Michael as when the man drew the crowd in and spoke from his heart. Everything was working.

But Michael was uncomfortably quiet as they packed their bags. He made no eye contact and often cleared his throat like he had something to say. Once, he walked out of the room and didn't return for an hour. Didn't even bring ice or a bottle of cola. He did, however, smell like bourbon.

"Okay, just spit it out," Ben finally said. "What did I do wrong? Must have been something big for you to not even want to look at me."

Michael turned red eyes to his son. "No! Nothing. You did nothing wrong. You're…" the man sighed. "You are perfect, Ben."

"So, what's with the silent treatment? We have lots to do. You got a call from the guy in New York, they've tripled your speaking engagements, added two days and a second venue. Is that going to mess up our schedule?"

More silence. Ben sat on the bed just waiting. Something was up, and his superpower wasn't helping one bit. Maybe what was happening didn't matter to the bigger picture. Maybe that's why he had no idea. "Dad?"

Finally, Michael sat and looked into his son's eyes. "I've watched you grow into an amazing young man, Ben. But hell, you were an amazing infant, and toddler, and student. It was a blessing to witness, but I missed the most important parts. The part where I could have been your father. Talked to you when you needed guidance, or taken you fishing."

"Fishing? You fish?" This was getting too heavy, all Ben wanted was to lighten things up a bit.

"No." Michael didn't even smile. "But if I was your dad, I could have. That's the point. That's what I gave up."

"To protect me. So…"

Michael's head shook. "Have you enjoyed this trip so far?"

"Yeah. Loved L.A. Really love sword training with you. Love watching you win over so many recruits. I honestly didn't think it would go so well. Dad… I'm kinda proud of you."

"I'm proud of you, too, son."

Silence. Ben glanced at the clock near the beds. "So, what time's our flight tonight?"

Michael took another deep breath then looked at Ben with determination. "I fly out in an hour for New York. You—"

"Wait a minute. What? No. I'm going with you,"

Michael shook his head but smiled. "No, you're flying to North Carolina in the morning. A car will take you to Ocracoke."

"Why? If I didn't do anything wrong, why are you sending me away?" Ben's gut twisted and he rubbed it.

"Use your head, Ben. Gracie needs help. And… it's time for you to live your life. I'm grateful we did this, you know. It was fun for me, too."

"Wait," Ben stood and paced the room Was his power of perception ever going to kick in and help him with this? "I understand, maybe, that I can help Gracie, but I can help you just as well."

"Use the power, buddy."

"Obviously it's taken the day off." He stood, hands out, eyes glaring.

"You might be a little afraid of what you know."

"Like what? Wait. Wait! Start living my life? Isn't that what you said? Isn't that what I'm doing here with you?"

"No," Michael said as he shuffled through the courtesy bar, cracked open a tiny bottle and downed it. "What you're doing here with me is feeding my selfish need to be a father. Think about it. If I was your dad your whole life, exactly what would I be doing right now?"

Ben blinked.

"I'd be sending you off to live your life. Ben, there might not be a whole lot of life left for any of us. This could be the Counting to end it all. You need to take the time you have left and enjoy it."

Already, Ben knew he wasn't going to win this argument. "War isn't exactly my idea of enjoying life."

"With your sword skills? Seriously?"

"Who will I spar with on that tiny little island?"

"Warriors far more skilled than me." Michael closed his suitcase and lifted it.

"Who's going to help you now?"

"Chester has agreed to travel with me, set things up, take care of the details. He's probably no better at it than you are, but…" He shrugged and grinned. "I'll call, let you know how things are going. Keep your cell phone charged."

"I only forgot once." Ben stood and embraced Michael. "I love you."

"I know. Your flight leaves at nine tomorrow morning. Do not miss it."

"Now you sound like a headmaster."

"Wonder why?"

Ben watched Michael melt down the hallway and into the elevator, knowing full well that the next time he laid eyes on him, could be on the battlefield. On the other hand, it was the first time in his whole life he was completely alone. *Cool!* He ordered room service and considered taking a walk but it had started to drizzle. Looking out the window at the city lights and the Golden Gate Bridge, he wondered what would actually happen to everything if they failed. Everything was in danger. He imagined devastation and destruction, earthquakes, tsunamis, desperate humans everywhere. He thought about dying on the battlefield, about losing the fight that couldn't be lost. He heard the cries of the wounded and smelled the death all around.

A knock at the door sent a shockwave through his whole body. "Can't be thinking that shit," he whispered, acutely aware it was his imagination and not his power of perception at play. Things were bad enough without making them feel worse. Another knock. He looked into the face of the person standing in his doorway. "You're not room service. What the hell are you doing here?"

Kevin pushed past and walked inside. He dropped a suitcase at the foot of one of the beds then flopped onto it with a bounce, sporting his patented irresistible grin. "I'm going to Ocracoke with you."

"Why the hell would you do that? Aren't you supposed to be helping Chester? Why didn't you go to New York with them?"

The guy grunted and sat on the edge of the mattress. Ben stepped around to see his face. It looked odd. "What?"

"Chester and I… we're finished."

Something pinged in Ben's chest. Something he had no idea how to deal with. Finished? Finished? What did that mean? "You talk like he was your girlfriend or something." It wasn't the right thing to say, but still, even though his perception had just kicked in full throttle, he wasn't sure he could handle what he knew.

Kevin looked around the room, at his hands, then up at Ben whose knees were going a little weak.

"What did Chester say?" Ben had to know.

Kevin rolled his neck. "He said 'Old men shouldn't have shiny new things'."

"What's that mean?" Ben had to sit, so he lowered to the other bed, facing the man who was changing his life—giving him the life his father wanted him to enjoy.

"Man, I know you're afraid. This is the beginning for you."

"What're you talking about?" But Ben knew exactly what Kevin was saying. He even knew what he'd say next. All Ben had to do was allow it, instead of doing what he wanted to do which was to run like a crazy man out of that room. Ben leaned in, waited, and he prayed it wouldn't be too hard to move ahead.

"A first time, a first awakening to what you are, and I'm not talking about wings and weapons, Ben." Kevin was silent for a moment, then ran a hand through his hair and licked his lips. "I know, man. I know I've been a real pain. I've been acting like a real prick but honestly, it was all an act for Chester. I didn't want to hurt…" He blinked then focused on Ben's face. "I didn't want him to know. Ben," he shifted to the very edge of the mattress and leaned forward. "All I know is that you are spectacular. And… I'm sure I'm falling in love with you. Really, truly, deeply."

"Uh…" How could he have no words after that? "I, ah, I'm…"

"The words are hard at first. Trust me, I know. Let me help. Are you… attracted to me?"

Ben nodded.

"Are you feeling something bigger than friendship?"

"Yes."

"Hey, I know you're not ready for anything more right now. I get it. I've been there and it's fine. I'm a patient man. Ben Allerton, you are worth the wait."

"Oh. So…" Ben squirmed. "So, what do we do now?"

Kevin's smile was radiant. His hands cupped Ben's face and he leaned in. His lips were soft and strong at the same time, and the kiss ended quickly.

Ben blinked. "Oh."

"That okay? Because what we do now is just take it slow. I can wait. You can be sure of it."

"Okay," Ben actually wanted to laugh, shout, dance. "Hey, can we go out and do something? I mean, I'm only eighteen. Can't legally drink yet and Dad left me no bail money, but there must be something fun to do in this city."

"Sure, there's a cool coffee house. How's your poetry tolerance level?"

"Hate poetry, but it sounds like fun." And Ben leaned in this time, kissing the man who'd been driving him mad for nearly a week. He didn't like Kevin or hate him. He was in love with him. How could it happen so fast? With such surety? Remembering Gracie's disappointment when she wanted to make love ached inside his chest. Now he knew what it felt like to love. Luckily, he didn't have to deal with rejection. Poor Gracie. Now he loved her even more.

"So, Kev, you think I'm spectacular? Wait until you stand face to face with a Pure Nephilim."

"I can't wait." Kevin's arm dropped over Ben's shoulders and they walked three blocks to a coffee house that served lousy coffee and presented even worse poetry. The most upsetting thing about the place was the many battle heat demons roaming around. Ugly, slimy, black as night. One even clapped after an especially terrible poetry reading.

It was a rude awakening in the midst of his overwhelming happiness. War was coming. They left soon after, climbed into separate beds, but talked all night.

~*~

Parkland was right. It felt more like a fantasy than a dream or a memory, and all I could do was wonder how much of the creative images in front of me were my doing, and how much came from somewhere else? I felt like Alice, and everything became curiouser and curiouser. Oh, I could hear his words clearly, the timbre of his voice, the cadence of his sentences. At times he seemed to strategically stop talking while I formulated pictures and colors, even sounds and physical sensations. Tickles. Chills. Fever. Floating. Falling. Crashing. It was all there, somehow telling me things in a new language of symbolism far more pleasant and easy to decipher than Metatron's book.

Parkland's power was mystical, strategic. Remarkable. When I found a moment to catch my own thoughts, they always slid and slapped around, then dissolved in the gloaming. Everything made sense. He'd said that the images were not his, they were from my own mind, my own soul. Every now and then I caught a glimpse of Metatron's teachings in the midst of my observations. Other times, I skimmed down a muddy hill toward things I didn't want to face, but would have no choice once I reached the bottom.

There was growing and crashing, spinning vortexes of color and light, gritty energy that felt like stinging bees. Sensations morphed into images that shifted precariously out of sight, then around again. My mind examined everything meticulously until a new scene unfolded, blasting cold as ice all around, then it drifted like a raft on calm waters. Sounds wafted everywhere, some demanding, some slithering around my ankles, others tinkling like wind chimes or gonging like monster bells. Wave upon wave of color clashed and dispensed, then everything went a soft blue, radiant and pulsing like a heartbeat.

I reached out to touch the air and it recoiled then embraced me with warmth. My environment shifted and I was standing in the center of a pure white cornfield. White stalks, white husks, white kernels. Then, inexplicably, there was a squirming, chubby infant, warm in my arms, and my heart wanted to burst with the amazement of it all. I turned full circle taking in all that purity and my enchanted journey came to an abrupt end. Wonderland was closed and I opened my eyes.

"Holy shit!"

Parkland laughed. "What do you know now that you didn't know before?"

"Everything. Nothing. Mr. Parkland, that was astounding. I fundamentally know what I am, who I am, *why* I am! And the most important thing…" I stood and actually wrapped my arms around his neck in a hug. "I'm not afraid anymore. I know the value I have for our race. Thank you."

"You're welcome. Now wash those dishes." Parkland left for the guest room.

14

slept better than I had since the day we learned Ariel's Gate would close. Fragments of my experience with Parkland's superpower drifted into my dreams. The weight of the coming Counting had eased and my shoulders relaxed. Several times I rolled around on the bed, still sound asleep, but clearly aware of my massive wings, fluttering, shifting, gentle all around me. A soft ringing called, but I couldn't find it in the dream. The noise became more and more demanding until I woke and discovered my cell phone, vibrating like crazy on the bedside table.

"Hello?" I was breathless, like I'd just ran a marathon.

"Gracie. Sweetheart. It's me."

"Cole! Are you alright? Are you hurt? What's happening? When are you coming—"

"Whoa," he chuckled and the bubbling sound made my heart leap. "I'm fine. Got myself into a little mess here, and I may be heading for another one. I just needed to hear your voice."

"I love you." It was a soft offering, but I hardly believed I said it.

"How are things there?"

I filled him in with the goings on, the growing camp, Parkland, and what I now knew about Jenny's death. He listened, didn't interrupt, but I could feel his need to get moving. "You're not going to get a chance to come here, are you?"

"I want to. I might. I don't know. I've got a shot at sixteen million Free-Winged, and possibly another few thousand, just from this trip to New York."

"That's amazing!"

"It could be, if it works out."

Silence.

"Did I wake you?"

"Yes, but it's good. I needed to hear your voice, too. Things are evolving here. There will be powerplays and you might be surprised when you see it all."

"Nothing surprises me anymore. Listen, I gotta go. Remember, you're strong and important, baby."

"I know." I smiled wide, wishing he could see it.

"I love you. I'll try to call again soon."

"Oh, Cole! Wait! I have something for you."

"What?"

"Allerton's phone number. Parkland gave it to me today. Maybe you can let him know how things are going. If you need help, he's going to be in New York soon."

"I know. You should see the signs. You'd think the guy was a Wall Street guru. Priceless. Text me the number." Cole's voice was ragged. "But the kind of help I might need… I don't think Allerton can offer. Hey, go back to bed, Gracie."

"Good night, Cole. *Caalii sausha,*" I said in the ancient words I'd taught him before he left.

"Caalii sausha," he whispered. "You be brave, too, my love."

There was no more sleeping in the cards for me. Only three in the morning, but I wanted fresh air. Sitting out on the porch, I enjoyed the autumn coolness. At Ariel's Gate, tucked neatly in the West Virginia mountains, we'd be freezing our butts off in early November, but the night was around fifty degrees and I was comfortable under Cia's yellow afghan.

Across the darkness, the camp was growing massive and a line of smoke lifted from campfires kept burning day and night. Parkland said that sometime tomorrow or the next day, the camp and house would be put under a protective veil, making it invisible to humans, demons, and outside Nephilim. I'd need to let Cole know how to get under the veil when he finally came home. My heart ached for him. I hoped he'd be back soon, but I knew how much there was to do, knew it more than I ever understood before.

Numbers. Numbers. It was all about the numbers. Something I learned in my father's book made me wonder. There were sacred ways of looking at numbers, using numbers, and manipulating numbers, but I hadn't quite grasped it yet. In some situations, the bigger the numbers, the better, but for other things, smaller numbers counted more than the big ones. Yet in other circumstances, it was all about the combination of numbers. Numbers like seven, four, and sixty held great importance. Numbers like three and fifteen were warnings. Who could figure this crap out? But somehow, I suspected that our coming Counting was a pretty straight forward, down and dirty, us versus them, and the team with the biggest posse would win.

Losing to Esther and the devil wasn't an option, at least not for me. For me, it was personal. Half of me hated her for serving Lucifer. Half of me hated the devil because he'd manipulated her into doing what he wanted. That's how he works. Right?

With that thought I pressed my hands to my ears, fighting a slight pain that made me gasp. It was over quickly and I shook my head to clear it.

Candy.

I blinked, slowly turned and looked right into the eyes of a three-headed demon, standing just on the other side of the porch railing.

Candy. Candy. Candy.

I heard that, clear as a bell. Its mouths weren't moving but I could hear a demon. It was actually talking to me. Here's the weirdest thing about it, I wasn't the least bit afraid. In fact, I decided to test my theory. "You want candy?" I asked the garish creature and three, count 'em, three, heads nodded. "Okay, wait here."

I went inside, praying Ryan hadn't eaten all my M&Ms. Cookie gave me two giant bags designed for Trick-or-Treat. One was gone, but thankfully, the other was still unopened. Grabbing a handful of little packages, I wondered if I was actually asleep and dreaming. Then my shin cracked into a table turning a corner. Nope. Wide awake. And I wondered, how far could I take this?

Opening a package, I set the loose colorful candies on the railing and watched as fingers gathered and mouths chewed.

"Doesn't Lucifer give you candy?"

No.

My heart fluttered. I was having a conversation with a demon! "Does he feed you?"

No need.

"But you like candy?"

Yes.

Now for the big question. "How many of you are there?"

Legion.

"Do you know the number?"

The creature jumped up and down, several fingers pointing to the place where candy once sat. I poured several packages out for it and repeated my question. "Do you know the number? For how many of you there are?"

Legion.

I listened to crunches and slurps as blackened tongues slipped out and licked cracked lips. "So, how many is legion?"

Too many.

I watched a tear roll down one ruined burn-blackened face.

Thank you, Gracie. It turned to leave but one head looked back. *Esther loves you.* Then another head turned to me. *Cia is gone.*

And my heart broke with both bits of information. The amazing thing was that I had been given a new quickening power. I could hear and understand the demons. Now what?

~*~

The East Gags Pub smelled as expected, of beer, and puke, and cigarette smoke. Clearly the criminal Nephilim element cared as much about laws and governmental restrictions as any other felon hiding in the dark corners of America. A whiskey bottle flew across the room, smashed against a wall and laughter wafted from the back of the bar. It was so dark, the bar was lit by nothing but a red and yellow neon sign. *East Gags is gonna get you!* Far to the other side of the room, a red exit sign winked and Cole wondered if this plan wasn't such a good idea.

Letting his eyes adjust to the dimness, he strolled to the bar, shouldered his way in, and ordered a whiskey, straight.

"We don't got no crooked whiskey," snorted the bartended as he poured. "Who the fuck are you?"

"Name's Masters. I'm looking for Nunzio."

Cole could have heard a pin drop in the following silence. He sipped, casually flipped a five-dollar bill onto the bar then turned to scan the crowd. All faces were aimed at him, glowing red and yellow in the odd light. "So?" he shouted and everyone blinked. "Where the hell is he?"

"What do you want?" The voice came from far to the left. Men and women, all Nephilim, created the perfect pathway until Cole was looking right at the man. Unfortunately, Nunzio's scraggly black beard was half burned away and angry blisters decorated that side of his face.

Cole walked up to the table and looked down at him. "I want to talk to you."

"You got McGuire back." Nunzio returned all his attention to his beer and the struggling, unhappy woman tight in his arm.

"Raping one a day? Is that your quota?" Cole growled.

Nunzio pushed the lady away and dragged a chair closer to his table with his boot.

Cole didn't sit.

"What do we got to talk about?"

Cole shrugged, glanced around. All attention was on them. "You like living, Nunzio?"

All three hundred pounds of Nunzio sat straight up. "That a threat? Cause I got a lot of men behind you that can shut your lights off with one nod from me. Hear me? *Behind* you. I don't recall seeing no fire blasting outta your ass, Masters."

Cole tilted his head and gave a thoughtful grin. "It can be arranged." When the man didn't react, he held out his hands. "Seriously, I need to talk to you. It's about all of us surviving."

"Surviving what? Your crazy fire voodoo trick?"

"No, stopping the end of the fucking world. Don't be an idiot, Nunzio. Give me ten minutes to explain what we're all up against."

"Who's this *all* you're talking about?"

Cole sat and glared directly into the man's eyes. "Every single winged being on this planet. You," his arm swept the room, "them, McGuire's gargoyles, the ones you see in suits on Madison Avenue, winged women on the subway. Every single one of us. All of us."

Several moved closer and leaned in to listen.

"Nunz, that's the fucking dream I had!" A voice rose from the smoky dim room.

"Shut up, Geezer."

"But Geezer's dreams are real, they happen. They always do!"

Cole sat back to see where this would go, hoping it led closer to his proposal. The raging conversation came to blows around four o'clock, altered into terrifying speculation before the sun rose, then finally settled with Cole and Nunzio, nose to nose in negotiations.

"It isn't about being a good person or a criminal, it's about standing together, whatever we are."

"And that bitch will stand with me? I raped her more than once, ya know." His eyes twinkled.

Cole leaned back. Thought. "No, you didn't. I know Carla. You might have been violent during her captivity, but she was willing any other time. I'm right, aren't I?"

Nunzio actually shrugged. "Maybe. She's a wild one. Too bad she's on the other side."

Cole slammed a palm on the table, making the big man jump then growl like a dog. "There are no sides! We're all on the same side, or we all die. Are you too damn stupid to understand?"

"Diplomacy ain't your strong suit, Masters. I ain't stupid. I been surviving all along without all you other winged beings. No *nephiliminium* thingy ever stepped up to help me or save me. Why should I step up now?"

Rubbing his eyes raw, Cole leaned back, his head dropping so he could only see the filthy ceiling. "Nunzio," he repeated. "You like living?"

The pub door crashed open and for a moment, Cole feared it might be the cops. Together he and Nunzio stood and watched as McGuire stomped her way inside.

"Well?" she shouted.

"Well what?" Nunzio asked. Cole expected an old wild west standoff, ten paces and pistols in the middle of West 116th Street.

"You in?"

"You?"

Slowly Cole sat on his chair, wishing he had a camera to film the event.

"Yes, the gargoyles are in."

"How many you committing to this fiasco?"

"It's a war, idiot. All sixteen point eight million."

Cole's heart almost stopped. Sixteen point eight million?

"I gotta talk to Petie and Freeze, but I'll match that."

The battle for superiority was on, Cole wished he had a fresh beer.

"You can't match it. Bring what you got, and you and me, we'll have a deal."

"*The* deal?" Nunzio stepped closer to her, his hand affectionately pushing back her hair. She pulled away and he said softly, "About yesterday. Sorry. Never again."

"You bet your ass, never again. At least never again until we make sure the damn planet is going to survive. Then we'll talk."

She turned to go and he pulled her arm, spinning her into a kiss worthy of a Hollywood romance.

"Wait!" Cole stood. "I hate to mess up this tender moment, but Nunzio. You said Petie and Freeze."

"Yeh, they're my territory commanders. Don't worry about them, they'll fall in line."

"No, I have another question… for both of you. Are there other Free-Winged coalitions? Around America? Mexico? Canada?"

"Greedy little shit, ain't you?" Nunzio shook his head. "Yeah, twelve other groups, none as big as McGuire's or mine." Carla snorted. "Okay, none as big as hers, but they're out there."

"Can you connect me with them?"

"We can do better than that. Carla here can call a meeting. All the leaders in one place. All we need is cash to make it happen."

"How much do you need?" Cole opened his backpack and filtered through the remainder of the ten-thousand bucks Allerton had stuffed into the van's glove box.

Both Free-Winged reached for the backpack.

"Will five-grand do the job? Get them all here? Quickly?"

"Well…" Carla said thoughtfully.

Nunzio grabbed the cash from Cole's hands. "That'll be just about right." He grinned, then noticing Carla's expression, handed her half and whispered, "We can use the extra, and you know it. You can buy food for your people, and I can bribe Petie and Freeze if they give me any flack."

"Good. Now, how soon can we have this meeting?" Cole's heart raced.

"I'll get right on it." And Nunzio, walked out of the bar.

"You really are a dumb ass, Cole. Two-grand would have done the job." She shook her head. "And, I'll do everything I can to get the leadership together, and the ones I work with and the ones, he does. Three days."

Cole's brows shot up. "That soon?"

"No need for planes and trains or busses. I've got a connection with lots of technology expertise. We'll hold a cyber meeting and get this ball rolling."

"Carla, I think I love you."

"Too late. I'm promised to Nunzio." And she snorted again. "Like that's ever gonna happen."

15

urprisingly, I wasn't a bit tired. The sun rose slowly, deliciously, elegantly and I took a walk to the beach. Recalling life on Ocracoke as a little girl made me nostalgic, soft, like I was listening to my favorite music all alone in a safe room. When three demons arrived, kicking sand and running from the coming soft waves, I almost smiled. Once those creatures were Nephilim and loved the things we all love. Chocolate. The beach. Friendship. It was awful to think about what happened to them.

When Wally tore himself free from his demon counterparts, it was the ugliest, most horrifying thing I'd ever witnessed. He was killing himself to reverse his blood vow to the devil. Dead. Wally was dead because of his free will choice. So was Jenny. Death… so final. In Wally's case, he hoped beyond reason that he could return to his Nephilim existence. According to Raphael, Wally was the first demon to ever do such a thing. He was courageous. A hero.

The demons left, strolling down the beach like anyone else might on such a lovely morning. I wondered about free will. Why we have it. How it works. It may have been simplistic, but an idea came to me, one so huge it almost exploded my brain. If we use free will to choose something bad, then why can't we just use our free will to choose something good? To reverse it all. Why do we think we have to stick with the bad choice? Why do we think the bad choice is forever? We make promises to God all the time. *If you let me pass this test, I promise to never cut gym class again. If he kisses me, I'll never walk around angry at the world again.* Promises, promises, promises, and we break them all the time. So, what made a promise to Lucifer bigger and more permanent than a promise to God?

Chewing on those thoughts, my mind dug deeper. What made us think evil was stronger than good? It wasn't. So, reversing a free will bad choice is not only possible, it makes sense. Wally did it. Sure, there would be repercussions and penance, but at least we'd be free of the bad choice. Right?

Okay. Yeah, I know. Simplistic.

I sighed and walked through the trees toward the camp. Like the sky, it too had come alive. Birds chirped and the scents of sizzling bacon and coffee drifted on the breeze. Every camp had a cook, but now they'd all come together and meals had become communal banquets. Cookie worked diligently with all the other cooks, developing menus for every meal, each preparing their specialties. Each cook shined, sweating, talking, and laughing. Standing inside the dining tent and watching them, I discovered that the flawless, harmonious symphony they created was strangely similar to the demons playing on the beach. Life was joyous and no one wanted to see it all end.

I'd been hearing about the meals at camp and wanted to join in. There was a strict breakfast dining schedule. Leadership at six, specialists and performers at seven, maintenance at eight. I stood there, looking at the posted list, determining where I belong. "Six it is," I said aloud and sat at a table.

Slowly, leaders and dignitaries drifted in.

"Gracie!"

I turned to see Dawn rushing toward me, wearing that smile that could launch a thousand ships and one wooden horse. "Hey, how are you?"

She sat beside me and leaned in. "You look different."

I blinked confusion. "I just saw you three weeks ago. I've been up at the house, why didn't you come visit?"

Her expression darkened and she rubbed a swelling tummy I hadn't noticed when she walked over. "Tobias," she whispered. "He feels we should leave you alone. Besides, you have Parkland up there. He's no friend to the Emmaus warriors."

"That's not true! He's behind all your cash and information flow."

"He's snubbing Tobias."

"Well, Tobias can be… you know."

She sighed.

"Hey, congratulations. When's the baby due?"

Dawn leaned close to my ear. "He doesn't want it. I think he knows we'll fail and it will never have a chance to live."

I gripped her wrist to keep her from walking away. "Dawn, I know, really know, we have a great shot at surviving this Counting. Trust me. This," and my hand ran tenderly over her belly bump, "this is a good thing. He'll be thrilled after all the hard stuff is over."

"I wish I could believe you."

I gripped tighter and she squirmed.

"Stop listening to him!" I hissed. "He has no right to take this joy from you."

She nodded sadly, and walked away. Tobias had arrived.

For some time, I sat alone wondering if any of the leaders would acknowledge or join me. Rashee was the first, smiling and sliding elegantly onto a chair across the table. As she chatted about performers and the weather, Raphael sat beside me. Then came a few people I didn't know.

Parkland completed the table, grinning. "I don't like to cook all the time," he said then reached out a hand to Rashee.

The diners at my table looked a little like a world tour. A beautiful Native American man with hair, long and straight, shining so black that blue sparks wove through it, smiled. He was Bold Eagle, leader of the Tiospia Powwow Warriors. When I asked what it meant, he showed his white teeth in another handsome smile and explained, "Tiospia means lodge, or home."

Next to him sat a tall, grey-haired man named Wardo. He played Merlin in his Round Table Performances and lead the Merlin Knights. There was an Italian leader named Joe Carducci, who commanded the Roma Victa Army. A black warrior called Akkii, was leader of the African Wonders Warriors. There was a stunning man, Juan, who lead the Mayan Fighters. And finally, sitting at the end of the table wearing a plaid wool kilt and puffy shirt, Walter McTavish who led the Fighting Highlanders. These were all Americans, boasting their heritage and being an integral part of the melting pot.

Rashee was the only ancient at the table, the rest were Nephilim. Each ran a carnie show, led life as gypsies and rogue warriors, and stood ready to die for the Nephilim race. Conversations raced around the table, most of them including me in their discussions. A few asked my opinion, and surprisingly, I had something to say each time. Whatever Parkland had done, really worked. I was beginning to believe I was leader of this amazing army. My thoughts were sharp as polished blades and clear as a bell. A few times a leader nodded thoughtfully, considering my suggestions regarding camp necessities and available resources.

I had finally climbed my way into something I never had. Confidence, but it was based on a blessed deluge of learning from Metatron, Raphael's lessons, and Parkland's unique power. All I needed now was experience.

~*~

Tobias couldn't eat. So much frivolity. No one knew it was the end. He ignored Dawn and her inconvenient pregnancy, pushed aside a full plate and snarled at Garta when she asked if he was feeling unwell. Across the room little Gracie laughed and chatted up her new friends, all the weakest of the rogue warriors in his opinion, except for that Native American guy. Tobias had once seen him fight. Bold Eagle was not one to mess with.

Eighteen tables were filled with leaders and dignitaries and not one of them offered respect to Tobias. The last Counting was different. He had been the leader of them all and they came through it just fine. Since then, his hands had been repeatedly, foolishly, tied. He blamed Parkland. Yes, the cash came regularly. Yes, bits of information came to Tobias from the man's spies. However, if Tobias and the Emmaus warriors weren't luckily traveling so close to Gracie's Acclimation location, he was sure he'd have never been part of such an important event. His directive came from higher up than Parkland, so his sense of superiority was justified. No one seemed to care that it was he, and no one else, who found Allerton and collected the newly acclimated Nephilim, including the last living Pure Nephilim. Why did no one care?

Tobias sat until everyone had left, deep in his angry thoughts. He slammed his mug on the table, splashing coffee with his frustration and walked out. The sound of shuffling tables and clacking folding chairs followed him out. As the cook tent was set up for the next, much larger breakfast crowd, Tobias entered the silent trees and this time, he headed north, far from the peach grove.

There were demons everywhere. Too many, and he wished he was armed. He'd find great pleasure in cutting down the enemy while they were so passive and unthreatening. Ah, but that might be counter-productive to his goal, so he walked by, ignoring them as they, and all of the camp, ignored him. Of one thing he was most pleased. He would establish the protective veil soon. He alone controlled who entered and left that veil. Things would be different then. Respect would come. Still, he had to make his proposal first. That way he could protect them all and hopefully, eliminate the Counting all together.

More sure than ever of his intentions, he waited until he was alone, no Nephilim, no people, no demons.

"Where are you?" he hissed. "Are you such a coward you can't acknowledge a man praying to you? Show yourself, Lucifer!"

This he repeated and repeated until his voice became raw as soot and his head ached.

"Won't you give me a chance to make a proposal you can only benefit from? It's an incredible deal." He leaned against a tree and waited, then turned and took a piss. "I never thought the great Morning Star was afraid of a mere ancient," he said as he closed his trousers. "A coward." He stepped into a small clearing. "A complete, fucking, coward!"

"You talk that way to me?"

The voice boomed so loud, Tobias tumbled to the ground and covered his ears.

"Is that how you talk to the Father?"

"I… I—"

"QUIET!"

Tobias, on hands and knees, bowed his head to the dirt and stilled. "I have a proposal, Lucifer."

Nothing.

"Please, let me explain. I can help you, and help the Nephilim at the same time."

Not a sound, even the birds and creatures of the woods had gone silent.

He remained still until his back trembled, then he stood, brushed off his hands, and nodded. "Alright, Morning Star… another time. Tonight. Tomorrow morning, as many times as it takes. We need to talk."

Returning to camp, he felt more tired than ever. He retired to his camper to rest. Then he heard the gunshot.

~*~

Halfway back to the house, I spun a circle and took in the camp and everything around it. The house, tents and campers, chocolate-loving demons, the scent of cooking fires, and sounds of people. Life. The energy floating around it all seemed to radiate from the magic willow tree and encompass everything in a positive warmth. I wasn't so naive as to believe that all was well with the world, but it felt close to well at that moment. Especially when I focused on the two men walking toward me.

His walk, his coloring, there was no denying who it was. Excitement charged and I ran as fast as a woman with a club foot could. He ran too and met me, arms out and embracing like we'd been apart for years.

"Gracie!" Ben set me on my feet and pushed me arm's length away, eyes scanning every inch of me, while I checked out the handsome man joining us. "Gracie, you're as beautiful as ever! Man, I missed you."

"I missed you, too."

"At least you aren't alone," he said, taking in the huge camp behind me.

"I was for a while. Who's this?"

"Oh… ah… Gracie, this is Kevin. Kevin, this is the incomparable Gracie Caine."

My hand shot out. I'd become a hand-shaker, and I liked it. The touch of his palm to mine made him solid, real. It was the energy between Ben and this man that vibrated deepest into my heart.

"Gracie," he leaned in and spoke softly. "You're as spectacular as Ben said… maybe more."

I smiled and Ben stepped toward the camp. "Wow, Gracie. Look at this! Come on, show us around."

He raced ahead and I gripped Kevin's arm. He looked at me and I spoke words I sure as hell never expected to say in my life. "Mister, it's Ben who's spectacular."

"I know. He is extraordinary in so many ways."

"So, you'll understand when I tell you that if you hurt him, I will kill you. Kill you dead."

With another flash of his smile, Kevin took my arm and walked me to camp. "You re a good friend, Gracie. I hope one day you can be my friend, too."

"Oh, I can. But—"

The sound of a pistol blast thundered and for a split second, everything seemed to still. Then I ran, Kevin raced to catch up with Ben. Everyone was rushing every which way but I had a feeling I knew exactly where the sound came from. I saw Koeffer tucked in the kitchen area. He's hard to miss wherever he hides.

I passed three demons, staring and pointing in the direction I was heading.

He's in pain.

He wants revenge.

He wants to die.

Praying it wasn't a gunshot, but instead some kind of cooking accident, I plowed into the dining tent.

A tall black man in an expensive suit and tie stood, arm out, his pistol shaking, aimed at poor Koeffer. Already blood ran from the big man's arm. I feared he'd charge the judge, but instead, he spoke softly, compassionately.

"I am so sorry for your loss. She was a beautiful, vibrant young woman who fell to her death. If I could have saved her, I would have."

"You killed her, because I—"

"Put down the weapon," someone behind me shouted. With a quick glance I noticed several people pushing their way into the tent. Stepping silently behind the grieving father, stealthy Ballister Green reached out and caught Fennimore's hand, then wrapped his other arm around the man. The gun fell to the ground and Tobias blasted in with a roar.

"What the hell do you think you're doing?" he shouted into the judge's face.

At that moment, Parkland stepped to my side and whispered, "Lead, Gracie. It's time to lead."

Without thinking twice, I stepped forward, thanked Green, then asked him to take Judge Fennimore to the house.

"Koeffer, can you get to Garta?"

"I'm fine, Gracie. I don't need to waste the healer's time."

"No, you're bleeding. Go to Garta."

Tobias stepped up. "Gracie, you don't talk to a grown man like that."

I could sense Ben preparing to jump in and defend me like he'd done most of my life. I set my hand on his arm.

"I'm talking to a wounded man who needs to be healed before the Counting. Now, I would like leadership to gather at the house so we can work through this situation."

"What situation?" Tobias shouted and Raphael leaned close to whisper in his ear. The ancient wasn't listening. "A man came into camp and wounded another man, with full intentions of killing him, no doubt. What's to work through? He's a prisoner of war."

"Don't be a fool," I actually said. "Even a man who doesn't believe there's a Counting coming, is needed."

"Not that man!"

"Every man," I said quietly and all eyes were on me. "Tobias, gather the leaders for a meeting at the house… or don't. Come… or don't. Decisions need to be made and I want all the leaders' opinions."

"Our opinions?" He looked around like he'd fallen into an alternate universe. "You mean our guidance. Our expertise. Our decisions, which you will follow, little girl." Raphael gripped Tobias's arm and tried to pull him away. Like a rock, he wasn't moving an inch.

"No, Tobias. Your opinions. I will make the decision." I looked to the people gathered. "Please tell your leaders, all the leaders to come to the house." People scurried and I turned and walked away.

My knees shook so hard I had to still myself and take several deep breaths. *Don't throw up, don't throw up, don't throw up,* I kept thinking.

"What the hell?" Ben said with a gasp. "Where'd that come from?"

"Things have changed a little." I said, focused on walking steadily and the massive challenge ahead.

Kevin hooted. "That was amazing! Can we be in that meeting?"

"Are you a leader?" I snapped. I didn't mean to. I was just so shaken. He stepped back and walked alone behind me. Time to get a grip. I leaned close and bumped hips with Ben. "Tell him yes, but you two have to sit outside the window. It's not a very big house."

Ben grinned. "Things really have changed. Do your thing, Super Woman. We'll be outside if you need us."

PART TWO

Lead me from death to life, from falsehood to truth.
Lead me from despair to hope, from fear to trust.
Lead me from hate to love, from war to peace.
Let peace fill our hearts, our world, our universe.

~ Satish Kumar 1937 –
Prayer for Peace (adapted from the Upanishads)

16

ole carried a wriggling toddler in one arm, and a sleeping newborn in the other. It had taken half the day, but finally all of Carla's gargoyles were back in their original home. The fire damage was not as bad as Cole feared, mostly at the entrance. He wondered how the smoke from his angel fire escaped notice out on the street. Wondered if there was more to the fire magic than he knew. He fully expected police to be investigating, searching through or removing the homeless gargoyles' property, but nothing had been disturbed.

Lowering to place the infant into his mother's waiting arms, Cole set the toddler on her feet and watched her run and spin like a whirling dervish. A smile tugged at his lips. What would a child of Gracie's look like? How much fun would it be to watch it play and learn? Then he shook his head to clear away the fantasy. This was not the time for such thoughts.

Carla walked Old Mamma to her favorite corner and helped her pull a blanket over her legs. The gargoyles talked and laughed, but most curled up to sleep. None felt safe in the Harlem garage. They were thrilled to be back where they belonged. It had taken all day to transfer everyone safely, his and Carla's eyes peeled for danger or confrontations with humans or the ever-present demons. Like all homeless, they moved in the shadows, and often waited until people walked by before advancing. Strategically, they'd left the most difficult to move—the handicapped, elderly, and mothers with small children—for twilight and after the pedestrian rush had passed.

"We got them all?" Cole asked, following Carla to the entrance where she prepared to sweep and scrub away the soot. He rolled up his sleeves to help.

"Can't find ICe, but other than that, all are well and accounted for." She dumped soapy water from a bucket and he began to sweep, slushing soot and sludge toward the opening. Outside the door she turned to Cole. Checking to make sure they were alone, she whispered, "My connection says we can do the meeting Thursday at midnight, 2628 Troy Avenue, East Flatbush in Brooklyn. Don't be even a minute late. We have this timed. Only an hour, that's all we get."

Cole nodded, scribbling the information on the back of his cheat sheet portal map. "How many are we expecting?"

She shrugged. "Maybe sixty leaders will get to computers and be with us, but they'll pass on the information. We won't have an estimate of committed warriors for a week or so, after the news gets around."

"Thanks so much, Carla. You're doing the right thing."

"Yeah, but listen, don't count on Nunzio. Some of his groups might join in, mostly for the fight, but don't get too confident. He's not a reliable resource."

"I can tell. So, my speech is going to have to be really good on Thursday."

"You're going to have to be phenomenal, especially if you hope to get any of Nunzio's coalition. My people will follow me, but his are combatant and quick to argue. It's likely to be a battle for the loudest voice."

"Got it." Already Cole was rethinking how he'd present his information.

He'd need to add an edge the criminal element found most attractive, yet keep Carla's loyal followers in mind, too. It would be tough, but he was planning to get some help.

Cole was heading to Ocracoke and Gracie. She'd know the balance required to be successful, but Carla's warning weighed heavy. If he could convince all sixteen-point-eight million members of her coalition, plus all of Nunzio's ten million, he'd have made a major dent in building an army of Free-Winged. On the high side, Carla estimated that Thursday's meeting could win over another twenty million from additional, scattered coalitions around the country. Or, none at all, she cautioned, suggesting that he might need to get face to face with more coalition leaders. Be more convincing. Show his fire.

The problem was time. No one really knew how much time remained before the call for the Counting. Falling in with two of the largest Free-Winged coalitions in the continental United States was a lucky break, but it just might not pan out as well as he hoped. While he was in Ocracoke, he'd explore portal locations for Mexico and Canada on Blackbeard's maps. His next trip to New York would be for the cyber meeting, and if it went well, he'd need to head south and north of the border. Damn, and he didn't speak a lick of Spanish. No one said it would be easy, but this could be impossible.

All that aside, his heart thumped hard and strong. He was on his way to see Gracie, and he couldn't wait.

The house front room was packed to the walls with camp leadership. Cookie had sent coffee and tea, even sandwiches in case the meeting went late into the evening. I, for one, was grateful. It had taken nearly seven whole hours to get all the leaders to the house. Obviously, a mess of discussion took place before they decided to follow my order and join in. Of course. I expected it, but few, if any, appeared negative or unfriendly while they shuffled and shifted to fit in the tight space. I dragged in kitchen and dining room chairs, even a vanity chair from Esther's bedroom and finally, all who wished to sit were seated. Those, like Tobias, who chose to stand, were back against the walls.

Judge Terry Fennimore sat next to me on the sofa. Parkland stood, leaning at the dining room archway. He gave me an encouraging wink, but I didn't need it. My sense of fairness was solid from all those years at Ariel's Gate. Right and wrong were never a question. Battling those who were blind to it was always the issue.

Outside the window behind the sofa, Kevin and Ben were blessedly sitting out of sight but I could hear them whispering. "Quiet!" I called out, mostly to my friends, but also to silence the noisy crowd. "Bring in Peter Koeffer, Ballister Green, and Ryan Sutcliff, please."

People scrunched back from the opening door as the three men, one almost bigger than the doorway, stepped in.

"This is ridiculous," Tobias said with a snort.

"You're welcome to leave, Tobias." Did I really say that?

"I most certainly will not!"

He glared at me in a way that made everything feel gritty and dangerous. Suddenly I heard those voices.

Banish Tobias.

Demons were close by and passing on information.

Banish Tobias.

The problem with demons is that each one is more than one brain, so often, the messages were muddled, contradictory, and downright confusing. These were not.

Banish Tobias.

Now how the hell does one do that? Without losing all of his warriors? I glanced toward the downcast, broken judge at my side and an idea sparked.

"Tobias, one more outburst from you and you will be removed from this meeting."

His mouth opened but Rashee turned and pointed at him. "Hush!"

The room quieted and I proceeded to go through all the questions Parkland asked the day we'd learned the truth about Jenny's death. Ballister Green spoke, then Koeffer, and finally, Ryan. Through it all, I watched Fennimore shake with sobs. I set my hand over his and he squeezed my fingers.

"I'm so sorry," he said.

"So are we. I loved Jenny, too. We grew up together. She was my roommate and we knew everything about each other." Not the truth, but I wanted so much to comfort the man. "It's over, now. Please, go upstairs and rest."

He nodded, looked to Koeffer and apologized again. The giant embraced the grieving father and we all watched him climbed the stairs. My heart ached. He'd lost his powerful beliefs in the Tribunal system, lost his position as an Honorable Judge, and lost the daughter he'd tried so hard to protect. The whole world might crumble, but poor Jenny's dad was already in shreds.

Chairs shuffled and people started to move, so I stood and raised a hand. "We're not finished here."

All eyes on me, I lowered to sit again, swallowed hard, and waited for complete silence. This time, I didn't even look to Parkland for reassurance. I wasn't certain he'd agree with what I was about to say. With a deep cleansing breath, I raised my chin and spoke as clearly as I could. "Leaders, I've decided that there will be no protective veil over this camp."

"Are you mad?" shouted Tobias.

"Quite the opposite. I see no reason for such an undertaking. It will drain valuable power from too many important warriors and—"

"No! Not at all." He jumped like a bouncing ball for a moment. "The veil can be maintained by myself, Garta, who can hardly fight at her age, and Beauty Low. That's all!"

"That's too many," I said. "Even Garta, who can't lift a sword, is valuable for the Counting. Besides, a healer is far too valuable to have her power wasted on a protective veil we don't need."

"Don't need?" spouted the Arabian leader. That man was dark and striking, as sleek as the pure-bred horse he might ride through a golden desert. A stern man who was also pretty agitated. "Have you seen the demons roaming around our camp?" he asked with a hiss.

"I'm sorry, we haven't met," I said softly, determined to make sure the coming debate wouldn't dissolve into a shouting match. If that happened, I'd be the emotional little girl, not the leader they needed.

He gave an elegant bow. "Apologies. I am Abdalmalek, Miss Gracie."

"Abdalmalek," I pronounced carefully, "has any demon attacked you or any of your warriors?"

He looked to the other leaders, all shaking their heads, and finally he answered, "No."

"So, tell me, Abdalmalek … where is the threat? Where is the reason for a veil? One that restricts our coming and goings at such a crucial time… steals power from warriors who need all their strength… and hides us from the things we need to know?"

"Perhaps—" Abdalmalek began but Tobias jumped in.

"Parkland will send spies with information we need."

"And Tobias," I looked right into his dark, wild eyes, "when exactly will the Counting take place?"

"Little girl, no one knows that." He snorted a chuckle, but no one joined in.

"Exactly. So, how do you intend to get food, and water, and other supplies purchased and delivered to this camp until the Counting? As I understand it, every time you breech the veil, it becomes weaker. What if we need to wait months? Years? How long before that veil completely dissolves, never to be regained?"

"Those are ridiculous—"

"Enough, Tobias." Parkland grunted then settled beside me on the sofa.

"We all know the veil is not necessary as long as the demons are docile."

"And when they're not?" Tobias looked like he'd explode.

Parkland spoke calmly. "Right now, we have gathered more than five thousand warriors in this camp. That's five times the year-round population of this entire island. I haven't seen more than thirty demons at any given time. You don't think our battle-trained warriors can take on thirty demons?"

Abdalmalek stood. "And if they do attack… would we be without protection afterward?"

"That's something we'll discuss… if, and when there's an attack." I spoke with confidence and he sat without argument. "Listen," I continued. "At this moment, I see no reason to waste resources on a protective veil. That could change. I'm not interested in losing anyone to demon scrimmages. Until there is one… no veil." I looked into each leader's eyes and except for Tobias and Abdalmalek. Most nodded agreement.

"Idiocy!" Tobias yanked the door open so hard it slammed against the people near it and left.

"I am sorry Tobias is unhappy." I really wasn't, but I needed to keep everyone calm. "This is an important decision for a number of reasons I can't explain. Please, all of you, be careful in camp. You know to avoid touching a demon. Don't try to instigate anything with them. It's important. Very important."

"Demon lover," someone said quietly and I stood.

"Whoever said that should remember exactly what those demons are. They're us! Nephilim caught in Lucifer's trap. I have seen a Nephilim physically tear himself free of the demons he was attached to, and it was… well, it opened my eyes. There's something of us in those damaged, ruined creatures. Until the Counting, our job is to gather warriors and be prepared. No demons are cutting down our numbers, and we will cut none of theirs. Am I clear?"

Rashee leaned into the opening from her chair and looked down at her locked hands. "Gracie, forgive me, but we have only known of the death demons can bring. We only know what we've seen. I can tell that you are seeing something very different, and we are willing to move with your choice. But trust me… if even one demon attacks, none of our warriors will stand back. There will be hell to pay."

"Will I be doing the paying?" I asked with a tilted head and bold expression.

"No, but the warriors will take control. You may lose your high position."

"My position means nothing. Only the Counting, Rashee. Only… the… Counting. Nothing else matters." I looked around. "Anyone else?"

"Gracie." Bold Eagle stood. "Where are you getting your information? How did you come to make such a decision? It's counterintuitive. Something you had to know would cause controversy."

I smiled. "My father is Metatron. This book…" I held it up and everyone's mouth dropped, recognizing the relic as true and real. "Inside, once a week and sometimes more, Metatron writes and teaches me. Raphael teaches me. Mr. Parkland has been invaluable with his personal powers of perception. Bold Eagle, a lot is happening. There's way more than just this camp. Our small demon infestation is nothing compared to the work going on all around the planet to help us show strong at the Counting."

He put up a hand in acceptance and sat, head nodding and looking around at his colleagues.

"Anyone else? Please, I want to hear from all of you."

"You haven't asked for our opinion about this demon problem."

I searched the crowd for the woman's face. I knew her to be Malinda Dooly, leader of the Shield Maiden Warriors. I had heard so much about her, I already had kind of a girl crush the moment she stood and looked at me. This was an Amazonian Nephilim with energy that heated the whole room.

"I'm sorry. What's your opinion, Ms. Dooley?"

"My opinion is that you're right about the veil. It's an ancient thing the ancients like to use, but will be far too limiting in our situation. It also gives all the power to those managing the veil."

Several snorted and grunted.

She continued. "No one would be able to leave or enter without Tobias' permission and control. Good call, young woman. However, we need more than a few directives about how to deal with the demons."

"What do you suggest?" I was on the edge of my seat.

"I think each camp should assign two or three people, round the clock, to respectfully, peacefully, police their own campers, and the demons moving around. Just to make sure it doesn't get ugly… and someone doesn't think a demon reaching out to steal a piece of chocolate is a threat."

My heart thumped. So, I wasn't the only one feeding the strays.

"How do you all feel about that idea?" she asked, looking around the room.

Heads nodded and heads shook. "I'll do it," one said.

Another said he felt that policing would make the threat seem real and could create the opposite reaction.

Malinda repeated. "I said *respectfully*, *peacefully* policing both our people and the demons."

"I can see that working," Rashee agreed and more and more comments floated to the surface.

Finally, I stood to quiet them. "How about this? A show of hands. Whichever side has the most votes, we will all agree to. Will that be acceptable to everyone?"

"Tobias isn't here," Abdalmalek said with a grunt.

"Then your vote will count for both your and Tobias's camp." Rashee was really sticking her neck out with that, but since Abdalmalek seemed to be most in line with Tobias's views, everyone accepted the double vote.

I raised on my toes to see better. "Alright, who agrees with assigning people, round the clock, to respectfully and peacefully police both their camp members and any demons moving within their camp? A show of hands."

Hands rose and one by one the word "aye" was spoken. I bit the inside of my mouth and asked, "And how many against?"

My gut rolled and as happy as I was, I felt sure a brawl was about to break out right in the Cia's parlor. I cleared my throat and announced, "Thirty-two ayes, ten nays. The ayes have the vote. All will respectfully and peacefully police their people and the demons within their own camps, including Tobias. Thank you all."

As they filtered out, I stood at the door and smiled to everyone, even the naysayers. The last to leave was the woman warrior. Malinda shook my hand and leaned down to my ear. "Can you hear them, too?"

"Yes."

"I thought so. Many of us can, it's why your vote was so strong."

"What does it mean?"

She shrugged. "You're the Pure Nephilim. Ask your father. Maybe he knows."

Malinda didn't know that it didn't work that way, not unless I was face to face with Metatron. And his visits stopped weeks ago. All I had was the book, and Dad's writing was never conversational.

On the porch, Ryan and Ben were having a reunion while Kevin stood aside. He smiled my way and gave a thumbs up. Well, Ben's new boyfriend approved. What was Tobias going to do?

17

Esther slid another Big Mac across the table and watched ICe eat. "I was so worried when you weren't home. I looked everywhere. What happened?"

He ran a napkin over his mouth then slid half the sandwich inside and chewed. "We stayed in Harlem last night," he said, his voice muffled with all-beef patties and special sauce.

It never paid to ask ICe too many direct questions, so she leaned back and paced herself. "So, you had a little adventure?"

He nodded and sucked soda from a straw. "Cole burned up some guys."

Sitting straight, she recalled the blackened entry to the gargoyles' basement. "Cole? Did he hurt you?"

"No!" His face brightened. "He saved us all. He saved McGuire! Cole's a hero. Can I have more Coke?"

She took his cup and refilled it, her mind racing, curious, thunderstruck. What did Cole save them from? Had Nunzio tried something again? Sitting at the table, she sipped her own soda. "Cole Masters?"

"Uh-huh."

"What's he doing in New York?"

"We're going to help him count. You know, like numbers. I ain't so good at numbers, but he said I'm important."

His grin was so endearing Esther wanted to cry. So, Cole had cracked the code. If he collected all of McGuire's Free-Winged, he had definitely improved his chance at success when the time came. She leaned back and shook her head.

"You feeling good? Are you better?" ICe was finished eating and looking content as a giant Cheshire cat.

"Yes, I'm perfect. Thanks to you. I'm so glad McGuire's okay."

"Yeah. We had to fight. I fought, Esther! Like a real warrior. I fought hard."

"You are a real warrior. Listen, I need another favor."

ICe opened his eyes wide. "Something is still missing. Something's gone from you."

"Yes, remember, the baby. I lost the baby."

ICe was getting agitated. "No, I know. You should be… you should have… McGuire says that when a gargoyle turns eighteen, they get stuff. I can't remember what, but important stuff."

"Yes, I know. Calm down, it's okay. I'm fine, honest I am."

Tears gathered in his eyes. "Come count with us. I'd feel better if you were safe with us."

Patting his hand, she sighed. "That's kind of what I want to ask you, ICe. I need a really big favor. Will you come somewhere with me?"

"Where?"

"Just trust me, it'll all be okay. Will you come?"

"Yes. For Esther I would do anything!" ICe smiled like the world was a perfect place.

Fifteen minutes later, he was shaking so hard she didn't know what to do. Inside the portal, standing in the alternate plane, it took all of her strength to hold him still. The last thing she wanted was to draw attention from passing demons or, God forbid, Cole Masters.

"Hush, hush. Listen, ICe. Listen. It's quiet here. So quiet. You like when it's quiet."

His breathing slowed and his eyes darted up and down, left and right, then he started to cry. "I don't like this place!"

"We're only going to be here a minute, but I need you to listen to me. ICe, listen to me."

"Did I die? Someone's going to hurt me. I don't like this place!"

"No," she said evenly. "Can you try to focus on me, Ice? Just look into my eyes. I need a favor and this is the only way you can help me."

~*~

The evening drifted down quietly and the air was still warm. Cicadas sang all around, and the last thing I wanted to do was sit alone inside the house and think about the leadership role I've been playing. Fake it until you make it, I guess. I knew inside my heart that I was ready, but my head wasn't on team Gracie Genghis Khan yet.

For a while I sat on the porch, watching Ben, Kevin, Ryan and Raphael goof around like kids at school. Nothing lightens a heart more than hearing laughter, no matter how unfunny the comments generating those guffaws and snorts. Then, Raphael stood and reached out his hand. I took it and walked with him all the way to the weeping willow tree. Dad's tree.

"It's time for your next lesson," he said, sweeping aside the long, dramatic drooping branches. Inside was a different world, and I knew no one would disturb us. We weren't on earth anymore. We weren't on the strange plane where the Counting would happen. We weren't in heaven and we certainly weren't in hell. We were in a safe and perfect place I knew well from my childhood, and from my time with Metatron.

We sat and Raphael just watched me for an uncomfortable few minutes. "Speak," he said softly.

My gut rolled and I shifted, seeking comfort at the base of the big tree. "Can I say no?"

"To what?"

"To this, right now?"

He watched me like I might grow horns and a tail, so I shrugged and continued.

"Just for now. I feel good, really good, for the first time in a long time. Can I just sit back and enjoy it?"

"So, you're asking me to put off today's lesson? It's an interesting one. The Trickster's War."

"It sounds interesting." I looked up at the crystal brilliance flashing through the strange translucent leaves. Fighting tears, I nodded. "Okay. I guess it's childish to want to just… you know… be happy."

"Gracie, it's not childish. It's vital. It's what you're all here for. Humans, Nephilim, all here to find joy and peace and happiness."

"Just not now, right?"

"My dear, I chose this moment and this location because I believe this lesson will give you more joy, more happiness, more strength and clarity. But it's your choice."

My choice? My choice. Why was everything my choice and my responsibility. The archangel grinned like he knew what I was thinking. I really liked him, and I knew that if I pushed the issue, he'd postpone the lesson. I also knew that I needed to hear it. I needed to know everything I could about my race and our struggles because, if we survived the Counting, I wanted to make sure we did this Nephilim stuff a lot better.

Raphael tossed his golden tresses and whistled a happy tune. How could I fight that?

"Alright! Alright! But only if you stop whistling."

He smiled and leaned back on his arms, his feet crossed and legs stretched long. His wings filled most of the space under the tree.

"Are you going to put me to sleep?"

"No time. I'm just going to tell you about The Trickster's War, then I need to send you back. Things will be happening at the house."

"Oh." I straightened. "Good things or bad things?"

"Just things. Ready?"

"Should I take notes?" He shot me a glare but I was serious. Would I remember everything he told me? I hoped my expanded brain was up for the task. "Okay, shoot."

Humans know nothing of this, but there were many, many versions of this earth, its surface, and the beings that populated it. Some were very sophisticated, others, mere nomads. All, intelligent. And each time they lived, it was with the continuation of the Nephilim vow to protect the human race and the planet. With each ending of the world, some survived. Chosen humans and Nephilim. A few ancients. All charged with continuing the vow, propagating the planet, and protecting the balance of good and evil.

One of those was the time of Nahimi, and for five thousand years all was peaceful and good, pleasing in the Father's eyes. The time of Nahimi was the one and only time when God the Father walked among his people. It would be many, many worlds later… your world… when he would send his only son to do the same. Rashee is the only living ancient to have seen the Nahimi era. It is nearly impossible to guess her age.

This Nahimi era was glorious, productive, creative, beautiful. This planet was green from top to bottom, cooler at the poles, but wrapped in gentle weather year-round. The humans were exquisite, pale and gentle, yellow and feisty, red and selfless, black and powerful. All were peaceful to a fault, but beautiful to behold. For a time, the Nephilim outnumbered the humans, but the courses of disease and the earth's growing tectonic shifts brought the disproportion to a correct balance. Like always, the Nephilim race was secret and apart from the human race, yet playing human to do their job best.

Under sunlit skies, beautiful cities rose and fell, aged with time and replaced by progress, but the biggest change came with the Trickster. See, during the Nahimi era, the Father sat at tables and walked many miles with the human race. He talked at length with the Nephilim, He monitored the balance. When finally, deciding that the Nephilim race was ready to carry the vow they'd made a million generations earlier, He bowed and took his leave.

That's when Peeklin arrived. Lucifer believed that if the Father could dine with the natives, so could he. Instead of simply whispering into an unexpecting human or Nephilim ear, he could deceive them face to face, and gain much, much more. He named himself Peeklin because it was an unassuming, gentle name. Then he infiltrated the population and did his worst.

The good thing about the Trickster's War is that the humans used their free will to stick with the status quo, avoiding Peeklin at all costs. Nephilim, however, fell into the Trickster's trap, leaning toward world improvements the devil liked best. Peeklin introduced government, prostitution, sins of grand proportions, such as adultery and the worship of a particularly sweet image of the Trickster himself. It was gold and looked like a kitten playing with a ball of yarn. Every Nephilim household had one, but the humans refused to take to the cat. They were dog lovers, but dogs were nothing like they are today. They were much more self-sufficient then and a real help-mate to humans.

I was not self-sufficient living as your bulldog. I was a pet. I liked it very much.

And Raphael grinned ear to ear.

"And?"

Yes, so the imbalances grew and grew, but this was not an imbalance caused by all free-willed beings, only the Nephilim. And thus, the troubles grew, where Nephilim battled Nephilim for greater honors, bigger homes, more money, women, power. Peeklin fed into the insanity until it became full-out warfare.

What occurred during the Trickster's War is that Lucifer himself was tricked. While the devil wasn't looking, the Father so shook the earth, that many, many died and many looked to their wealth, realizing it had no worth.

But the damage had been done. God chose his few humans, Nephilim, and ancients. He carefully set them aside in a hidden world we now call the alternate plane, and then he brought the fires. Everything was destroyed. Nothing remained. Not a bone, not a splinter of the beautiful, spiraling structures or homes, not the animals or plants. The Father would start again.

But in this blast, Lucifer, pretending the benevolent Peeklin, was caught unawares and burned, too. If you see him today, he appears beautiful, strong, handsome, alluring, but beneath his illusion is the bubbled, hideous mess of charred celestial flesh and bone.

He has never forgiven the Father for that indignity. Yet he still battles, day in and day out, tirelessly determined to prove God wrong for bestowing free will upon the human race, and in turn, the Nephilim race because of their human DNA.

But here's the most valuable part of today's lesson… The Trickster's War ended with most of the Nephilim race shifting their free will choices back to goodness.

"So," I was so excited. "It's possible! Possible to change our bad choices!" My brain had uncovered something on its own. I knew this already. I thought it was simplistic, but it was not only possible; it had happened before.

"Yes."

"And that's what Wally did, right?"

Raphael's eyes saddened. "Perhaps Wally was a victim of the trickster in Lucifer and he made his blood vow by mistake, making his commitment weaker than most. Please remember, Wally was one in a trillion, Gracie. Anyone who bought, whole-heartedly, into the devil's blood vow could never—"

"Why not?" All I could think about was all the demons talking to me.

Those demons were not that committed, or they wouldn't be munching M&Ms and recommending that I banish Tobias. Unless. Unless. It was all a trick. But. "Really, why not?"

"I've watched humans and Nephilim walk this planet since the Father first breathed life onto it. It would be unlikely. It would be impossible. Lucifer always has a plan, and when it fails, he returns with another plan."

"So, what happens at the Counting? If we win, are we all allowed to live? Or are we all, except for a chosen few, going to end?"

He sat up and gripped my shoulders with his powerful hands. His eyes were intense on mine. "This is an extraordinary time laced with remarkable events. Anything could happen. No one can predict the Father, and no one can predict my brother, Lucifer, either."

"I thought you said this was going to be a good story, one to make me happy."

"Gracie!" The archangel stood and gazed down at me, smiling wide and radiant in the strange light. "Many, many Nephilim sought redemption before it was too late! All the humans had shunned the devil's advances! And… it was the first time The Morning Star was ever punished for his actions. That was a good story!"

I supposed so. He pulled apart the drooping branches and headed toward camp without so much as a goodnight. And I wondered, had he been the trickster? Making me think his story would make me happy? Or maybe I just didn't get it yet.

As Tobias walked into the dark trees, he wondered if he was going mad. Madness was common among ancients after a certain number of centuries, but Rashee was solid as stone, and Tobias wasn't about to admit weakness in comparison to that woman.

The night was warmer than previous nights, and he was mainly hiding from Dawn. The girl had taken to crying for his attention. He'd learned long ago that this particular manipulation always led to his demise in any dispute. He would not have sex with her until after the Counting was over. He'd told her that a thousand times, and still she begged for closeness, comfort. Holy hell, what do women want? You give them a child and they hate you for it. Give them power, and they use it against you. Give them compassion and they deem you feeble. There was no winning. He knew when he took the pretty Nephilim to his bed, this would happen. It always did.

But the comfort she gave to him during the uncertain times, times when he knew the toughest Counting ever was ahead, times when he feared no Nephilim would join the cause, times when he worried for his warriors and often, seriously considered taking them all somewhere else. Ending them all like any other cult mass suicide. Perhaps there was still time to do that? Maybe he could. But not before giving his plan a few more chances.

"God damn it, come and talk with me!"

"You are an impertinent ass." The voice was a deep, rumbling hiss mixed with the chatter of leaves in the island breeze.

Tobias swung around. No one was anywhere in sight. The voice was Lucifer's, he knew that now. Knew by its resonance, its thunder. Then, the air around him heated to unbearable temperatures and Tobias thought he'd die. He felt his blood boil and skin crisp.

"I just want to talk to you!" he shouted and gasped for air.

As suddenly as it started, coolness wafted over him.

"Three nights from now, at exactly this moment, at the peach grove I will hear your offer."

Tobias straightened, pushed his hair away from a sweating brow, and attempted a bow. "Thank you, Morning Star."

"Call me Peeklin." And the devil laughed.

Tobias moved slowly. Each encounter with the devil seemed to weaken him more. He needed his strength. So, he would sleep as long as he liked the next morning. No one needed him in camp, apparently.

He could rest until it was time. With luck, he could accomplish all he wanted three nights from now, at the exact moment, at the peach grove.

"What the hell kind of name is Peeklin?" he said aloud, then chuckled, unknowingly passing Raphael in the darkness.

The archangel cried.

18

aphael's lessons always left me with a lot to think about. I wondered if he was right, if Wally was one in a trillion, or if maybe, a much larger percentage of Nephilim-turned-demons were ready, willing, and able to switch teams. But, how would they do that? The ripping apart of multiple Nephilim from the body of a single demon wasn't pretty. And, it's deadly. I would never want those willing to change their bad free-will choice to suffer like Wally did, but maybe that was the cost. I recalled the phrase, there, but by the grace of God, go I. Any one of us could have been lured into a blood vow with Lucifer. We all wanted out of the orphanage, we were starved for freedom. Ryan wanted to play college football. Jenny wanted to see the world. Even I wanted out so bad I could taste it.

I walked home in the darkness but felt safe. A demon kept pace with me but at a distance. The moon was smiling down and I tried to regain my earlier feeling of wellbeing. I was almost on the porch when I noticed him. A big man with a child's face. He huffed and stood. I leapt back with a small squeal. He backed up in response and covered his face. I'd never seen anyone like that guy before. Not in the world, not in camp. I looked around, prepared to scream for help but there was no one near enough to hear. He was between me and the door and really big, really strong, even if he looked more afraid of me than I was of him.

He sniffled. "Are you Gracie?" It was a soft whisper.

I stepped forward and gently touched his hand. It dropped from his tear-stained face and he looked into my eyes. "Yes, I'm Gracie. Who are you?"

"I'm ICe. Big I, big C, little e." He nodded, pleased as can be.

"Hello, ICe. Um… where did you come from?"

He pointed to the peach grove and trembled so hard he sat back down on the chair. "That strange place."

I looked around. No one. The camp glittered with fire and lamp lights, but was quiet, settled for the night. There were a few demons roaming around not far from the porch, but none offered any information about my visitor. They appeared as curious as me.

"Ah!" ICe squawked as one demon stepped closer then moved back.

"It's okay, they won't hurt you."

"No?"

"ICe, where were you before you went into the… strange place?" I sat beside him, hoping to keep him calm.

"New York."

"Did Cole send you?"

His head shook, eyes focused on me. "Esther sent me. She said you're the woman Cole loves, and I'm supposed to protect and take care of you. I can do it. I can fight. I fought for Cole. He said I'm a warrior."

So much pride glowed in his eyes, all I could do was smile. "So, my sister sent you to watch over me? What else did she say?"

"It's very, very important to protect you. Oh… and she said she loves you."

Damn. The message of Esther's love had now arrived from two different sources. The demons and ICe. Was it time to believe? I so wanted to believe. "ICe, is Cole alright?"

His head nodded emphatically. "He said he wants me to count with him, Esther said this is the place to be, but Gracie… I can't count so good. Is that okay? Oh, don't cry. Please."

I couldn't help it. A sudden warmth filled me and I knew the important things of life, for the first time in my life. Love. My sister did love me, and to prove it she'd sent ICe to protect me, and I sensed he'd do it to the death. He was here for the Counting, and instead of taking him to Lucifer, Esther sent him to me.

Raphael's lesson resonated in my heart. Could Esther change her free-will choice? Was it worth hoping for? Did she want it bad enough? Or was she just showing a little compassion for her gimp of a sister? Either way, I had another houseguest. It was likely ICe would never sleep in camp, so far from me. I stood.

"Do you want to come inside?"

"No. I'll guard from here." He eyed the demons and cringed.

"Are you sure? It might get a little cold tonight."

"I'm used to the cold."

Of course. Poor ICe was homeless like his brother and sister Free-Winged in New York. "Okay, wait here." I rushed inside and returned with a blanket and a handful of little candy packets.

"Oh, M&Ms," ICe said with a grin.

"Are you hungry?"

"No. Esther bought me McDonalds."

"Well, you can have some of this candy, but mostly it's for the demons. If they come to the porch, open a little bag and set the candy on the railing, like this. They'll just eat it then go away. Alright?"

"They eat candy?"

"They love it. Are you sure you won't come inside?" Already his mouth was full of M&Ms, so I brought the whole giant bag out. "Remember, they're for the demons, too."

"Yes. Sleep good, Gracie."

~*~

Ben turned and rolled in his sleeping bag, stared up at the pitched roof of the nylon tent and sighed silently. Earlier, he and Kevin went into town and purchased the tent. Now, Ben's mind crashed in on itself, wondering what can of worms he'd opened by agreeing to share a single tent. He knew how he felt about Kevin, knew it fully and without question, but what came next was nowhere in his experience. He pulled on his jeans and tee shirt, then slipped out for a walk.

Images and fears battered in his heart. He had no clue how to proceed. He didn't want to lose Kevin, and he was a perfect candidate for messing the whole thing up by making the guy wait too long. Ben's mind wasn't focused solely on sex, either. What did he know about real committed relationships?

His father had hid behind the disguise of headmaster all of his life. Cool as it was to finally have a dad, Ben couldn't deny, he'd rather it not be his school principal turned recruiter and phenomenal sword warrior. Couldn't it have been an average dad? One with flaws? Michael Allerton wasn't that. Ben's heart thudded with pride and frustration. At least his power of perception made him the better swordsman, but this wasn't a competition. It was supposed to be a father/son relationship.

Then there was Gracie. She was his best, his only, friend at Ariel's Gate. As small children, he liked her because she was different. He liked her sharp mind and how she never let her bad foot stop her from anything. As he grew older and began to uncover the truth about himself, he liked Gracie even more because she never asked questions. She always treated him like a normal guy, and he had to confess, for some time he especially enjoyed their deep friendship because spending time with Gracie kept others from noticing that he didn't like girls that way. He felt guilty for using her, especially when she expressed serious interest in him.

He stopped walking, looked around and took in a deep breath. He'd always feel bad about that, and he wondered, could he have loved her? Given her what she wanted? Maybe, but it certainly wasn't what Gracie deserved. So, his mind had gone full circle, back to Kevin.

He turned before walking into the woods and decided to circle the camp again, following the edges of it, nodding to the camp guards and avoiding the occasional demon.

Again, he slipped inside his own heart and pondered. If Kevin had decided that tonight was the night, why did he insist on pitching their tent so close to everyone else? Why didn't he choose a more private area? Gracie suggested they camp behind the house and Ben particularly liked that suggestion. They could help watch over and protect her while Cole was away, and have some peace and quiet to… to … explore.

His heart thudded in his chest and he imagined how things could have progressed. Then he heard a disturbance. Shuffling. Like a bear pushing his way into civilization, someone walked into camp from the trees. Ben's mind spun visions, he stilled and held his breath. Spying Tobias slipping into his camper made him shiver. Something ugly was coming and the ancient was behind it. There was no question about it. Then the vision expanded, defined itself, washed like fire across his brain and he could hardly breathe. How was this possible? Could Tobias do that? Why would he think something that stupid could work?

Recalling everything his father had explained, and how focus alone helped refine his knowledge, Ben stood still as death and almost forgot to breathe. Without a doubt, this was a significant piece of information. It required immediate attention, but who on earth was qualified to help? Kevin wouldn't understand. Gracie had enough on her plate. He couldn't confront Tobias alone. Then he knew not only who to talk to, but who could actually change the trajectory of Tobias's dangerous plan.

Ben ran to the tent Raphael used. Empty. Then he rushed to that odd weeping willow tree where the archangel and Gracie disappeared under earlier.

"Raphael! Raphael!" He hissed as loud as he dared, afraid of waking anyone camping nearby.

"Come under, Ben."

The moment he passed through the long thin branches, everything, even the air changed. He spun on his heel. "What the hell?"

"No, not hell. But we can talk safely here. How can I help you?"

Usually, even in scruffy clothes, the archangel blazed with undeniable strength, vitality, and good humor. If he didn't know better, Ben might have thought poor Raphael was coming down with something. He was pale, his hands trembled slightly, and his eyes were rimmed red.

Ben tried to start, but where to start was the question. "I… I um…"

Raphael waved for him to sit and he lowered, cross-legged to the ground, sensing the energy rise from the earth and embrace him with comfort and assurance. Maybe that's what Raphael needed. A little comfort. "Maybe I can come back another time. You look… tired."

"I am tired. I am in pain. My heart aches. But I imagine you may shed some light on my misery. Ben, I can see that you've been quickened with the power of perception. Tell me what you know."

Steadying his heart, Ben spoke slowly, carefully, trying hard not to overplay or underplay his information. He talked in a whisper and Raphael leaned close, his eyes closed tight against the onslaught of evidence. When he finished, he waited.

A tear ran down the archangel's face and he nodded. "So, it is confirmed."

"Pardon?"

"Parkland… he has the same gift… he spoke with me earlier… gave me the same news."

"Can Tobias do that? No one asked him to do that and—"

"Tobias has written his own script for more than a thousand years. He imagines he can do anything."

"This?"

"No."

"So, what do we do?"

Raphael stood and led Ben out into the real world beyond the tree's magic. "You've done your part. Get some sleep."

"I don't think I can sleep knowing this."

"Then you'd best learn how, fast. Your gift only intensifies with life, and you are a young man… lots of life ahead."

"If we don't screw up the Counting."

"Yes, Ben… if."

Crawling into his tent, he discovered that Kevin had zipped their separate sleeping bags together making one large, roomy bed. One side was flipped down for him to slip under. He undressed and tried to keep his heart calm. As he lay still, he listened to Kevin's rhythmic breath. "Are you sleeping?" he whispered.

"Nope."

Kevin rolled over and dropped his arm over Ben's hip. His eyes opened and he raised a brow. "You look bad. Like you did before Michael started training with you. Did you learn something?"

Ben nodded.

"Something bad?"

Another nod then he turned away and closed his eyes.

"I'm here if you need to talk. Sleep well."

After several silent moments Ben sighed. "I'm sorry."

"About?"

"I figure you wanted… you know."

"I just wanted to be close. There's time for… you know. Later."

If, Ben thought. Only… if.

~*~

Raphael returned to the tree and prayed, begging desperately to be released from his responsibilities. Long, long ago, he bargained with the Father about Tobias. He promised to walk at the ancient's side and guide him through the maze of forever life. Then he was called to do something else, to watch over one of the only remaining Pure Nephilim until the Counting. He did that for nearly a hundred years, trotting around Ariel's Gate as a personable, smelly English Bulldog, just waiting for Gracie to arrive. Until just a few weeks ago, he had not seen Tobias for a century. Tobias had changed, had become corrupted, oblivious, apathetic to the human and Nephilim condition, especially facing the troubles ahead. There were still three days. Three days to decide how to handle the Tobias issue, and three days before he must leave the earth realm. The Counting was growing near, and it pained him to have to leave. Raphael had been earthbound for a very long time. He'd grown to love the planet, the humans, animals, the softness of the air, the quiet of a starlit night. There was a lot he would miss, but there were things to do first.

With a lot of luck and persuasion, he might be able to save Tobias from himself. There was a terrifying chance Lucifer already knew what the ancient planned. There were demons everywhere. Many were calm and relishing the closeness to Nephilim energy, but some could be spies. He wondered, what would a spy know and where would they get their information? Parkland knew to speak to Raphael under the tree, and that's why he waited for Ben in the same place. Nothing could be overheard from there. Only Tobias could tell someone his intentions, and he'd broken his connections with everyone, even his lover. Even Raphael.

Contrary to Tobias's beliefs, the idea he loved so much had, in fact, been offered before. In the Nahimi era, one ancient made such a proposal to Peeklin. The devil pretended to accept the deal. It's a deal made time and time again with Lucifer. The Devil went down to Georgia, and many, many other places. Many humans, Nephilim, and even ancients have tried to bet with the devil. All have failed. All will. The question on Raphael's heart was whether to save Tobias before he sold his soul to

Lucifer, and possibly destroy any chance for the Nephilim to save their race from extinction. Or? Or?

Tobias wasn't listening. Following the ancient into the woods confirmed his dark intentions. Intentions designed to beat the devil and place himself above all once the deed was done. He imagined he could win a guarantee from Lucifer to never again tempt the human or Nephilim races. Tobias had always had that fantasy. To save the world then rule it. For centuries and centuries Raphael had soothed his desires. This time it might be too late. Tobias may have already gone too far.

Three days was all he had to turn the ancient from his folly. Three days.

Raphael decided to start immediately. Lucifer was not the only archangel with the ability to whisper into the human essence. Tobias slept inside his camper, his back against the wall just beneath the window. Raphael leaned his back and ethereal wings against the camper, willing his energy to travel through the thin metal and into Tobias. He prayed and prayed then simply spoke the words, soft and with hopeful intensity.

"It's time for the performances, Tobias. No one can set things up for such a tremendous show but you. You are the leader of them all, and these performances will prove it. It's time to prepare for the show."

Tobias rolled his head in his sleep. Raphael leaned to look into the window and watched the man's growing smile. "Time to prepare for the show," his sleep voice softly said.

Raphael went to his tent to pray more. Preparations for the performances would at the least improve Tobias's mood, and at most, take his mind off the pending meeting with the devil. Perhaps Raphael could arrange a few performance faux pas to keep Tobias on his toes and away from the peach grove. That was most important because the Trickster was already prepared for the likes of Tobias.

19

Getting out of New York was far more challenging than Cole expected. Brutally sidetracked by Nunzio, demanding more cash to assure his people would even consider attending Carla's cyber-meeting, the man and his minions roughed Cole up. He'd given them most of the cash left in the backpack, but they wanted more.

"Not going to blackmail me," he grunted between slams into his gut. "This is about your survival! Do it or don't! I don't give a fuck anymore!"

"Good," Nunzio said after stopping his goons. They'd dropped Cole to the filthy pavement not far from the gargoyle's basement. "Just so you know, Masters. It's my, and only my, choice." He gripped Cole's head by the hair and glared into his eyes.

"Fine."

His head thumped back to the ground. Cole groaned then located a public restroom, and one glance in the mirror confirmed the mess. Blood gushed from his face and nose, so what he saw wasn't a pretty picture. He couldn't stop the bleeding with all the wads of paper towels in the dispenser. The emergency room was only a block away, and blessedly it was a quiet night. Four stitches later, thin black lines elegantly etched across his left cheek, and a black eye blooming beautifully, he cleaned up and finally walked through the portal at East 106th Street.

His trek across the weird plane was uneventful, with almost no demons in sight. However, once he stepped into the peach grove and looked toward the house, his breath caught. The camp was huge, quiet in the near dawn, but there were more demons present on the property—some sleeping in heaps, others just sitting together in groups—than he'd seen in days.

Curious. His goal was the house and Gracie, but not before a few more surprises.

"ICe?" He gently shook the man's shoulder. "What the hell are you doing here?" The porch was littered with M&M wrappers.

"Cole!" The big, sleepy face smiled. "I'm watching over Gracie. I'm helping you."

"Yes, you are, but…" No point in asking more, the man's eyes were already drooping closed again. "Come on inside. It's warmer."

The pre-dawn air was brisk. ICe stood, shivering and holding his blanket tight at his neck. Inside, he sat on the sofa and was already leaning toward the armrest before Cole could say another word.

"Thanks, buddy," he whispered then kicked off his boots and tip-toed up the stairs.

He'd have never peeked, but the first bedroom resonated with a rumbling snore. Cracking the door, there was a lump sleeping in the bed he'd used before leaving. Further down the hall, leaning close, there were huffing, masculine snores coming from behind Esther's closed bedroom door. No one was in Gracie's room, so he quietly slipped into Cia's bedroom, hoping beyond hope there wasn't another man sleeping in there.

He could actually feel her energy and sense the dynamics of her massive wings. He knelt at the bedside and ran a finger down her nose. Pale light stole into the window and her face was so young, so lovely. "Gracie? Sweetheart, I'm home."

She woke and stretched slowly then opened her beautiful hazel eyes, the flecks of amber in them catching the first glow of morning sunshine. "Cole," she whispered and with soft hands, pulled his face to hers, kissing him with unbelievable tenderness. The kiss became deeper and Cole relished every moment. She slid over and pulled him onto the bed with her. Still kissing his lips, his neck, his face, then, noticing the bandage, she sat up and turned on the lamp.

"Oh, Cole! What happened?"

"Nothing to worry about."

She carefully lifted the tape to see the damage. "Your beautiful face!"

He settled his head in hand and gave a grunt. "Was it?"

Another kiss, then another. Looking at her was like seeing a whole different woman and he marveled. Gracie, no longer just a pretty girl, no longer afraid or confused. This was Gracie as she was always meant to be. Before he could grasp the physical and emotional changes she'd undergone during his absence, his hands began to participate in the activities. "Gracie," he warned. "Come on, slow down, baby."

Her fingers ran through his hair and her lips skimmed his neck, wet, warm, alluring.

"Slow down. Gracie, don't push me too far… so far I can't stop… Gracie, sweetheart, I need to go sleep in the other room."

"Stay with me, Cole."

His heart gripped, his body trembled. There was nothing on the planet he wanted more, but was it the right time to love her? Would it help or hinder her? He'd be leaving again in a few days. Was this wise?

"Stay with me," she whispered in his ear then licked down his neck.

It was on, but first he needed a little clarification. "Are you fully awake?"

She giggled and placed a kiss over his heart as she helped him tug the tee shirt over his head.

"Okay, you're awake, so you know what we're doing, right?"

"I know. I want you. I love you, Cole."

His jeans were loose but stuck at his hips so he awkwardly kicked and kicked until they flew across the room, never taking his hands from her flesh.

"Okay… okay…" he said through gasps. "Last question… why are there so many men in this house?"

"I'll tell you later." She sat up and swept her nightgown off. In an elegant flurry it joined his jeans somewhere on the floor.

Cole Masters believed himself to be a damn good lover. He'd had enough practice, with sweet women, rough women, prostitutes, older women, and younger women, but nothing prepared him for sex with a woman he dearly, fully loved. It was at first a struggle to be gentle, remember it was Gracie in his arms, that she was a virgin, to keep her comfort in mind. Then, with her repeated proclamation of love, it all went out the window. They moved like fish racing through water, dashing and chasing, slipping away then regathering their flesh together. Every touch was exquisite, every breath, a gift. She was bold yet timid, strong yet gentle with him, and Cole's last lucid thought was to wonder if she'd imagined this as many times as he had, as completely, with detail and desire. Then nothing registered, his body had officially overtaken his mind.

When they melded into one being, he felt her wings and his mingle, twisted together, holding on as tightly as their arms. He prayed he wasn't hurting her. He hoped her gasps and moans were of pleasure more than pain. He finally released himself, forever connecting Gracious Caine to his soul.

She lay, covered in sweat, slippery and heated in his arms. Catching his own breath, he ran a finger along her arm and down the length of her hip. "You are spectacular," he said with a sigh then collected her into an embrace. "I am so glad you've forgiven me."

"For the thing with Esther?" She snuggled into him. "Oh, no. I'll never forgive you for that. It's my ace in the hole."

He pulled apart to look into her playful eyes. "Shit, Gracie. I thought you were serious."

"I am. Sort of. How else will I be able to torment you?"

"Loving you is enough torment. Worrying all the time, thinking you're being taken advantage of, used."

"Oh, I let them all think so. It's how I torment the camp leaders."

Now she was giggling and he playfully gripped her tightly. When she gave a quiet squeal, he freed her and whispered, "Torment me forever, okay?"

"So, some day, you might maybe marry me?"

Cole sat up and pushed back his hair. "Is that what you want?"

"Only if you do."

He nodded. "Sure, but maybe we should save the world first. Just a thought."

"A good one."

She smiled and looked away, straightened the sheets over her body, and he could feel a building tension. Maybe she didn't mean to talk about marriage. Maybe she didn't know he'd do it in a heartbeat for her. Maybe she was just beginning to grasp the depth of what they'd started. She sighed and glanced into his eyes, regaining her playfulness.

"Now," she said, "about my guests. I have ICe from New York."

"Him, I know. Good guy, but what's he doing here?"

"Esther sent him to watch over me. He's a sweet man, but not much of a bodyguard."

"Don't rule ICe out. I've seen him rage a mean slap fight."

Gracie laughed then leaned against his shoulder. "Then we have Mr. Terry Fennimore, High Black Judge of the Eastern United States Tribunal."

"What? Why?" Cole was alarmed. That Tribunal had once imprisoned Allerton.

She leaned back and gave him a reassuring look. "The Tribunal has dissolved. The more Nephilim learned about the situation, the angrier they got. It was all kept from us. So now, the Tribunal has no more power. I don't think anyone will ever give them power again. Fennimore's here because… well, he's Jenny's father, and he suspected foul play in her death. It was resolved. A terrible accident. So sad."

Cole hugged her close, recalling the crazy girl, and powerful Nephilim Jenny was. "Now, who's the other guy?"

Gracie's smile turned mischievous. "You won't believe it. That's Gregory Parkland." She squinted, like she wanted to make sure she said the man's title correctly. "He's Regent of the Americas, and head of the Nephilim Worldwide Intelligence Bureau. It's like the Nephilim secret service. He's got some serious powers, and not just politically."

"Is he my competition?"

"Eww!" She grinned and punched his arm. "He's old."

Slipping his arm under her, he tugged her beneath him and smiled down into her beautiful face. "I'm not old, and I want more." His voice was hoarse, desperate, begging, and she arched up into his body, welcoming. They were as quiet as possible, but he could hear people walking past the room and down the stairs. Oh well, busted, he thought, but truly didn't care. With Gracie in his arms, nothing else mattered.

Facing the devil was never easy. Even when she thought she loved him Esther harbored deep fear of what she'd agreed to. There was no contract to review, no paperwork as proof, all she had was her memory. A thirteen-year-old girl making promises. She recalled wanting to be out from under Cia's protective thumb. She adored the freedom Lucifer gave her to wear the clothes she liked, color her hair any way she fancied, pierce anything and everything she wanted. It was refreshing, until the actual blood vow was made. At thirteen, sex wasn't even a blip on her radar. She wanted to play, and live, and be happy with fun people all around her. The sex wasn't pleasant at all, but afterward he let her run free as a lark.

What was her promise? She never recalled offering any part of herself outside her body for his carnal requirements, but somehow, deep in her soul she knew there was more. Things she ignored or forgot, things he tricked her out of, things he now possessed. Things, missing.

Esther would never forget the first time she encountered a battle heat demon. She was walking toward Luc's workroom. The creature rushed out the door and right at her. Frozen with fear, disbelieving what she was seeing, it neared at breakneck speed. Two heads, four legs, only one arm, it moved like oil, fluid and fast. Then she heard the voice of the devil, loud and demanding.

"No!" he shouted and suddenly the demon exploded into a mess of greasy black slop, splashing against the walls, floor, and ceiling. She'd just escaped being splattered when she jumped back. Bones and organs throbbed in the gunk. Two voices cried out in agony then silenced. One head, eyes wide and blue as the sky, deep in the ugly blackness, stared up at her.

Before she could scream Luc had her in his arms, sweeping her away from the mess. "Never, ever come near my laboratory." His eyes explored every inch of her, making sure she was unharmed. "It's too dangerous, my little one. Stay away from here, and my demons. One touch and you will burn to death."

She pointed, still trying to still her heart. "Did you kill it?"

"Yes, I did. To protect you. But now I have wasted valuable time, and energy. Don't come near this place again. Is that clear?"

Esther remembered feeling so grateful. Thrilled he loved her enough to destroy his creation to protect her, but in retrospect, she also recalled him asking her to bring his current favorite book to him at the lab. She was instructed to leave it on the floor outside the door, and she had full intentions of doing so. She clearly remembered the spine of that book, Vonnegut's Galapagos, still readable but sizzling in the slime that was once his demon. So, was he protecting her or once again teaching her a lesson? That he could kill her without even trying?

The demons scared the hell out of her. They were like nightmares come to life, so strange and hideous, unnatural, unpredictable. But she knew, even at such a young age, to keep fear at bay. Control it. Be strong in the face of it. From that day forward, she chose to see the demons differently. Rather than living with constant distress, she chose another path. She decided to be casual around them and give the illusion of befriending them, repulsive as they were. If they thought they didn't bother her, maybe they wouldn't try. Sometimes she'd even talk to them. Naturally, they never talked back, but at least they never again approached her aggressively. Most skirted her, a few even did something oddly human, like wave to her from a distance.

It horrified her to imagine how Lucifer might have created his race of demons. Were they made from scratch? Were they a collection of humankind's malevolent thoughts and ideas? Were they pulled from the ether and actually an illusion? No. Losing Cia to demon burns obliterated that theory. She'd heard him boast that he'd often sent them out to fight the rogue warriors. That they were so diabolically formed, no Nephilim could kill them. Another of Luc's lies. Once, in Arizona, she watched a Nephilim warrior kill three demons with one swipe of his soul sword.

For the last few days Lucifer had been MIA, working on something original and interesting on the earth, he claimed. Something about gambling with the ancients, just for a little fun. Knowing Lucifer had a new project, she worried for Gracie and the Ocracoke camp, but she also knew it was the perfect time to learn everything she could. It was time to learn exactly what the devil had taken from her. What ICe worried over. What exactly was missing.

Stepping closer to the door, she wondered if he'd know she was snooping. If he'd punish her. Esther didn't care anymore. He had ravaged her body and destroyed any chance of motherhood. He'd disrespected her in the name of love, yet never actually cared about her. What was he doing with her, anyway? If she was so unimportant, why did he keep her so close?

The door was unlocked. In fact, several demons waited for her inside. One nodded then led her slowly down the pristine white hallway and opened the double doors for her to enter.

Everything inside her mind knotted in a twist. She sensed the agony experienced in that room. Then she saw it. A laundry cart loaded with, of all things, wings. Blue wings, red wings, black wings, white wings, all bloody at the point where they were violently torn from the body. All big enough for a human to wear. Nephilim wings. Many, many Nephilim wings. Could they be from the Nephilim she routinely brought back as recruits, confident Lucifer had sent them all off for intense military training on a secret, distant alternative plane?

"Oh! Oh, no! Oh, God!" she cried out so loud the demons rushed to close the doors and danced around to silence her.

The demons Lucifer was so proud of were not created from the ether. They were all Nephilim, tricked by Lucifer, just as she had been, to give up all of themselves and fight for his cause. Tears flowed, but beneath them boiled anger so great all she could do was laugh. Didn't it make sense? Didn't she deserve to feel this way? How could she have been so stupid? The demons were as much her doing as his. Rumbles of madness bubbled out of her, burning tears rolled from her eyes and still she laughed. One demon actually pushed a glass of water toward her, making her laugh even more.

"I am so sorry," she said to the creature. "I didn't know. I was such an idiot, I didn't know!"

As she prepared to leave, hide herself somewhere on earth and figure out what to do next, the demons blocked the doorway and pointed to the back of the lab.

"Esther, come to me," a strained voice called. "Come."

The room seemed to arch and waver. Her knees weakened but taking a long deep breath, she moved forward. The smells of the workshop could have been found in any chemical plant or hospital. Strong. Ugly. Stinging. Sanitary. Focusing on the floor, pacing her steps to match the foot-wide blocks of flooring tile, she intuitively knew when to stop and look up, but her tear-filled eyes and raw heart could hardly take anymore. Slowly it came into focus. There it was.

The giant bell jar was the most chilling thing she'd ever seen in her life. Inside that glass stood… herself. Her other part. Six magnificent wings fluttered, unable to fully expand inside the trap. The face, pure and clean, glowed with joy. It looked like Gracie but radiated Esther's soul and energy. This pleased her and calmed her at once.

Unable to speak, she raised her hands and placed them onto the glass. Inside, the translucent Pure Nephilim part of Esther did the same. As the heat of their hands gathered, emotions and painful thoughts of loss and fear flowed from inside the bell jar all the way into Esther's small, human brain, aching, throbbing, and expanding it. The knowledge pouring in was agonizingly bright, like looking into the sun, but she grasped the fact that only the most important bits were being conveyed. They couldn't stay connected like that for long; Lucifer would be returning soon.

Now Esther knew not only how the devil had deceived her, but that there was no way out. Her heart begged for answers. A flicker of an insane idea flashed—to just shatter the bell jar, take her better half, and walk away from Lucifer—but that was impossible. Was it? But when? How? There was too much going on. Even with his gambling dalliance, Lucifer was more intense than ever, on top of every detail and focused on results. Since her last miscarriage, he'd taken to doing the recruiting she used to do, bringing in hundreds at a time. Every thought and word he had was fixated on the Counting, the war, the destruction of the Nephilim and human races.

Once the call came, once she stood between Lucifer and her Pure Nephilim half at his side of the battlefield, it would be too late. She had to try something, anything. She looked into the eyes of her other self. "Even if we die, we try," she whispered.

Nothing could be trusted. Lucifer could have set up the encounter, knowing she'd make some heroic attempt to change things. Knowing he could tighten the noose around her neck and keep her even closer to him. Now she knew why. She was important after all. Without her, her Pure Nephilim half could not exist. Breaking free was hopeless, and she knew it. Her heart wished she could experience her rightful celestial existence, but until the time was right, if it would ever be right, it couldn't happen. What had her childish foolishness brought her? She watched tears drip down the beautiful celestial face.

"Be brave," she said to her angelic half.

Esther ran from the lab and did find a safe place to hide, carefully tucked in the cubby ICe loved so much, and taken care of by McGuire's gargoyles until they would receive the call. Then her only option was to return to her place at the devil's side. What other choice did Esther Caine have?

20

ole's few days with Gracie would prove trying, not because of her, but because the coming Counting revealed itself to be very different than he'd planned or expected. They had a plan to bring as many of the Free-Winged as possible. They'd foolishly imagined they were in control of that misunderstood Nephilim component, from Alaska to the southern tip of South America. Sitting around the crowded breakfast table, he could tell it was now in someone else's hands.

The food was great, so he knew Gracie didn't cook. Cookie had been regularly feeding the special guests at the house. Was it at Tobias's orders? Or someone higher? The someone higher sat across from Cole and grinned. Dapper guys shouldn't grin like that, but maybe forming instant judgment about Gregory Parkland, super-duper secret service dude with wings, wasn't going to prove productive. So, Cole assumed the role of a good soldier and listened carefully.

"Cole, you've done a stupendous job." Parkland lifted another loaded fork to his mouth.

"Am I fired... sir?" He had to know, and he was ready to fight to keep his job.

The fork dropped. "Hell no. Cole, I'm going to help you with Free-Winged recruiting. I hear from a good source that the Counting is very near. We need to work fast."

"How's this going to work… sir?" Cole could see Gracie's face bouncing back and forth between him and Parkland. To her credit, she never interrupted.

"You can drop the 'sir' stuff, Cole. We're all in this together. I just have a few more resources than you do."

"Like?"

Ah, there it was, a kick under the table from his beloved.

"First of all, I've located a former Free-Winged military police officer. Turns out he's been taking care of the Mexican and South American Free-Winged for a decade… from Mexico City all the way down to southern Argentina. He's the Spanish-speaking version of your McGuire. Honestly, if not for your and Gracie's activities with the Free-Winged, I'd have never realized the numbers there. You two opened my eyes at the right moment, just as the Tribunal hand-tying disintegrated. You've done an extraordinary job."

"Yeah, thanks. What about Canada?"

"Covered."

"So, what am I supposed to do now?"

Parkland leaned back and sipped coffee, eyed everyone around the table, then cleared his throat. "First of all, you need to complete your work with McGuire on Thursday, draw in as many as possible from her coalition and the other one. Nunzio, right? I've prepared another stash of cash for you. Pay any bribes you have to. Whatever it takes. Then… after that, you will immediately return here and start working with the two hundred Nephilim who have volunteered to guide the recruits into the portal at the right moment."

Cole blinked, mouth open.

"This is a promotion, buddy. You're the only man who can organize this effort."

"Two hundred?" Cole blinked. "How can I possibly—"

"Later today, special equipment will be installed here at this house. This will be command central with live video access to every guide. I've provided the technology for them all to be just a single click away. This way, you can stay here and get each guide to their respective portal, so they'll be ready when the call comes."

"And where will you be? Ouch!" Again, she kicked him. He glared and she glared back. Parkland just laughed.

"It's good for him to ask all the questions he has. I'm leaving in a few moments. I will do my best to get back here in time to enter the portal under your command, Gracie."

Then he turned to Cole. "Where will I be? All over the place. Many of the volunteers have spent decades in underground Tribunal prisons. They need some Acclimation and adjustment assistance. Many are elderly and ill but determined to be part of the efforts. There will be a lot of assessing to do. Oh… and this gentleman is Terry Fennimore… your first volunteer. I suggest you take him with you to New York. Let him help you, and get a grasp of how the portals work."

Cole eyed Fennimore, a beautifully dressed, elegant, tall black man. "Buddy, you really need to dress down. The Free-Winged are homeless. They'll be real suspicious if you look like that."

"Understood." He smiled and Cole could see Jenny in that smile.

"Now," he addressed Parkland. "What does Gracie need here that I can help with until I leave for McGuire's meeting?"

Parkland stood and set his plate in the sink. "You can monitor the demon activity for her. Make sure it's not escalating, or becoming aggressive."

"I noticed we're treating them like pets."

With that, Gracie snapped. "You don't understand, Cole. As long as they're passive, we don't attack. Something is happening and I want them to know this is a safe place."

"Gracie, no place is safe. Don't you remember the battle after the Emmaus show?"

"I do. This isn't that."

"It might be."

"It's not."

He looked to Parkland and the man shrugged. "She's right. Something major is at play here. My sense, and another with the same quickening gift of perception, can tell. There's something important happening. We have to let it happen without interference. This is only speculation, but perhaps the demons that have experienced time in our camp will walk through the portal and stand at our side."

"You think that's possible?" Cole's gut twisted.

"Anything is possible. Maybe it's that, maybe not, but something's brewing where the demons are concerned. My sense of perception… and… Gracie's order, is a solid wait and see."

"That's a rather vague gift you have there," Cole said with a snort.

Parkland laughed. "Here." He tossed a loaded backpack across the table.

Inside, Cole fingered what could add up to thirty thousand bucks in twenties. "This will help."

"Good. Also, I'm bringing Michael Allerton here to the island after his engagement tomorrow."

"Why?" That time it was both Cole and Gracie in unison.

"Because he's done the job, and the news has raced like wildfire. There's no longer a need to send him anywhere else to recruit. Nephilim fully committed to being part of the Counting have miraculously regenerated their own swords and contacted us. He's done very well, as expected."

Cole thought. "And, this way he can spend more time with his son."

"I like the idea of keeping family units together before the Counting.

There's a certain synergy to it. All of you Ariel's Gate people should be together, preparing, praying, working, enjoying each other. Makes sense, doesn't it?"

Cole had to agree.

"Good. Gracie, my sweet." He reached out and she stepped into his embrace. "I will see you soon. If not here, on the Counting field. Keep leading. They're following beautifully. Oh, and I would like you to put Dawn St. Mary in charge of supplies management. She has a knack for managing things, and she needs something to focus on. Tobias has never taken advantage of her skills."

He shook Cole and Fennimore's hands, then walked out of the house to his waiting limo.

"Who was that masked man?" Cole teased, but Gracie shook her head.

"What?" He called after her as she went out to wave farewell. Maybe that guy really was his competition. If not in bed, definitely in strategic matters. Cole Masters, former Marine and committed Nephilim, knew better. Always follow orders, even if it had been fun to run the whole show for a while. Either way, Parkland had not only given him an important promotion, he made sure he and Gracie could have a little more time together.

He went to the door and gave a solid salute before Parkland returned it and drove away.

~*~

Tobias woke feeling invigorated and empowered. His discussion with the Morning Star went very well last night. He had an infallible plan, a solid appointment to propose that plan, as well as the strength and determination to see it through. All would be well, but before that spectacular finale to Lucifer's meddling, Tobias had a show to put on.

This would not be any average show. This would be the last of all shows. No more carnie rogue warrior bands, no more recruiting, no more war or stress over the future. This would be the be all and end all, so it had to be beyond expectations.

In the past, he'd arranged the performances for just before the Countings. At first, it was just a bunch of carnie folks showing off. But with each subsequent Counting, it became more of a competition, a platform to display the excellence of many and showcase superiority of a few. For a while, the same ancient leaders' groups repeatedly won, other times, new ancients came along with new ideas and blew the competition out of the water. This time would be most interesting, as only a handful of the groups were led by ancients. Newer groups led by Nephilim had emerged over recent years. Were ancients becoming obsolete? Or were the coming performances about to prove otherwise?

Tobias dressed, smiling ear to ear, listening to the normal sounds of the camp outside his door. Little did they know that this time, this performance, would set the bar and keep it right where it lands. With no need to hide and live the gypsy life, there would be no need to create stupendous performances to draw in the Nephilim for the fight. The system would die out, like so many he'd seen in his long lifetime. The tribunal was gone, though it was the shortest-lived control system Tobias ever knew. He feared the orphanage system would regenerate. There would be no need for such protection of Nephilim children with Lucifer retired. So much would be different. He couldn't wait for a comfortable, quiet life. Perhaps he could give his humanity a rebirth. Love again. Raise a family again. Join the people around him in the activity and simplicity of living, moment by moment. It will be grand. He just knew it.

After dinner in the communal tent, he quickly commandeered three of the large tables and set them tightly together. With rolls of paper, he covered the tables from end to end. A set of colored pens stood waiting and a stack of index cards poised for their assignments. He dragged a chair close, closed his eyes and allowed his mind to visualize the show he would plan. An annoying shuffle of tarp and canvas interrupted his thoughts and the ancient glared as Dawn walked in.

"Whatever you want, not now," he growled like a bear.

"Tobias, I just wanted to make sure you don't need anything else. I know you're busy, I don't mean to bother you."

"So," he said without looking up. "Stop bothering me."

"Okay, well, if you need me, I'll be down at the house. They've asked me to handle the purchasing and management for the camp."

"Fine. Go."

She didn't leave so he looked up, one brow raised, and the other in a nasty scowl.

"Isn't that cool?" She smiled, running a hand over her growing middle. "That they want me to handle—"

"So, go do your job and leave me to mine."

Still she stood. She was a beauty, but her belly gave him pause. He would not be blackmailed into being her puppet just because her womb was fertile. He had other plans for now, and for later. This thing with Dawn St. Mary had to end. He squared his shoulders and shouted at the top if his lungs. "Get the hell out of here! And stay at that damn house. I want nothing to do with you!"

Tears fell before she swung a turn and slapped his face with a rousing crack, then left the tent in a huff. Rubbing his cheek, he nodded. "That should do it."

Getting down to work, he wrote out one card for each group in camp. The list was long, but with what he'd seen thus far, the best performances would be among the top sixteen of the forty-one troupes present. He wrote carefully. With each card he wrote, he sat back and thought long and hard about what he knew about them.

Emmaus Warriors – Tobias, ancient. Tobias had no worries. He knew his people better than any other leader in camp. They were loyal and competitive to a fault. He almost felt it was unfair for them to go against any other troupe.

Arabian Knight Warriors – Abdalmalek, Norema Nephilim. Fifteen years ago, Abdalmalek was one of the Emmaus Warriors. He was still extremely loyal to Tobias, but felt the need to take his culture and use it to pull in Nephilim of the Muslim faith together for

performances, training, and the coming threat, for the Counting ahead, and battle.

Rashee Mystic Warriors – Rashee, ancient. What was there to say about Rashee? Tobias was, as always, unsure of her or her troupe's ability to actually fight. They were fundamentally committed to peaceful solutions at all times. It had been Rashee's philosophy for longer than Tobias was alive. Much, much longer. This would be the most fun, seeing her people perform in competition with another troupe. It could be eye-opening, or it might just confirm his convictions about her.

Tiospia Warriors – Bold Eagle, Calanine Nephilim. Basically, Tobias liked Bold Eagle. He was straight forward and pulled no punches. He'd never seen the Tiospia Warriors' show, but he had once fought at their side when battle heat demons attacked a few years back. They were brutal, efficient warriors from the bone and spirit to the flesh. Bold Eagle's people had Tobias's respect.

Merlin Knights – Wardo, Norema Nephilim. Everything Tobias knew of Wardo and his Merlin Knights was hearsay. They seemed to have captured the alchemy of old-world wizardry and integrated it into their style of fighting. Their show was said to be mystical beyond anything anyone was doing. Wardo had collected more Nephilim recruits than any other group in camp.

Roma Victa Army – Joe Carducci, Norema Nephilim. Joe Carducci was recruited by none other then Ballister Green a decade ago, but was instantly drawn to creating his own show, his own troupe, and his own way of recruiting. He spent five years moving around from troupe to troupe until he was sure of what he wanted and how he wanted to do it. Tobias respected that, but in truth, always expected Joe to crawl back home to the Emmaus Warriors. The Roman Victa Army put on a spectacular show of old Roman pageantry and flair. Joe didn't do too badly in the recruiting department either.

Mayan Band Warriors – Juan, Calanine Nephilim. Juan took over the

Mayan Band Warriors from his father, who took it over from his father. It was truly a family driven operation, but culturally, called out to the Mesoamerican Nephilim living in the continental United States. He had a consistently strong group of good fighters, and the scoop was, a damn good show, too.

Fighting Highlanders – Walter McTavish, Norema Nephilim. Walter McTavish was not born in the United States. In fact, he didn't have a green card and had never even imagined seeking citizenship. He was a true outlaw living and recruiting among rogue warriors. His goal was to gather together the Scots of America and make a great showing when a Counting came. Highlanders can fight, so Tobias had no qualms fighting at McTavish's side. What wasn't clear, was if the Fighting Highlanders had a show worth seeing. Would people outside of the Scottish community find it interesting? Did they have the elements that shine bright in performance competition? But then again, did Walter McTavish give a damn about competition? He'd spent his life focused on building a band of warriors, drinking whisky, and standing ready to fight at the drop of a hat. He was an unknown factor, for sure.

Gypsy Fighters – Nicco, Norema Nephilim. Nicco and Garta were good friends. She originally traveled with Nicco's great-great-grandfather before shifting to Tobias and offering her healing services. Whenever the two troupes crossed paths, it was old home week for the old woman. She was like a grandmother to young Nicco, only thirty, but already a dynamic fighter and showman. No one put on a show like a real, live gypsy.

African Wonders Warriors – Akkii, ancient. Akkii and Tobias had never crossed paths in either of their very long lives. The tall black man with scarred markings across his face was off-putting to Tobias. It was always easier to be welcoming then get the hell out of that man's way. What he could tell of the African Wonders Warriors was that they trained constantly, fought well, and looked like disciplined performers. It was yet to be seen how great a show they put on.

Romanoff's Warriors – Francis Karonoff, Calanine Nephilim. Descendants of the real Romanoffs, Francis held true to his culture, focused on historical Russian dance and music, and put on one hell of a show, complete with Rasputin, played by his elderly brother, Richard. The group could fight but the show gave Tobias the creeps. The performance used mystical manipulation of the mind, pulling viewers emotionally into their message while reenacting the historical Romanoff family disaster with flare and embellishment. In Tobias's mind, it was gory to the point of distasteful. For all his years of presenting carnie shows, he still believed that entertainment should be entertaining. Shock appeal never sat well.

Rasta Fighters – Bobby, ancient. Bobby was an interesting ancient. Every hundred or so years, he changed his name, his show, and his focus. In his current version, he was most popular with younger Nephilim. He recruited like nobody's business, mostly through concerts featuring Reggae music, but powerful magic was there, always enticing the newest generation. Could these guys fight? Tobias had no clue, but he did like the sound of steel drums.

Dead Heads – Ben and Jerry Martin, Twins, Norema Nephilim. These guys had been recruiting like crazy since the beginning of the Grateful Dead's reign in 1965. All those people following the group, camping on the side of American highways and roads, cheering on the music, were recruited Nephilim. Some still remain the same. Others have moved on to serve under other leaders, but the performances were unreal, like seeing an acid trip live and in front of one's eyes. Could they fight? He hoped so. Just in case those damn battle heat demons hanging around turn ugly.

Shield Maiden Warriors – Malinda Dooly, Norema Nephilim. Malinda Dooley was born a Free-Winged Nephilim in Wisconsin. She was recruited by the original leader of the Shield Maiden Warriors and taught to fight by some of the best female fighters of the Nephilim race. Their show explored the ancient Viking pantheon, and was said to be mind blowing. Tobias, for one, couldn't wait to see them perform. He loved beautiful women, especially when they were completely unattended by men, and completely able to defend themselves.

Soul World Searcher Warriors – Barkley Parson, Calanine Nephilim. Soul World Searchers were once an entire community of Nephilim based outside New Orleans. For three-hundred years, generations of them lived quietly in the low country, on one of the few remaining Nephilim breeding grounds, much like the Ocracoke land where they currently camped. But, over the last thirty years they came out of their quiet existence and explored ways of recruiting, aware of the Counting ahead. Their performances tended to pontificate on the natural resources of the planet and preserving the beauty of it. The imagery was fantastic and often hard for Tobias to puzzle out. They had a knack for twisting magic and reality in knots, producing breathtaking shows. Of course, they recruited well, and resonated with many Nephilim of like mind.

The Fortune Tellers Squad – Coleen, ancient. Coleen was another ancient who loved to reinvent herself, her show, and her approaches to recruiting every so often. There's something to be said for an ancient who moves with the times, but those times were long gone for Tobias. Colleen was only six hundred years an ancient, at the most, so it was still fun for her. She and her performers told outrageous fortunes that turned out to be true. It might prove to be quite a show. Tobias just hoped he wasn't present when they did their prognosticating. His secrets were his alone.

Satisfied with his sixteen primary choices, he shuffled through the cards. Tobias had a vision of seeing more than just performances the troupes had already perfected. He wanted more, and he wanted performances going on two at a time, pitting one group against another in the massive two-ring tent waiting in the center of camp. At first, he thought to pit the ancients against each other, then let the Nephilim leadership fight it out after real superiority was established, but a sense of fairness washed over him. He wanted this to be a tough challenge for all the performers and leaders. He wanted real effort.

These performances would strengthen and fortify the warriors for a possible coming battle, even though Tobias knew there'd be no battle. No Counting. Just himself, standing alone in the peach grove, holding Lucifer's relinquished sword and ready to help the world reorganize and be a better place. However, the warriors had to believe there was war on the horizon. They had to be challenged. And so, he began.

Seeking out similarities and differences between each of the top groups, he decided to set same against same, unique against a completely different unique, then let the shows begin. The remaining twenty-five troupes would bid to perform against the winners of the first eight shows. The performances would start at noon, and end around noon the next day, leaving Tobias more than enough time to slip off and do what he intended. When he returned, if the shows were as amazing as he expected, he'd sit and enjoy them until the end before making his announcement. If they were boring, he'd stop the performances and share the good news. That he, Tobias, was their savior.

He glowered and set out the cards in order, each settling over a circle representing one of the two performance rings. The synergy and simplicity of it pleased him. He'd explain the plan to the leaders the next morning at breakfast. They'd have one day to prepare and rehearse. No more.

The matches he created excited him. His own Emmaus Warriors against McTavish's Fighting Highlanders. The amazing Arabian Knight Warriors with the illusions of live horses, would perform against the Native American Tiospia Warriors and their similar live horse illusions. The Rashee Mystics against the Soul World Searcher Warriors. Wardo and his Merlin Knights would face against the Shield Maiden Warriors. Roma Victa would face off with the African Wonders Warriors. Just for fun, he pitted the Mayan Band Warriors against the Rasta Fighters. The amazing Dead Heads, would battle performances against The Fortune Tellers Squad. And finally, the Gypsy Fighters against the Romanoff Warriors. He carefully stapled each set of competitors together.

Next, he tossed the cards into the air, then picked them up randomly. Whichever pairing came up first, would be the first to compete, and so on, and so on. He marked a time on each set of cards, then set the remaining twenty-five cards aside. When the time came, he'd shuffle them and permit each troupe to bid for the opportunity to compete against one of the eight winners. A little gambling, a little posturing, a lot of high energy. He laughed aloud. This was going to be fun.

21

en's chest knotted like a rope about to shred and split into pieces. He sat up, tried to breath then closed his eyes. Again. It was happening again. His quickening power was trying to kill him.

At his side, Kevin woke with a start, reaching out, but Ben couldn't tolerate being touched. He jumped up and ran out of the tent. Looking around, he heard nothing but the cries of terrified voices, shrieking, rattling his bones, all in a vision far away. Shaking, Ben turned a circle, unsure of which way to run.

"Focus!" Kevin shouted. "Focus, Ben! You can control this."

Still, he ran, bare feet scrubbing over rocks and dried weeds, his face scratched as he raced through shrubs and trees. Where was he going? The visions wouldn't go away, they followed him everywhere, even sleep couldn't silence them.

"Focus!"

He heard that. The voice of someone he loved, someone who loved him. Stumbling into a heap on the ground, Ben tried just that. Focus.

But on what? The terror? The screams? No. The place. Where was this happening? Because sure as hell, Ben knew it was happening that very moment. He did his best to steady his breathing, eyes squeezed tight, fists balled. Details slowly emerged. Battle. Somewhere there was a battle going on. Who was fighting? Or maybe it was a massacre? He saw images more clearly, more details came, swimming at the edges until he could identify them. No demons. No Nephilim. Only humans and… "Oh shit!"

He gasped, desperate to hold on to what had been revealed. There was a city, bright lights, neon everywhere. There were sounds, loud music, people writhing in pain and fear. Shots rang out and panicked the crowd. What was happening, and why did he need to know? Then he saw it. Something he could have never even imagined. The Image of a man, no a Nephilim, no an archangel, burned to a crisp, his skeletal wings dripping black tar, his face so repulsive, Ben turned and wretched in the dirt at his knee. Lucifer. He stood like a conductor, leading an orchestra of terror and fear.

When Ben's heart slowed and regained normal function, he could do nothing but sob and allow Kevin to hold him tight. They slowly walked back to their tent. "What the hell?" Ben cried as campers came out to investigate the noise.

Kevin waved them away. Many were familiar with Ben's episodes. They gave a solemn expression of distant yet caring support and left. The only creatures remaining were the demons, inching closer and closer. Kevin shooed them away, too. "Your dad's coming soon. Michael's coming. He'll know what to do. Come on, you need some sleep."

Panic raced across Ben's eyes and Kevin braced for the coming assault. It passed slowly, so slowly. He had to do something, so he babbled mindlessly, saying anything that might catch and hold Ben's attention.

"Did you hear, the Nationals won it? Oh… and what about that roast Cookie made for dinner? So damn good, wasn't it?" Ben nodded absently. "Hey, and tomorrow, let's move the tent closer to the house. It's still quiet there. Something in the camp might be triggering this crap."

Ben took Kevin's hands and held them warmly, sufficiently stopping them from further cleaning and dressing all the bloody minor wounds on his face and feet. "It's not being triggered. It's being… um… transmitted. It's information we need to know. Can you do something for me?"

"Anything."

"Bring Raphael here. He needs to know what's happening."

Kevin left but Ben's visions continued, stretching his brain and pressing agony through his head and neck. He cried out so loud he feared everyone would hear. "Stop! Stop that!" he was shouting at the devil who elegantly orchestrated the disaster in Nashville, Tennessee, wounding nearly a hundred, killing thirty thus far, and enjoying every moment of it. At one point, the evil entity looked directly into his eyes and laughed. Ben's screams became louder and louder until he could scream no more.

At the house, Gracie heard the cry and raced down the stairs, through the house and past ICe. The monster was awake too, and could run far faster than Gracie's twisted foot would carry her. Instead of passing her in the field, he gripped her under one arm like a sack of potatoes and raced forward. At the tent, Ben struggled, shook and trembled, his mouth foaming and eyes rolled back in his head.

"Ben! Oh God, Ben!" Gracie shouted, freeing herself from her protector and crawling closer, but ICe simply slipped past her, crouched like a giant in the tiny tent and settled his massive palm on Ben's brow. The seizure stopped immediately and Ben seemed to drop from a high place onto his sleeping bag.

ICe slid Ben out of the tent and lay him out under the stars as Kevin and Raphael sprinted closer. The big guy never took his hand from Ben, and before anyone could say anything, the patient looked up with a grin.

"Thanks, man," he mumbled with a voice that sounded as raw as he looked.

"It's in his head," ICe said shyly, retaining contact with his patient. "Someone has to fix this."

Garta walked toward them and shook her head. "Someone, indeed. However, my friend, you are the most powerful healer here. What do you suggest?"

Poor ICe just shrugged. "Dunno. Can I just keep my hand on him?"

Garta lowered to sit on the ground beside them and nodded. "As long as he needs you to."

Ben chuckled. "I'm okay, now. Sorry for all the fuss. Raphael, Lucifer is instigating death and riots all over Nashville. Can we stop him?"

"I'll do my best. But if he's playing with humans, it might explain the demons' behavior. They're not receiving direct orders from him right now."

"Or," Ben shuffled and lay his head on Gracie's lap. "Maybe they don't want to listen to the devil anymore?"

Raphael smiled and shook his head. "My brother always has a plan. Stirring up the human race is part of it. Losing the loyalty of his demon race, I assure you, is not."

Ben sluggishly sat up and leaned against Gracie's shoulder, her arms around him like she'd never let go.

"You're okay, now," ICe announced.

"Am I? The visions are still there. Why are they sometimes just there, and other times, taking over my whole body?"

"Honor to your quickening, young Ben," Garta said softly. "But yours is a power that grows as the need grows. It will never free you completely, but it shouldn't eat you alive, young man."

"How do I control it?"

No one spoke for several moments, moments that almost caused him to doze off and sleep. Then Raphael released a long sigh. "Ben," he spoke almost in a whisper. "You simply need to become a man. You're only a boy yet, as far as your power is concerned. Focus helps, but maturity is the only way you'll understand how to use this gift."

"Maturity?" Ben offered a tired guffaw. "I've spent the last eighteen years avoiding such a thing."

Raphael didn't laugh and even Gracie hugged him tighter.

The archangel nodded for the others to leave but Gracie refused.

"Ben needs his rest," Raphael said directly to her and she tightened her lips, prepared to argue. "You should be with Cole. He leaves in the morning."

Resigned, she nodded and stood. "Don't do that again!" she hissed at Ben then walked to the house, looking back several times.

Finally, alone, Raphael placed a hand on Ben's shoulder. The skin there tingled and even throbbed, then felt like a sledge hammer had struck it.

"Um, ouch."

"I need you to pay attention. Your gift is so powerful it can, and will, kill you if you don't get your act together, boy. Your race needs you, now and after the Counting, so don't be such a child."

"What? I'm just trying to survive this shit, man. I can't handle it any better than I am, no matter how hard I try. I—"

"You are not trying," hissed the archangel. Then Raphael leaned back and glanced toward the tent. "What are you denying yourself?"

"Huh?"

"What are you refusing?"

"I don't know what you're talking about. I'm tired, Leave me—"

"You are a dead man if you don't learn a few things very quickly. One," an angelic finger rose, "you are not alone. Your power can only be contained when you back it against another's power."

"But—"

"Two, you aren't living, and that's all you have, Ben… life, as your Creator gave it to you. Peace isn't just found. Joy isn't just dropped into your lap. But the signs are always there. You're ignoring the signs and playing the victim."

Ben stood quickly and dropped right into Raphael's arms.

"I've been watching you your whole life, Ben. Hiding. Pretending. Hoping, yet never living fully. Now." He looked into Ben's eyes. "What are you denying yourself? That is the answer to your problem. The only answer."

Raphael released Ben to thump on the ground, then stomped off like a pissed off housecat. Ben wondered if the archangel was right. What was he doing, trying to handle his gift alone? Where the hell was his dad? Michael should be helping him, right? Helping him like before, with swords and focus. Right? He leaned toward the tent. Inside it was silent.

Raphael's voice resonated inside his mind. What are you denying yourself? What are you denying yourself? "What am I denying myself?" Ben whispered, and the silent answer was so powerful that for a moment, he feared another seizure.

On his knees he shuffled closer to the tent. "Kev? You asleep?"

"Hell, no."

"Let's move the tent, okay? To the back of the house. Let's do it now."

Dragging sleeping bags and pulling tent pegs before he even answered, Kevin grinned and said "Will do, but you rest here."

"Yeah, I'll rest here." Ben's head dropped to the cool grass and he sighed, amazed at how quiet the visions had become. They were still there, terrifying, funny, strange, and bloody, fifty of them, hundreds of them all at once, just not sitting on the front of his brain. He was focusing on something else.

~*~

Raphael would never understand human beings. They were given everything—joy, love, procreation, beauty, creativity, the opportunity to live on the cutting edge of the expanding universe, and most of all, free will. All of it, and what did they do? Squander life on worry and despair, and propagating more of the same by living that unfortunate reality. It takes little to step apart from oneself and take inventory. Ask if he or she is happy, then change things to be happy. So little. That was the gift the Father gave them all. A gift that permitted them the strength to take care of everything else. But humans and Nephilim tended to forget the important things. Love. Joy. Happiness. They went right for the jugular. Fear, desperation, poverty of spirit. If there was one thing he hated about the human race, it was their struggle to ignore the truth of their existence. To simply enjoy it.

He stomped into the peach grove, through the portal and across to the Nashville portal. Standing next to Lucifer on the edge of a downtown honky-tonk roof, he shook his head. "What the hell are you doing, brother?"

"Ah, Raphael!" The devil turned and embraced him, his flesh lumpy and scarred, blistered and black. "Good to see you! What am I doing? Well, I'm having some fun. Look," he pointed. "There. See him? Abiyus. Remember him? The ancient? He used to fight for the Nephilim, now he has a country music obsession, wants to be famous and sing sad, twangy songs. He sold his soul to me for three hundred bucks! After walking the earth for more than two-thousand years, can you imagine he would do such a thing? Humans are just so unpredictable, aren't they? Three hundred bucks for a cheap, used guitar. Abiyus was so sure his song would be a big hit. Nope. He tried and tried, really put in his blood and sweat but, seriously, it was an especially bad song from start to finish. Now, he's mine. And he's aiming and shooting to my heart's content."

"You're wasting your time, Lucifer. Don't you have more important things to do?"

"Not really, it's all in hand. I have twice your number in demon warriors. I have the Pure Nephilim twin sister of your gimpy Gracie. Oh, and soon I will have the soul of Tobias. Now that's a coup, isn't it?" When he grinned, his ugly face appeared almost as radiant as it once was.

Shots rang again, screams and terrified bellows rose. The street crowd grew as terrified people ran from different establishments, collided in on themselves, unsure which way to run.

"Stop this," Raphael spat.

Lucifer shrugged then smiled. "I'm getting bored anyway. Let's have some coffee. I have a chalet in Aspen. Beautiful this time of year, all those colorful leaves."

Raphael shook his head and glared.

Lucifer employed his power of illusion, regained his beauty and splendor, stretched out his pure white wings then sighed. "Who's the new Perceptive?"

Raphael remained silent.

"He's a powerful one. He stood right where you are and looked right at me." The devil rubbed his hands together. "That one's more powerful than Parkland. Maybe the most powerful I've ever seen walking the earth."

Still Raphael stood quietly, watching the mayhem below.

"He will die of it, you know. The human half will destroy his angelic nature. He might not even make it to the Counting." The Morning Star gathered air beneath his wings and rose several feet like a feather on a warm current, the starlit sky twinkling behind him. He looked down at his brother. "Are you sure you won't join me for coffee? I have a few ideas for after I win this. Most certainly a place for you, my brother."

"Luc, man, you won't win. You will never win. Father is not weakening."

"Ah, but his free-willed people and Nephilim are. Have you seen my army? All Nephilim who came freely to me… more come every day. I will show Him, Raphael. I have to. These beings have no right to hurt Him the way they do. They should be obliterated."

"You… will… never… win."

"Oh, I will. Very possibly this go around."

And in a blink of the eye, the devil was gone. Raphael closed his eyes and said a prayer, begging for medical and police assistance to arrive soon. Then he heard the shot that killed Abiyus. It rang louder than any other sound and lifted to the sky. The danger was over. For now.

Returning to the silence of camp rattled his nerves. Weary, he sat at the central fire, a worshiping fire that burned day and night, rain or shine, and stared into the flames. Both he and Lucifer were correct. Ben would die of his power if he didn't get a grasp on how it worked, and soon. Raphael would do all he could to assist. Garta was on board. ICe turned out to be the surprise healer of the century. And Gracie, poor Gracie was about to feel the real demands placed on her fragile shoulders. Serious challenges lay ahead for her. Lots was happening all around him, and for the first time in a very long time, Raphael wished he had drawn a quiet management job at a desk somewhere in heaven.

Across the camp he watched lights darken in the dining tent. Tobias walked out, stretched his arms high and yawned. The man had a glow about him, and Raphael knew it had everything to do with the coming performances. The shows were his pride and joy. Was it too much to hope the shows would keep him away from Lucifer?

No. That bounce in his step had to do with far more than putting on a few shows.

22

"Didn't you hear that?" I asked. Cole was staring at the big new tables that now lived in my dining room and living room. No more comfort, no more cushy couches, no more Ocracoke hospitality. My house was now command central, and Cole seemed to be deeply entrenched in his assignment. It was, after all, the only way he'd get to see the Free-Winged project we started through to its completion. However, he seemed to forget everything else when he worked like that.

"Cole? Didn't you hear that?"

"Uh, hear what?"

Finally, he looked up at me. The tables were covered with maps, both Blackbeard's and new maps of various cities. All around the room were computers and, on the table, sat a monitor, constantly scrolling with the growing list of Nephilim willing to guide others through the various portals.

"Didn't you hear Ben crying out?"

"Oh man, no. It happened again? Is he alright?" His hand reached across and gripped mine.

"I don't know." I tried to be brave. "I don't think so. He had a seizure this time."

Arms wrapped around me and I felt Cole's warm breath on my neck. "I'm sorry, sweetheart. Was Garta able to help him?"

"No. ICe stopped it. The guy's gift is healing, but I don't think he can stop this crap from happening. Good God, Cole. I don't want Ben to suffer like this."

Cole sat on a stool and pulled me onto his lap. Everything about life had changed, but becoming lovers had shifted our reality. We'd started to think alike. Sometimes we didn't even have to use words. Maybe this was normal, maybe it was Nephilim, but either way, it was a comfort and terror beyond reason. My heart grew and broke every moment. If this was love, how did people survive it? His hands were soft on my back, and his lips found mine. Gentle yet strong, he held me captive inside his big heart. Then he leaned back. "Maybe Garta can help figure it out? Raphael? Or maybe," he looked into my eyes. "Let's go to the tree and see if your father has any ideas."

"Exactly!" I was out the door before he could even stand up. As I approached the tree I wondered if Cole would actually be able to cross into that other world with me, or if he'd be left behind. I stood, eyes squeezed tight, hoping we could do this together. His hand slipped into mine and I nodded, then we stepped through the drooping willow branches.

"Oh dear!" I whispered. Something was wrong. Different. Unexpected. Soft, fluffy snowflakes drifted in the crisp air. I wrapped my arms around my shoulders and held my breath. This was not the same place I usually went.

"We're not in Kansas anymore, are we?" Cole said at my side.

Behind us I heard two masculine voices, deep in discussion. I turned and there he was, my father, Scribe of God, Metatron. "Um…" I never saw the archangel with him before, and he didn't seem to care that I was even there. "Metatron? Dad? Do you have a minute?"

My father turned and smiled and I did what I always did, walked into his open arms and enjoyed the depth and power of an angelic embrace. "Dad, we need your help."

He eyed Cole carefully, freed me then walked a full circle around him. Poor Cole looked a little afraid. Then he did the stupidest thing. He shot out a hand and said, "Nice to meet you. I'm Cole Masters."

Dad chuckled and shook Cole's hand then turned. "Makha'el, come. Be social. Meet your grandson."

My heart stopped beating for a second. Makha'el? God's warrior chief was Cole's grandfather? Cole looked just as shocked but another handshake broke the ice.

"Forgive me," Makha'el said in slow, broken English. "Much to do."

He tenderly patted Cole's shoulder and nodded seriously, then disappeared into the snowstorm.

"Why's it so cold?" I shuffled from foot to foot and Metatron tilted his head.

"Cold?"

I looked at Cole and he at me. "We need your help." Cole spoke directly, his voice shaking. Imagine meeting your grandfather Makha'el?

"How can I assist?"

"It's Ben," I said, and Metatron blinked. "Um, Michael Allerton's son? My best friend since, well, forever."

Finally, Dad nodded and waited patiently for my request.

"Can you help him?" I sighed and thankfully Cole continued for me.

"He's struggling with his quickening gift… perception. Really powerful perception. He's suffering, sir. We fear for his life."

Metatron flipped through a few pages of paper in his hands, most likely killing time before having to give us the worst news ever.

"Children… the Father gives no gift unless He knows you can manage it. It's for your friend to decide. To choose. He may choose to end his life rather than control such a powerful gift. Free will, my dear." He looked at me sadly. "It is all his choice."

I wanted to shout that Ben wasn't as strong other Nephilim, that he was special, unique, loved, but none of those words came out of my mouth. Only tears dripped down my face.

"I must go. Gracie, keep a clear eye out for Esther. Keep your head. The Counting is very near."

Poof.

He was gone and we were standing under a plain old weeping willow tree. Boy, those archangels can really piss me off. That was it? All the help he could give? If Ben wasn't functioning right, how could I function right? Watch out for Esther? Keep my head? What kind of angelic advice was that?

We pushed out from under the tree and noticed Ben's tent was gone. "Maybe he finally decided to put it behind the house?" Cole must have sensed my mood. He wasn't about to discuss what just happened. Best to let it pass. Not for me. I started to pace back and forth in front of him, a hobble that made me look like a confused Quasi Moto.

"Why are they doing this? Why won't they help us? It's their fault we're even here in the first place. You'd think they'd want us to succeed, but no, all they want is for us to keep a stiff upper lip and plow ahead."

Cole's head followed me, back and forth, back and forth. He didn't reach out, didn't try to argue for or against my point. Just waited. Then when I stopped, I noticed how his face glowed.

"What?"

"Let's go make love."

Half of me wanted to argue, ask if sex was going to be his solution for everything, but hey, maybe it was the solution for everything. After all, he was leaving tomorrow to finalize the North American Free-Winged arrangement. I do love him, and well, I did really want to make love.

He left the light on in the dining room. His maps and materials waited on the table as we passed, and I knew that later, when I slept, he'd return to them. I was discovering that Cole was an intriguing person. He had an ability to recognize a special moment and squeeze everything he could out of it. His quickening powers were extraordinary. While normal men could decipher and solve problems, stretching their imagination to create or invent solutions, he could see portals that were poised to save all our lives. While other men could use their fists and weapons to defend themselves and those they love, Cole could produce angel fire, which was way more effective and spectacular. He was always precise and thoughtful, even when he was being a guy. As he lowered over me on the bed I understood, for the first time, that Cole was a real catch. And for the first time, I really knew that I wanted both of us to survive the coming Counting. This guy, this love, and the life I could have with him was too good to lose.

In the quiet moments we whispered. He told me about Carla and how they'd met years ago. I told him that I could hear the demons talk to me, that others could, too. He mentioned the danger Nunzio presented, and I declared that the idea of watching for Esther to come to our side felt like a fairy tale. We kissed and caressed. We managed to talk about a future, living there on Ocracoke, or living somewhere else. We joked about raising pigs and chickens, or adopting an English bulldog and naming it Raffie. We touched and we laughed, then we cried and comforted each other.

"We're going to survive this, right?" I asked.

"Yes," he whispered and took me again.

Curled under a slimy blanket that smelled bad and danced with fleas, Esther hid deeper, avoiding the coming morning light seeping through an opening in the crumbling wall. A spider worked there, diligently spinning a stunning web big enough to cover the whole wall, but not thick enough to block the coming daylight. She sighed and rolled over, covering her head. With a little luck, no one would bother to check on her. She'd been with the gargoyles for two days. Hiding in ICe's favorite corner, eating little, aching, and sleeping. A sickness had taken over every part of her, an all new misery outside of Esther's experience.

The cook at the Hell to Pay Pub suffered this way. She took several pills a day to make life easier for her. Lili was weak, in Esther's eyes. With a name like Lili, how could she be anything but fragile? A woman with a good strong name like Esther would never fall prey to something as stupid as depression. But she had. When Lili complained, Esther laughed and told her to grow a backbone. Where had Esther's backbone gone? To hell in Lucifer's arms.

She sat up, frustrated. Pushing her grimy hair from her eyes she noticed her feet, filthy, crusted with dirt and grime. She had become homeless, had grown the shell of such a being in forty-eight short hours. But Esther would not cry. She had too much to figure out.

Unfortunately, she couldn't summon her brain to think. Her head constantly ached, her body rebelled, her appetite had disappeared, and her heart, her poor broken heart, had decided to take some time off and just beat. Not feel. Not react. Not sense.

She reached over and checked inside of her boot. It was still there, a long, sharp shard of broken glass. Why she was hiding it was a mystery. Glass was everywhere, broken, crumbled, shattered. So were old rusted nails and metal pieces, old pipes big and small, stacks of cement and cinder blocks. Nothing made that piece of glass special, except for the job she had planned for it.

Maybe. Maybe not. If only she could think clearly. I only she didn't feel like the salvation of the entire world was on her shoulders. If only she didn't feel like such a monumental failure. But how had she failed? Really?

Inspecting the sharp point and edges of the glass, she watched in wonder as the sunlight flickered off of it, through it, splayed the beam into colors on the walls that disappeared with the slightest movement. Tiny adjustments could change everything. Everything.

She had options. She was nothing but a plain old human, so why couldn't she just join the human race? Walk out of the basement and down the street. Find a job. Meet a man. Make a life. Should she do that?

Did she want to do that? She was a sight for sore eyes, the light brown roots of her hair growing bold in contrast against the black and fuchsia dyes she loved so much. Her black nail polish was chipped and her nails were broken. She'd forgotten to look to herself, had forgotten how much of Lucifer's illusion power was at play in her life. If she looked better, would she feel better? Did it matter?

There was the issue of her other part, too. The Pure Nephilim part stolen from her. She wasn't actually only human, and as long as her Pure Nephilim elements lived in Lucifer's captivity, she could never be anything, not even human.

Could she get her angel part out? Rescue it? She considered asking the demons for help to lift the giant bell jar and free her other part, but that would be impossible. They didn't understand her and she didn't understand them. Lucifer must have destroyed their brains as much as their wings. There could be no effective communication for such a strategic operation.

Desperation and loss threatened to overtake her mind, but Esther quickly moved it along. She could break the glass bell jar, take her winged part and run from the lab. Maybe run to Gracie. Maybe Gracie would know what to do next—but if Lucifer split her apart, was it possible for anyone else to put her back together?

Maybe nothing was possible and she was too far into the evil's grip. She considered staying the path and standing at his side. That would put her Pure Nephilim power at his command. That would pit her against her sister. The world. Everything. If Lucifer won the Counting and the war, he would make himself king of the earth. He had always promised she'd be his queen. When she was thirteen, she imagined the Disney queens, the nice ones. She'd wear a gown and a crown, sit on a throne at his side and smile a lot. The reality was that being queen to Lucifer's king would not be such a blessing. She would be as she had always been. His slave, his lover, his toy. He would never return her angel elements to her. They would be forever held captive to control Esther's actions.

Her belly ached and she rolled to her side, gasping for air. She carefully wrapped the glass in a piece of the nasty blanket, then cuddled it like a comforting Teddy bear. She had something the Morning Star did not have. Esther had free will. All she needed to do was use it.

If she lived, her angel elements lived. If she died, her Pure Nephilim parts would die with her. If she managed to control even that part of the coming Counting and war, she would have accomplished much. Esther needed to get a grip on herself, make a clear plan, and do what she had to do. She couldn't continue like this. Hurting, afraid, sad.

First, she had to clean herself up. Drawing a deep breath against her misery, she stood, hid the wrapped glass shard in her pocket, then tugged on her boots and left to locate a public restroom where she could clean up. She had cash, so she'd try to eat. She'd drink coffee, lots of coffee. Then she'd decide.

Outside the air was warm and lovely, bright as oranges against the inside of her lungs. Mid November and Indian Summer had come to visit the Big Apple, and the leaves in Central Park were waving banners of gold and orange. People strolled casually, sporting summer clothes that belied the season. Shops displayed Halloween costumes and decorations. Children played and laughed, while parents smiled and took in the wonder of being alive. New York smelled like it always did, and that felt good, consistent, eternal. It was a beautiful world. She had to help save it.

Looking in the mirror at a diner's restroom, she observed her own gold flecked hazel eyes. Pulling her hair back tight into a ponytail, more of the brown hair showed than her silly hair color. It had been a rough few months, and she had let herself go. The last time she colored her hair was weeks before Gracie showed up at Ocracoke. Esther looked more like Gracie than she realized, but it made her smile. She was a twin, part of two, and had always loved her sister. How far she had gone to hurt Gracie at Lucifer's demand, tormented and tore at her heart.

A sadness pulled heavy at her and she could hardly walk all the way back to her cubby with the gargoyles. More than once a passerby asked if she was okay. She smiled and brushed them off. She needed the safety of ICe's cubby. She had free will. She had a plan. She just had to rest a bit before she acted upon it. Just a few hours. A little sleep. That's all. A little sleep and a lot of courage, and Esther could change everything.

23

eaving Gracie behind wasn't quite as difficult as it had been in the past. Cole witnessed her strength and abilities to run the camp, he'd become her lover, and he'd found his heart for the first time ever. It was hiding in his loneliness, just barely keeping him alive until she tapped into the power. He was confident she'd be fine without him, yet a little afraid she no longer needed him. Whether that was a good or bad thing, only time would tell.

As he stepped through the portal in New York City, he chose to feel confident and sure of things back in Ocracoke. There were concerns to consider right where he was. Would Nunzio follow through, or would Cole lose a huge number of Free-Winged to ego, street politics, and power plays? Worse yet, would Nunzio's cronies end up becoming Lucifer's demons? Surely, a fate worse than death.

He arrived a few hours early, choosing to spend some time alone in Central Park, but it didn't look like that was going to happen. The day was so beautiful there were people everywhere, not a park bench empty. Didn't people work? It wasn't a weekend. It was a Thursday afternoon.

Trying not to be annoyed, he walked deeper along the paved path, seeking a little solitude. The pressure to succeed made his fingers twitch and his mind race. He felt like the quarterback, fourth quarter, and well past the two-minute warning. It was all up to him. If he threw the pass correctly, accurately, perfectly, he could be the hero. If not?

He needed a few moments to settle his thoughts and turn hope into faith. A loner by nature, Cole wanted so much for his life to change. Kicking a soccer ball back to a gaggle of playing kids, he wondered at the shift Gracie had brought him. She was their leader, their salvation, their path to victory. Remembering the handicapped little girl he almost refused to acclimate, he could do nothing but smile. What a journey his heart and soul had taken.

Recalling that dilemma and his unfounded concerns, he realized there were two different words to correctly describe a Nephilim's Acclimation. There was the word acclimate, which basically means to adjust or become accustomed to something new. However, there was also the word acclimation, which is an act, a liturgy, a chant, kind of like a celebration. It's an announcement expressing acceptance, loud, with shouts and excitement. Of all the Nephilim he knew, no one held that truth more than Gracie. From the moment of her awakening, six massive wings spread wide, she was the embodiment of an Acclimation. She stood as the true representative of what they all should be.

He sat on a stone wall and looked up at the glowing tree above him. The blue sky fluttered through orange leaves, teasing him, creating a kaleidoscope of color and light. Closing his eyes, he listened to the sound of the leaves, the shouting kids, the calling parents. They deserved to live. They were God's people, given free will and real life. Nothing to hide, simple human existence. In the past a sensation of envy would have crept into his heart, slipped and slid over the things he had to hide. His angel fire, his ability to see portals, his need to hide the fact that something was different about him. Was it Gracie, or the current situation that had changed that envy into an eager commitment to protect the human race? It wasn't their fault the world was in so much danger. It wasn't completely the fault of his own race, either. It had always been so easy to blame

God, or the devil, or someone, anyone, else. Things get out of balance. It happens after so many centuries. Granted, the Tribunal system had a lot to do with it this time, and the Nephilim afraid to acclimate their young were responsible for the Free-Winged issue. Cole found little desire to blame the orphanage system. It had given so many a happy, healthy, positive childhood. Things didn't get ugly until after Acclimation, and only for a few. Being one of those few, he'd learned to let that go and move ahead for the cause.

Demons lurked everywhere in the park. Slithering behind trees, walking among the crowd of unseeing humans, even looking directly at Cole and other Nephilim walking briskly past. They were docile, so Cole choose to ignore them. To breath in the autumn air and enjoy the peacefulness. Time moved like warm water, slowly and with a soothing effect. He was as ready as he would ever be.

Glancing at his watch, he headed back to the portal to await his assistant. This would be Terry Fennimore's first test—to get though the correct portal and meet Cole on time. He'd walked him into the strange plane then right up to the exact New York portal several times. The alternate plane was terribly disorienting, but he was hopeful the man could do it. Now he'd know.

One minute late. Two. Three. Cole began to pace. The sun was setting and he wanted to connect with McGuire's techie no later than eight. It was ten minutes after seven before a rattled retired High Black Tribunal Judge stepped onto East 106th Street.

"You okay?" Cole asked, watching the man wipe sweat from his face. "Everything okay at camp?"

Fennimore's head shook. "Trouble with the demons."

"What kind of trouble?" Cole fought the urge to run back to help.

"One Nephilim wounded, two demons dead as doornails." Fennimore looked around, obviously astounded to be standing in New York City, yet only steps from Ocracoke Island. "Young Miss Gracie took care of it, but things are tenuous. I'm pretty sure the altercation was instigated by Tobias, but he swears not."

"This is bad."

The old man nodded. "I stuck around to see if she might need assistance, but she's got this."

"What did she decide?" Cole asked as they headed toward East Flatbush and their techie contact.

"She decided to segregate the demons from the Nephilim. Needless to say, Tobias is fuming over the decision, but the camp vote was unanimously in her favor. Especially after several of those present, including Gracie, announced that they could communicate with the demons, and the creatures were willing to comply with the new rules."

"Segregate? How?"

"You'll see when we get back. So, now what?"

"Now we do what we came here to do."

They walked several blocks to the correct address and Cole looked around. They were early, but the neighborhood seemed kind of dead. Unnaturally quiet. Clouds had gathered and wind pushed dead leaves and loose trash around in loops. Darkness crept out from the alleys and dark corners. Stepping into the door, he located the correct apartment and buzzed. A second door opened and he climbed the steps, listening to Fennimore's footfalls right behind him. Something didn't seem right. He checked for the pistol he'd tucked under his jacket. It was there, ready for trouble. The door of the top floor apartment was open and he cautiously stepped inside, raising a hand for Fennimore to hold back.

"Come on in, Mr. Masters. Mr. Fennimore is welcome, too." The voice was female and elderly, confusing Cole even more. How did she know their names? Even McGuire had no clue Fennimore was coming.

"Yeah, okay. Who are you? And how do you—"

"Sit down, have a beer. Relax."

"No." Cole glared into the old woman's face.

"Jeeze, relax. Like you, I'm a new employee of Gregory Parkland and his fancy-dancey worldwide organization. Sit."

Cole sat on a chair but Fennimore stood, looking out the window.

"Name's Wiggie. I'm sure McGuire told you I have a thing for technology. Thanks to Parkland, I have better equipment today than I had yesterday. We're set for midnight, but I expect everyone will be early. All channels are open and ready. I just need to pull the attendees into a singular system."

Cole blinked. She had to be ninety, but her thin fingers flew across the keyboard with nimble accuracy. He leaned in to see what she was typing, but code was never in his wheelhouse so he leaned back and rubbed his eyes. A buzzer went off and he listened as people trod up the steps. Wiggie was right, they all showed up early—McGuire, Nunzio, and the illusive Petie and Freeze, both men of girth and strength, not to mention, annoyed expressions. They did the questioning and Cole sat for his interrogation.

"What do we get if we help you?" Freeze asked, or maybe it was Petie. He couldn't tell, they looked so much alike.

"You get to go on living."

"That a threat?" the other said with a snort.

"Nope, a fact. Nunzio, man, I thought we were past this shit."

Nunzio grinned, his teeth rotted and black but his expression that of sheer pleasure. "What can I say, Masters? I tried to convince them, now it's your turn."

Cole shook his head. "To hell with this. Leave, go, help, don't help, I don't give a damn anymore."

Agitated, Nunzio stepped between Cole and his buddies. "Hey, hey. We're making a lot of money. Right, Cole? Like, how much?"

"Forget it." Cole's gut knotted and he stood to glare at the three men. "I'm not buying an army. I need people who want to live, who want to help the human race, the whole planet to survive what's coming… not idiots who see this as a money-making scheme."

"What'd he call me?" Petie or Freeze blasted.

Cole leaned in, nose to nose. "I'm calling you a dead man who doesn't have the foresight to do something good with your life before it ends."

"And who's gonna kill me? You? You puny fucking freak?"

"Yoh… Freeze… you don't want to push this guy too far," Nunzio shouted.

Freeze tried to push Nunzio aside but found himself slammed against a wall.

"Hey! Hey!" Wiggie shouted but Nunzio leaned in and hissed a whisper to Freeze.

Freeze blinked, glared at Cole, then back at Nunzio. "Him? Nah. He ain't got nothing special about him. Look, he's a fucking waste of air."

"No man," Nunzio gripped Freeze's arm, holding him away from Cole. "You saw Bob and Moe's burns. He's the guy. Him."

"Him?"

"Yeah." Nunzio drew a sigh of relief. "Now, are we here to get our money and find out where and when we go to fight… or not?"

Freeze and Petie looked to each other. Shaggy brows and twitching black beards rose and fell and rose again, a whole conversation without words. Finally, Petie shrugged. "Fine. Now, how much we talking?"

"I said… no money." Cole spoke calmly, then sat on Wiggie's sofa. "I am not here to buy fighters, I'm here for loyal, committed warriors."

"Be surprised how loyal and committed me and my people can be for the right amount of cash." Nunzio gave a grunt.

Cole huffed, watched McGuire, sitting quietly in the corner, allowing Cole to figure his own way out of this mess. The answer was simple. He'd purposely left the loaded backpack behind. He was going against direct orders, but suspected that hired guns simply wouldn't be counted. After all, it was all about the vow. He felt strongly that he was on the right track. Bringing several thousand skeptics and un-vowed soldiers was not what the Father was expecting. If Lucifer's warriors were committed to him, then the Nephilim's warriors would have to be committed to the cause.

Freeze turned to leave but Nunzio called him back. "Hey, we just got off on the wrong foot, that's all. Let's get back to what's important. We need money and you need fighters. Right?"

"Wrong. I need warriors who believe in what we're doing, not fighters who believe in nothing but themselves."

Nunzio drew in a long breath and shouted his response. "Look at you! You sure don't look like you've missed any meals, Masters. You got an education. You got a good life. We got nothing and we need… we want… money to do what you want us to do!"

A vibration began in Cole's chest and he sat straighter. "You're right. Some Nephilim have had great advantages, some have had none. I understand. I've met Free-Winged before, worked closely with the gargoyles. It's not fair but it's life. Tell me something, are you willing to earn the money?"

"You mean fight first, maybe even die, then maybe get paid? Nope."

"Do you want to live, Nunzio?"

"Quit asking me that!"

"Then give me a fucking answer!" Cole bellowed.

The trio blinked, then leaned in and spoke quietly in a huddle. Finally, Nunzio turned and faced Cole. "If you got answers, we might be interested. See… shit's happening all around us that we can't figure out. Those black creatures only we see? They can kill us… did you know that?"

And so, it began. Nunzio, Petie, Freeze, McGuire, Wiggie, and even Fennimore asked question after question and Cole answered. Surprisingly, his knowledge was broad and satisfying to the growing concerns of the Nephilim in front of him. It took nearly two hours, and with no reasonable explanation Cole could identify, six vows for the cause were collected, and six shocking soul swords were generated—a bit of a safety hazard where Nunzio and his minions were concerned. A major shift had occurred. They were not only committed to stand and be counted, but hopeful that after their success, a new, better life could be created for the Free-Winged.

~*~

His body tingled and his brain buzzed constantly after the generated swords appeared. Midnight had arrived and it should have been easy from there. It looked like the recruiting was about to go smoothly. McGuire had already gained commitment from her gargoyles, one and all, but just as Wiggie was tuning in to the group video with more than thirty Free-Winged already waiting, the coming storm wracked the entire building. Outside the window, all of Flatbush was whipped into tiny tornados of dead leaves, rain, and wind. Lightning and thunder rumbled and rolled around and around, intensifying with each turn. Then everything went dark. Every light in Cole's view went pitch black. The only brightness came from repeated lightning strikes.

"What the hell!" Wiggie yelped as her screens went dead and something sparked then smoked behind one monitor.

Cole and Fennimore pulled all the plugs they could find while McGuire smothered the sparks and tiny fire.

"Now what?" Wiggie groaned in the darkness.

McGuire called, "Masters, where are you?"

"Here." He reached out an arm but got a handful of Wiggie's wiry grey hair. "Ah, sorry… I'm behind Wiggie."

"Okay, my question… Nunzio, you and the others still here?"

"Yeah," they said in unison.

"Okay. Masters, I think we got what we needed here. You've gained vows from the leadership. We can talk all to our people and bring them into the fold. Can you come back and make these swords?"

Cole grinned, ridiculously confident in his answer. "No need. You say what I said, feel their commitment, ask for their vow, and the soul swords will appear."

"Even over the internet?" Wiggie asked.

"Yes."

"You sure?"

"Positive," Cole sighed in the dark. After all, if it worked for him and he wasn't even trying, it would work for them, even over the damn internet. Hope, after all, had turned into faith and he knew, without a doubt the problem was solved.

"Good, cool, now… how much time we got?" That was either Freeze or Petie.

"Not a lot. Less than a week, I'm guessing."

Silence, he assumed heads were nodding but couldn't be sure.

"And, who's gonna lead us into that Counting place you talked about?"

"That would be me. Terry Fennimore."

"You the tall black dude?" asked one of Nunzio's minions.

"Yeah."

The storm settled as suddenly as it came, then dissolved to a light but persistent rain. The lights flickered on and there was a scramble to get all the computer plugs back into appropriate outlets. Within seconds monitors glimmered then brightened and Wiggie gave a sigh of relief.

Cole looked around the room. "Wiggie's your information source. I'll be sending her all the instructions about when and where to meet. Terry will bring you through and take you where you'll need to stand."

"What about these… things?" Nunzio raised his sword and everyone jumped away.

"I wish I had time to teach you how to use them, but the most important thing about that soul sword is that it knows you. Trust it. If a demon attacks, use it. Otherwise, keep it hidden from the humans or you may find yourself in jail. Trust me, we have no time for jail."

All heads nodded. There was nothing else to say, nothing else to do. Cole nodded to Terry and they headed out the door while Wiggie gathered the men around the monitor to start their meeting. He wondered if he should stay to make sure everything went well, but chose to prove his confidence in them and head back to camp and Gracie.

Cole pulled his collar up against the fresh, clean chill in the air. Fennimore hugged himself and pushed rain from his eyes.

"Wait. Masters, I need your help with something." McGuire masterfully hid her sword in the fabric of her long skirt. Watching her come closer Cole realized there was far more to Carla Shreveport than he originally imagined.

"Were you really Free-Winged?" he asked as she stepped close.

"Good eye. I just took the wrong vow. Then I figured I could help with the poor, homeless Free-Winged. I never knew this was possible. Thank you, Cole. Thank you with all my heart."

"Sure," he said with a grin. "What do you need?"

She looked at Fennimore. "No need for you to come. I'll only need your boss for a little while." She turned to Cole after the tall man walked off. "There's something you have to see."

The carnie performances would begin before Cole got back if he didn't leave now. He wanted to see those performances. He wanted to be with Gracie as much as possible before the Counting. He wanted nothing more than to get back to Ocracoke. Looking into McGuire's face, he also knew her need was something he couldn't ignore.

24

"Well, hell," Esther whispered weakly as she slowly awakened. Opening her eyes just a crack, she glanced down at her pristine-white bandaged wrists and let the tears fall. She wasn't in ICe's cubby where she'd sliced her wrists. This place was brightly lit, and she was laying on clean white sheets and fairly comfortable. The only problem was, she wasn't dead. She heard low talking, quiet footsteps, like whoever was approaching didn't want to disturb her, so Esther decided to play along. Eyes closed, she listened for clues.

"When did she do this?" A man's voice. Fairly recognizable. Who was that?

"About three hours before I met you at Wiggie's."

That voice she knew, and shame creeped into her heart. McGuire.

The man leaned close and she smelled his aftershave. His finger tenderly pushed hair from her brow. "How the hell did you get her taken care of?"

"That part was easy. There's a free clinic a few blocks away. Old

Mamma and I caught her in the act, and they cleaned the wounds and stitched her up before she'd lost too much blood."

Ah, now she remembered.

The man groaned. "How did you get her out?"

"Yeah, that wasn't so easy. The doc had already called the cops to take her for observation. A threat to herself, you know. Custer and Joe Grissom created a diversion. Using cat blood, Joe covered Custer's wrists and ran in screaming for help. That's when I grabbed this girl and ran. I don't know why I did it. Maybe she should be in a looney bin but I just couldn't leave her at their mercy. She's just a poor troubled human."

"No, she's not. You did the right thing. Wake up, Esther. I can see your eyeballs moving. You're not sleeping."

"What if I want to be?" She looked into Cole's face. Ah, she knew she recognized that voice. "What if I want to be dead?"

"Then it's the wrong thing to want. Come on, can you sit up?" He leaned forward and held out a bottle of water for her to sip.

Glancing around she realized why the place felt so different. She was in McGuire's space, but everything in there was covered with clean new sheets, making it look sterile and hygienic. Several big flashlights were on and aimed at the ugly ceiling, unbearably brightening the space.

"What do you want?" she said with a groan, then let him help her sit and settle into a comfortable white cocoon.

He gave McGuire a glance and she left them alone. "Are you comfortable?"

"Yeah."

"Good, now explain yourself."

She glared, but tears seeped through belligerence, giving her away to the one person she never wanted to be exposed to. All she wanted was to stop Lucifer's control over her and her Nephilim. To make things safer for Gracie and her people. How did it come to this? Being a burden to McGuire? Making explanations to Cole Masters? Was this hell? "What do you care?"

"Me?" He shrugged and settled closer to her on the floor. "I don't, really. But your sister will go nuts when she hears about this. Are you crazy? Trying to kill yourself?"

"What do you know?" She turned away.

"More than you think. I tried the same thing at least three times. Never worked. Someone always saved me."

Slowly she turned to look into his sincere eyes. "Why? Why would you try?"

He snorted and leaned back on his arms.

"I mean, you have everything! Amazing powers, happiness… my sister."

"Didn't always have that stuff, Esther. Tell me why the hell you would do such a thing? At a time when we need every Nephilim we can pull together for the Counting?"

"Oh, maybe you didn't realize this, but I'm blood bound to Lucifer." She glared.

He glared back. "So? You have free will, woman. You can change your damn mind and I'm pretty sure you already have. Sending ICe to protect Gracie showed your real colors. Seriously, why try to kill yourself?"

An ache soared through her chest and she gripped the sheets, making the stitches in her wrists pull and hurt. Glancing into his face she wondered, did he really not know? Was that possible? "Look at me, Cole," she whispered.

"I see a scared girl who can be a powerful warrior if she chooses."

"No, you don't. I'm not Nephilim. Only human… maybe not even that. I'm an empty shell stuck in a terrible mistake I made when I was fourteen. So yes, maybe I can change my mind, use my free will to walk away from the devil… but … but he…"

She collapsed into a mountain of shaking sobs and he gathered her into his arms. "What did he do, Esther?"

Nope, can't talk to him, not Cole Masters, her sister's lover, not while crying like a baby in his arms. She pulled away, cleared her throat but let the tears continue to soak her face. One deep breath, then another, and finally she could do it. Make the ultimate confession. But not eye to eye. She couldn't bear to look him in the eyes while explaining her failure. Her massive, stupid, terrible failure. This, she had to approach carefully, if only to protect her fragile emotions.

"Tell me about Gracie's Acclimation."

"What? You know that's personal, Esther."

"I know nothing, Cole. I need answers before I can tell you what happened to me. I need to understand."

"Okay." He sat up, cross-legged and thought a moment then began. "Usually Acclimations are done privately, between a guide and the acclimate, but since Gracie and her three friends were the last to acclimate… anywhere… all the others were dead, murdered by the demons… uh… I felt it might be safer to acclimate her with witnesses who could help protect her."

"You sound defensive about that."

"Maybe I am, a little. Not protocol, you know." He examined his hands like he might find approval in the lines of his palms.

"I know nothing about protocol. What you did sounds rational to me. I was aware of those murders, you know… many thousands of them… I watched Lucifer give the orders. What the hell was wrong with me?" More tears. Good Lord, when does a body run out of tears?

"Maybe you were under a kind of spell or something."

Her head shook. "Gracie's Acclimation."

"Yes, right. I told her the story of our race, our past, our responsibilities. I explained that we are not human—she had some trouble with that, actually laughed at me for a minute. Then, as midnight came, she changed, shifted… even the way she looked slightly altered. Her face was radiant, magic flowed from her center, a sparkle, a brilliance that amazed me each time I guided an Acclimation, but with Gracie, I swear, it was shocking, powerful… extraordinary. When her wings emerged it was painful, but she was a real trooper, focused on what was going on inside her soul and allowed her truth to shine. Then she did something astounding. Her six magnificent wings unfurled and with gentle movement they lifted her from the ground and all the way to ceiling. Esther, it was something to see. When she lowered to the floor, I asked for her vow, and her glistening soul sword was generated. Gracie vowed to serve God and the human race." He fell silent, eyes closed, recalling the incredible experience. "Then we came to Ocracoke to do what we had to do."

Esther was quiet until he opened his eyes to take her in. The man gulped hard, seeming to suddenly understand why she would ask about Gracie's Acclimation. He looked right at her chest where there was no light. No Nephilim energy. No brilliance. She was sure he understood that it wasn't that she hadn't made a vow, it was that she never had the chance to.

"My God, Esther… How could this have happened? How the hell did he take away your Pure Nephilim? No Celestial being has the power to do that! How—"

"He didn't. I think… no, I'm pretty sure… I gave it to him."

Cole blinked.

"He kept telling me how painful and damaging the wounds would be, how much it would hurt. That he could take care of all that. Eliminate the fear and the agony so… so I let him. He put me to sleep, and when I woke, I was perfect, no pain, no damage, no stitches or scars. I felt great, but it wasn't until recently that I put two and two together and discovered that I didn't have what other Nephilim have. ICe pointed it out. He kept saying that something was missing. I didn't believe him because I felt powerful and strong, but Lucifer could do that, cast spells that made me feel like I was as good as, or better than, any Nephilim. Better in fact because of my vow to him.

"When I searched for what was really taken from me, I found her. Cole," she sobbed again. "He… he has her trapped… she's in a big ass bell jar in his lab… the lab where he makes his demons from poor misguided

Nephilim who give him a blood vow. Did you know the demons were actually Nephilim? Their wings torn off and bodies mutilated and remade into monsters?"

"Yes."

"How? How did you know?"

"One of Gracie's friends, one of my acclimates, ran off before making his vow and turned up later, part of a demon. That kid actually tore himself free of the monster he was connected to… he lived a few hours but no more. Wally, his name was Wally Dean. I failed him."

"You at least tried. What have I done?" Esther pushed hair from her wet face and thought. "Wait… what do you mean he tore away and lived a few hours? How can that be?"

"No clue. The burns and physical damage from tearing free killed him, I guess."

"But… how could he, part of a multiple demon, retain his individuality? Decide to free himself? Have his own thoughts?"

Cole sighed. "Maybe Lucifer didn't do a perfect job with that one. Maybe he didn't do perfect jobs on a lot of them. Gracie can hear them talk to her. Many of the Nephilim in camp have that gift and the demons are talking sense, making decisions, communicating. For all I know, they're hanging around the camp to be close to other Nephilim."

Esther endured a flood of misunderstood memories. How many times had the demons guided her away from danger or led her to the truth? The demons who brought Cia to her looked guilty, but probably weren't even the ones who burned her in the first place. They looked like they cared about Cia because she cared about her. Esther couldn't hear them, but they surely knew what they were doing. Then her heart sank.

"Even if Lucifer knows he has a few flawed demons, he has so many… and they are fully faithful to him. Controlled by his desires. Way, way too many, Cole. It's hopeless."

The following silence was deafening. Finally, Cole spoke, but with a spark in his eye that wasn't there before. "Wait. No, not hopeless. You said you gave your Pure Nephilim to Lucifer, even though you weren't aware of it, right?"

Her head nodded and she sniffled.

"Well, all you need to do is use your free will to take it back. You can change your mind and choose a different path, Esther. That's what free will is. The devil has no real control over you. He can't keep anything you choose to take back. He is NOT in control!"

His excitement spread like flooding water into her and Esther blinked. "How, when, what do I do?"

"It's about faith and commitment. I can't regenerate your soul sword for you because you're not complete, but I will ask you now... Esther Caine, are you here for God, or is God here for you?"

"For God. Definitely."

"It's not just words to escape punishment, is it?"

"No." Her heart beat strong and loud in her ears. "I want to stand with you and Gracie for the Counting, and I want to be complete when I do it."

Suddenly she feared her brain would burst, so frantic were the ideas floating and exploding there. "How," she whispered, wiping her face with the clean white sheet covering her. "How am I going to do this?"

"Keep the commitment you just made, Esther. Hold it holy, close and tight. And… trust the demons, the ones that follow you around. They want to help. Talk to them, they do understand. They'll help."

"What if they run and tell him?"

"Just be careful. Time things carefully. Trust in your soul. I know you can to this. It will be made clear to you when you need to take action."

She nodded, wanting to thank him for his help and guidance, wanting to beg him to bring Gracie to her, or take her to the camp with him. Without her Pure Nephilim half, there was no point. She had work to do. For the first time in her eighteen years of life, Esther knew what she wanted.

~*~

The sun was setting as the Harley roared its way into camp only to find it quiet, except for the center where there was a huge performance tent and cheers rising to the sky. Michael revved the engine and rode all the way up to the big top, zigging and zagging around tents and campers, feeling like a twenty-year-old and reveling in the vibrations zooming through his body. Before he could climb off and walk inside, Gracie strolled up with Dawn and gave him one of those you should know better looks.

She finally smiled and gave him a hug, then Dawn, glowing and a little rounder than usual, offered her wide-open arms, too. He squeezed her, feeling the definite swelling at her belly. He knew better than to offer congratulations; that could only get a man into trouble. Best to wait for the announcement.

"You look sexy as hell wearing that Harley, Headmaster Allerton," she whispered in his ear and his face reddened.

"So, what's happening here? Where's Tobias? Where's Cole? And most importantly, where's my son?" The look on their faces made his heart thump. "Ben's okay, right?"

Gracie took him aside and spoke clearly. "We have to talk. Let's go to the house."

She really was in control like Parkland said. However, he didn't intend to be handled. "Just tell me."

"Ben's resting. The visions are really causing him trouble. The seizures were bad, but Garta seems to have them under control. He just doesn't sleep at all, so she gave him something to help him rest." Her hand squeezed his. "Mr. Allerton… Michael… we're all doing everything we can for him. He seemed to be better this morning, and he should be even better after he sleeps a little more."

Michael shifted from foot to foot, unsure of the lay of the land in this camp. He cleared his throat. "Gracie… are you telling me I can't see my son?"

"No! I'm trying to take you to the house to be with him."

Finally, his heart felt like it might beat regularly again. He swung a leg over the bike and grinned. "Hop on."

Settling the proffered helmet on her head she wrapped arms around his middle and asked, "Where did you get this thing?"

"I bought it," the engine revved and he shouted, "from Cole."

~*~

Tobias noticed Michael Allerton's return and thrilled that everything had come together just as he'd intended. Allerton would feel no leadership control, because he was worried for his son. That's the inherent job of an Orphanage System Headmaster, to worry for the poor children. Tobias grinned wider. Cole Masters' computer regime down at the house would end when the threat was over. Tobias worried little over the other ancients in camp, even Rashee. Nothing was getting in his way this time. Not even common courtesy. Let them think he was mad. They would all adore and worship him when he proclaimed dominance over evil forever. Now that would be an eternity he could live with. One he controlled simply by being its true and real savior. He had laid low for far too long. The time had come.

All around him spun a kind of chaos only a real showman understood. Nothing had started on time, and that was by design. After all, without assigning the performance matchups until that very morning, there were a thousand negotiations to take place. Who would have the right ring? Who would perform in the left? Which troupe would perform first? Or should they perform at the same time? Who would be the judge? That one gave Tobias a chuckle. After polling the audience, he, of course, would make the final decisions, but only after he'd defeated the devil and returned to camp. This was going to be a very long night, and he was thrilled about that.

Early that morning he'd sat in the woods alone and let his mind wander. It wasn't the mind he'd started with many thousands of years ago. Back when he first walked with Raphael, the world was new and lovely and he was a vibrant young man. At least, it was new for the fourth or fifth time. Tobias never worried for the actual facts, only that with each beginning, he'd have another chance to prove himself to the Father who made him an ancient. Maybe earn his way to an end, but not yet, not back then, not even now. Not even with so much danger all around.

Ah, but he lived for the Countings, each and every time. The past few centuries though had shown him something different. In the beginning, he was a brash and impulsive man, a radical leader, a true believer. Over time it all became rote, the same again, and again. Somewhere between the last ancient he made out of anger, and the one he made out of love, he became more and more calculated, realizing that it was far easier to appear as the Nephilim expected him, than to be the man he really was. He cultivated the illusion of kindness, but only with sure rewards.

He encouraged his people. Beauty Low, who should never hold the high position of Ring Mistress, but had the mystical power to help him create protective veils and specific illusions. Ballister Green was given a lot of control over the camp. Green had been able to generate soul swords since his Acclimation, and Tobias knew how valuable that was. It also helped the Emmaus crew believe they had something very special. Not true. Tobias in his very long life knew full well that any Nephilim could generate, or re-generate soul swords. He just convinced the other ancients and rogue warrior shows that it was the gift of only a few. Rashee never contradicted him. Such a stupid woman.

Unknown to her, Tobias had turned Garta into an ancient out of pure spite. Her healing powers were only revealed after her change. It took a lot to recruit and keep her close to him. She was his in more ways than one. He needed a healer. He'd built his show that way, only accepting qualities he needed and subtly, quietly, eliminating the Nephilim useless to his plan. He had no regrets. Murder was not outside his capacity, as long as he would save the world in the end.

And now, everything was in place. The show must go on, so when the time was right, he'd give Beauty Low a nod and step back to watch. At least until exactly 3:15 the coming morning, when he would slip away and meet with Lucifer. Tobias smiled and closed his eyes, wondering what name the world would give him. Redeemer? Savior? Earthly God? Those would all be just fine with him.

25

"My apologies, Esther," McGuire said, looking down at her own hands.

Esther had asked to talk to her, but the last thing she expected was an apology. Esther should be making the apologies. "Why?"

"I didn't know… never realized you were Nephilim."

"How could you know?" Tears threatened and Esther cleared her throat. "Listen, you've already done so much for me, but I need a little more help."

McGuire sat on the floor and waited. And waited.

"Um… okay. I know ICe was your healer here with the gargoyles, but I sent him to Ocracoke to watch over the camp, well, more specifically, my sister."

"Yes."

"So, I kinda need you to find another healer. One who can help me gain my strength and get out of here like, now."

McGuire raised one eyebrow. "You think I haven't thought of that already? Nunzio has a good healer, a woman named Frey. She's on her way, but might not get here for a few hours."

"I don't have a few hours. Lu… someone will be looking for me and I have to get back." She tried to stand but almost folded in half. Thank goodness for McGuire's strong arms.

"Okay, okay. Listen, we do have a minor healer here." The woman grunted as she lowered Esther back to the sheets. "She's already worked on you. She almost stopped the bleeding before we got you to the hospital."

"Old Mamma?" Esther thought it was a dream, being jostled down the street, that sensation of magic weaving lightly around her wounds.

McGuire nodded as she stood and called out for the old woman. "Nothing says it won't take Old Mamma a few hours to get here, too," she teased.

"I thought she might be a healer. Did she help ICe?" Esther's heart thudded. "Did I do the wrong thing? Sending ICe away?"

"All Old Mamma did was befriend Isaac and give him confidence. She helped him hone some of his powers. There's a lot more there than any of us know. Ah, here she is. Old Mamma, this girl has asked for energy, strength to leave and get on with things."

The woman looked a hundred years old, but Esther knew from her experiences with the gargoyles that age creeps up faster among the homeless, and it creeps up in more ways than just appearance. McGuire called Old Mamma a minor healer. Did that mean her powers were fading like her vitality and strength?

"Can you really help me?"

The woman must have been a beauty in her day. Her cheekbones were high and sharp, her eyes, blue as a spring sky. Though her hands were gnarled and swollen, they moved with a kind of grace and elegance. She eyed Esther then grunted.

"Can try. You shut up, lay still. Eyes closed."

"I can—"

"I said shut up!"

Esther shut up and closed her eyes, imagining ways to repay the gargoyles for all their help. Then she couldn't imagine anything but floating on a deep blue sea. Her wrists bobbed up and down, and the warm water wafted over her like silk. Above hung a sky too blue to look at, so even in her imagining, Esther's eyes closed. Then it started, a throbbing deep under her flesh that started at the tips of her fingers and toes and slowly, with agonizing rhythm, pulsed inward, inward, until it gripped her heart like a bolt of electricity. For what felt like an eternity, her body arched and vibrated, then calmed. Her flesh was heated, her skin felt sunburned, her mind raced over everything she had to do. She needed to devise the perfect lie—one the devil would believe. She needed an infallible plan to reunite with her Pure Nephilim. And she needed the help of Lucifer's demons. That was a lot, and she sensed there wasn't a lot of time. Opening her eyes, she asked, "How long have I been out?"

"Out?" Old Mamma grunted to her feet and hobbled away. "You ain't been out at all. Now go do what you gotta do."

Esther looked to McGuire.

"You heard the lady."

Esther tugged her bandages down. The stitches looked fresh, but the wounds did not look severe at all. That would work. Her heart was beating at a strong rate, and her body wanted to move. None of Lucifer's illusions had ever felt like this. This was coming from inside herself. "How can I ever thank you?"

"Do what you can and get your Nephilim back. Cole says we need it for the Counting."

He must have told the whole story, and Esther was grateful. Knowing she had allies among the campers in Ocracoke and the New York Free-Winged gargoyles, made her feel even stronger.

~*~

Michael expected the absolute worst—his son sleeping off a deadly illness no one could save him from. As he turned the corner and stepped into the bedroom, he paused, mouth opened and head tilted. Ben wasn't sleeping. He wasn't even in bed. He was sitting on the floor with Kevin and a big oaf of a man Michael had never seen before. They were laughing and talking and completely engaged in being young and alive.

"Ah," he said then cleared his throat. "Anyone know where the sickly boy is. Ben's his name."

"Dad!" Ben stood and reached Michael in two long strides. The embrace relieved some of the fear in Michael's heart. He pushed Ben to arm's-length and looked him over from head to toe. This was not the boy he'd sent to camp. This was a man. One who'd obviously solved his own life-threatening dilemma.

"Tell me everything," Michael said, scanning across the other men in the room. He sat on the bed while the younger bucks plopped on the floor, all grins and vigor. Nope, this was not what he expected at all, and his gratitude for that moment warmed him to the soul.

"It was bad, really bad. I couldn't sleep, couldn't think… nothing worked. Garta gave me a sleeping potion, no… she's not a witch, what did she call it?"

"A draught ," Kevin corrected.

"Yeah, that crappy tea knocked me out for almost a whole day and night. Then when I woke up, it was all still there but I wanted to be with… um… Kevin and I wanted to…"

"Get some lunch," Kevin offered. "That's when we got to talking with ICe."

"Ice?" Michael was getting a little confused.

"Oh, yeah. Dad, this is ICe. Big I, big C, little e. ICe, this is my father, Michael."

Shyly the big man looked up, but didn't take Michael's offered hand.

"Hello, ICe. Nice to meet you."

Looking down again, the oaf shrugged.

"Anyway, Kevin and I were talking about how to get some control back. Like when you and I worked with the swords? We've been doing that a bit, but that's not right. See Dad, that's not focus... it's distraction."

Kevin jumped in. "So, we were wracking our brains trying to figure out what to do next. See, ICe is a healer and he kind of sticks close so when things get ugly for Ben, he just puts a hand on his arm and, well, voila, all better."

"Really?" Michael looked at ICe with new eyes. One would think after years of working with young Nephilim, he'd know better than to judge so quickly. "Thank you, ICe."

"Yeah," came quietly from the big man's mouth.

"He's more than a healer," Ben took over again, "he's a genius! See, we tried all kind of ideas, just tossing out anything that might help me focus. Stuff like video games... did you see that equipment Parkland sent for Cole? There have got to be some amazing games on that equipment! Then we thought about trying to ignore the visions, you know, pretending it's all my imagination. I didn't think that was going to work. We talked about maybe marijuana, but no one has any here in camp. Then we talked about stronger stuff, again, not easy to get."

Michael's brows knotted and Ben sat straighter.

"Oh, don't worry. It was just talk, things we thought might help. We even thought maybe I should take up an instrument, learn to play the tuba or something... or maybe something cooler. Something, anything that would take all my attention, but again, that would only be a distraction.

"Then ICe said the simplest thing in the world. He said, 'free will, Ben. Think about what you want to think about.' Isn't that right, ICe?"

"Yeah, I said that!" excitement brightened his face and made his large hands twitch. "I figured... he can pick what to focus on. Nobody said he has to pay attention—"

"To everything at once! You are a genius, young man!" Michael wanted to drop to the floor with them and celebrate, but looking into Ben's eyes he struggled not to ask the next question.

"Yes Dad, it's working. And no, I have no idea if it's the right thing do, but I need to choose, one at a time, or these visions will kill me."

Michael sighed.

"Trust me, I can tell you a dozen things going on right now. They're all there, playing out like a wall of television screens inside my head. But I'm consciously choosing which one to focus on at any given moment."

Michael remained silent.

"It's working. I'll get better at it. Parkland offered to help me when he gets here. Offered me a job when this is all over, too."

"Ah," Michael raised his hands. "An employed son. Every father's dream come true."

"I know, I know. You're worried that I have this gift because I'm supposed to warn the right people at the right time. I think so, too… but until I master it, this is the best I can do."

Ben looked concerned and Michael laughed. "You idiot. All I'm thinking is how amazing you are. You… and ICe, figured it out. You're going to survive this gift, Ben."

But, Michael thought silently, will Ben mistakenly ignore the vision warning us of real danger? Will we survive the Counting? Will any of it matter if we've failed?

"Good. I'm hungry. Cookie's made dinner, let's eat before the shows actually start." Ben stood and walked out with ICe.

Kevin shrugged. "It's been hell, Michael. I'm just grateful he feels like living again. He worries about missing important cues, but I'm trying to convince him that he'll know which things to pay attention to and which things aren't so important. We have to trust his instincts. It's the best we can ask from him."

~*~

Esther slipped through the portal, stomped into the beautiful New York penthouse Lucifer had concocted in the alternate plane, and plopped on the white sofa with a bounce. Outside the windows, a fake Manhattan twinkled in at her and she realized how familiar she was with the city—how unfamiliar Lucifer was. Crossing her fishnet covered legs at the ankles, she tapped her dirty biker boot on the pure fabric and groaned.

"Where have you been?" Lucifer growled, looking up from the Washington Post and glaring right at her.

"Long, long ass story." She sat up abruptly and glared. "You remember that congressman you told me you wanted? The guy from Alabama?"

"Stotlar. Yes, have you made contact with him?"

"You can say that. I wooed and he wowed. Took me four days to get his full attention then finally, he said he was taking me someplace special."

Lucifer set the newspaper down and stood. "And?"

"The bastard took me to his 'playroom,' if you know what I mean." She had Lucifer's full attention now, even making air-quote fingers at him. "He tied me up with wire, Luc! Wire! Can you believe it? The place was like a medieval torture chamber, he—"

"Did you get his vow? Where is he? He's a very powerful, very valuable Norema, Jophiel's great-great grandson! Tell me you got him?"

"He's a dud! I couldn't get him no matter how hard I tried… the damn guy is impotent! In this day and age where a little blue pill could—"

"You failed?" His nostrils flared.

"Failed?" Tears fell on cue. "Look at me?" she stood and tore off the bandages. "He hurt me! Left me there, tied up for more than six hours. A maid came in and cut the wires, like she was used to cleaning up his messes."

The devil tenderly held her wrists in a hand then kissed each one in turn. "My poor little dear. You tried so hard. I must reward you."

"Can you make the scars disappear?" She knew he couldn't, knew it irritated him, too.

"These are beautiful scars showing your courage and bravery, your commitment to me. You must keep them. I will put diamond bracelets on both wrists to commemorate the day, my dear."

Or will they be diamond hand cuffs, she wondered.

"I am so sorry I failed you. I just couldn't fight my way free."

"Hush now. Listen," his eyes glittered. "I have to be someplace for the next few hours. I'll be back around four at the latest."

"Four in the morning?"

"Yes. Clean yourself up, dress beautifully. I've stocked your closet with lovely things, choose whatever you like. Maybe do something with your hair, Esther."

"I know, the roots are showing," she grinned apologetically.

"Make yourself beautiful and I will take you to dinner when I return."

"Dinner? At four in the morning?"

"It all depends on where you are, my little one. It may be four in the morning here, but it will be nine on a balmy night in The City of Lights."

"Paris!" she squealed with all the counterfeit delight she could muster.

"Paris. Perfect for a celebratory dinner."

"What are we celebrating?" Her gut twisted. Did he know something she didn't? Or worse yet, did he know what she did know? Was it too late?

"We will be celebrating what I will accomplish tonight. Something that feels like the cherry on top of the sundae. Frivolous, yet oh so satisfying."

"I can't wait to hear all about it." She leapt into his arms and let him kiss her deeply. Terrified her repulsion would show, she slipped to the floor and rushed toward the bedroom. "I need to start getting myself ready!"

And poof, like a Vegas magic act, he was gone.

Her mind spun. Twenty minutes to color her hair, fifteen to shower, another twenty to dress and put on some makeup. That gave her all the time she needed to set her real work in motion.

She walked through the penthouse front door and down the hall, directly toward his lab. First there were two, then six, then ten demons following her. She spun around and eyed them as well as possible, considering none of their heads were in the same place or at the same level. After a long, deep breath she spoke. "Okay guys, I'm told you can understand me even though I can't hear your responses. So, we'll figure something out, okay?"

Weirdly, heads nodded. Some from side to side, some up and down. The view was almost comical, if they weren't so hideous and dripping with deadly black ooze.

"Are you happy with the blood vow you made?"

Heads shook, some violently.

"Are there more of you that are unhappy?"

Fingers pointed back down the hall and heads nodded. Some of the demons jumped up and down. Hopefully that meant what she was hoping, so she continued.

"I need your help."

One demon approached. Esther cringed but stood still as stone as it reached a long finger to tenderly touch one of the bandages at her wrist. The gauze blackened where the fingertip landed, but the demon looked up into her eyes, pointed to itself, then to her.

"Oh, good. So, we're a team, right guys… and ladies too, I guess? Now, I need to talk to the Pure Nephilim in the bell jar." Together they walked ahead. "Oh," she turned to her strange followers. "Make sure no one tells Lucifer about this."

26

ichael had recently dined in some of the best restaurants in America—Le Bernardin in New York, Melisse in Santa Monica, Quince in San Francisco, Topolobampo in Chicago, August in New Orleans. He'd eaten barbecue in Texas, Kansas, and North Carolina. Tasted specialties from the best cooks alive. He could hardly remember most of the places or food, but of the twelve cities where he recruited and dined, nothing compared to Cookie's meat loaf and mashed potatoes. Nothing made him feel so comforted and complete. After chocolate cream pie, Michael's taste buds could have sworn that everything was going to work out just fine.

Sweeter still was watching Ben and Kevin occasionally catch each other's eye. He'd done the right thing sending Ben away. It was time for the boy to be a man and learn to live as the man he was.

ICe was a conundrum, though. Kevin explained that Esther, Gracie's twin, had sent ICe to protect Gracie. That was confusing enough, since as he understood, Esther was on the bad guy's team. There'd been little protection of their fearless female leader so far from ICe, but a lot of care given to Ben. By his estimate, ICe was probably a high functioning autistic with a quickened gift of healing. His heart was in the right place, but his control of the world around him was not. The big man couldn't be in better company, though. There were several occasions, just sitting in the dining tent, when ICe could have easily lost control. Once when a folding chair crashed to the ground as people pushed their way toward the buffet and again, when the band started a rousing march with loud brass cymbals and blaring trumpets just outside the tent flap. Each time, an instant before the noise occurred, Ben settled a hand on ICe's shoulder. "Look at me, buddy," he said and instead of panicking, the big man simply took several deep breaths then grinned a silly grin.

Pride pulsed in Michael's chest. For eighteen long years he'd never revealed himself to his son, but he did have a lot to do with the kind of person Ben had become.

"I'm guessing they're really going to start the show now," Kevin announced, gulping coffee and gathering plates for the dishwashing tent. "Let's go!"

The first round of performances was supposed to begin at noon, but there we were, nine hours later and still being entertained by the various camp clowns and musicians. I was pretty sure something was way off-kilter, I just couldn't figure out what. Were the performers just not ready? That seemed impossible to me. I'd been around these performers for almost a month now, and trust me, they're always ready. Some wear their costumes or stage makeup all the time. Others broke into acrobatic moves without warning, even while walking around camp or following orders by their leaders.

Tobias was oddly calm, showing no irritation at the long delays. His brows bobbed and head nodded when he talked and even when he listened. He was constantly surrounded by bedazzled, shiny, and brightly dressed performers but showed no frustration. That should have been my first red flag, but like everyone else in the biggest big top I ever saw, we all just wanted to see the show.

Darkness had wrapped all around us and I realized that the year was quickly moving toward winter. Soon it would be Thanksgiving and my mouth watered, wondering how good Cookie's feast would be. Then my heart skipped a beat. Something deep in my gut knew the Counting was coming soon. Before I could savor turkey and gravy. Maybe before any of us could even see the shows we'd been waiting all day for.

Hundreds of white lights brightened, and me, like a silly idiot, worried briefly how I'd ever pay the electric bill. One name slid across my mind. Gregory Parkland. That's how the bills would get paid. I marveled at the energy the tent took on as lights wavered and sparkled, long cords of them waving gently on a soft breeze crawling into the tent. I could sense everyone's collective hearts beat faster.

Weeks ago, Beauty Low said, "The show is the thing!" The biggest opportunity for the rogue warriors to display their powers and learn who was the best of the best. I loved the fact that we could witness such an exhibition. The tent was a patchwork quilt telling the stories of many, many rogue warrior troupes and the gypsy lives that led us all to that moment. I already knew that the Emmaus Magic Show was spectacular. I also knew they were strong and efficient warriors. I'd fought with them. My guess was that everyone in camp was extraordinary in many ways. But to see them perform meant something more. It felt like the last hurrah, the last chance to sit back and smile and laugh, to clap and be joyous before the hard part started.

Looking around, I found myself wondering how on earth I got there. Not so long ago I wanted to go to Radcliff. I wanted a normal life with a normal job in a normal town. Laughter bubbled out and Cole turned to me. He'd just gotten back and I was finally relaxed, knowing we'd done everything we could to recruit the Free-Winged.

"What's funny?" he asked.

"Life," I said and he kissed me, full on the lips, right in front of Headmaster and Ben and everyone.

"Get a room," Ben teased.

Michael's eyes were a little less delighted and I just shrugged.

"Sorry," Cole teased. "Maybe you need a woman, Michael."

"Maybe I need to stop thinking of you all as… kids."

"That could work," I said and squeezed his hand. "Because we're not kids."

"No, you are powerful warriors. Keep reminding me, Gracie. I still remember you as a teary-eyed five-year-old looking up at me."

"I remember that, too." I remembered everything, and sometimes I wish I didn't. For years, at least until I was ten, I hated Michael Allerton, believing he'd bought me, or stolen me from my mother. I was just a kid wishing for a better life, but what better life could I have ever had? He made sure we were all educated and taken care of. That we had as much freedom as was practical under the circumstances, that we were loved, even though he never said the words "I love you," even to his own real son. It was time to change that. I leaned close and he lowered an ear to hear me over the ump-pa-pa music.

"Headmaster Allerton," I said. "Thank you. I love you for everything you did for us."

Moving away I saw tears actually slide down his cheek. He nodded. "Ditto," was all he said.

With a sigh, I looked across the ring at the entire set of bleachers filled with demons. There had to be at least two hundred of them. I hoped beyond hope that I hadn't made the wrong decision, letting them stick around camp. Letting them stay for the performances. They were respectfully apart from the Nephilim, segregated, munching popcorn and candy, eyes glued to the still empty rings. Recalling the first show I ever witnessed brought sharp memories of what happened afterward. After the beautiful performances, after the amazing Ballister Green generated soul swords for his new recruits. The noise, the sudden terror of a demon attack. The battle. The blood. The losses. And the returning of poor Wally to us, burned and ripped to shreds because he wanted out of his blood vow to the dark.

All those memories tore me in half. The demons were evil. The demons were us. The demons were harmless. The demons were dangerous. What was truth? Had I done the right thing? Ben turned to me from the bleacher bench below. I sighed. He knew what was happening at all times in many places.

"Did I do the right thing?" I nudged a chin toward the demon audience.

"Yeah. They're supposed to be here, Gracie. Later it could be bad or good but right now, it's cool."

Cole's hand tenderly rubbed my back and I leaned into his warmth.

Not a word was spoken. Esther tenderly set her palms onto the bell jar and received the heat from her Pure Nephilim's hands on the other side of the thick glass. We can do this, Esther thought. I'm just not sure how. I have an idea. Stick with me, okay?

The celestial in the bell jar turned her head suddenly, glazing across the room. Panic soared through Esther's veins. Was Lucifer back? Was he watching her? What on earth would he do to her? Stick her inside a bell jar, too? But there was no one across the room, only a large door. Stepping closer, the demons actually made squawking noises. Were they encouraging her or trying to stop her? Either way, she had to see what was behind that door.

It moved like lead through water, heavy and huge, but finally she slipped inside. There was a short hallway with a door to the right, and one to the left. Both doors had a window. Slowly she glanced into the one on the right. Bloody wings and body parts were strewn everywhere. Something moved in the far corner. Half of a Nephilim, headless and bloodied, pulled itself by broken knuckles, trying to reach the wall. In less than a heartbeat, it was still and dead.

With quick reflexes, Esther leaned back against the wall and drew in several deep breaths. How long had the poor thing been trying to escape? How long had it suffered? How could she possibly let this continue?

Worst yet, did she have the courage to look into the door across the hall?

As slow as possible, she stepped toward the door and leaned to see inside. There were bars, and a whole lot of Nephilim behind those bars. "What the hell?" Stepping inside she took in the scene. It was a really big holding cell with more prisoners than she could count. Some were playing cards, some were talking, others sleeping. There was even a couple copulating in the corner. Were there more than a hundred? Quite possibly. What to do about it loomed large and she just jumped into action.

"Listen up!" Esther shouted and all heads rose.

Comments and grunts blended with insults and gnarly sexual propositions.

"Quiet!"

One man stepped forward and leaned against the bars, a slimy grin on his face and eyes twinkling like there were a million stars inside them. "What can we do for you, pretty lady?"

"It's more about what I can do for you. Tell me, why are you locked in there?"

"We ain't locked in here. We're in a holding pattern… that's what Master called it. We're all shipping out for special training. We'll be fighting on the winning side for the war to win the entire fucking planet."

Her heart thudded. It was what she used to tell her recruits. She paced in front of the wide set of bars. "So, you think you're all going to be elite soldiers? Heading out for special training? Do you realize who told you that?"

"He's our master, so that's what we call him."

"He is Lucifer, you fool. The devil. There is no elite fighting team. Look." She pointed to the demons gathered behind her. "What do you think they are?"

The man snorted. His eyes had stopped twinkling, though. "Those are his crap crew. He sends them to clean up the messes."

"And you believed him?"

The man became more agitated. "Why the hell would he lie?"

"He's the fucking devil, you fool! Look closer at this demon!" She pointed to the one standing closest, the one who had burned her bandage, the one who always seemed to be near her. "Look closely!"

"So? Whatever it is, it ain't our concern." Nervous shouts and grunts of agreement rose behind him but she focused on his face without wavering.

"Look closely, because that will be you. The demons are Nephilim… Lucifer's recruits. This is what he does to you. This," her hand waved toward her demon followers, "is his army!"

The prisoners became deadly silent.

"Prove it," the man demanded, looking a little squirrely.

She glanced around, spying a large ring of keys hanging on the wall like in an Old West jailhouse. Leave it to Luc to be so damn campy with his imagery. She tried three keys before the barred door swung opened. A large number of captives tried to push their way past but the demons slipped closer, slightly burning a few of them.

"Just you," Esther commanded. Bright Eyes slipped out of the door and followed her while the demons formed a tight wall around the cell.

"Now you got me alone, sweetie, how about we see what we can do?" He reached for her but she slipped his grasp and pointed to the windowed door across the hall.

"How about you look in there first."

He squinted down the hall, possibly considering a run for it, then sauntered to the door and gawked in. For several moments he stood there, blinking, breathing heavy, then he turned and threw up, splattering vomit across the wall and floor. "What the fuck?" his eyes turned fiery and terrified. "What…"

"That's what he's doing with Nephilim. That's how he's building his army." She pointed to the prison room and they entered, him wiping his mouth and Esther, hands on hips, glaring at him. "Now, tell them."

He jerked away as Esther's demon slipped closer. "She ain't lying.

We gotta get out of here. Can you get us out of here?"

"That depends," she said feeling calm and sure for the first time in a long time. "You have free will. All Nephilim have it, even the Free-Winged." She was sure many of those in the cell were Free-Winged, but also that many were educated, and possibly wealthy people. Average Nephilim men and women trying to cope with the world and its difficulties. Lucifer was an expert at pulling them to him. Now they needed to know how to free themselves from their vow.

"What do we do?" That screech came from a woman too far behind the crowd to see.

"Each and every one of you gave Lucifer a blood vow, a vow to the dark," Esther began.

Silence.

"You did it of your own free will, right?"

Quietly heads nodded.

"So… change your free-will choice right now. Decide to vow to support God and the cause. Step away from Lucifer. You can do this."

"Wait!" bellowed a big man in an expensive suit. "Just wait a damn minute. The world is coming to an end. The Counting is coming and you want us to join the losing side… to just give up? I'm not for that for anything. I plan to live and sit at Lucifer's side. My vow, all of our vows, stand, little lady."

Tears gathered in her eyes but she shouted, "Are you mad? Do you think for one moment the devil gives a damn about you? Or you?" she pointed. "You're losing more than your life here… you're losing your soul. Open your eyes!"

"Who's with me?" yelled the Wall Street broker. "Who wants to survive?"

But the crowd of prisoners were split. Many pushed against the bars, begging to be freed, to get away.

"Who chooses to use their free will?" Hands and voices rose. Esther opened the bars and pointed to the side of the room. "Anyone else?" She'd counted fifty-six. Just fifty-six. It was heartbreaking. As she was about to slam the bars closed, three demons stepped inside the cell. Leading her recruits for the cause out of the jailhouse and down the hall, all Esther could do was try to ignore the screams behind her.

At the edge of the hallways she led them all into the alternate plane. "These demons will lead you to safety."

"Those demons can kill us," cried a small woman.

"They won't. They're going to take you to a camp on Ocracoke Island. Talk to a man named Cole Masters. He'll take care of you."

"How? Is he going to punish us? If so, I'll go back and take my chances with the others."

"Okay, go back." She gave a glare.

"Uh, no. Just tell me, is he going to punish us?"

All eyes were on Esther. "He will receive your vow to serve God, then generate your soul sword for battle. Trust me, where I'm sending you is the true elite warriors' camp."

She watched them melt into the portal's strange light and rushed back to the apartment, knowing full well that the demons would take all the heat for the jailbreak and the carnage inside the cell.

27

Tobias looked at his watch. His body vibrated with excitement as his time grew closer and closer. Three in the morning. Darker than dark. The depth of night just before a promise of dawn, but this dawn would arrive with a new life for all. A free, safe, protected life. No more Lucifer, no more battles, no more demons. Tobias breathed deep and smiled wide.

The performances had been better than even he could have imagined. The matchings were spectacular, and the audience was wild with enthusiasm. Already groups were playing political games to push their favorite troupes ahead. Such fools. Believing that being named the best would matter in the least.

Fifteen minutes and he would leave. Watching the crowds cheer and the amazing mystical Shield Maidens show unfold before him, he couldn't help but look back at all he'd accomplished in his long life. He had fathered hundreds of children, although he never actually was involved with any of their brief lives. When one sees centuries rather than decades, nothing really matches the entertainment of the moment. He'd fought in a million battles and saved thousands of lives. He watched the world push itself to the edge, then rebuild after full disaster. Again. And again. And again. But this time it would be different. It took him an ancient's entire number of days to realize that he was powerful beyond words. Strong beyond reason. Deserving above all.

He'd sacrificed since his beginning. He had walked many centuries at Raphael's side and learned everything the archangel had to teach. He needed no archangel any longer. Needed no Nephilim, no human, no God to define who and what he was. The time had come to set things straight.

The music rushed to its fruition, ending the final original matchup competition. The winner was sure to be The Deadheads led by the Norema twins, Ben and Jerry. Tobias blinked and laughed aloud, for the first time catching the joke of their names. It had been fun, all of it, but he couldn't help but mourn the loss of battle and powerful warriors. The new world would need nothing like that. Naturally he'd want a large army of the best of the best around him as he guided the world ahead. He could pick and choose, and already knew where to get them. They'd been performing for hours right in front of him. It was a show like no other and the best warriors in grease paint and sequins would find their place in his army. No one else deserved such honor.

The troupes awaiting their opportunity to compete circled him and he randomly handed out cards for each. The show would continue without a hitch now. The winners of the first round would perform against the second round. That should take at least six hours, after which camp voting would take place and the winner would be announced.

Of course, by that time none of it would matter. Tobias would have already defeated the devil and stopped the madness that has run the world since the beginning. Tobias marveled, why hadn't he thought of this before? Timing was everything. Now, he was ready. Now he was sure. Although he felt painfully alone in his decision, apart from his warriors and separated from Dawn. Perhaps he should have been gentler with himself, allowed himself a little carnal pleasure, permitted himself a few loyal guards to cheer him on as he faced Lucifer, blade to blade.

Maybe he should have considered letting Raphael in on his plan, but to what end? Lucifer was the archangel's brother after all. Tobias always suspected there was a strain of fraternal loyalty to the devil there. Best to approach this alone.

Tobias glanced around. All eyes were on the lighted rings and activity going on there. He slipped through the tent flap and walked directly into the woods, intending to travel, hidden by the trees, all the way to the peach grove.

~*~

Ben accepted a vision that caught his breath. More than choosing which vision to allow front and center attention, he had to start passing them on to the right person so that he could be free of them. As the next performance started, the music slow and elegant, he stood and looked toward Raphael, waiting at the edge of the tent for a sign.

Raphael nodded then stepped out into the darkness.

~*~

Every moment revealed something else I'd never seen before, and may never see again. Anyone who doesn't believe in magic should witness these shows. Movement and light, color and air, even sound and scent melded together for illusions that couldn't be explained.

Realizing that each Nephilim warrior had received at least one quickening gift, there was no end to what these performers could do. My heart raced, then stalled with delight and terror time and time again. At one point a beautiful woman from the African Wonders Warriors suddenly leapt straight up and all the way through the top of the massive tent, then returned, splattering like raindrops into a little kiddie pool on the ground. In the blink of an eye, there she stood, wet, whole, and unharmed. I had no words, just the ability to clap until my hands hurt.

Kevin was beside himself and Ben and I laughed. The poor guy had no clue what to expect. Well, none of us really did.

289

~*~

"Tobias," Raphael called. "Hey, man. They need you back at camp."

"They're fine. Let them figure it out, whatever it is."

The archangel jogged up behind him.

Looking over his shoulder, Tobias glared. "Sometimes a man has to take a piss, Raphael. He might want to do it alone, you know."

"If you were taking a piss, you would not be running so hard." Raphael magically appeared right in front of him, causing Tobias to stumble and drop his weapon.

"And why do you need a sword to piss, my friend?" Raphael lifted the bulky weapon and slowly examined it. "Remind me, where did you get this?"

"Raphael, go back to the show. They need you back there. They look to you for guidance and—"

"Why is that, Tobias? Why are they looking to me? To young Gracie? To Cole and Michael?"

Tobias shrugged, glance in the direction of the peach grove and huffed his frustration.

"Is it because you have become a royal pain in the ass, and even your own people don't care to listen to you anymore?"

"What the hell are you talking about?" Finally, all his attention was on the archangel who continued to examine the sword, holding it, swinging it, spinning it gracefully.

"Where did you get this weapon? Julius Caesar?"

Tobias began to pace, growing more and more agitated. "You know full well who gave me that weapon."

"I do. A good man. An honorable Roman. Hadrian. So, what are you planning to do with this sword, Tobias?"

"What do you care?" Tobias reached for the weapon but Raphael's magic made it vanish into thin air.

290

"Talk to me, Tobias. What are you up to?"

~*~

Gracie was totally engrossed, and who could blame her? It was so good to see her smile and laugh. Things had been heavy on her frail shoulders, but Cole could not have been prouder. She was their leader, no one could deny. Many looked to Raphael, but most came to Gracie for practical solutions. She always came through, whether it was managing supplies with Dawn, ordering the digging of more latrines, or negotiating peace between the camp and the demons. Cookie had taken to asking her advice on menus, and Garta spent more time than expected making sure she was serving the camp's needs in ways Gracie saw best.

Frank Pincer climbed up the bleachers and tapped him on the shoulder, whispering that there was something he had to see. Cole slipped away without a word. If there was a need, he'd alert Gracie.

Outside the tent stood a lot of strangers. He counted fifty-six in all and looked at Pincer. "Who are they?"

"They said that some lady named Esther sent them. They're ready to take the vow."

"Shouldn't Ballister Green do it?"

Pincer shrugged. "They asked for you. You've done this. Do it." He grinned wide and stepped back.

Cole led them all to a clearing further from the tent. "So, where did you come from?" There were men and women, well dressed and poor, big and small.

One man stepped forward. "You don't want to know, buddy. All I know is that she said we got free will and can make this new decision. So, can you take our vow?"

"Do you mean it? Or are you just afraid of the alternative? Penalty? Hell?"

The spokesman, wearing raggedy jeans and cowboy boots, shrugged.

"As I see it, this is likely to be the losing team, so the fact that we're here to fight anyway should tell you everything."

"I need to explain," Cole paced in front of them, all eyes on him. "If you don't mean the vow… if you're not committed, it will be for nothing. Take a second… really go deep into your soul and find the answer to my question. Because when I ask if you're here for God, you need to really mean it."

"I mean it," several people said.

"First, you have to tell me where you came from."

They looked at each other for a moment, then another spokesman stepped forward. "We're from everywhere, cities and farms, rich and poor. Esther found us all waiting in a jail cell for… for… well apparently, to be turned into demons. She asked if we wanted to change our vow and let us out. A demon brought us here. We were vowed to Lucifer. Can we vow now for God? For good?"

"Did everyone come?"

Heads shook.

"How many didn't come?"

"About a hundred, maybe more."

Cole blinked. So, this was how it was going to be. Many would follow the dark, and few would follow the light. The Counting was near, and every Nephilim was needed, even those who once believed they wanted to fight for the devil. These few risked everything to come to camp.

"Kneel," he instructed and they did. He walked along the line of varied and interesting Nephilim and asked each one if they were here for God. When every single Nephilim answered, he closed his eyes and let the air drift from his lungs. A sensation of electricity and heat floated around him, music from the performance reached his ears, and a cool breeze chilled his body. Then he heard the gasps and opened his eyes. Each Nephilim lifted their soul sword in wonder, awed that it was in their hands, out of nothing but a vow for the cause.

Satisfied, Cole turned and almost crashed right into Pincer.

"Not bad, Masters! Good as Green could've done, any day."

Cole lowered his head. "Can we make accommodations for these people to sleep in the dining tent for tonight?"

"Absolutely." Frank Pincer smiled wide and looked to the new recruits. "Name's Pincer. Let's get you all settled in, then you can watch some of the show."

As they followed Pincer, Cole returned to his seat beside Gracie and wondered. How was it all going to work? If Esther was correct, the good guys had already lost the Counting.

~*~

Tobias stood defiant, hands on hips and ready to fight. "I don't have to answer to you, Raphael. You are disloyal and not worth my time."

"You are so important now?" Raphael laughed and walked slowly around the man. "You forget, my friend. I recall your terror and fear, your stupidity and misguided youth. Your ego. When I left you a century ago for a new assignment, I was so sure you were reformed. Made whole. What have you become? This is disappointing."

"Give me my weapon."

"So, what's your plan. Do you really think Lucifer can be felled with this paltry piece of steel?" The sword was once again in the archangel's hand and Tobias stepped back. "And do you truly believe you can defeat him? Alone?"

"Join me! We can stop this insanity for good."

Raphael shook his head, long golden hair swaying in the speckles of moonlight reaching down through the leaves. "Have you learned nothing?"

"I've learned that someone has to do this!"

"Do what, Tobias?" Raphael stepped closer and closer until the man was up against a tree.

"Back off!"

"I have wonderful news, my very old friend. The Father has called you home."

"No! Give me that sword. I'm going to do this!"

Raphael leaned closer and closer, the sharp, glistening blade firm with steady pressure against the man's neck.

Tobias tried not to panic, but his arms were frozen at his side and unable to move. "Back off, damn you!"

"Don't you understand? You've done all you can do and the Father is grateful for all your good work with the Nephilim race. He has called you home. Called you to your well-deserved rest." The blade pressed harder and drips of red blood slid down Tobias's neck.

"No!"

"Yes, my dear friend." Tears ran down the archangel's face as he pressed quickly, praying not to cause the man he'd known for many millennia any more pain than necessary.

"Stop," Tobias said with a gurgle. "I can end the evil."

"Don't you see? There can be no good without evil. So, even if you could defeat Lucifer, which you can't, evil must continue. It's how the world is designed. Free will doesn't work without contrast. Only contrast can show the light and the dark. Go home to Father, Tobias. I cannot bear for you to lose your soul to Lucifer when he ends you."

"So… so… you will… end me?"

"I have been asked to send you home. The Father has called you…" The weight of Raphael's whole body pressed against the blade that sliced clear through to the man's spine, then snapped that as well. "Home," the archangel whispered. Then gathered up the destroyed body and sobbed helplessly, rocking Tobias in his lap like a beloved child.

~*~

As amazing as everything before me was playing out, something was itching inside my mind. It was as though I was reading my father's book. A message was clear and precise and.... I stood and left the bleachers, aware of Cole and Ben and the rest of my posse following me.

Outside, the air was crisp and cool. I looked to Ben and all he did was point. Lord knows I had to get someplace fast and my stupid twisted foot wasn't about to accommodate. So, for the first time ever, I chose to bring my wings, massive overkill as they were, into play. At first, I shot into the sky, but what I had to see was happening in the woods. Low to the ground, my two perfect feet brushing against the grass and dirt, my wings swept me fast and sure into the trees, the lowering closer to the earth I ran with the added push of wind beneath feathers.

Where was it? What happened? But I saw it, was looking right at it. Disbelieving even as it registered, I couldn't wrap my mind around it.

Raphael sat, leaning against a dead tree and holding a very dead Tobias. I wasn't sure what to do. Approach? Run away? Pretend I didn't see it?

"Gracie, come closer," the archangel said, his voice raspy like he'd been crying. A bloodied sword, massive with a shiny wide and very bloodied blade, lay at his side.

If you can't trust an archangel, who can you trust, right? I stepped closer and found the courage to ask, but only after a gulp to calm my nerves. "Oh God, Raphael. What happened?"

His eyes were red rimmed and glassy but his words were clear.

"In a few minutes," he said, "you must go back to camp and tell them that Tobias has been called back to the Father. That after his very long life, he's finally home."

"Okay." I tried not to look, there was way too much blood. "Did you?" I pointed to the severed head in his arms.

"Gracie, the Father has called him home. He had to leave and he had to do it now."

I nodded, glancing around and hoping someone would show up. Surely someone followed me, right? Someone who could make sense of this? "Okay. I'll go back and tell them now."

"No, first my dear Gracie, I need to give you your final lesson. The last lesson. It's more news than a lesson, but I hope you can learn from it. Then, after that, you must stand with me for the passing-on ceremony. It'll only take a moment. Then…"

I waited and waited but he didn't finish. He just looked at his dead friend. "Then… what?"

"Then I will be gone. There will be no more help from any of us. Gracie, the call for the Counting is only hours away." He stood and I stood. Wiping his hands off on his raggedy tee shirt, he reached out and took my hands. "This is what you must know. Share it or don't share it… the lesson is for you."

His eyes closed and my heart started to thump so loud I feared I might not be able to hear him. I struggled to ignore the carcass at his feet, the terror growing in my belly, the uncertainly of my true place at that moment. Raphael was obviously distraught, in agony over what he had to do. The demons had warned me about Tobias. Perhaps this was a good thing. Perhaps there would be no friction as we prepared for the Counting. The Counting that would be sometime tomorrow. How would we ever be ready?

Finally, Raphael raised his face to the sky just as wispy clouds covered the moon and gentle rain misted over us. His entire body changed into the archangel he was. His wings huge and flowing, his face glowing, his whole body brilliant and radiant. "Gracie," he said, his powerful hands still holding mine and my wings still fluttering nervously at my back. "This will be the final Counting. There will be no more. You must make sure that every vow is genuine, that every heart is strong and committed, for those not fully committed… will not be counted.

"Be brave, my dear. Hold your courage like a shield. Pray that Esther may join you… she could be a great help to you. Have confidence that you've done everything you could. Others have, too. All will be proven on the Counting field. Do not lose hope. Do not lose faith. Because if you do, if any of you do, the Nephilim Race will be no more. It will be lost forever."

My breathing accelerated, my fingers twitched, my wings wanted to pull me away from the truth. We would be lost forever if we aren't true to our vow.

"Do you understand, Gracie?"

"Everything is up to me?"

He smiled and it was amazing, pushing energy right into my heart. "All you need to do now is lead them all onto the Counting field. And…"

"Pray."

Raphael drew in a long, sad breath then knelt to straighten the dead body of his long-time friend, Tobias. Then he spoke the ancient words, and as he spoke, I whispered the translation, so that I would never forget.

This man.

This soul.

This body.

This conscience.

This energy.

All belongs to You, Father.

Take this man to Your heart.

All belongs to You, Father.

Take him to Your loving heart.

The mangled, bloody mass that was once a vibrant, egotistical, and powerful ancient slowly dissolved and lifted to the heavens. Speckles of blue light accompanied each cell of the once living figure on its journey to the place where it would be received, high above the earth and my reality. I turned to look at Raphael but he too was dissolving.

"Raphael," I cried out. "Tell my father I will do my best."

"Metatron loves you, Gracie. The Father loves you. We will all watch with prayers for your success."

And he was gone. Really and truly gone. I walked my slow, hobbling gait back to camp, my wings too sad to stick around, and my heart, too broken to even imagine how I'd explain it all to the warriors.

28

ucifer paced in the trees, his footsteps vibrating along the earth. He waited and waited, but apparently Tobias had let him down. After all the devil had done for that weakling—all the guidance, all the intercepted messages, all the strategic directives that led Tobias closer to the promised land—he didn't even show up to take his medicine and relinquish his soul. Everything had a price, and Lucifer hated when a human, ancient, Nephilim, or the boring generic kind, skirted reciprocation and refused the devil his due. Free will was a boon, and a curse.

No one was immune to Lucifer. Everyone hears, and listens, and often acts upon his whispers. But Tobias, he thought he was above the fray. Beyond the standard. This result was a design flaw that repeatedly irritated Lucifer. An ancient was not required to give a vow to God or Lucifer. They only needed to seek out their chosen deity and move in that direction. Many of them leaned toward the light because of the Nephilim wings and what they represent, but Lucifer knew, full well, there were as many corrupt Nephilim as there were corrupt humans.

The devil huffed. The soul of a strong ancient like Tobias would have given him a marked edge, but it mattered little at this stage of the game. Like all archangels, the coming Counting was imprinted on his very being and he sensed that it was near. He already had far more recruits than the combined worldwide Nephilim camps. No need for one more ancient.

Lucifer raised a frustrated glance to the sky. Tobias had obviously chosen redemption. So be it. To hell with Tobias and his rotten soul. He had better things to do, and a soft, lovely woman waiting for him. Dinner in Paris sounded far more pleasant than making Tobias beg and bleed. Afterward, there would still be begging and bleeding, only from that same soft, lovely woman. Such satisfaction made his mouth water. This would be his last time to enjoy Esther.

Things were about to change, big time.

I heard the sing-songy calliope music and followed it to the big top. Ben stepped near, but I couldn't explain. Not yet. There was so much to consider. When I couldn't stand it another minute, I whispered to Cole, who'd been watching me like a hawk, biting his tongue and respectfully allowing me time before asking anything. He left for the house, then I walked to the two rings and stood between them with my hands high. The spotlights aimed, the music stopped, all eyes were on me, and I gulped hard. Around me were nearly four hundred warriors, four remaining ancients, and about a hundred demons. I had to do this right.

"I… I have …" One of the stage crew rushed forward and handed me a microphone. I gripped it like a lifeline. "I have very sad news," my usually quiet voice boomed.

Everyone silenced, making it even harder for me to speak. Ryan and Ben stood right in front, offering all the support I needed. After all, we were the last of our generation. The unlikely leadership. No longer kids or children to be protected. I cleared my throat and spoke.

"The Father has called Tobias to his rest."

Gasps and cries rippled through the gathering and after a moment, I raised a hand.

"Raphael has also left… but he has informed me that we are mere hours from the Counting." I waited, but didn't receive the shouts of panic I expected. The panic I felt. All I saw before me were committed Nephilim, ready to move ahead at my command.

"Those working with Cole, please go up to the house. Efforts have begun to place recruits and guides at all the portals. We don't know exactly when the call will come, but we must be ready. Everyone, please get some sleep. If the call hasn't come by morning, do everything you can to secure and shut down the camp.

"Oh… and anyone seeking weapons training, um… Pincer? Can you please help with that? Just for a few hours, then send them for some rest."

Pincer stepped near and actually gave a slight bow. "Of course. We have new recruits, and a few from inside the camp who can use a refresher. My honor to serve."

I gripped his hand before he could leave and whispered, "I'm so sorry for your loss."

His eyes glowed with pooling tears.

"And finally," I turned to the audience and spoke into the mic. "I would like to see the camp leaders in the dining tent… immediately."

Leaving the big top, I saw them, streaming like a black river into the peach grove. The demons had deserted us, and my heart broke. It was a silly pipe dream to hope they'd stand on our side. Still, tears stung my eyes.

Walking to the dining tent felt like trudging through quicksand. How was I ever going to be able to do this? Settled before me were the leaders from each camp, and Ballister Green as representative for the Emmaus warriors. They were quiet and calm, but I was shaken to the bone. Then Ben stepped into the tent and gave me a nod. Did that mean I was doing the right thing? Or, that he just wanted to be there for me, like he'd been most of my life? Damn if I knew. I closed my eyes and concentrated on the situation, the efforts so far, the committed nature of every warrior in our camp. I imagined it multiplied by all the camps around the world, and all the recruits Allerton and Cole had secured, as well as Parkland's international efforts. We'd done everything we could.

"I have something to say, I just don't know exactly how to…"

"It'll be fine, Gracie," said Malinda Dooley, looking like the Viking shield maiden she'd just portrayed in the ring. "Just tell us."

"This is a message for all of us, but I'm hoping to hear the ancients' thoughts about it. See, I've been informed that this will be the last Counting… ever. We either win here, or we are lost forever." I waited while my words sank in, each set of eyes reacting differently, some with disbelief, others with pure dread, a few with tears. "Can any ancient here tell me what this means? Rashee?"

She stood, her elegant body moving like water and her face hard as stone. She turned to the other three ancients around the table. They all shrugged then nodded, so she spoke. "My child," she said. "It's either the end, or the beginning. Every Counting I have participated in ended with a time of judgment, where only a handful of Nephilim and ancients were chosen to continue. What Raphael has conveyed is that should we lose this Counting, we will all end. It's been a long battle to justify the existence of the Nephilim race… to prove your value as the guardians for balance on this planet."

She was silent for so long I began to tremble. "And?"

"And, we mustn't tell the others. It could cause our warriors to lose heart."

"Or…" I almost shouted. How dare she give up so easily. "It could make them fight harder. As I understand it, if we lose the Counting, we get to fight for the chance to continue, right?"

Rashee, leaned across the table and settled her warm hand on mine. "That has been so in the past, but it seems the rules have changed this time."

"Not fair! I mean, I just got here. I just started to work for this cause. It's wrong to just pull the rug out from under—"

"Gracie," Rashee shouted to be heard over my tirade. "Listen to yourself? Remember who you're talking about. The Father can change the rules anytime he pleases. It's his game, child. Not yours. Not ours. All we can do is stand and show our commitment."

Wow. Talk about a reality check. Slowly, all my nerves slipped back into place making the puzzle that is my life, whole again. "I'm sorry. I know. I know. So, where does that leave us?"

"Rashee is correct," the tall African ancient stated. "It's best to keep this bit of information to ourselves. I have seen warriors run before the Counting actually began, just because they heard we may not have gathered enough recruits for a favorable outcome."

"Keep it a secret?" Even to myself that sounded sarcastic.

The ancient's heads nodded agreement.

"But, if they want to run, don't they have the free will to do that? Shouldn't they have the information to make that choice?"

All four ancients shook their heads, but the Nephilim leaders looked confused. They leaned close and whispered. After only a moment, the verdict was announced.

"I, for one, will be passing this information on to my warriors," Walter McTavish announced.

"A most unwise decision, young man," Rashee said with grandmotherly kindness.

McTavish stood and faced her, leaning across the table to get his nose close to hers. "Perhaps unwise for you," he said with a hiss. "We are the Nephilim. We are the cause, and we intend to justify our existence as guardians for balance." He shouted and snorted and the other Nephilim gave a grunting cheer. "Old woman, you may have led many Nephilim into many Countings and many battles… but this is our first Counting and our first battle. You have never had the likes of us at your side! I will be passing on the critical information to my warriors."

His Scottish accent was so thick I had to squint to understand it. No one else seemed confused though. One by one, every Nephilim leader followed suit. The ancients had no other choice but to align with them.

One slip of a tongue could cause terrible repercussions. Desertions. Disloyalty. Distrust.

As they left, my heart suffered another blow. We'd lost the docile, chocolate-loving demons that had become a part of our camp. We'd lost Raphael and his valuable guidance. And now, the ancients were super unhappy with me.

Ben sat beside me and bumped his shoulder to mine.

"You knew this was going to happen, didn't you?"

"Yep."

"I hate my job."

"No, you don't. Now follow orders and get some rest."

"What are you going to do?"

He looked into my eyes. Maybe I shouldn't have asked. He knows so much. Finally, he blinked and smiled. "I'm waiting for Parkland. He's on his way. We've got a few things to… um… decipher."

Choosing to leave that to the guys with perceptive skills, I headed for home and my empty bed, sure I'd get no sleep, waiting every single moment for the call.

It took a while but Esther, dressed elegantly and a half hour early, stood at the mirror and carefully weighed the risk. She just had to go. It was almost impossible to stay away from her Pure Nephilim half ever since she discovered it. Her body and soul craved closeness and connection, but Lucifer had put a wall of thick glass between them. When the Counting came, he'd have no choice but to free the thing he'd stolen from her. In the meantime, the bell jar was like candy. She had to be near it.

Looking around she decided to take the chance. Just a brief visit. Just enough to give her strength for the night ahead.

She walked, stiletto heels clicking on the floor, all the way to the lab. As always, the sight of the restrictive bell jar made her tremble. The ethereal angel within smiled with sad eyes, then settled her hands on the glass. Mirroring that action, Esther leaned in and lay herself against the glass, wanting as much of the Pure Nephilim power as possible to seep through the barrier and into her. Warmth calmed and settled her mind and heart.

"I've been thinking a lot about this," she whispered. "When the call comes, we must stand at his side and appear fully committed to him. If we stay focused on our vow, and each other, I believe something magical will happen. At least, I hope."

Esther had made so many mistakes, but she stood willing to die to correct them. Looking into the eyes of her Pure Nephilim, she sighed and leaned her brow against the glass. "We can do this. We can do this. We can. I know we can."

A chill raced across her body and her gut rolled, a sensation that told her Lucifer wasn't far away. She slipped out of the high heels, gripped them in one hand, and raced back to the apartment, all the time begging her mind and heart to be still and calm.

Great. Now she felt sweaty, worried her hair was messed and lipstick smeared. Positive Luc would be angry, she rushed toward the bedroom just as he entered the apartment. What followed resembled an I Love Lucy scene as she twisted and turned, trying to look innocent yet trying to get back into the bedroom before he got a good look at her.

"Oh… um… jeeze… I've been trying so hard to be ready and I can't decide! I was thinking maybe the red would be prettier," she said, her voice surprisingly cool and sure. "Maybe that sleek black dress? But the gold one is stunning, too."

Lucifer stood in full tuxedo, sharp and beautiful, diamond watch aglow, and shoes so shiny they could blind a person. He tilted his head and eyed her up and down, then walked all the way around. Esther had colored her hair a shiny black. The deep blue satin of her dress seemed to spark and reflect in the gleaming strands. Her amber-flecked eyes glowed. Slowly, a smile crawled across his handsome face, lighting his whole expression and showing off his pearly whites. Lucifer was pleased, almost too pleased to waste time eating dinner.

Esther knew that look. She also knew that she was going to have no choice but to give him what he wanted, whether it was that moment, or after dinner. Perhaps in the men's room at the restaurant. Outside in an alley. Nothing was beneath the devil. Resigned, she almost reached behind to unzip the beautiful gown, but he surprised her.

"Put those sexy shoes on," he said, still circling her like a starving tiger. "Let me see how you look."

She'd almost forgotten about them. Esther dropped each stiletto dramatically then stepped into them, slowly, sensually, one at a time. They took her up, made her taller, almost able to look directly into his eyes. It was a new view of the gorgeous man she fell in love with once. Or maybe it wasn't love. Maybe it was something else. Something he'd manipulated, just like the image he was wearing.

Like his inability to heal wounds, Esther knew of his other failure, the devil's true image—the mutilated, seared, ugly visage of an angel burned to the bone. She only saw it once, when he was too tired to bother with magic and climbed into bed beside her. That single glimpse of Lucifer's truth had caused her many nightmares.

She forced a smile. At the moment, none of that mattered. What mattered was that he was pleased, and he was playful, and he wasn't hurting her in any way.

With a soft chuckle, Lucifer tenderly turned her to the view outside the window. The Eiffel Tower sparkled.

"Oh! So beautiful."

"Like you, my little dear." He kissed her neck.

Too hot. His touch was way too hot but she didn't pull away. Instead she went for playful. "Dinner," she chimed and leaned back against him.

"First, for just a few moments, I have a few things to finish in my lab."

Esther's heart stopped and she coughed to get it pumping again.

Facing him she spoke with the slightest irritation. "Really?" She blinked her eyes for effect, pouted a bit, then spoke sadly. "Can't it wait until tomorrow? It's been so long since we've had time to be together. I miss you… and I'm so hungry."

Lucifer shook his head, a sexy grin on his face, eyes twinkling, fingers twitching. Was he thinking of her, or the coming victory? Did it matter? As they left the apartment to stroll the streets of his fake Paris, she was grateful for a few things in particular.

First, that this would be the last time she'd have to deal with Lucifer, ever. And second, that a nice long dinner would give the demons time to clean up the mess and do whatever they could to keep Esther clear of any wrong doing in the jailhouse.

And she wondered. Was she sinning? Was there any other way to do what she had to do?

~*~

As expected, sleep was not going to be easy. Activity downstairs in Command Central wasn't quiet, and outside my window, most of the camp was not following orders. Obviously, nobody could sleep, so why should I even try?

I sat up and wondered about ridiculous things, like how would we hear the call? Would cell phones ring and an automated message be played? Would our soul swords brighten like light sabers? Would all the birds start screaming? How would we get that all important call? And, was it going to be a sneak attack? Like when I'm in the shower, or making love, or eating?

"Oh!" I gasped, feeling something deep in my heart, an ache that seemed to grow then calm, then grow again. Was that the call? Panic pulsed in my veins and I knew, without doubt, that the original sensation was sadness, and more importantly, it was not my feelings or emotions. It was someone else's. Sitting on the edge of my bed I attempted to breath evenly and without a hitch, but that was getting harder and harder.

Someone was so sad, so devastated, I had to do something. Rushing to pull on jeans and a tee shirt, I kept trying to figure out what was happening. As yet another emotion raced across my being I understood, but what kind of sense did it make? Why would I receive a quickening power now, at the very end of the game? What did it mean, and more importantly, what was this power?

Who could I ask? No one. The ancients were pissed at me. Everyone in camp was busy. Looking out the window, dawn had crawled up from the trees in the east and there was movement everywhere. All I knew was that someone needed me. Many someones, in fact. Rushing as fast I could down the stairs, I noticed my wings had arrived and were pushing me ahead. Maybe they'd help me. Maybe they knew what I was supposed to do. My first encounter was Cole at the computer screens. He looked up as I sped past, then called out, "Honor to your quickening, Gracie. I only have another hour or so here, then I'll…"

I couldn't wait to hear the rest—I ran to the door and took flight. From above, I noticed several warriors looking up at me. Some waved, others just returned their focus to what they were doing. Many were practicing with their soul swords. Many were working to pack up the camp. Cookie was feverishly preparing simple meals for the day. I landed in front of him and he jumped, then laughed a gut-hearty guffaw.

"You surprised me, Gracie. So, how's this, boss? Scrambled eggs and cheese wrapped in soft tortillas for breakfast, cold sandwiches and chips for lunch, same for dinner?"

"Perfect," I smiled, but still my heart was calling me elsewhere. I just hated to walk away from Cookie and his beautiful mood. The joyous energy that flowed from him, an energy that had probably always been in him, but I never noticed before.

Mood? Energy? Was I suddenly empathic? Was I really picking up other people's emotions? And was I supposed to try to help them? Or maybe, it was more important to just know where each Nephilim's heart sat. Fearful, sad, excited, or unsure?

Munching a tortilla wrap, I stopped and almost doubled over. The sadness brought tears to my eyes. Looking around, trying to see beyond the crazy activity, I felt more than saw her. Dawn. Alone. Walking without direction.

We sat together silently for a little while. She whispered only once about mourning Tobias, and how much she worried for her child's future.

I knew that if the Counting went badly, as we all suspected it might, battle was in play. "Dawn, maybe you need to stay behind. Let us fight for you and the baby. It's too dangerous—"

"No." Her lovely face glowed and red hair caught the sun. Fingers reached for mine. "I am committed. I stand to be counted... and I fight for the survival of our race. You and I both know that Allerton raised us right. Raised us to know what to do and how to do it. I stand with you when the call comes."

She squeezed my hand and I wanted to cry my own tears. A true commitment to the cause had just been solidified. All around, the warriors were doing the same, any way they could. I walked the camp, allowing emotions to wash across me until one dug deep into my soul. Without looking for anyone in particular, I found the pain sitting at the central fire. "Michael?"

"Gracie," he said without looking up, then tossed another log on the flame.

It was Michael's pain, Michael's agony, and his fears that had called to me the most. "Talk to me, please. Otherwise I might explode from everything you're feeling."

Looking into my eyes he smiled. "It's a good quickening power... empathy... but maybe you should use it elsewhere. I'm sure someone needs your ear more than me."

"I'm sure not. Please. Talk. While we still have time."

He leaned back in the frayed lawn chair and sighed. "Gracie, if I hadn't sent them away, hadn't let the other Orphanage System headmasters follow my lead and sent their young ones away... if I hadn't done that... let them be murdered..." For a full moment he sat in silence. "If I hadn't done that… remember, we're talking thousands of souls, our race's future… My God Gracie, what else could I have done?"

"Nothing," I said softly. "I know you. You never do anything unless it's the absolute right thing to do. The correct thing. The moral thing."

He shook his head but I laid a hand on his shoulder. He still wouldn't look at me, but I kept talking.

"You chose Cole to guide us into our Acclimations. You did that. No one else agreed but you knew. You turned yourself in because you took my dad's book, even though you knew it could cost your life. You did it because it was the right thing to do. You sent Ben here with Kevin. You always know the right thing to do. And… you know this isn't the right thing to do right now… feeling bad about something that can't be changed. Isn't there someplace else you'd like to be? Like, maybe, with Ben?"

Finally, he turned. This man was more than a father to me. He was a guide, my strength, and the reason I had become the person, the Nephilim, I am.

He shrugged with a grin. "Ben's busy. He's leading the weapon's training. He doesn't need me around."

"But he does."

Michael gave a chuckle of denial.

"I can feel it. He wants you near. Go and help him train the warriors, Michael. Be what you are. His dad and a real leader."

He stood and shook his head then huffed. "I always knew you'd be something special."

"See. See… you're always right!" And I watched him walk away, shoulders squared and head high, sensing the ache in my heart subside.

Now what? Walking deeper into camp, I stopped outside Beauty Low's massive camper, spying her inside, still, and quiet. Usually she played her radio loud. In the past, I've even seen her dancing all alone in the cramped space. "Beauty?" I called.

"Come on in, Gracie."

She didn't wait for me to explain anything. "Honors for your quickening. But don't worry about me. I'm just thinking about all my human friends, especially my human family."

I blinked and she continued.

"See, I was adopted as an infant. I suppose I'm kinda Free-Winged, but none of my family know or care about any of that. They just cared for me. Loved me. Gracie, I'm worried for them. I don't want us to fail… because I'm committed to this cause… the Nephilim vow, but also because I want my human family to survive this. They don't even know what's coming."

Her eyes glowed and I leaned back, sipping the sugar-free lemonade she'd slid across the table to me. "Wow," I said, seriously in awe of her and her story. There we were, all preparing to go to war together, but we didn't really know each other at all. "I want the same thing… for the cause… and for your human family."

Beauty grinned and sighed then pulled a box of cookies from a small cabinet. "To hell with the diet. Let's indulge. Have some."

I laughed and crunched, loving the fact that Beauty's worry was drifting away from my heart and her own. And I marveled, it took so little to truly connect with people.

Cole was probably still toiling at the computer screen, so I strolled deeper into camp. My heart started to jump with joy and I looked around for the source. Benny Beans, still covered with the grease face paint of a clown, swinging his soul sword beautifully and moving his compact dwarf body perfectly. I'd hate to have to fight him. This was one clown who lived for the fight.

As I walked on, I sensed the emotion of pride warm inside of me, so I turned, unsure of what I'd see. Bold Eagle, dressed in full Lakota warrior regalia, stepped forward and handed me a feather. It was distinctively white at the tip, fully black from there down.

"Eagle feather. One must earn the right to carry one. You have, Gracie. A gift from spirit." He bowed slightly then turned and walked away. How cool was that?

I strolled further from camp and toward the various circles of fighters. I sensed ICe's excitement as he held his sword and moved with careful precision. I noticed the joy radiating from Kevin as he sparred with Billio, the snake man's arm and chest tattoos rippling with strength. I watched Ben and Michael work together, guiding the new recruits on effective swings and stances.

Malinda Dooly called out to me. Everyone there felt so confident, so strong, I was sure no one needed anything from me. She tossed me a sword, and magically, as it touched my fingers, it morphed into my own soul sword. My wings burst forth and I lifted slightly above the ground. Glancing down I noted my favorite part of getting winged—that both of my feet were perfect. Silly pride, but it felt really good.

She drifted up on her wings, grinning from ear to ear. I laughed and lunged, spun and thrust. Metal clanged against metal and my heart raced. Soon this would be more than just practice. Soon we'd be fighting for our lives, fighting for the continuation of our race. My attention focused and the sparring became more intense. A circle of Nephilim cheered us on and I ducked then swung, just missing Malinda's head. A few clips of her hair actually drifted in the breeze, free and loose.

"Enough!" I called out and we both lowered to the ground, wings cupping tight against our backs.

"That was great, Gracie! We had no clue of your fighting skills."

"Well," I blushed. "Those were my soul sword's fighting skills. I'm way better in the girl-slap fight category."

As I turned to leave, I felt his desire, running hard and strong. In the blink of an eye, Cole gripped my hand, waving farewell to everyone on the field and pulling me back to the house.

~*~

All Cole wanted was to feel Gracie in his arms, tight and warm and safe. How did he find her? Taking risks he'd never allow, swinging a lethal weapon and, well, winning. Was he right to worry that Gracie might not need him anymore? Possibly, but what Cole needed most at that moment was assurance that she wanted him.

They were totally in sync, shoes were off before they reached the bedroom, clothes fell and flew before the door was kicked closed. And the warmth, the magnificent depth of Gracie's love covered over him like the sweat growing across their flesh. Her fingers moved smoothly and gently, as his adored and worshiped every inch of her flesh. Was this love supposed to last forever? And would they get the chance to find out?

Having her in his heart, so close he could feel her pulse thrum with his own, he understood that it was a gift. It was all a gift. Birth. Life. Ariel's Gate. Allerton. Parkland. And most of all, Gracie. How could he be sad about that? Many get far less in a full lifetime. Some ancients never find as much over centuries of existence.

He slowed his pace, moving into her with honor and dignity, giving his own gift. Forever might end in mere hours, but there was an eternity in those moments, the fullness of their physical and emotional love for each other.

Cole sighed, holding her close as she finally drifted to sleep. How on earth did he deserve this? He was a lost soul, terrified of what he was and what he could do. Now, all he wanted was to do his best for his race, and for the woman in his arms.

~*~

Kevin woke with a start. It was almost sunset, but what he heard was loud and clear. Beside him, Ben stood and dressed. A trumpet had blared. The call had come.

~*~

Not a sneak attack, but sneaky all the same. Cole and I had just dried off after a fun shower. We were dressing and I heard it.

"Was that?"

"Yes."

I never dressed so quickly. Cole retrieved our swords from the corner of the room, and together we walked out of the house. I carried Metatron's book in my arm, the beautiful eagle feather tucked inside. The pages were ominously empty, but I knew I had to protect it. Or maybe I was hoping it would protect me, protect us all.

The whole camp stood at the peach grove, awaiting. Making a path for us, we moved to the front as many warriors bowed or whispered encouragement. All a moot point. We either had enough for the Counting, or we didn't. As I passed Dawn, looking determined and far from afraid, I set my hand on her growing belly. "You will count as two," I said and she smiled.

Michael, Ryan, and Ben stepped behind us, and after our Ariel's Gate warriors stepped Parkland and the ancients. Then the Emmaus Warriors, then everyone else.

Knees shaking, I turned and whispered to Cole. "Caalii sausha." Be brave.

"Caalii sausha," he replied, and together we stepped into the alternate plane.

29

nside, the usually vibrant, confusing sky settled into what looked like a cloudy grey fabric fluttering high above. Parkland whispered something to Cole and pointed.

"So… Parkland and Ben scouted the best place to stand, not physically scouted, you know," Cole explained. "Like Brainiac, I guess." Even now, my guy could joke.

We climbed to the top of the chosen rise while thousands and thousands of Nephilim flowed in from hundreds of portals, gathering to our right and left. I imagined their choice, their concerns, their courage, and could do nothing but be proud for them. They fell into place, twenty, fifty, maybe a hundred deep on our side of the enormous Counting field—so many that I couldn't see from one end of our line to the other. The distance seemed unfathomable.

Before us was a clear ribbon of land, the distance of a football field and marked with a brilliant, glowing center white mark at what would be the fifty-yard line. The dead center. On the other side, looking right at us, was the enemy, Lucifer and his demon army. Darkness boiled as far as the eye could see.

We were facing the end and I wanted to be an empowered leader. There was no place for fear, only courage—something I was learning about but had definitely not mastered. I trusted we would show as well as possible, we'd done the best we could. Behind me, the ancients were unnaturally silent and I wondered if it was their hope that we really did fail. If they were that angry with me. But, if we failed, they would too, so that didn't make sense. I shook off the paranoia, struggled to think clearly. This would be the last Counting. The ancients could have stayed behind, been safe, but they came and stood for us. That said it all.

Looking around, the mind boggled. So many Nephilim continued to stream in and stand brave, my heart grew with joyous accomplishment. We might be outnumbered, but we would show our vow with grace and dignity.

But across the field there were way more demons standing there. We were going to lose the Counting, but the emotions of every Nephilim and ancient on our side vibrated in my soul. We were solid, dedicated, and prepared. We would give our lives to win the battle, should we get the chance.

Thunder rumbled in the strange sky and I slowly, bravely, focused on the real enemy, standing on his own rise and glaring across at me. Lucifer was powerful, his wings massive and wide. At his side stood my sister, small and frail, her hair loose and black, blowing in the heated breeze. Beside Esther stood an almost translucent version of her Pure Nephilim.

I wanted to jump. I wanted to laugh. I wanted to sob. "Oh, God! He took it from her! This was never her choice!" I cried out. Cole put an arm around my waist and pulled me close.

"Yes, and she's way stronger than you think."

Just as I was about to turn and ask "how?" vibrations rumbled underfoot. The Counting had begun. Far to my left, miles and miles into the misty distance, a yellow strip of light blazed across both sides of the neutral field. Deliberately, like a controlled laser beam, it slowly slid over everyone, creeping closer and closer. Until that moment, there had been cheers and jeers, shouts and threats coming from the Nephilim, but silence fell hard as everyone stood still as death and waited to be counted.

Inch by inch, the ribbon of light glided closer and closer. Then I noticed a slight movement from the corner of my eye and I gazed across the field as my sister subtly, miraculously, melted into her Pure Nephilim. The movement was so slight, Lucifer hadn't perceived anything amiss. He only responded when she took to the air on six magnificent wings and soared toward me.

Terror streaked through my belly and I screamed for her to hurry, sure Lucifer would do something to stop her. He didn't. He stood, roaring her name and shouting obscenities while his rather handsome continence dissolved into something hideous and sickening. Something as destroyed as his soul.

The instant Esther's feet touched the ground at my side I couldn't get my arms around her fast enough. I burned to have all of her tight against me, to regain all the years I'd lost with her, all the love we should have shared, I wanted it all at once. My sister. My twin. My other half had come to stand with me at the most desperate moment of my life. Lucifer's bellows continued, loud and frightening until another sound came louder and more frightening.

Just before the Counting light reached us, the racket rose among our warriors to my right. I witnessed something I couldn't understand or explain. Hundreds, then thousands, then probably millions of demons broke rank and rushed toward our line.

Poor ICe, determined to protect and defend, ran right at them, crossing the white center and meeting them head on.

"Hold the line!" I bellowed and Cole added his voice to mine. "ICe, no! Hold the line!" I shrieked, but to no avail. Esther cried out, too, but even the calls of our own warriors couldn't deter him. Horrified, we all watched as our gentle giant was engulfed in blackness and could be seen no more beneath the swarm of deadly demons. Lost, forever. Burned by the creatures I told him he shouldn't fear.

The Counting light slipped over Cole, me, and Esther, feeling like brittle cold water then it was gone, moving further down our line to the right. We three had been counted, but what was about to happen below? My command to hold the line was obeyed, every Nephilim, even those desperate to call ICe back, followed orders. I didn't want to watch. The demons were about to attack and kill a majority of our recruits before the counting light even reached them. Was Tobias right? Should I have banned them from camp? They had witnessed our respect and soft hearts and now they were about to annihilate us.

I wept, tears covering my face, but Esther just stood and watched, holding my hand tightly. Cole was silent, his hand on my trembling shoulder. Wiping my eyes, I witnessed an event I could hardly believe.

"Yes!" Esther shouted with a fist pump.

As each demon passed the center point of the field, that brilliant white fifty-yard line, they tumbled, broke into pieces, and before my very eyes their flesh returned to normal and missing limbs were restored. Removed wings suddenly regained position and took flight as the regenerated Nephilim dropped elegantly on our side of the Counting field. They had changed their vow, used their free will, and come to the light.

Esther cheered and I glared across the field. Red light blazed from the devil like fire and the stench of burned flesh drifted on the air. Lucifer knew all was lost. More than half of his army had come to our side. When he aimed a gnarly finger directly at us, I felt the searing heat of his anger, the power of his frustration. Esther laughed and pointed her own finger right back at him.

Lucifer dissolved into thin air and was gone before the Counting was even completed.

~*~

It felt like we had fought in the most draining battle of all times, but not one soul sword had to be lifted. Only one life was lost. Only ICe, and it was devastating. Everyone was silent, waiting. Wondering. Was it safe to feel safe? To believe it was over? That we'd done what we had to do?

The once-demons gratefully accepted bits of clothing from my warriors. The sun shone bright and the sky cleared. Not one cloud floated in the strange sky that appeared ridiculously normal. Normal in the alternate plane where nothing was ever normal.

After cheers and joyous shouts, the Nephilim circled the rise and I looked down at them.

"We have another chance, my friends." I could hardly speak. "A chance to do this right."

More rousing cheers rumbled all around and I glanced toward my sister. "Anything to add?"

"Just to watch out, the devil doesn't stay in hiding for long. He will be back."

I squeezed her hand, then directed everyone to return through the same portals they'd entered, to go back home. To be good and always remember their vow. Without warning Cole swung me into an embrace, kissing me deeply and with intention.

I smiled at those chuckling around us, trying not to blush or look stupid. Trying not to think about all the work ahead, now that we'd earned another chance, our last chance, to keep our promise to the Father. To protect the balance for the human race and the planet.

I stepped through the portal first, then gasped. Cole stood stunned beside me and Esther stepped forward in disbelief. As our warriors poured out of the portal, they too gawked in silence.

The camp looked as though it had been torn to shreds. The house, dilapidated to begin with, appeared on its last legs. Trees were torn out by their roots, and the air felt charged with electricity.

"I want to talk to the ancients," I said through a tight throat. They'd been through Countings before. Maybe they could explain this mess.

Ballister Green stepped close. "They're gone, Gracie."

"What do you mean? They can't be, they live, like, forever. Where's Rashee?"

Green shrugged.

Cole turned. "I'll get her," he said with a growl then walked toward what was once a portal and right into a peach tree. "Shit!" His nose bled and his eye was turning black. "What the hell?" Adding insult to injury, a healthy peach dropped right on his foot.

"Are the portals gone? Could that happen?" Did I really sound that desperate?

"Anything can happen," Cole said, covering his embarrassment and mopping blood from his face.

"Hey!" Esther shouted to a man walking at the far end of the property. She stomped toward him and we all followed.

The man stepped back, blinked, then smiled. "That you, Esther?"

She turned to me. "This is Mr. Garson… he owns the gas station."

"Well, I used to. Hey, we filed a missing person's report, you've been gone without a trace for so long."

"How long?" I asked.

He shrugged. "Esther's been gone for more than a year."

More than a year? My heart skipped a beat. No, more than one beat. "What year is it?"

He chuckled. "What are you, time travelers or just stupid? It's January 2021. Happy fucking New Year."

I felt like I was going to throw up. No one said a word and we all looked around like we'd just dropped onto a strange planet. Mars, maybe?

Then the man stepped closer and leaned in. "Listen… I ain't had a drink since the second hurricane, so I know I ain't hallucinating. So… can you tell me something? Why do you people have wings?"

To be continued…

A GOOD KINGDOM

Book Three: the Lost Race Trilogy

DEBORAH RILEY-MAGNUS

ONE HOUR AGO

ate Bedlow lived quietly in her Iowa farmhouse. Sixty-two and retired, she'd lived the extraordinary life of a Pulitzer Prize winning journalist and rabid (her own description) activist. The farmhouse was her great grandmother's, but the painful concerns and loneliness were all her own. No cats for Kate, she was a dog gal, but like her husband of forty years, the canine found her way into a grave two months after Walter. Moving to Iowa was supposed to be their well-earned withdrawal from public life. Now all she wanted was to withdraw from everything.

The funerals, both Walter's and Dingle's, were only weeks before the whole world changed. Over the past year, several newspapers called or showed up at her door to beg her out of retirement, but she just didn't have the heart, or the interest. People were struggling, suffering all over the world, and Kate could only think of her loss.

It had been fourteen straight months of hell. Climate and seismic disasters including earthquakes, landslides, hurricanes, tsunamis, fires, floods, and volcano eruptions darkened not only her heart, but the skies for months. Nothing like this had ever happened in human history, and oddly enough, the last thing on anyone's mind was war. The Middle East quieted, North Korea went silent, and China and Russia had gone dark. No nation asked for help, and no nation offered.

For months the basic requirements for comfort and normalcy were out of reach. Electricity took nearly a year to spark because each time it did, another round of earth anger raised its ugly head. Iowa and the center of America had held its own, far from live volcanos or oceans but plagued with wildfires and drought. It had nearly stopped raining, but come winter, snow as high as six feet had taken, and saved, many lives. The water table held strong after the spring thaw, and Kate prayed for another hard and cold winter on the plains.

She had survived on her own garden and chicken coop. Some farmers were stable enough to help desperate neighbors, but everything was in short supply.

Then two months ago the electricity and even the internet returned to the living. Televisions lit up to actual broadcasts, mostly news from around the world. Radio stations started to play music. Cell phones began to ring, and slowly, cautiously, people reopened what they could of their businesses. Maybe it was over. Maybe it wasn't. Who knew? Surely Kate had no clue.

The phone rang loud. "Yes?" She'd never cultivated that warm-and-fuzzy way of answering phones.

"Kate, it's Marty Wolf."

She gulped.

"From the New York Times? You can't have forgotten me, woman."

"Nope. Close my eyes and I can still see your nose hair, clear as a bell."

"How are you doing out there in the middle of nowhere? Ready for big city life again?"

She gave a grunting laugh that ached in her ribs. Tossing another log on the flames in her fireplace, she settled on the sofa. "Is there still a city, Wolfie? I saw those pictures on the news. Looks nothing like the New York I knew."

"I need you, Kate."

"Ah, so this isn't a casual call, is it?"

"Seriously. You're the woman who fought discrimination and injustice. The one who uncovered Representative Scott Pillior's Texan white-supremacist organization. You exposed crimes in—"

"I know what I did… the operative word… did."

"Come do it again. The whole world has lost its mind!"

"Of course, it's lost its mind. Everyone refused to listen to the warnings. This planet has had enough of us. We're an itch it wants gone."

"Come back, Kate. People need your guidance."

Kate snorted and watched soft snow flurries drift outside her window. "Get someone else, Wolfie. I'm retired."

"You're alone and too talented to just sit there and waste away."

His words melted as she stood and squinted through the frosted glass. The house across the field had been empty for over a year and suddenly there were lights on in the kitchen. That couldn't be right.

"I need to go."

"Kate! Kate don't—"

She'd already hung up. The house was too far away to just sprint in the freezing January air. Boots, gloves, scarf, hat, coat. "Jesus!" she shouted as her wool covered hands struggled to turn the doorknob to get outside.

She trudged as fast as she could, trying hard not to think of everything she'd lost. A year ago, her neighbors across the road had died in a house fire. A month later, another neighbor's child, a fifteen-year-old genius, froze to death attempting to run away. No one knew what was happening, or if it would ever stop happening. Three farms down, Pete Chambers and his whole family hanged themselves from the barn rafters. That was late summer when all their crops had failed. Failed or not, there was no one to buy soybeans, no one to process corn, no way to make sure the cows didn't starve to death.

Last November, just before all hell broke loose, the house she was nearing went dark. Joel and Maggie Fielding were a young couple, just starting their married life. They left a note in Kate's mailbox telling her not to worry, that they were off for a trip and would pop by when they got home. Kate worried a lot, terrified she'd lost them too as the planet convulsed and attempted to kill everyone on it. Where had they gone? Were they safe? Were they home, or had someone desperate decided to camp inside their lovely refurbished old house? She wouldn't blame them. No one should freeze to death. Most people were good… but the rest, not so much. Kate wasn't an idiot. She'd seen a lot. She just had to know who was living so close to her.

Darkness came early these days, but she was grateful there was light at all. Three o'clock in the afternoon and already the sky was black as night. There was movement inside; she could identify shadows and shapes. She walked around to the door and knocked hard.

"Joel? Maggie? Is that you in there?"

"Yeah?" But the door didn't open.

"Let me in. I'm fucking freezing out here."

The doorway cracked slightly and all she could see was a silhouette of a head.

"I have my cell phone… I'll dial 911 if you're not Joel."

"I am, but Kate, can you come back tomorrow?"

"No. Let me in, damn it!"

He did. At first the brightness of the light blinded her. Then, as her vision adjusted, she blinked, then gasped. "Holy shit!" she whispered before passing out cold. Her last thought was that it had all been a terrible dream. That the world had come to an end long ago. She just didn't know until that moment when the angels had come to take her away.

But wait. Angels. Joel and Maggie might be nice people, but angels? Her eyes slowly opened and confirmed what she knew was impossible. Wings. Those were wings. On the backs of both Joel and Maggie Fielding. She'd known them since they were kids. They never had wings before. Was this the story her old pal Wolfie wanted her to cover?

"Water?" Maggie offered a glass, pure fear in her eyes.

~*~

Watch for A Good Kingdom
Book 3 of The Lost Race Trilogy, coming soon!

AUTHOR BIOGRAPHY

Deborah Riley-Magnus is an author and an author success coach. Her fiction is creative and magical, beginning with the Twice-Baked Vampire Series books 1 and 2, Cold in California and Monkey Jump. A fascination with the battle between good and evil plays out in fantastical worlds built for her specific stories, worlds that deliver childlike curiosity, dark explorations of human nature, and the struggle to remain strong in the face of danger and loss.

Deborah lives in beautiful Pittsburgh Pennsylvania, and writes in her quiet home office overlooking the sparkling city with three rivers. Seeing that view has spurred fantasies of mystical Native American peoples who lived along those rivers, the constant what if? and the occasional shifting vision of dragon tails whipping around the glass castle spires atop the PPG building. Are there trolls under the million bridges? Does a monster dwell in the fourth river beneath the Allegheny, Monongahela, and Ohio rivers? Does the ghost of a little girl really sing in the hundred-year-old hallway behind her as she writes? This is where real fantasy come from. And it makes this author smile.

OTHER BOOKS BY DEBORAH RILEY-MAGNUS

FICTION

The Orphans: Book One, The Lost Race Trilogy
Cold in California: Book One, The Twice Baked Vampire Series
Monkey Jump: Book Two, The Twice Baked Vampire Series

NONFICTION

Write Brain / Left Brain: Bridging the Gap Between Creative Writer and Marketing Author
Cross Marketing Magic for Authors: New Avenues for Advanced Book Marketing
Author Marketing Playbook #1
Author Marketing Playbook #2

AUTHOR INFORMATION

FICTION

Fiction Website: drmagnusfantasy.com/
Angel Moments Blog: angelmomentsweb.wordpress.com/
Pinterest: www.pinterest.com/deborahrileymag/
Twitter: @MyAngelMoments

NONFICTION

Writaholic Blog: rileymagnus.wordpress.com/
Teaching Website: theauthorsuccesscoach.com/
Twitter: @rileymagnus
Facebook: www.facebook.com/deborah.rileymagnus
Facebook Coaching Page: www.facebook.com/authorsuccesscoach/
LinkedIn: www.linkedin.com/in/deborah-riley-magnus-4ba15ala/